TURNING THE TABLE

Helen Nielsen was a master of the ...
stories rarely end on a predictable note, rarely going
where you think they are going to go. These fifteen
stories, originally published from 1957 to 1991 in the
pages of *Alfred Hitchcock's* and *Ellery Queen's
Mystery Magazines*, display her wide range of
storytelling at its best.

As editor Bill Kelly points out in his introduction, her
full range is represented here, from mystery puzzle
story, police procedural, domestic malice, trial drama,
cozy, comic mystery to one story that might almost be
classified as pure horror.

Anthony Boucher once observed in his *New York
Times* column that Helen Nielsen wrote "in a vein of
quietly observant realism, underlined by sustained
emotional horror."

She certainly never wrote the same story twice.
Here are fifteen of Nielsen's very best.

Turning the Tables:
The Short Stories
of Helen Nielsen

EDITED AND INTRODUCTION
BY BILL KELLY

STARK
HOUSE

Stark House Press • Eureka California

TURNING THE TABLES: THE STORIES OF HELEN NIELSEN

Published by Stark House Press
1315 H Street
Eureka, CA 95501, USA
griffinskye3@sbcglobal.net
www.starkhousepress.com

The Perfect Servant: *Ellery Queen's Mystery Magazine*, November, 1971
Witness for the Defense: Ellery Queen's Mystery Magazine, September, 1963
The Perfectionist: *Alfred Hitchcock's Mystery Magazine*, November, 1967
Pattern of Guilt: *Alfred Hitchcock's Mystery Magazine*, July, 1958
Murder and Lonely Hearts: Alfred Hitchcock's Mystery Magazine, May, 1958
Death Scene: *Ellery Queen's Mystery Magazine*, May, 1963
The Master's Touch: *Alfred Hitchcock's Mystery Magazine*, April, 1966
Henry Lowden Alias Henry Taylor: *Alfred Hitchcock's Mystery Magazine*, July, 1960
The Very Hard Sell: *Alfred Hitchcock's Mystery Magazine*, May, 1959
Don't Sit Under the Apple Tree: *Alfred Hitchcock's Mystery Magazine*, October, 1959
The Affair Upstairs: *Alfred Hitchcock's Mystery Magazine*, July, 1961
Won't Somebody Help Me?: *Ellery Queen's Mystery Magazine*, January, 1959
Cop's Day Off: *Ellery Queen's Mystery Magazine*, August, 1961
The Deadly Mrs. Haversham: *Alfred Hitchcock's Mystery Magazine*, October, 1957
Your Witness: *Alfred Hitchcock's Mystery Magazine*, December, 1958

"Introduction" copyright © 2022 by Bill Kelly

ISBN: 978-1-951473-99-0

Cover and text design by Mark Shepard, shepgraphics.com
Proofreading by Bill Kelly
Cover photo: Leora Dana from *Alfred Hitchcock Presents*, "Your Witness" episode

First Stark House Press Edition: September 2022

Contents

Introduction

By Bill Kelly

Helen Nielsen (1918-2002) was the author of 19 novels and over 50 short stories, making a significant contribution to 1950s/1960s American crime fiction. This is the first collection of her short fiction since *Woman Missing and Other Stories* (ACE, 1961). Nielsen also scripted several teleplays and provided story source material for other television and movie scripts. Of the fifteen stories included in this collection, four were adapted as teleplays (Appendix A provides list of these stories and their teleplay details).

Stark House Press has previously published five of her novels, four appearing as two-fer editions. The two-fer volumes feature introductions that provide information on Nielsen's life and writing career. See Appendix B for further information.

Helen Nielsen published her first novel, *Gold Coast Nocturne* (also published as *Murder by Proxy* and *Dead on the Level*) in 1951. Her first published short story was "The Murder Everybody Saw", appearing in *The Saint Detective Magazine* in October of 1954. Nielsen would continue to alternate her contributions to both the mystery novel and short fiction forms throughout the 1950s, 1960s and early 1970s. Her last two short stories appeared in 1987 and 1991. Her final novels, *The Brink of Murder* (1976) and its predecessor *The Severed Key* (1973) were not published in the US, but found a home with her long-time UK publisher, Gollancz.

Nielsen avoided creating a series character for novel (or short story) publication until the mid-1960s, when she created Simon Drake, a rich lawyer-detective working from his Southern California mansion and only taking a case that he finds sufficiently stimulating. Nielsen had scripted two episodes for the Perry Mason television series in 1961 and 1962, so she may have been at least partially motivated to create Simon Drake (who appeared in five novels) by her work on this series, or as is often the case, the creation of a successful series character can supplement a writer's income and hopefully lead to television and movie productions.

All fourteen of Nielsen's novels published prior to the Simon Drake series are standalones and none of her short fiction features a series character. Based upon a reading of her work, I suspect that a primary goal of Nielsen as an artist was to avoid repeating herself. I find it extremely difficult to find echoes of plotting or characterization in her novels or short stories. Each story is fresh and each characterization is unique, even for "minor" characters. She does have several themes that she explores more than once and she will definitely show proclivities for airing (subtly) attitudes for various social mores and customs. For example, juvenile delinquency—its manifestations, adult attitudes toward, and society's "cures" for this phenomenon, regarded then as a crisis unique to the times, would often appear in her work. Never wielding a heavy-handed social club, Nielsen would often take an amused peek into the minds of those disturbed by "rampaging" wayward youth, that truth be told, was an American social condition that actually preceded the 1950s by nearly a century. Nevertheless, today is often regarded as new and unique by those experiencing a disturbance and many observers of the "j.d" crisis of the time would have wildly varying perspectives on "root causes", among them, one from a Nielsen character: "… no wonder so many kids are going wrong. They come home from school and find their mothers dressed up in a sack with a belt at the bottom. That's enough to drive anyone out on the streets." (from "Pattern of Guilt", included in this volume). On the other hand, as we see so often in her work, Nielsen is not locked into any particular viewpoint or development of a topic or theme. In this volume, the stories "Cop's Day Off" and "The Very Hard Sell" show adults resisting the easy way out through philosophy or lecturing and take risks to ensure that young people in trouble are given the opportunity to turn their lives around. This is but one example of Nielsen taking multiple approaches to exploring situations and themes that lesser writers often treat one-dimensionally.

This collection of fifteen Nielsen stories displays a wide range of story-telling, characterization and thematic perspectives and clearly demonstrates that Nielsen consciously pursued a goal of giving her readers something new each time they read her fiction. Several crime fiction sub-genres are represented: mystery puzzle story, police procedural, domestic malice, trial drama, cozy, comic mystery and one tale, "Won't Somebody Help Me?" that would not likely be classified as a horror tale, but its situation is as close, I think, as most of us want to come to the real thing. Themes explored by Nielsen in these stories include: personal and professional ethics, justice (particularly legal vs. moral), personal affirmation, revenge, and communication between the sexes. And there are stories that may bring a smile or two.

Exploring the short story form is beyond the scope of this essay, but Nielsen was of course aware of the basics of the form, in particular the rigid stripping from the prose form any element that does not advance characterization or story. Ideally, each paragraph, for example one that is primarily descriptive of a woman's rose garden as in "The Affair Upstairs", will also provide insights into the woman's character that will enable the reader to both accept the ensuing events of the story and most importantly, the resolution of the story.

For most of the stories in this volume, Nielsen employs the "turnabout" resolution to her endings—what might have been expected to happen or what usually happens—doesn't happen. This technique, of course, has to be made believable so that the plot points appearing in the story are reasonable and are true to the nature of the characters themselves. Each of the stories in this collection will have a "surprise" type ending, or if the ending is somewhat expected as in "Henry Lowden Alias Henry Taylor", its path will be strewn with puzzles that put the "foregone conclusion" in doubt, e.g., there is a third Henry added to the mix in the story "Henry Lowden Alias Henry Taylor".

Nielsen uses the turnabout resolution repeatedly, but explores a wide range of thematic material while doing so: reversal of held power (the weak overcoming the strong); comeuppance (extra-legal/personal justice & the "dumb" besting the "smart"); mentoring (the strong assisting the weak) and pride goes for a fall (best laid plans by those in control being foiled) all make an appearance. But in Nielsen's stories, the just do not always triumph and good intentions are not always rewarded. Nielsen's palette, however, is not composed entirely of dark colors. "Murder and Lonely Hearts" and "The Affair Upstairs" could be described as "serio-comic", while "The Master's Touch" is an O. Henry-like tale whose humor is ironic and generated from characterization, rather than the author relying on generic comical situations.

Helen Nielsen may never be regarded as a master of the American mystery short story form in the same league as Edward D. Hoch, Jack Ritchie or Stanley Ellin, but I believe no one will feel cheated by her efforts and most will find satisfaction in her linear plotting, rich characterizations and most of all, in her humanity.

Much of her short fiction has been considered worthy of being anthologized and as mentioned, adapted for television (Appendix A). One story in this volume, "Pattern of Guilt" was produced twice, with the original *Alcoa Premiere* production being rebroadcast on the *Kraft Mystery Theater*. Pretty good mileage for a short story.

The following paragraphs provide a brief summary and sometimes a "flavorful quote" for the stories included in this collection, in the order in which they appear:

"The Perfect Servant" describes the dilemma of a woman, recently widowed and unemployed, who secures a job with a doctor, hoping to attain some security in life. She has a strict moral code which is challenged by the doctor, forcing her to walk a fine line between her need to survive and her conscience. — "[the death of a patient] was a small event in the life of a young doctor who was slated to become the most popular society doctor in the area, but it destroyed Maria's last vision of Camelot."

"Witness for the Defense" finds a mentally challenged young man on trial for a crime he was emotionally compelled to commit, but is he to be held accountable? The characters struggle with the challenge of legal justice vs. moral justice, as the defense attorney, at wit's end, calls on a witness whose testimony may actually end up condemning his client.

"The Perfectionist" concerns a businessman on the rise looking for a way to eliminate his wife, who bars his way to her money and to acquiring the woman of his dreams. — "the creative part of his mind would be checking and rechecking his plan for any possible bugs. There was nothing morbid in this. [his wife] had already become an inanimate object. She existed only as the central character in the soon-to-be-presented drama of her death."

"Pattern of Guilt" features a reporter and a detective pursuing a serial killer, but the reporter (Keith) finds a way to use the killer as a means of solving his own problems. By nature weak, selfish and impulsive, will Keith find it within himself to finally put his life on its proper course? — "You only married me because you couldn't have your cake and eat it, too. That's your big weakness, Keith. You want to have your cake and eat it, too!"

"Murder and Lonely Hearts" is the bittersweet story of a lonely man (Herbert) who must decide to remain in his rut with a wife who ignores him or convert a pen-pal romance into a life of true romance and adventure. — "Herbert wasn't ambitious. If he occasionally felt a vague stirring or uneasiness within, he stopped off at the drugstore for a bicarbonate and forgot about it."

"Death Scene" is an eerie tale of a young lady-killer (Leo Manfred) who believes he has struck it rich when he meets a woman of Hollywood royalty residing in a decaying mansion. The young man has plans for both the lady and the real estate. — "For a man like Leo Manfred, time was short. He had a long way to travel to get where he wanted to go, and no qualms about the means of transportation."

"The Master's Touch" is a lighthearted tale of an unemployed magician and a dentist on his uppers who secure the services of a paroled safe cracker to make their dreams of easy wealth come true.

"Henry Lowden Alias Henry Taylor" follows a man seeking to prove the innocence of an ex-con whom, as a prison guard, he has been forced to kill during an escape attempt. — "The coming [to town] brought memories of Sunday School picnics with ripe watermelons and bottled pop kept cool in gunny sacks plunged into the water; of girls' laughter and the plop of a baseball in a catcher's mitt, and of all the other rich remembrances that hadn't been so far behind Arnold Mathias when he died with a bullet in his back."

"The Very Hard Sell" finds a detective investigating the alleged suicide of a man whose son had lost respect for his father, whom the boy describes as a "chicken". — "[the detective's] eyes held the boy's for a few seconds and then dismissed him. [the boy] went out, but long after he'd gone [the detective] stared after him. At least the boy had inadvertently explained what was behind his mother's refusal to face the obvious. 'Chicken,' he repeated to himself. It wasn't much of an obituary."

"Don't Sit Under the Apple Tree" is the story of a woman who has worked very hard to climb the corporate ladder and secure an ideal mate—her boss. Her new husband has put her on a pedestal "where life expectancy was so short", but will she be able to maintain her position without losing him when she begins to receive phone calls suggesting blackmail?

"The Affair Upstairs" is a serio-comic revenge tale of a landlady whose involvement in the affairs of her tenants goes a step further than she wishes. — "When something is too large," [he] said, still staring at [the landlady], "it has to be cut down."

"Won't Somebody Help Me?" explores the difficulties of a woman living with a man undergoing personality disintegration, her primary problem being that everyone else believes her husband is normal. — "beyond violence is a quiet place where all cries fade to muted whimpers in the mind—until nothing remains but staring silence and no hope at all."

"Cop's Day Off" reveals the motivations behind a workaholic detective less interested in solving a crime than he is in rescuing a potential suspect who is unaware of the dangers his chosen road in life hold in store for him.

"The Deadly Mrs. Haversham" is a serial confessor to murder who pursues justice for the murderer of her own husband. — from Mrs. Haversham's psychiatrist: "she really understands why she felt compelled to confess to crimes her nature would never have allowed her to commit."

"Your Witness" portrays the struggle between an abused wife and her powerful lawyer husband whose penchant for destroying the people around him must be addressed. — "The innocent must always be made to appear guilty. This was [her husband's] secret of success."

Appendix A: Stories from this Collection produced as teleplays:

"Your Witness": *Alfred Hitchcock Presents*, Season 4, Episode 31, 1959 (Nielsen story credit; teleplay by William Fay)

"Henry Lowden alias Henry Taylor" (as "Letter of Credit"): *Alfred Hitchcock Presents*, Season 5, Episode 36, 1960 (teleplay by Nielsen)

"The Very Hard Sell": *87th Precinct*, Season 1, Episode 11, 1961 (teleplay by Nielsen)

"Pattern of Guilt": *Alcoa Premiere*, Season 1, Episode 11, 1962 (teleplay by Nielsen); rebroadcast on *Kraft Mystery Theater*, Season 3, Episode 14, 1963; dramatized by Robin Chapman for *Tales of the Unexpected*, Season 5, Episode 8, 1982

Appendix B: Stark House Publications of Helen Nielsen's Novels
Link: starkhousepress.com/nielsen.php

Woman on the Roof, Black Gat Edition #9, November, 2016, ISBN 13: 9781944520137
Borrow the Night & *The Fifth Caller,* May, 2019, Introduction by Nicholas Litchfield, ISBN 13: 9781944520724
Sing Me a Murder & *False Witness*, November, 2021, Introduction by Curtis Evans, ISBN 13: 9781951473518

—Mesa, Arizona
September, 2022

Turning the Tables:
The Short Stories
of Helen Nielsen

\- - - - - - -

The Perfect Servant

Lieutenant Brandon was trying to bridge a generation gap when the woman walked into the police station and deposited a wad of currency on the counter. The trio of teenagers he had charged with collecting hub caps that belonged to irate citizens seemed unimpressed with the idea that they had committed theft, and then the woman, who was in her middle forties, shabbily dressed and wearing a look of quiet despair in her eyes, relinquished a cheap money clip containing the bills and said, "Please, who is the officer I see about this?"

Brandon nodded for a uniformed officer to take away the teenagers, grateful for a release from the pointless conversation, and asked the woman to state her problem.

"I was walking down the street—down Broadway," she stated, "and I saw this on the sidewalk. I picked it up. It is money."

Brandon pulled the bills out of the clip. There were three twenty-dollar bills, three tens, and two fives. "One hundred dollars," he said.

"Yes," the woman agreed. "I counted, too. That's a lot of money for someone to lose."

It was a lot of money, and the woman looked as if she had never had her hands on that much at any one time in all her life. Brandon called the desk sergeant to fill out a report and explained to the woman that the money would be held for thirty days, during which time the real owner could report his loss, describe the bills and the clip, and have the money returned, or, failing a claimant, the money would then become the property of the finder.

"Your name?" asked the sergeant.

She hesitated. "Maria," she said. "Maria Morales."

"Occupation?"

"I have no work now. When I work I am a domestic."

"Address?"

She gave the number of a cheap rooming house in the Spanish-speaking section of town. She told them she was very poor, unemployed, and without any property of her own. When the report was offered for her signature she placed both hands on the desk. A plain gold band adorned the third finger of her left hand.

"Just sign here, Miss Morales," the sergeant said.

"Mrs. Morales," she corrected. "I am a widow."

Brandon caught the desk sergeant's eye and shook his head in wonder.

"You should get those cocky young kids back in here to see this," the sergeant suggested.

"Waste of time," Brandon answered. "They wouldn't appreciate anything this square. Don't forget now, Mrs. Morales, in thirty days you check back with us. Chances are you'll get the money—or at least a reward."

"Thank you," she said in a very soft voice, "but I would rather have a job."

A young reporter from the Tucson daily came into the station just as Maria Morales was leaving, and Brandon, the bitter taste of the cynical teenagers still in his mouth, related the incident of the honesty of Maria Morales. It was a slow day on the news front and when the morning papers came out, the story of the unemployed widow and the $100 was written up in a neat box on the front page.

By noon Lieutenant Brandon was flooded with calls from people who claimed the money, and also with job offers for Maria Morales. Having developed a protective interest in the widow, he took it upon himself to screen the offers and decided that the best prospect was Lyle Waverly, a bachelor and a physician with a lucrative practice among the country club set.

Waverly needed a housekeeper he could trust. He owned a fine home in one of the better suburbs and entertained a well-heeled social set. He offered Maria a home, a good salary, and free medical care for as long as she remained in his employ.

Brandon approved the credentials and gave Waverly the woman's address, feeling the kind of inner warmth he always got from delivering Christmas parcels to the Neediest Families.

Maria Morales was extremely pleased with young Dr. Waverly. He was easy to work for. The house was large but new, and there was a gardener to help with the heavy work. She was an excellent cook but, aside from breakfast, the doctor seldom dined in. He was a busy man in more ways than one, which was only natural for one so attractive and increasingly affluent.

It soon became apparent that the doctor's love life was divided between two women: Cynthia Reardon, who was 23 and the sole heir of Josiah Reardon of Reardon Savings and Loan, and Shelley Clifford, ten years older, who had an additional handicap of being already married to Ramsey Clifford, the owner of Clifford Construction Company. Clifford was a burly man of fifty who had too little time to spend with a lovely wife who liked younger men.

Maria observed these things with professional silence, and long before Dr. Lyle Waverly was aware of his destiny, she knew that Cynthia had the inside track and would eventually get her man.

Life was pleasant in the Waverly house and Maria had no desire to return to the kind of employment she had recently known. She began to plot a campaign of self-preservation. When the doctor gave her an advance on her salary, she purchased fitted uniforms with caps and aprons for the frequent cocktail parties he gave for his wealthy friends and patients.

He soon learned that a caterer was no longer necessary. Maria's canapés became the envy of every hostess, and she herself became a topic of conversation not unwelcome in the tension created whenever Cynthia and Shelley were present on the same occasion. Shelley had the prior claim—a fact made obvious by the way she took over as hostess. She was the "in" woman fighting against the inevitable successor, and only Clifford's preoccupation with business could blind him to what anyone else could see. Of the two women, Maria preferred Shelley, who was no threat to her own position as mistress of the house. Shelley wanted only Lyle Waverly; Cynthia wanted his name, his life, and his home.

"Maria is a miracle," Shelley explained at the second party. "Imagine finding someone with her divine talent who is honest as well. Why, she's a perfect servant!"

"An honest woman?" Cynthia echoed. "Impossible! No woman can be honest and survive! Maria must have a few secrets."

Maria smiled blandly and continued to serve the canapés.

"I refuse to believe it!" Dr. Waverly announced. "All my life I've searched for a pure woman and this is she!"

"Perhaps you'd better marry her, darling." Shelley said. "You could do worse."

That remark was aimed at Cynthia, and Maria didn't wait to hear the reply. She returned to the kitchen and began to clean up the party debris. It was sometime later, after most of the guests had gone home and even Ramsey Clifford had taxied off to catch a late plane for a business appointment, that she heard Shelley berating Dr. Waverly for his interest in Cynthia Reardon. Maria returned to the living room to collect abandoned glasses and saw them alone.

"You needn't think I don't know what you're doing," Shelley was saying. "You needed me when you were beginning your practice—you needed my contacts and influence. Now you want a younger woman."

"Shelley, please." the doctor begged.

"No, I'm going to have my say! You want a younger and a richer woman, don't you, darling? What better catch than Josiah Reardon's sexy daughter? You'll never hold her, Lyle. She'll wear you like a pendant until she's bored with you. She's used up half a dozen handsome young men already."

"I'm not a child!" Waverly protested.

"No. You're a man and vain enough to think you can use Cynthia Reardon. I'm warning you, you'll be the one who gets used!"

"You're jealous," Waverly said.

"Of course I'm jealous. I love you, and I need you, Lyle. Now I need you—"

Maria retreated quickly to the kitchen before she was noticed. Sometime later the doctor came in carrying the glasses. All the guests were gone. He loosened his tie and drew a deep breath. "The things they don't teach you in medical school!" he sighed. "Maria, you are the only sane person on earth. You must never leave me."

"I'll fix you a hot milk," Maria said.

"Oh, no—"

"A bromide?"

"Brilliant idea. Are you sure you never worked the social route before?"

Maria's face darkened. "I worked for women," she said. "I didn't like it. They talk about you in front of others. 'You just can't trust anyone these days,' she said with savage mockery. 'They'll steal you blind and expect to get paid besides!'"

Waverly laughed. "I think I understand why honesty is so important to you. By the way, the thirty days are up. Did you ever go back to claim that hundred dollars?"

"Tomorrow," Maria said. "Tomorrow I go."

"Good! I hope it's there. If it isn't I'll give you a bonus to make up for losing it."

Maria returned to the police station the next day. Lieutenant Brandon gave her a paper to sign and then handed her the money which was still held in the money clip made of cheap metal with a silver dollar for decoration. None of the claimants could identify the exact denominations of the bills or describe the clip, so, the money was now legally hers.

"How's the job?" Brandon asked.

"The best one I ever had," Maria said.

"Now, that's what I like to hear! There's some justice in the world after all."

"Yes," Maria said, and slipped the money into her handbag.

Her position at the Waverly house continued to improve. She had her own room and, with an adequate household budget, was able to buy food less fattening than the starchy diet of the poor. She soon replaced her uniforms with a smaller size and had her hair done twice a month. She was beginning to feel and look more like a woman. Waverly soon took notice.

"Maria," he said, "you never told me about your husband. He was one lucky guy. What was his name?"

"Wa—" she began.

"Juan?"

She smiled softly. "Yes," she said, "his name was Juan."

"Handsome?"

"Of course!"

"And a passionate devil, I'll bet! What do you have going for you now? There must be a boyfriend somewhere."

The doctor had been drinking. He slipped a friendly arm about her shoulder.

"No boyfriend," Maria said.

"No? That's a shame! What's the matter? With legs like yours you could still do a fancy fandango. I'll bet you've done many a fancy fandango in your day."

"In my day—yes," Maria admitted.

"Then get back in circulation. Take a night off once in a while. Take tonight off. I'm going out with Miss Reardon."

"In that case, I think I should make you another bromide."

"No, you don't! I'm just a teensy-weensy bit drunk and I need much more fortification tonight. I'm going to ask Miss Reardon to marry me."

"She will accept," Maria said flatly.

"That's what I'm afraid of. You see, Maria, I've never been married. I'm afraid of marriage. I like women but I like my freedom better."

"Then why—?"

"Why marry? Because it's the thing to do. It's stabilizing. It builds character. It's what every rising young doctor should do, Maria, but I'm still scared. I don't like to be dominated."

"Then don't be dominated," Maria said. "Be the boss."

Waverly picked up his glass, "I'll drink to that," he said.

But it was Maria who feared the marriage more than Waverly. No sooner was the engagement announced than Cynthia began to reorganize the household, and Maria began to worry again about her security. Waverly caught her reading the want ads and demanded an explanation.

"What's the matter? Aren't you happy here?" he asked.

"Do you want more money?"

"No," Maria said.

"Then what's wrong?"

"Things will change after you marry."

"What things? Don't you like Miss Reardon?"

"It's not what I like. It's what Miss Reardon likes."

"Stop worrying. Nobody's going to treat you the way you were treated before I found you. I like you and that's all that matters. I'll tell you something I was going to keep secret. I've had my lawyer draw up a new will—a man does that when he gets married. I've made a $5000 bequest in your behalf. Now do you feel more secure?"

Maria was reassured, but she had lived long enough to take nothing for granted except money in the bank. Dr. Waverly was impulsive and generous, but Cynthia Reardon was a spoiled, strong-willed girl and Shelley Clifford's description of her character was more accurate than anything a prospective bridegroom was likely to see. What's more, Shelley didn't give up the battle simply because the engagement was announced. The mores of Dr. Waverly's social set, Maria learned, were more liberal than her own.

Shelley immediately developed symptoms requiring the doctor's professional attention at indelicate hours—particularly when her husband was away on business. There were surreptitious calls going both ways. When Waverly finally refused to go to see Shelley again, she came to see him. Traveling over an unpaved, circuitous drive, Shelley's small imported coupe made the trip between the Clifford estate and the doctor's house with increasing frequency.

It was a shameful thing, Maria reflected, for a woman to cling so to a man. As much as she had loved her husband, she would have let him go the minute he no longer wanted her. But no matter how many women Walter might have had before their marriage, he was faithful to his vows. Walter—not Juan. Juan Morales was the name of the father Maria barely remembered. Walter Dwyer was the name of the man she had wed. But when one must work as a domestic for the Anglos, it seemed better not to let it be known that she had once been married to an Anglo, had once lived like a lady.

She had been hardly 20 when Walter married her, but Walter was a gambler and gamblers die broke. After settling with the creditors, there was nothing for the widow Dwyer to do but return to Tucson and again become Maria Morales, domestic.

She had nothing left of the past but what Walter had called her "Irish luck," but her mind was no longer servile. She saw things now with the eyes of Mrs. Walter Dwyer, and what she saw was troubling. When a woman lost at love it was the same as when a man lost at cards. If she cried, she cried alone. What she could never do was cling to anything that was finished.

If Cynthia Reardon knew what was going on, she showed no outward sign. She might even be enjoying Shelley's humiliation. If Ramsey Clifford knew what was going on, he was indifferent. Eventually Dr. Waverly had it out with Shelley in a verbal battle over the telephone. Maria didn't eavesdrop. It was impossible not to hear him shouting in his study.

"No, I won't come over tonight!" he shouted. "There's nothing wrong with you, Shelley, and I won't come over tonight or any other night! I suggest that you get another doctor. I have no time for a chronic neurotic."

It was cruel, but it seemed to work. The telephone calls stopped. Two weeks before the scheduled wedding, Cynthia Reardon moved into the doctor's house and Maria's moral values were again updated. It seemed to be accepted practice in the young doctor's circle and Maria made no comment.

But her worst fears about her future status were soon confirmed. She couldn't please the new mistress who took Maria to task on the slightest provocation. The good days were finished. Cynthia was vicious. She would get whatever she wanted on her own terms either by using her sex or the lure of Josiah Reardon's wealth and prestige. If there was any doubt of who would rule the Waverly manse, it was decided the night of Josiah Reardon's prenuptial dinner party.

Once a week Dr. Waverly spent a day at the local free clinic, and, because Cynthia didn't care about these things, he sometimes talked about this work with Maria. It was the one thing of which he was genuinely proud, and because of it she was proud of him. A twelve-year-old Mexican boy had been under his care for some time. Minor surgery had been performed and confidence carefully built for the major surgery which, if successful, would restore him to a normal life.

Half of the battle, Waverly assured her, was in the rapport he had established with the frightened boy. On the evening before the scheduled major surgery Reardon gave his dinner party. Maria heard the doctor try to get Cynthia to change the date.

"I have nine o'clock surgery," he said. "It's imperative that I get my rest."

"You're not the only doctor at the clinic!" Cynthia scoffed.

"But this is a special case!"

"And Daddy's dinner isn't, I suppose! Lyle, you must be mad. You know Daddy doesn't change his plans for anyone, and this is a very special occasion. You see, darling, you're the first man I've ever known that Daddy liked. He thinks you're a stabilizing influence for me. I happen to know what his wedding present is going to be. What would you think of fifteen percent of the Reardon Corporation?"

Dr. Waverly thought through a few moments of absolute silence. "You're dreaming."

"Then I must have dreamed the papers I saw Daddy's lawyer drawing up. That's what the dinner is for tonight—the presentation of the gift. Now I know you can get somebody else to take over for you tomorrow. It's not as if you had a paying patient. It's just one of those clinic cases."

Maria held her breath and said a silent prayer, but she lost. Waverly went to the dinner with Cynthia. It was almost two a.m. when he returned and, minutes later, Cynthia was at the door. Maria heard them laughing in the entry hall.

"You shouldn't have come here," Waverly said. "The old boy doesn't know we've jumped the gun, and he might not like it."

"He would loathe it—but who cares? Darling, isn't it wonderful? You see, I didn't lie to you. We've got something to celebrate."

"It's so late—"

"A little nightcap—please."

Maria, listening from the kitchen, sighed and went back to bed. In the morning she arose, made a pot of coffee, and carried it up to Waverly's room. He was asleep. Cynthia opened one eye and then threw a pillow at her.

"Nobody called you!" she whispered angrily.

"The doctor has a hospital call—"

"Cancel it! Tell them he's sick or something. Can't you see that he's asleep? If you don't call the hospital this minute, I will!"

Maria retreated from the room. She went downstairs and phoned the hospital to inform them that Dr. Waverly couldn't perform the nine o'clock operation. It was noon before the doctor came downstairs and that was just a few minutes after the hospital called to tell him that the boy had died on the operating table. It was a small event in the life of a young doctor who was slated to become the most popular society doctor in the area, but it destroyed Maria's last vision of Camelot.

She remembered that Walter, who was crude and uneducated, had once left a game during a winning streak—and that was the one thing he had taught her a gambler should never do—to donate blood to the black porter who parked his car at the casino each night. The friend who took over Walter's hand had lost everything, but that hadn't mattered because the porter lived and Walter came back as happy as a schoolboy playing hooky. And so Maria was thoroughly disenchanted with her position at the Waverly house even before the night that Shelley Clifford returned.

It was four nights before the wedding. Cynthia, tired from rehearsals of the ceremony, had gone up to bed and taken two sleeping pills. The doctor was preparing a deposit slip for the visit to the bank that he wanted Maria to make for him in the morning. Maria went to the front door when the bell rang and there was no way to keep Shelley out of the house. She had been drinking and was hysterical. One eye was blackened and she had a cut on one cheek. Her husband, she explained when Waverly hurried out of the study, had learned of their relationship and beaten her. Her story might be true or untrue, but the doctor's reaction was firm.

"You can't stay here!" he insisted.

"Just for tonight," she begged. "Ram's been drinking, too. I'm afraid to go home."

"I don't believe you," Waverly said. "Ram Clifford doesn't drink."

"He did tonight. I'm afraid, Lyle. I'm afraid he'll kill me!"

Maria watched the doctor's face. He looked as if he thought that might be a good solution. Firmly he took Shelley by the shoulders and turned her back toward the door.

"Then go to a hotel," he said.

"Why can't I stay here?"

"Because I won't let you."

Waverly was trying to keep his voice down. When Shelley noticed him glance apprehensively toward the stairs, she sensed immediately what he was trying to hide. Her eyes widened. "She's here, isn't she? Cynthia's here!" And then she laughed and pushed Waverly away from her. "You couldn't even wait for the marriage! Oh, that's beautiful! Now wouldn't old Josiah Reardon love to know about this! His daughter may be a swinger, but the old boy's a stickler for the proprieties! And there's nothing more conservative than a savings and loan corporation, darling. When they hear about this you may not get that partnership and seat on the Board of Directors."

"Get out of the house!" Waverly ordered.

"Oh, I will, I will—just as soon as I've run upstairs to check—"

She lunged past him and started to run up the stairs. Waverly was about two steps behind her when the liquor, the shock, and the injuries caught up with Shelley. She was more than halfway up the stairway when she stumbled and fell against the railing. She shrieked and grabbed at the air and then, as both Waverly and Maria watched in horror, she plummeted over the railing and fell to the marble floor of the entry hall. There was a sickening sound as her head struck the marble. She was dead when Dr. Waverly reached her.

For a few moments he was too stunned to speak. Then he turned to Maria. "You've got to help me," he said.

"What do you mean?" Maria asked.

"You saw what happened. It was an accident—she killed herself. But I can't have her found in my house like this. Can you drive a car, Maria?"

"Yes."

"Good. Cynthia's asleep. The pills I gave her will last until morning. I'll get my car out of the garage and you follow me in it. I'll take Mrs. Clifford's body in her car and leave it out on that shortcut she uses."

Maria hesitated.

"Do you understand what I've said?" Waverly asked.

"I understand," Maria said, "but suppose the police come—"

"Out on that unpaved stretch? No chance. Anyway, I'll be the one taking the risk. I'll have the body with me. If you see a police car, just keep going."

"Still, there could be trouble," Maria said.

"Maria, there's no time to argue! I'm not going to hurt Mrs. Clifford— she's already dead. But I can't afford a scandal now. This is a matter of self-preservation!"

"With me, too, it is a matter of self-preservation," Maria said coldly. It took the doctor a few seconds to understand Maria's words. He had taken her for granted too long a time to make a sudden change without a certain anguish. When he finally did understand, he asked how much self-preservation she had in mind.

"A will is risky," she said. "Wills can be changed. Five thousand dollars in cash is more reliable."

"I don't have that much money in the house," he protested.

"I'll take a check," Maria said.

Minutes later, the doctor's check tucked away in her handbag, Maria drove Waverly's sedan at a safe distance behind Mrs. Clifford's little sports car. There was no traffic at all on the narrow road. When they reached a wide shoulder forming a scenic view over a ravine, Waverly stopped the small car and parked off the roadway. Maria stopped the sedan and watched him carry Shelley Clifford's body to the edge of the shoulder and toss it into the shrubbery.

Waverly then returned to the car and emptied Shelley Clifford's handbag of all cash and credit cards. Leaving the emptied purse on the seat, and pocketing the items that a robber would steal, he then took out his pocketknife and jammed it between the treads of one rear tire, letting out the air. The scene was set: a flat tire on a seldom-used road; a passing car hailed and a grim harvest of murder and robbery. Waverly folded his pocketknife and walked to the waiting sedan. He drove the car back to the house himself and then he and Maria scrubbed away the bloodstains on the marble entry floor.

When they had finished, Waverly said, "Nothing happened here tonight."

"Nothing," Maria agreed, "except that there's a bloodstain on your coat sleeve, Doctor. Give me the coat and I'll sponge out the stain before I go to bed."

Waverly pulled off his suit coat and gave it to her without hesitation. "Don't call me in the morning," he said. "I'm going to take a couple of sleeping pills myself."

Maria took the coat to her room but she didn't sponge out the blood. She turned off the light and tried to sleep. When that didn't work, she got up and packed her bag. In the morning, she got the doctor's bank deposit from his study, the suitcase and the stained coat from her room, and then, because the keys were still in the ignition, drove the doctor's car to the bank. Ordinarily she would have taken the bus. Today was urgent. Because she was so well known at the bank, and particularly after having made the doctor's deposit, she had no difficulty cashing the check for $5000.

On the return trip she took the unpaved shortcut. No other cars passed and she reached Mrs. Clifford's abandoned coupe unseen. Drawing alongside, she tossed Dr. Waverly's coat into the front seat, and then drove on.

Both Waverly and his fiancée were still asleep when Maria returned the doctor's sedan to the garage. Then, bag in hand, she walked to the bus stop.

Shelley Clifford's body was found early in the afternoon. The story of her death was on the evening television newscasts. An apparent victim of a casual murderer, her death inspired urgent editorial demand for increased police patrols and an end to permissive education. Ramsey Clifford offered a $10,000 reward for the apprehension and conviction of her murderer. It wasn't until the third day after Shelley's body was found that Lieutenant Gannon came to Dr. Waverly's house. He carried a small bundle wrapped in brown paper.

"I've been doing some checking. Doctor," he said. "I understand that you and the late Shelley Clifford were very good friends."

"You've picked up some gossip," Waverly stated.

"I don't think so. We didn't release all the evidence we had on her death when the body was found. We needed a little time to check out something that was found in the seat of her car—" Gannon ripped open the package and held up Waverly's suit coat. "We've traced this to your tailor, Dr. Waverly, and we've matched the bloodstains to Mrs. Clifford's. Now all we want from you is an explanation of what it was doing in her car."

On the fourth day after Shelley Clifford's death a smartly dressed, middle-aged woman checked into a hotel on the Nevada side of Lake Tahoe. She signed the register as Mrs. Walter Dwyer and then took a stroll through the casino because the atmosphere of a gambling town made her feel closer to Walter. Later, upstairs in her room, she studied the Tucson newspaper she had picked up in the lobby and was amused to learn that the police of that area were conducting an intensive search for her body.

Confronted with his bloodstained jacket, Waverly had told the truth—but he wasn't believed. When it developed that his housekeeper had last been seen on the morning of Mrs. Clifford's death cashing a $5000 check at Waverly's bank, Lieutenant Gannon formed the theory that Waverly had used Maria Morales to get him some ready cash in the event the doctor was linked to Mrs. Clifford and had to leave the country, and had then disposed of the woman so she wouldn't talk.

It was all nonsense, of course, and Maria was sure that Gannon could prove nothing. No crime had been committed. The worst that could happen to Dr. Waverly was that his marriage would be called off. That was a little sad since he deserved Cynthia Reardon as much as she deserved him. The other thing that would happen—and this was the reason she had placed the doctor's coat in Mrs. Clifford's car— was that the community would be made aware of Waverly's true character. This was imperative, in Maria's mind, in view of the nature of his profession.

Mrs. Dwyer remained at the hotel for several weeks. By that time the Tucson papers no longer referred to the Shelley-Clifford affair, and she could assume that it was in a state of permanent limbo with no need for her reappearance to save Waverly from a murder charge.

Before leaving the resort, Mrs. Dwyer put a down payment on a smartly furnished condominium apartment which, the salesman assured her, would bring a prime weekly rental in high season. Mrs. Dwyer explained that she traveled in her work and would occupy the apartment only a few months of the year, but that it was nice to have roots somewhere and a woman did need a good investment for her retirement years.

A few days later, a shabbily dressed woman, wearing a look of quiet despair in her eyes, entered the Tahoe bus station. She carried a cheap suitcase and a handbag containing $100 in a money clip. The bills were old—in fact, they were the same bills in the same money clip that Maria Morales, who was then 19 and the prettiest cocktail waitress on the Strip, saw drop from Water Dwyer's pocket as he bent over a casino gambling table. Maria had nothing of her own but a $10 advance on her salary, and when she returned the $100 to Dwyer she was so impressed by her honesty, and other attributes, that he took her to dinner. A week later they were married and the marriage was for love—not the cheap bargain that Dr. Lyle Waverly had tried to make with Cynthia Reardon. The money and the clip had been Walter's wedding present.

"Keep it for luck," he said.

"Your Irish luck ..."

In the bus station Maria bought a ticket to Sacramento, the state capital of California. There would be many wealthy people in that area who were so nervous about their own corruption that they would be eager to hire a housekeeper honest enough to go to the police station with $100 found on the street while looking for a job.

Walter had taught her never to walk out on a winning streak.

Witness for the Defense

The woman in the hall sat alone on a backless wooden bench, her cotton-gloved fingers laced over a large pouch bag, her sensibly shod feet set flat on the marble floor, her ramrod-straight back stressing the seams of a heavy tweed ulster purchased before the added weight of middle-age, and her Viking-grim face staring ahead at the soiled plaster wall with eyes that saw nothing—and remembered much. Her name was Martha Lindholm, and she was the sole witness—with the exception of three psychiatrists—for the defense of Larry Payne.

Larry Payne was a murderer.

He was twenty-three years old, handsome in a weak, boyish way, and only partially aware of what was happening to him. It had been a complicated trial, so full of legal ramifications that, the once sensation-hungry spectators had gradually lost interest, and the press, represented by three locals and one correspondent from San Francisco, had to tax their imaginations to make readable copy for the daily editions.

Now the trial was almost over. The double doors leading to the courtroom of Superior Court Judge Dwight Davis were closed; behind them an empty chamber awaited the return of a jury which would decide if Larry Payne were to live or die. The jury had filed out at four p.m. It was now ten minutes past midnight.

Except for the woman on the bench, the hall was empty. All was silent outside the press room where four newsmen and one female observer from the Department of Sociology at the local university lingered over a stale game of draw poker.

The female sociologist raked in the pot.

"Beginner's luck," Mark Christy growled.

"The superiority of science over the seat of the pants," she said crisply. "The coming age, Mr. Christy. You romantics will soon be obsolete."

Her name was Lisa Wyman. She was about twenty-eight and would have been pretty, Mark Christy conceded grudgingly, if she hadn't been so scientific. He rubbed a handful of fingers through his unromantically thinning hair and shoved back his chair.

"Wounded?" Lisa asked.

"Weary," Mark said.

He came to his feet and walked across the room to a filing cabinet that stood near the hall doorway. On it was a thermos of coffee. He picked up a paper cup and glanced at the wall clock.

Morrie Hamlin of the Herald had sharp eyes. "You lose again," he said. "It's after midnight and still no verdict. You said it would take only two hours."

"I said," Mark answered acidly, "that no twelve sane adults would waste more than two hours before finding Payne guilty."

"The voice of retribution," Lisa intoned, "and after all those weeks of professional testimony!"

The other men in the poker game were Sam Jorgens, editor of a county weekly, and young Ed Combs on his first assignment since graduation.

"Please, teacher," Sam asked, "what did all that technical jargon mean? Poor Larry didn't have all the love and kisses and bright sunlight he needed when he was a little boy. Well, who did?"

"Dr. Wyman's right," Ed Combs insisted. "Payne's a sick man."

Mark Christy held the paper cup under the spigot of the thermos and filled it to the brim. "I'd be sick too," he said, "if I'd stuck a knife in a prison guard. Larry-boy can't be such a martyred saint or he wouldn't be in a place where they have guards."

"Payne was sent up on a charge of statutory rape," Combs reminded. "You know what that means."

"He didn't get a life sentence for statutory rape. He tried the knife at least once before he killed that guard."

Sam Jorgens was a philosopher. "Lincoln's doctor's dog," he observed. "I've got ten dollars that says Jay Bellamy gets an acquittal for Payne not because of the headshrinkers, but because of the corn he pitched to the jury." Sam's voice dropped mockingly. "Larry's parents abandoned him—he was left with a maiden aunt—somebody killed his little dog—"

"A dog he loved deeply," Lisa Wyman interrupted. "A child has to love."

"And he couldn't love Old Stone Face," Combs added. "Who could? Can you imagine what would happen if a man came near her?"

There was still a tinge of adolescent arrogance in Ed Combs's laughter. Mark Christy stood in the doorway with the cup of coffee in his hand. His eyes found the hall and the woman on the bench sitting exactly as she'd been sitting these many hours.

"She's still out there," Mark said softly.

"Knitting?" Lisa asked.

"Knitting? Why?"

"Madame La Farge knitted."

Ed Combs tittered appreciatively.

"I don't think that's fair," Mark said. "She did come all the way from Dallas to testify for Payne." He turned away from the hall and looked back over his shoulder. Lisa Wyman was dealing another hand.

"I have two children," she said. "If they were in trouble, I'd fight for them—and I mean fight! But that woman out there has no emotion at all—not a drop."

"If that's true—if she doesn't care what happens to Payne—what is she waiting for?" Mark demanded.

"The payoff," Combs said. "She got stuck with an unwanted kid twenty years ago—"

"I asked Dr. Wyman!"

There was enough late-hour irritation in Mark's voice to cause a momentary freeze. Then Sam Jorgens grinned.

"You didn't lose that much, Mark," he scolded. "Come on, pick up your hand and we'll give you a chance to break even."

Mark ignored the invitation.

"Why is she waiting?" he challenged Lisa Wyman again.

"Mr. Combs may be right," Lisa said, "although I'm inclined to think it's an expression of guilt. She has to punish herself for her failure to be a woman."

"Couldn't she be waiting out of love for Payne?"

"You heard her testify. Did she speak one loving word? Did she show one sign of compassion?"

There was no answer. Lisa completed arranging the cards in her hand, then looked up. Mark Christy was gone.

The woman on the bench didn't notice him at first, but the cup of coffee Mark held out to her gave off a tantalizing aroma. She turned toward him inquiringly.

"I thought you might be able to use this," he said. "Be careful—it's hot."

Her reflexes were slow. She stared at the cup for a few seconds, then unlaced her fingers and accepted it with one gloved hand. There was something very proper about the way she took the cup that reminded Mark of his own manners.

"I'm sorry," he said. "Do you take cream?"

The question might have been one of deep philosophical significance. "No," she answered soberly, "I don't. I haven't taken cream since before the war. For a long time there wasn't any—just canned milk—and I don't like canned milk."

She closed both hands around the cup and drank slowly. Mark watched her—fascinated by the one mystery remaining in a headline exhausted case. Did she think of the war because it was at that time Larry Payne was placed in her care? She would have been in her early thirties—an old maid by the standards of a small Texas community. By her own choice surely—she was a plain woman but not homely.

"It must have been tough," Mark mused, "stuck with a child nobody wanted."

She lowered the cup and looked sharply at him.

"You're one of those reporters, aren't you?" she asked.

Mark grinned. "Don't hold that against me. I have to earn a living."

But the confidence he'd hoped to foster was destroyed: She was now uncomfortable. She shifted her position nervously; and one foot scraped against an object on the floor. Mark looked down. It was a shabby suitcase.

"It's mine," she said quickly. "Checkout time at the hotel was two p.m., but when the jury went out at four I made them let me go without paying for another night."

Mark Christy scowled. There wasn't a hotel room in town expensive enough to justify so long a vigil on that hard bench—unless Lisa Wyman's analysis was correct.

"Look at her hands clutching that purse," Lisa had said. "Look at her tight mouth. She's miserly about everything—especially love!"

That was said the day Martha Lindholm took the stand, exactly two weeks after the trial had begun ...

Sutton County was a ranching and winery area. The old courthouse at Sierra Vista dated back to a time when the state Capitol was at Monterey, and the super highway that snubbed the city at the overpass was only a stagecoach trail to the booming settlement of San Francisco.

Many outward changes had come to Sierra Vista—a new front on the Vallejo Hotel, parking meters in the business district, a fruitful crop of television antennas stretching from Mexican town to the new Rancho Cresta subdivision. But inward changes came slowly. It was three days before Jay Bellamy got a jury that gave him any confidence. Larry Payne was a convicted rapist and a killer. To the ranchers and housewives and merchants of Sutton County these were the ugliest crimes in the human repertory of evil.

Bellamy was a young man—quick, alert, his hair worn in a close crew-cut. He was the scientific half of the law firm of Bellamy & Raines, appointed by the state to defend Larry Payne. Lew Raines was gentler—he brought a "bedside manner" to the courtroom. Women jurors were selected with an eye to Lew's talents.

"But there's no emotional side to our case," Lew complained. "The emotion will be on the other side. All Hastings has to do is unbutton his coat and show his galluses."

Fred Hastings, the District Attorney of Sutton County, was a rancher. He wore a big hat to the courtroom and placed it conspicuously on the table beside his briefcase. There was something steady and unchanging and dependable about that hat—it inspired confidence in nervous jury candidates.

"Do you believe in the death penalty?" Hastings asked.

The prospective juror was a small rancher. He held his own big hat tightly in sun-browned hands. After sober thought, he answered, "Yes, sir. I do."

"And do you understand that—because the defendant is already serving a life term for a felony offense—that a verdict of guilty calls for a mandatory death sentence?"

Quietly, "Yes, sir."

"Candidate acceptable for the prosecution."

Jay Bellamy approached the stand. There was no familiarity when he posed his single question. "What is your opinion of psychiatry?"

The hat twisted slowly in the rancher's hand.

"I don't know as I'm an expert."

"None of us is," Jay responded. "I merely want to know if you will honor the statements of qualified psychiatrists who will testify for the defendant in this trial."

A year ago it would have been stifling hot in the room, with only the sweep of the old ceiling fans to cool the court. But a year ago the county budget had provided for air conditioning. Perspiration now came from nervous tension.

"Well, sir, I have a son the same age as Larry Payne. He's stationed at Canaveral and he's expected to obey orders even at the cost of his own life. I don't go along with coddling murderers."

Tersely Jay said, "The candidate is unacceptable to the defense."

Even when the jury was finally completed, Jay Bellamy had misgivings. People liked a simple world with simple definitions. In 1843, fifteen English judges had defined legal insanity in what was known as the M'Naghten Rules. Roughly, they declared a person not criminally responsible for an offense, if at the time the act was committed, he was mentally unsound so as to lack knowledge that his act was wrong. In the light of modern psychiatry the law was obsolete—but that light had yet to reach the statute books.

"We aren't fighting Hastings," Lew Raines predicted ominously. "We're up against a hundred and twenty years of Anglo-American legal mythology. Look at the face of those jurors, Jay. I tell you, change the plea to self-defense before it's too late."

"Payne stabbed the prison guard in the back," Bellamy answered. "In the back, Lew. We have no plea but insanity."

"But it won't sell!" Raines insisted. "Think of Payne's record. For a conviction of statutory rape he was sent to San Quentin. For possession of a knife he was given an automatic life term. Now he's charged with a murder that never would have happened had he received proper treatment in the beginning. Legally we're not in the Twentieth Century, Jay. Legally we're in the Dark Ages!"

Bellamy picked up his briefcase and moved toward the door.

"I'm familiar with Payne's background," he said quietly, "but the plea is still 'Not Guilty by Reason of Insanity.'"

"Hastings will throw the M'Naghten Rulings at you."

Jay smiled wryly. "I expect he will, and then we'll find out."

"Find out?"

"If this is really the Twentieth Century—or the Dark Ages."

Larry Payne's face mirrored an innate innocence—as if the sordid crimes charged against him had been committed by a sleepwalker. He was brought handcuffed into the courtroom, then his hands were freed, and he was allowed to sit between his two attorneys. He smiled shyly for the press photographers. Mark Christy watched from the press row.

"How do you like that for a killer?" Mark said. "He looks more like an honor student from Sierra Vista High."

"It's the release," Lisa Wyman explained. "He's killed. He's had his release."

"That's great!" Morrie Hamlin growled. "All they have to do is turn him loose and he can go on using his knife for therapy."

Morrie's viewpoint was the wall of resistance Jay Bellamy had to break down. Their client's record was ugly one of increasing violence without any sign of reformation ... Methodically, Hastings laid out the mechanics of the crime before the jury.

The first witness was Carlos Ventura, Larry Payne's cellmate.

"Tell the court in your own words," Hastings said, "exactly what happened the day the prison guard, Warren, was killed."

Carlos Ventura looked out over the courtroom with bland, non-committal eyes. Only when his glance rested on Payne was there a flicker of contempt.

"Well, there was this trouble about a knife missing from the kitchen. Warren came to the cell to search Payne's bed."

"How did Payne react?"

Carlos Ventura's mouth formed a hard smile. To be a prisoner called to testify in court was to be nothing; but nothing was better than Larry Payne.

"Like he was scared," he said. "Warren knew it. You always know when a guy's scared."

"And then what happened?" Hastings asked.

"Warren told Payne to face the wall while he searched the bed. Payne turned around—then all of a sudden he whirled and made a dive for the mattress. That was it."

"What was it?"

"The way it happened—fast. Payne grabbed the knife and shoved it in Warren's back."

"Did Payne say anything? Did he give any warning that he intended to stab Warren?"

"He didn't make a sound. He dived for the knife and let Warren have it in the back."

Raines leaned forward, listening. Bellamy watched Payne for a reaction; but there was none—the prisoner's attention was elsewhere. A fly buzzed lazily above Judge Davis' head and then lighted, unnoticed, on his collar. It seemed highly amusing that a dignified judge should wear a fly on his collar. Larry Payne smiled. A flashbulb winked nearby. The morning editions would carry the photo with a descriptive caption like Payne leers as cellmate tells how he stabbed prison guard.

Anticipating Bellamy, Hastings put a psychiatrist for the state on the stand. Dr. Lodge testified that Larry Payne had been given exhaustive tests after the murder. The psychiatrist, a slight, intense man, stated firmly that he had found the defendant coherent, responsive, and fully aware of the nature of his act.

"And therefore responsible under the law?" Hastings pressed.

"As I interpret the law, yes," Lodge answered. "I found the defendant sane."

Raines was almost beyond restraint. He leaned across the defense table and tugged at Bellamy's sleeve.

"That's impossible," he protested. "We have the analyses of Toler, Britt, and Stauffeur!"

Bellamy calmed him with a gesture. He rose and came forward to cross-examine.

"Dr. Lodge, at the time you examined the defendant, had he received prior treatment of any kind?"

Lodge hesitated. "I'm not sure I know what you mean."

"Had he been under the care of a medical doctor?"

"I don't know that I can answer that question."

"But I can," Bellamy said quickly. "Immediately after knifing Warren, the defendant was taken to the prison infirmary where he was treated for hysteria. He was later transferred to the county jail—under sedation. There—still under sedation—he was questioned by the District Attorney. What I'm trying to establish is simply this: was Larry Payne under sedation at the time of your examination?"

"Yes," Lodge admitted. "He was."

"And you have never examined him at any time when he was not under sedation?"

"No, sir. I have not."

The admission was a telling blow—but there was no way of knowing how it registered with the jury—all juries are unpredictable. At the close of the day's session Bellamy reminisced while packing his briefcase.

"I once defended a car thief," he recalled, "who was caught in the act, chased by the police and wounded five times in a running gun battle. The jury found him Not Guilty."

"You've made your point," Raines admitted grimly, "but I think we missed something with Ventura—" Raines didn't finish his statement. He looked up to see Hastings in the aisle, and reticence wasn't one of Lew Raines's noticeable traits.

"How does it feel to ask for the life of a man so mentally ill he doesn't know what's going on?" Lew demanded.

Hastings smiled wryly. "I stopped feeling years ago," he said. "Now I just take the oath of office and try to do my job. If you can convince the jury that Larry Payne didn't know right from wrong when he killed Warren, you'll have done your job."

"Is that your criterion for sanity?" Bellamy demanded.

"It's the law's criterion," Hastings replied quietly.

"An obsolete law," Raines protested. "The M'Naghten Rulings were made over a hundred years ago—prior to Freud, prior to studies in compulsive behavior, prior to—"

"—prior to the existence of the drug that kept Payne rational while he confessed the murder," Bellamy added, "and you know that as well as we do."

For a moment Hastings met Bellamy's direct stare.

"Is that what you're trying to do—use Payne as a cause célèbre to get a new definition of insanity in this state?"

"What we're trying to do," Bellamy answered, "is to defend a client the state has charged us to defend. If, in doing so, we can help science force the lock on an antiquated mental dungeon and let in a little light, we're all the winners."

But dungeons, even with rusty locks, are not easy to open. Three of the finest psychiatrists available had found Payne insane. John Britt, young and explosive, likened him to a martyr—as much a victim of society as Jean Valjean.

"Who stole bread because he was hungry," Hastings commented.

"There are different kinds of hunger," Britt commented in reply. "Are you suggesting that a man has a right to take love by force, Mr. Britt?" Hastings thundered.

"No, sir. I'm stating that a child in a man's body—a mentally retarded child—attempted to satiate his hunger by force. At that point Larry Payne needed psychiatric help—not a sentence to San Quentin where he would go on repeating a destructive pattern."

The second defense witness was Aaron Toler, older and more poised. In academic language he explained the nature of Payne's problem. Payne was a challenge—a human guinea pig who, if spared, might help science unlock secrets of the mind.

"Or who might kill again?" Hastings suggested.

No one could answer that question negatively. By the time the third psychiatrist, Stauffeur, took the stand most of the spectators, foreseeing the outcome, had left.

Raines whispered earnestly to Bellamy. "We're not getting through.

Stauffeur sounds like a public accountant. The jury has to feel that Payne is insane."

"What do you want to do?"

"Recall Ventura to the stand. There's something missing in his story. I'm sure of it."

It was the last day of the second week of the trial. Something had gone wrong with the air conditioning and the fans were no longer connected. Carlos Ventura's face was bearded with perspiration as Raines approached the witness stand holding the death knife. Murder needed a trigger, and under pressure Ventura broke.

"All right," he admitted, "Warren called Payne a name before the kid went for the knife."

"What was the name?" Raines demanded.

For the first time Larry became aware of the proceedings. His eyes were fixed on Ventura.

"A name for what Payne is," Ventura said. "'You stand with your face to the wall,' Warren told him. 'Don't you move a muscle, you—'" and Ventura mouthed a shocking word.

Payne was on his feet. "Don't you call me that!" he screamed. "Don't you call me that again!"

He lunged forward, clawing at Ventura. A woman juror screamed. The bailiff and a uniformed officer sprang forward, but not before Larry Payne, the mild-mannered boy who smiled shyly at cameramen, had become an enraged animal. Still shouting, he was dragged from the courtroom as Judge Davis ordered a recess.

As the courtroom cleared, Bellamy turned on his partner.

"You overdid it, Lew!" he stormed. "You left nothing to the imagination."

"I proved that Payne was goaded into the attack," Raines insisted.

"Yes—but you also proved he's capable of killing—and that's what the jury will remember! Payne didn't need that kind of image. If only we had someone who liked him—just one person who could take the stand and make Larry Payne sound like a human being instead of a case history."

Jay Bellamy didn't believe in luck—or in magic. The sweat on his face was his luck, and the knowledge in his mind was his magic. But there were times when a natural sequence of events seemed the work of Providence.

The courtroom was now empty—the doors left open for ventilation. Moving toward the doors, Bellamy paused—intrigued by what he saw in the corridor. The woman would have been conspicuous anywhere on such a day. In spite of the heat, she wore a heavy tweed coat, a hat, and gloves. In addition to a large, unstylish handbag, she carried a cheap suitcase and a folded newspaper at which she kept glancing.

At the entrance to the courtroom she stopped.

"Is this," she asked timidly, "where Larry Payne is being tried?"

"It is," Bellamy answered, "but court has adjourned for the day."

The woman frowned, unsure of herself.

"Who did you want to see?" Raines asked.

"A lawyer—" She consulted the folded newspaper again. She was obviously near-sighted, but she didn't wear glasses. "—named Jay Bellamy. His name's printed here in the paper. I've come all the way from Texas to tell him the truth about Larry Payne."

Bellamy sighed.

Her name was Martha Lindholm. She was called as a surprise witness for the defense. Larry Payne was in court again—subdued and apparently oblivious to the furore he had caused. As the woman passed him, his face brightened with recognition. Starting up from his chair, he cried, "Aunt Martha!"

Martha Lindholm halted. She seemed under a great strain. Those close to her could see the muscles of her jaw tighten before she turned her head to give Larry Payne a cold stare and then move on. Bewildered, Payne sank back in his chair. He looked like a small boy who had been slapped and didn't know why.

From the stand Martha Lindholm's voice was firm and without a trace of emotion. Bellamy led her into the past to the day an unwanted child was placed in her care.

"I had no place for him," she said bluntly, "and no time. I worked as a practical nurse for five dollars a day. It wasn't easy to feed an extra mouth."

"How old was the boy when he first came to you?" Bellamy asked.

"He was five. Not old enough to work for his keep or even help around the place. Just old enough to want."

"Want?" Bellamy echoed.

"Things he couldn't have—a wagon, a bicycle, a puppy. I told him we couldn't afford to feed a puppy, but he got one anyway. It wasn't my fault that—"

She stopped abruptly, embarrassed.

"Your fault?" Bellamy repeated. "What wasn't your fault?"

"It died," she said. "One day I heard Larry screaming in the yard. I ran outside and found him holding the dead puppy in his arms."

"What happened to the dog?"

Angrily she retorted, "How do I know? It was dead, that's all! After that Larry hardly ever spoke to me."

The air conditioning was still out of order. There was an under current of irritation in the courtroom—silent but easily sensed. Lindholm's gloved fingers worked nervously at the catch of her bag, and relentlessly Bellamy continued to gouge out the past.

"As the boy grew older was he difficult to manage?"

"Very difficult," she answered. "I had to work nights a lot. I paid eighty dollars to have a high fence built around the property and I always locked it when I went out. But Larry found a way to get over it."

"Then the boy was left alone nights. At what age was that?"

"Off and on until he was fifteen." Quickly she added, "But he was safe enough. Sometimes the storms frightened him, but he wasn't hurt. Then, when Larry was fifteen, he got into trouble. He took some money."

In the press section, Lisa Wyman leaned toward Mark Christy. "Stealing," she whispered. "The classic symptom of the love-starved child. Look at her hands clutching that purse. Look at her tight mouth ... "

From the witness stand Martha Lindholm's voice droned on.

"... twenty dollars," she said. "I told the Sheriff the boy was getting too much for me to handle. Maybe twenty dollars doesn't sound like much, but it was a lot to me."

In a surprised voice Bellamy asked, "The money was yours, Miss Lindholm? You preferred the charges—?"

"It was my household money!" she said angrily, "Larry squandered it taking a lot of strangers to the circus. Not people he knew, mind you. Not friends. Just strangers he picked up in the street. When the Sheriff asked why he did that, Larry said he wanted somebody to like him."

All through her testimony Larry Payne looked bored. His gaze wandered to the jury box. A middle-aged woman with lonely eyes was staring at him in a strange way. He smiled at her and she looked down quickly, fussed with her purse, and took out a handkerchief. She patted her perspiring face nervously.

A complaining whine came into Martha Lindholm's voice. "I never understood Larry," she continued. "I gave him a good home, treated him like my own right up to the day he run off. But he never appreciated anything I gave him. What do you do with a boy like that? What can you do?"

The jury deliberated Martha Lindholm's questions until twelve forty and then the foreman, having solemnly tabulated the last ballot, informed the guard outside the jury room that a verdict had been reached.

Judge Davis was notified, Larry Payne was brought up from a lower floor cell, and the weary survivors of the long vigil reassembled in the courtroom to hear the quiet announcement that Larry Payne— by reason of insanity—was Not Guilty.

Minutes later the manacled prisoner was escorted back to his cell. A few steps from the doorway he paused and looked pleadingly at Martha Lindholm. She lowered her eyes, and Payne, shoulders sagging, moved on.

Mark Christy watched intently. Why had she not faced Larry Payne? Vengeance? Guilt? Remorse? Now that the trial was over, the woman could permit herself to show some emotion.

Mark felt he had to know why she waited. He lingered in the emptying courtroom as Bellamy and Raines greeted her.

"Miss Lindholm," Bellamy said cordially. "I'm so glad you stayed on. I called your hotel and was told you had checked out."

"It was eight dollars a day," she explained. Timidly she then added, "You promised to give me bus fare back to Texas."

"Bus fare?" Raines echoed. "After what happened here tonight? Why don't you take a plane?"

"There's no need for that," she said. "Do you have the money with you? I've been waiting a long time."

Mark Christy now had his answer. He turned away disgustedly. If he hurried, he could catch Lisa Wyman and the rest of the pressroom group at the corner bar and celebrate a victory for the Age of Science. The thinning of his hair, he decided, wasn't coming any too soon. He was losing touch with reality. He had almost believed there could be such a thing as an unselfish motive.

In the courtroom Jay Bellamy finished counting out the bus fare and placed it in Martha Lindholm's hand.

"I'm sorry for what I had to do," he said. "I didn't know any other way to make the jury sympathetic to Larry—except by turning you into a heartless ogre."

There was both sadness and warmth in Martha Lindholm's eyes.

"It doesn't matter what people think of me," she said, "just so the boy finally gets help. I told you the day I came, he's been sick in the mind for a long time. But in that little town ... in those days ... nobody knew what to do with him. And nobody cared."

"Except you, Miss Lindholm."

"I did what I could, but there was a devil inside Larry that made him do terrible things. I saw it the first time on the day he killed the puppy he loved so much."

Martha Lindholm folded the bus money and put it in her purse. The catch snapped loudly in the empty courtroom.

"And he did kill him, Mr. Bellamy," she added, "even if you wouldn't let me tell that part of the story from the witness stand."

The Perfectionist

It was almost two a.m. when Claudia Shane eased away from the last dedicated group of celebrants at the Solimar Point Country Club bar and, on the pretext of visiting the powder room, made her way to the locked door of the executive office. Claudia was thirty-one, slender and elegantly poised. She rapped smartly on the door and it opened from within.

There were two men in the room: Pete Kelly, a chubby white-haired Irish cherub with bright pink checks, who was holding a black attaché case clutched tightly to his dinner jacket, and Alex Ward, who was leading-man handsome and as instantly aware of Claudia's entry as if their psyches were connected by electric wires.

Pete Kelly was leaving. Waving the attaché case as he neared Claudia, he crowed, "How about that? Alex stages the annual Founder's Day brawl and we come out three hundred bucks in the black! First time in the annals of the organization. The man's a bloody genius!"

"Are you just becoming aware of that?" Claudia chided. "Goodnight, Peter, dear."

She eased him through the doorway with the grace of a queen dismissing an unwanted caller who would forever believe that his departure had broken her heart. Then she locked the door and turned to meet Alex, fitting into his arms as if they were home.

"Claudia, it's been too long!" he said.

"Only two weeks," she answered.

"Two centuries! Don't ever do that to me again. No more separations—trial or otherwise."

"You're sold, then?"

"You know it! You must have known months before you went to Palm Springs."

"But now we're both certain, aren't we?"

She stepped back and let him gaze at her, confident that he could see only what pleased him. She had picked up a tan at the spa, and it was strikingly set off by a simple dinner sheath that had come off the rack in one of the local shops. A woman with style had no need of an expensive couturier. Widowed at twenty-six, Claudia Shane had carried on with her husband's insurance brokerage and prospered with the Solimar Point boom. Energies that might have gone into homemaking and childbearing had blossomed in another direction, but not at the expense of femininity.

"Now that we've eliminated the last doubt," she added, "there's only one question left. When are you going to marry me?"

"Soon," Alex said.

"Darling, I hate to be forward but there's so little time! I've missed too much of life. So have you. I want to marry you now and live with you, and make love with you with the doors unlocked and the drapes open—"

"You're shameless," Alex scolded.

"About some things, yes. When, Alex?"

Alex feigned interest in his wristwatch, then exclaimed, "It's after two! I've been trying all evening to have five minutes alone with you, and now I have to go out to the office and close up shop. The caterers were paid only until two-thirty. I mustn't lose that precious profit. How about lunch tomorrow?"

Claudia protested, "I'm serious, Alex. It has to be soon or we close the doors. I'm not the Back Street type."

"Tomorrow at one. Same place. We'll set dates. I promise."

Claudia left the office. Alex waited five minutes, then followed. The ballroom was deserted now. The brilliant jazz combo the Founder's Club board of directors had whined so about importing from London were packing up their instruments and preparing to depart. They had been a bit too riotous for the old establishment group, but executives were coming younger these days and the portion that remained was the group that had drained the bar of its private stock and thus turned the annual ball into a profit-making function. It was simple logic. Alex Ward had made one million dollars in the past five years by using simple logic and hard-nosed driving power. There was no luck involved. It was good judgment, good timing and chutzpah. It was the art of being a perfectionist.

It was also because he had inherited, through marriage, the management of Harry Dragerman's realty business when the old man died five years ago, and that left one severe drawback to Alex's enjoyment of his well-deserved affluence: his wife, Phyllis.

When the ballroom was completely cleared, Alex signaled the janitors to clean up and then walked out to the parking lot. The combo's van, a service truck, and his own car were all that remained to give evidence of a successful evening. Alex went to his sedan and slid in behind the steering wheel. Phyllis, swathed in mink, was curled up in the back seat.

She rose up and blinked at the panel light.

"Feeling better?" he asked.

Her voice was a familiar whine. "I slept some," she said, "but I'm chilled through."

"I told you to call a cab and go home."

"Alone—at night? You know how nervous I've been since that Dorrit girl was strangled on the beach."

"That was two miles away and nearly a month ago," Alex said.

"But the police haven't made an arrest. Alex, why were you so long? You knew I had a headache."

Alex started the motor and drove out of the parking lot. There was no traffic at this level. What was still awake and lighted in the Point was spread out below them as they rolled toward the highland estates. This was land Harry Dragerman had leased out for pasture until Alex took over the business and turned it into prime white-water-view residential lots. As he drove, Alex watched Phyllis in the rearview mirror. She was terribly pale, and her face had become quite puffy with the passing years. In spite of the mink—and the Parisian gown beneath it—she was dowdy. She had never been a great beauty, but she had been cute and uncomplicated. But life wasn't uncomplicated. Now that he was a successful man, Alex wanted a more meaningful companionship with a woman. Deep down inside, Phyllis was still Harry Dragerman's little girl, and nothing was more irritating than a thirty-five-year-old teenager.

"I thought Dr. Kuperman said those headaches were cured," Alex said. "Psychosomatic and cured. God knows we paid him enough!"

"Let's not talk about it," Phyllis said. "I'll be all right as soon as I've had a hot bath. It was the crowd and that awful music—"

"It's the best beat of the day."

"I know. You're always right about business things, Alex."

Pathetic. Claudia had frugged with the best of them, but if she hadn't liked the group she would have told him so with no qualifications. There was no challenge left in Phyllis. She was as dated as the business concepts that had kept her father on the edge of survival for fifty professional years.

"Phyllis," he said abruptly, "I think Kuperman is right. Those headaches are psychosomatic—and I know why. It's our marriage. It's just not working out. Let's be civilized and call it quits."

He knew how Phyllis would react. She was completely predictable.

"Alex, no! Not that again," she begged.

"Why not? We know it's true. Divorce me, Phyllis. You'll feel wonderful!"

Phyllis drew the mink closer about her face. She was weak, clinging, adolescent and deadly, because she held the winning cards and knew how to play them.

"It's Claudia Shane, isn't it? That's why you kept me sitting in the car so long. You were with her. I saw her come out—"

"Phyllis, leave Mrs. Shane out of this. It's between you and me!"

The pale face in Alex's rearview mirror smiled knowingly.

"All right, then. If it's just between you and me, I'll give you the divorce," Phyllis said, "but that's all I'll give you. Absolutely all. Is that sufficiently clear?"

Alex's grip tightened on the steering wheel. His foot bore lower on the accelerator. They were climbing too fast, as if he could run away from that nasal whine in the back seat.

"I know you think it's unfair," she said. "You did make the fortune— but with the business I inherited from Papa. It's still mine, Alex—"

"Phyllis, shut up!" Alex said.

"You know it is. You know the law. Can you make another million, Alex? Are you sure Claudia will want you if you can't? Are you sure you can fit into her sophisticated world without a bankroll?"

"Phyllis, if you don't shut up—" Alex threatened—and then Phyllis screamed. Instinctively, Alex' foot found the brake pedal. They had swung around the curve and picked up a flashing red light in the headlight beams, then an ambulance jutting out from a wide driveway, and a big man in a leather coat who planted himself in the path of the sedan as it lurched to a stop.

"Alex Ward?" the man called out. "Is that you?"

It was Captain Jimmy Collins of the Solimar Point Police Department. He came to the side of the car and poked his face in the open window, his teeth clenched.

"You damned near hit my police car, Alex," he said. "I should run you in for reckless driving, but I don't have, time. You just pull around the ambulance easy and go on home."

The ambulance was now bathed with light. The rear doors were open and a couple of white-garbed attendants came out of the driveway bearing a covered stretcher.

"This is the Sandersons' house," Phyllis said. "What's happened Captain?"

Collins hesitated. He was a tight-lipped professional, and it was obvious that he didn't appreciate having his operation observed by unofficial callers. However, the stretcher was too close to be ignored. Then, to cement the situation, a lanky, hatless man wearing a battered trench coat and fogged bifocals emerged from the driveway and tapped the captain's right shoulder.

"All vacuumed and fingerprinted," he announced in a nasal voice. "Doubt if we have much more to go on than we did in the Dorrit case, but look in at the lab in a couple of hours to make sure."

"The Dorrit Case?" Phyllis, echoed.

"Ennis, shut up!" Collins ordered.

It was too late. The lanky man was Wesley Ennis, who constituted the one-man crime lab at Solimar Point Police Station. He was a man who loved his work; a crime buff who had lectured before the Founder's Club and every other organization within a radius of fifty miles that would have him.

His presence at the Sandersons' could mean only one thing, and it was Collins who told the story. The Sandersons had returned from the Founder's Ball to find Angie Parsons, their seventeen-year-old baby sitter, dead. She had been strangled with one of her own silk stockings—a repeat of the technique used on the Dorrit girl in the beach house murder.

Phyllis began to whimper in the back seat, and this time Alex couldn't scold her. He was feeling exactly what she was feeling: icy fear.

Ennis took a piece of pale blue tissue from his pocket, removed his glasses, and wiped them clean. His curly, steel gray hair was damp with fog, and his shoulders hunched against the chill. Having cleaned the glasses, he replaced them and smothered a yawn.

"Don't know why murderers usually strike at such ungodly hours," he said. "See you later, Captain."

As Ennis started to cross in front of the sedan's headlight beams, a shout came from the dark driveway, followed by a shot and the sound of running feet.

"Stop him! Stop that man!"

At that moment, a slender male figure in tight denim trousers and leather jacket dashed into the arc of light. Temporarily blinded, he stood pinioned by shock. Ennis seemed paralyzed, but Collins' reaction was automatic. He blocked the fugitive with a low tackle and sent him sprawling back into the arms of the pursuing officer.

Snaking free, the runaway yelled, "I haven't done anything! I haven't done anything wrong!"

He was only a boy, wild now with terror. He clawed his way toward the sedan and grabbed hold of the door next to Alex with clutching gloved hands.

"We found him in the garage," the officer said.

"I was asleep. I was cold. The garage was open so I went in and fell asleep. Then I heard sirens—Mister, help me! I didn't steal anything! I didn't hurt anybody! Help me. Mister, please—"

Collins yanked the suspect loose from the sedan and buried him in a blanket of lawmen, but not before Alex Ward had a good look at the face of the man who was going to set him free.

A civilized society must be based on law. Captain Collins was aware of that but, like all good law officers, gnashed his teeth at the shackling restrictions of the courts. The leather-jacketed prowler called himself Arne Farmer. He carried a thin wallet containing twelve dollars which, he claimed, was what was left of his last paycheck from a temporary job at a hamburger stand at the beach. The job was over. Politics, he said, which Jimmy Collins translated as emotional instability. Farmer was a drifter. He gave his home as San Diego and claimed to be an orphan. He could offer no local references, and Collins was well on his way to a confession when Alex Ward appeared at the Police Station—in a surprising role,

Prior to marrying Harry Dragerman's realty business, Ward had taken the time and trouble to pick up a law degree. As the member of several civic organizations, he announced that he felt duty bound to see that the suspect received adequate legal advice.

While Collins fumed, Wesley Ennis emerged from the laboratory and looked on with bemused interest. He had traded the trench coat for a white linen jacket, and his eyes were owlishly large behind the thick lenses of his spectacles.

"Mr. Ward," he said, "I didn't realize that a man of your stature took such an interest in justice. I thought you were only concerned with making money."

"There's nothing wrong with making money," Alex said.

"No, there isn't. Unfortunately, neither the captain nor myself have much experience in that field, but our work does have compensations.

The captain, naturally, is interested in an arrest and a conviction. The force of public opinion falls on him if he doesn't deliver miracles. But my interest is purely scientific: evidence. I'm sorry to say, Captain, that we have no evidence. I found no fingerprints in the house, no lint from Farmer's clothing, not even any of the dirt his boots picked up in the garage where he was found."

Alex Ward weighed Ennis' words. "Then it's Arne Farmer's statement against—"

"Circumstance," Ennis said.

"Then no formal charge."

"Not without a confession," Collins sighed, "and he's guilty as hell. I'm sure of it. He admits to being in the area for a month. He worked at the beach where he could have seen the Dorrit girl promenading in her bikini—"

"Jeanne Dorrit wasn't raped," Ennis said quickly.

"Was the Parsons girl?" Alex asked.

"No."

"Still," Alex reflected, "it's a sex crime, isn't it? I mean, the use of the girl's stocking—"

"You are observant," Ennis remarked.

"You probably noticed, too, that Farmer was wearing gloves when he grabbed hold of your car tonight. Even so, there's still no evidence to put him inside the Sanderson house, and that leaves the captain handcuffed. Farmer will go free."

"To kill again," Collins muttered.

"Very likely," Ennis said. "If he is the strangler, he will kill again. It's a compulsion. Not a pleasant thought for realty values, is it, Mr. Ward?"

"It's not a pleasant thought for the ladies of Solimar Point," Alex answered.

Ennis was right. Arne Farmer was held for three days until his statements could be verified and his fingerprints checked out of Washington. He was clean, no record of arrests of any kind. Lacking a confession, Captain Collins had no choice but to release his suspect, with an admonition to put distance between himself and Solimar Point. He drove Farmer to the bus depot to be placed on the first bus for San Diego; but there Collins was met by Alex Ward, who had telephoned the police station and learned of the captain's plans. He had given the matter of Arne Farmer some thought, he explained, and it didn't seem fair to the boy, or to the community, to hustle him out of town that way with so little hope of a productive future.

"Farmer's been printed and mugged," he explained, "and I'll wager you've alerted the San Diego police that he's on his way. The minute he tries to get a job, a check will be run on his background and he'll get a fast brush. Who will hire a suspected murderer?"

"So what do I do?" Farmer challenged. "Commit suicide?"

"I helped you the night you were arrested," Alex said, "and I still feel responsible. I've got a new property development opening up a couple of miles up in the hills. Construction's hung up in this tight money squeeze, but the field office is completed and the electricity and water are connected. I need a watchman. How would bed, board and fifty dollars a week strike you? The job's yours as long as you can hold it. By that time Captain Collins may have caught the strangler and you'll be really clean."

"You're taking a big chance," Collins warned.

Alex drew Collins aside. "Isn't it better to know where Farmer is as long as he's still suspect? Incriminating evidence may turn up, and San Diego's awfully close to the Mexican border."

Viewing the situation in that light, Collins agreed. As for Farmer, he had no choice. He was transferred from the police car to Ward's, and Alex drove to the new development. Farmer liked the big sedan. He stretched out his legs and stared at his boots for a few minutes and then began poking through his pockets for a pack of cigarettes. Alex offered his own open case with a crisp new fifty-dollar bill folded inside the cover.

"Go ahead, take it," he said. "It's not marked."

"What's it for?" Farmer hedged.

"An advance on your salary, but I advise you not to go back into town to spend it. Feeling's running high about those murders."

Satisfied, Farmer took the bill and stuffed it into his jacket pocket. He then took a cigarette from the case and got his light from the instrument panel, and this act brought his eyes in line with a chrome nameplate proclaiming: This car was made for Alex Ward.

Farmer emitted a high-pitched laugh. "Alex Ward—big shot!" he said. "Now that the fuzz is gone, why don't you tell me what this is really all about?"

"Would you like a matched set of twenty of these fifty-dollar bills?" Alex asked. "And a good job with a construction outfit in South America?"

"What happens if I don't like it?"

"Nothing—unless somebody fans up the hotheads in the Point and they come up to the construction office some night to make sure there are no more stocking murders."

After that, Alex and Arne Farmer had a perfect understanding. The construction office contained a hot plate, a cot and blankets, and enough canned goods to keep Farmer out of circulation for at least a week. It would take that long, Alex explained, to arrange for an air ticket to South America and a passport. The boy understood and seemed willing to follow directions, and Alex's only fear, as he drove back to the Point, was that the fifty-dollar bill might be too hot for Farmer's jacket pocket until it was time for the strangler to strike again.

The Red Sails was a smart bar and dining room adjacent to the new marina. Claudia's sports car was parked on the lot when Alex arrived. He hurried inside and found her waiting in their usual booth with their usual cocktails. He glanced at his watch. It was, oddly enough, exactly five o'clock.

"I am here, as promised," he said.

"And a good thing, too," Claudia remarked. "You stood me up for lunch. That sort of thing bruises the ego."

"But you know why that happened. It was that mess at the Sandersons'. Ran right into the worst of it on the way home from the country club."

Claudia knew about it, of course. The papers and airwaves were full of it, and Rumorsville had been working three shifts.

"They let the suspect go," she said. "I feel creepy. Think I'll buy a Great Dane or something for protection."

"Don't," Alex said. "I've already applied for the job as protector."

"Any references?"

"The best."

"Alex, really? Did Phyllis finally—"

"Yes, Phyllis finally agreed to the divorce. Now, drink your drink like a nice bride-to-be. Everything's being arranged."

She was Claudia, and Claudia was too sophisticated to cry, but her eyes were moist and her voice had dropped at least an octave when she said, "How? When? I mean, how did you do it, darling?"

"I'm magic," Alex said. "Seriously, Phyllis just decided to agree that we're both civilized people, and civilized people don't deliberately destroy one another. She took it rather well, as a matter of fact. You understand, of course, that she keeps the house, and there'll be a settlement. Anyone who has put up with me for fifteen years deserves more than a pat on the head."

"Alex, how can you say that? She was the one who was so ugly about the divorce!"

Alex leaned across the table and silenced her with a kiss. "Grudges get heavy," he said. "To a new life?"

They touched glasses and Alex watched her drink. He had no need of stimulation. Something electric had started generating the moment he took Arne Farmer off the bus. It was exciting, like opening a new development, or watching a sleeper stock take off and soar. For the rest of the evening he would enjoy Claudia, listen to her and converse with her, but the creative part of his mind would be checking and rechecking his plan for any possible bugs. There was nothing morbid in this. Phyllis had already become an inanimate object. She existed only as the central character in the soon-to-be-presented drama of her death.

On the following afternoon, Alex appeared at the police station to register a snub-nosed .38 calibre handgun. Captain Collins was in the office, and his reaction left nothing to the imagination.

"Now, why did a sensible man like you have to buy this silly private eye pistol?" he demanded. "Everybody's doing it, but I didn't think you would. Do you have any idea how many people get killed with these household arsenals every year?"

"It was Phyllis' idea," Alex said. "She's been a bundle of nerves since the Parsons girl was killed. That got pretty close to home."

Collins shrugged. "All right, I can't stop you from owning the gun. But I can appeal to your common sense not to be careless with it. Fill out the form."

Alex lied, of course. He already owned a service pistol, but he needed an excuse to return to the police station and remind Collins that Phyllis was nervous about the murder, and that he meant to fulfill his husbandly duty to protect her from harm. He also needed an opportunity to see Wesley Ennis again and make sure the authorities weren't holding back any important data on the strangler's modus operandi.

The lab was locked only when Ennis was working on tests. Evidence pertinent to unsolved cases, or cases pending trial, was locked away from prying eyes and damaging fingers. Alex found the one-man criminology department poring over an impressive tome which he immediately closed at the welcome sight of a visitor.

Like all men, Ennis had an ego. Alex fed it small, leading tidbits until Ennis unlocked the files on the two recent stranglings and displayed the murder weapon in each—a sheer silk stocking.

"A killer has a signature," he said. "We know the Dorrit girl and the Parsons girl were killed by the same man because of a small detail in technique. We don't know how the girls were initially approached. Perhaps they screamed, but the beach house where the first murder occurred was remote, and the Sanderson house is on a hillside where anyone approaching is usually driving at a good rate of speed, or in low gear."

"And the Sandersons had gone out for the evening," Alex added. "The killer had to know that."

Wesley Ennis scowled at him through those penetrating bifocals. This was his milieu and he intended to direct the dialogue.

"I think that we can assume our killer, lurking on the premises, could make that observation for himself. The Parsons girl lived farther down the hill. Sanderson drove down and brought her up to his house at about seven-thirty. There was nothing secretive about it. That's beside the point. Whatever happened before the girls were strangled, and there were bruises to indicate some struggle, the interesting thing is that each girl, while not sexually molested, was stripped of one, and just one, article of clothing: a pair of stockings."

Alex held the evidence in his hand, each of the strangulation nylons carefully protected by a sealed plastic bag.

"You said a pair of stockings," he said. "There are only two stockings here."

"Exactly," Ennis responded.

"That's one of the reasons Farmer was released. He didn't have the second stocking on him, and Collins' men couldn't find it in Sanderson's garage. We think he has both stockings—maybe more from other crimes we know nothing about—hidden away somewhere. It's a fetish. If so, he'll come back to them. Where do you suppose the cache is, Mr. Ward?"

Alex was uncomfortable. Ennis seemed to enjoy his macabre profession too much, and those owlish eyes had a way of making a man feel his subconscious was showing. "If you're trying to frighten me," Alex said, "don't bother. I'm already scared to a ghostly white."

Ward smiled thinly. "You should be. Have you ever seen a woman after strangulation? I have some photos here—"

Alex instinctively backed away. Murder was a crime of passion. It should be done in hot blood, with no time to contemplate such consequences as the ghastly distorted face of a victim.

"Not very pretty, are they?" Ennis remarked. "I have quite a collection of these photos. Victims of gunshot, knifing, even ax murders. We live in an age of violence, Mr. Ward. It's in the air, and you know how young people get caught up in trends. To me, the act of strangulation seems the most cruel and primitive. Bare hands, as it were. And the victim has time to know what's happening, hence the terror and distortion of the features, as you can see."

"I'm sorry," Alex said quickly. "I have to pick up Mrs. Ward at the medical center."

"So?" Ennis reluctantly put aside the photos. "Nothing serious, I hope."

"All in her imagination. Always is," Alex answered. "You know how women are."

"I'm not married—except to my profession, Mr. Ward. Do come back when you have more time. I have some interesting color slides, very interesting—"

Alex ran two stoplights on his way to the medical center. Ennis either took sadistic delight in shocking people, or was so engrossed in his work he couldn't appreciate other sensibilities. By the time he reached the parking lot, Alex' face was beaded with perspiration and his hands were clammy on the steering wheel. He sat there in the bright afternoon sunlight and tried to think rationally about the subject of murder. He had loved Phyllis once. Old man Dragerman's shabby little realty office hadn't sparked the marriage. He had taken Phyllis for the same reason any man takes a wife. He wanted to be free of her now, but he didn't want to see her looking like those photos in Ennis' file. He could try once more to reach her with persuasion.

Phyllis emerged from Dr. Kuperman's office, scanned the parking lot and then walked toward the car. She was definitely overweight, and had the knack of choosing clothes that accentuated the bovine in her figure, but for the moment Alex was oblivious to these faults. He imagined her as he had seen her fifteen years ago: soft, feminine and in need of manly protection. A wave of forgotten warmth swept over him. He leapt out of the car and held open the door for her entrance.

Phyllis glared at him. "What's the matter with you?" she demanded. "Did the doctor telephone you? Don't get over-mobilized, Alex. I may not drop dead for another forty years. I know how happy you are to hear that."

Alex' illusion dissolved abruptly. "Why should the doctor have called me?" he asked.

"Never mind. If he didn't think my condition was serious enough to tell you, I won't. You can get this prescription filled at the pharmacy on the way home, and don't brake the car so fast that I bounce around in the back seat the way I did the night you almost hit that ambulance. I slipped a disc in my back. Alex? Are you listening?"

Alex wasn't. He was thinking of the best way to handle Arne Farmer. The first step was to make a diagram of the house, showing the location of Phyllis' room and the means of access. Farmer wasn't a mental giant so the plan must be kept simple.

The visit to Ennis' lab had been a disturbing experience, but without it Alex wouldn't have known about the stocking fetish. He selected a pair from Phyllis' dressing room. True to form, she had taken to bed immediately after the visit to Dr. Kuperman. The prescription was for her heart and was kept on the bedside table. Alex encouraged the invalidism; it made her more accessible. In the years since her father's death, Phyllis had imagined herself the victim of almost every known disease and a few not yet diagnosed. One more added to her repertoire of ailments didn't alter his plan.

The important thing was to leave nothing that could be traced back to himself. He took off a day to drive into the Los Angeles International Airport and, on the pretext of being called to the telephone, enlisted another passenger to purchase a one-way ticket to Buenos Aires. He borrowed nineteen fifty-dollar bills out of the office safe so no withdrawal would show on his bank account, and then, carrying a small camera, returned to the construction office in the hills.

He found Arne Farmer stretched out on the cot, nursing the dregs of a bottle of soda pop. He had made a paper airplane of the fifty-dollar bill and sailed it across his torso while Alex displayed the diagram and explained the plan. At seven-thirty of the following evening, Alex would leave for a regular meeting of the realty board in the Solimar Civic Center. He would make certain the window to the service porch was unlocked. There were no resident servants; Phyllis would be alone. Farmer would go directly to her bedroom (she always kept a night light burning) and do the job as quickly as possible.

Alex produced the stockings. "I bought a pair," he said. "I don't want you poking about after the job's done. You can add the extra to your collection."

Farmer accepted the stockings without comment. He dangled them before his eyes for a moment and then stuffed them into his jacket pocket. "Whatever you say, boss man," he sighed.

"Now sit up and let me snap your picture. I've got an unexpired passport and a friend who can doctor it up to fit your description."

Alex was trying to make the setup look genuine, and Farmer had never seen the passport. He examined it closely between poses.

"When do I get the bread?" he demanded.

"Tomorrow night, after you've done the job. I'll leave the meeting at exactly ten o'clock. It takes fifteen minutes for me to drive home. Meet me at ten-fifteen on the rear patio, the one you use to get into the house. I'll give you the money, the passport and ticket, and a head start. I won't discover the body until morning. The police will be told that I rapped on my wife's door when I came home. She didn't answer and so I assumed she was asleep. By the time the third strangulation is reported, you'll be on a plane somewhere over Mexico."

Farmer returned the passport. "I want to see the bread first," he said.

Alex was prepared. He removed a long envelope from his inside coat pocket and let Arne Farmer examine the contents: the nineteen fifty-dollar bills and the ticket. But with Alex' coat open, Farmer caught a glimpse of the handgun in the holster.

"What's the iron for?" he demanded.

"Protection. I'm carrying almost a thousand dollars in cash."

There was an instant when Alex feared Farmer was getting wise. He counted the money carefully and studied the ticket. When Alex held out his hand, Farmer returned the money but retained the envelope and the ticket.

"Just in case you try to cross me," he said.

"Don't be so suspicious, Arne," Alex answered. "I'm helping you and you're helping me. We need each other. Now, let's run over the plan one more time."

When Alex returned to his car, he pocketed the money and locked the passport and camera in the glove compartment. They had served their purpose as props and wouldn't be needed again. He let Farmer keep the ticket, which was useless without the passport, because it gave him a sense of security.

On the following evening, Alex stepped into Phyllis' bedroom before leaving for the meeting. She was propped up in bed with an open box of chocolates in her lap and a confession magazine in her hand. The sight of her roused nothing in him but impatience to get the night's work done.

"I thought you would never come," she whined. "It's time for my medicine and there's no water in the carafe. You should hire a nurse for me, Alex. Dr. Kuperman said I shouldn't be left alone."

"Dr. Kuperman should have said that chocolates make fat, and fat's dangerous to anyone with a heart condition," Alex retorted. "He can't be too worried. As for leaving you alone, you do like all that money I make for you, don't you? You must like it or you wouldn't be so reluctant to let me get away with my share."

The needling brought no response. Alex picked up the medicine and stalked into the bathroom, but his nerves were tauter than he realized. The bottle slipped from his hand into the basin, and all of Dr. Kuperman's expensive prescription went rushing down the drain. It was as clear as the water coming from the tap. Alex faked the dosage with a few drops of mouthwash, refilled the bottle from the tap and returned to Phyllis. She took the medicine without protest. Having replaced the bottle on the night table, Alex then left for the meeting.

Alex was better than his word to Arne Farmer. At nine-thirty he excused himself on the grounds of his wife's frail health, and drove home. He cut the headlights and parked a short distance from the house, then walked to the rear patio. There were no lights showing except in Phyllis' room, and the service porch window rattling in the night wind told him that Arne Farmer was already inside the house. He took the handgun from its holster and waited. Action came faster than he expected. He heard a high-pitched yell, and then the rear door burst open and Farmer ran wildly across the patio.

"Farmer!" Alex called. "I'm here!"

The boy whirled about. When he saw Alex he stretched out both hands in a clawing gesture. "Man," he gasped, "give me the bread and the ticket!"

"Is she dead?"

"She's real dead! Look for yourself. Now, give me what's coming to me."

"I will," Alex said, and shot Arne Farmer through the head.

Farmer dropped. Alex leaned over him and felt his pulse until certain that he was dead. The long envelope containing the airline ticket was protruding from one of the leather jacket pockets. Alex transferred it to his own inside coat pocket, then walked into the house and down the hall to Phyllis' room. One glance told him all he needed to know. He went into the den and telephoned Captain Collins.

Later, at the police station, Alex made a full statement. "I left the meeting early because my wife was nervous when left alone in the house at night. I drove home and parked beyond my driveway because something was wrong. I had left the patio lights burning. They were off. I walked to the house and approached through the rear patio. There I could see the light in Phyllis' room and the open window on the service porch where Farmer must have entered. I heard a cry and Farmer opened the back door and came running out. He saw me and yelled: 'She's dead! I've killed your wife!' He looked insane, and I guess I went a little crazy too. I shot him."

The police stenographer stopped writing. From behind his desk, Captain Collins faced Alex with an unblinking stare. Ennis, whose eyes were lost behind the reflected light on his bifocals, slouched against the water cooler. Alex sat stiffly in a straight-backed chair. It was Collins who finally spoke.

"I wonder why Farmer said he killed your wife. He must have known she was already dead when he put the stocking, around her throat."

"Already dead?" Alex's lips felt dry. He wet them with his tongue. "But that's impossible! I saw—"

"Did you go into your wife's bedroom before you called me?"

"No—" Alex reflected. "I looked in at the door and saw her sprawled over the edge of the bed with a stocking twisted about her neck. I didn't want to touch anything."

"I'm glad you didn't. But that stocking was too loose to strangle anyone, Alex. Your wife died of a heart attack. No wonder Farmer came out of the house yelling. We'll never know for sure, but it's possible she heard him break in, felt an attack coming on and tried to get to her medicine. The cap was found on the bedside table, the bottle on the floor, empty. Dr. Kuperman verified the prescription, but what we can't understand was why the stain on the carpet had no medicinal content. It was just flavored water."

"I can explain that," Alex said. "I accidentally broke Phyllis' medicine bottle before I went to the meeting. It was too late to get the prescription refilled, so I used tap water. I didn't want to worry her, and I didn't dream the stuff was important. She's been a hypochondriac for years."

Collins listened. His expression didn't change, but when Alex was all through he said, "I'll have to take your gun, Alex."

"My gun?"

"I can hold you on the charge of carrying a gun until I get something stronger. That permit I issued was just a registration, not a license to carry."

Collins stepped forward quickly and peeled back Alex' jacket. He yanked the .38 out of the holster and, with the same motion, flicked the long envelope from Alex' inner pocket. "Now, what have we here?" he said.

Alex didn't confess until after Collins took the ticket out of the envelope. It had a grimy thumbprint on it that made Wesley Ennis' face glow in anticipation, and Alex had no cover story for the evidence Ennis brought back from his lab, or for the exposed film Collins found in the camera in the glove compartment of his car, or for Arne Farmer's fingerprints on the passport. Finally, when Ennis showed him a close-up photo he had taken of Phyllis before she was removed from the bedroom, Alex told everything.

After Alex was booked, Collins congratulated Ennis on his ingenuity. "I never would have thought to analyze that stain on the carpet or to search Alex for evidence," he declared. "You must be psychic."

"Not psychic—thorough," Ennis explained. "Criminals have patterns, as you've often heard me say. The stocking strangler's first two victims were lovely young girls in their teens. I took one look in that bedroom and knew that Mrs. Ward didn't fit."

Collins didn't pursue the subject, which was just as well.

Ennis returned to his lab and placed the almost-strangulation stocking in a plastic bag. It wasn't an authentic murder weapon, but it did belong to the Strangler Collection. Peevishly, because it was an abominable thing for one man to steal another's style, he examined the second stocking they had found on Farmer's body, then folded it gently and placed it in his coat pocket. Outsider that it was, he would still take it home and put it in the drawer with the stockings he had taken from the Dorrit and Parsons girls, having first deftly strangled them in a manner bespeaking a perfectionist who had no fear of leaving damaging evidence which he alone, in the course of duty, would later discover.

Pattern of Guilt

Keith Briscoe had never been a hating man. Disciplined temper, alert mind, hard work—these were the things that made for success as a police reporter, and in the fourteen years since he'd returned from overseas, too big for his old suits and his old job as copy boy, Keith Briscoe had become one of the best. Enthusiasm was a help— something close to passion at times, for that was the stuff brilliance was made of—but not hatred. Hatred was a cancer in the mind, a dimness in the eye. Hatred was an acid eating away the soul. Keith Briscoe was aware of all these things, but he was becoming aware of something else as well. No matter how hard he forced the thought to the back of his mind, he knew that he hated his wife. And the thought was sharp, clear.

It was Sergeant Gonzales' case—burglary and murder. Violet Hammerman, thirty-eight, lived alone in a single apartment on North Curson. She worked as a secretary in a small manufacturing plant from Monday through Friday, played bridge with friends on Saturday night, served on the Hostess Committee of her church Sunday morning and died in her bed Sunday night (Monday morning, to be exact, since it was after 2 a.m. when the crime occurred), the victim of one bullet through her heart fired at close range. Sergeant Gonzales was a thorough man, and by the time Keith Briscoe reached the scene, having responded with fire horse reflexes to the homicide code on his shortwave receiver, all of these matters, and certain others, were already established and Gonzales was waiting for the police photographer to complete his chores so the body could be removed to the morgue.

She wasn't a pretty woman. A corpse is seldom attractive.

"You can see for yourself," Gonzales said. "It's a simple story. No struggle, no attempted attack—the bedclothes aren't even disturbed. The neighbors heard her scream once and then the shot came immediately afterward. She should have stayed asleep."

She was asleep now. Nothing would ever rouse her again. Briscoe glanced at the bureau drawer that was still standing half-open. One nylon stocking dangled forlornly over the side. He fingered it absently— and then, without touching the wood, stuffed it inside.

"Fingerprints?" he asked.

"No fingerprints," Gonzales said. "The killer must have worn gloves, but he left a pair of footprints outside the window."

There was only one window in the small bedroom. It was a first-floor apartment in one of the old residential houses that had been rezoned and remodeled into small units, but still had a shallow basement and a correspondingly high footing. Violet Hammerman must have felt secure to sleep with her one window open and the screen locked, but that had been a mistake. The screen had been neatly cut across the bottom and up as far as the center sash on both sides. It now hung like a stiffly starched curtain, that bent outward at the touch of Keith Briscoe's hand.

"Port of entry and exit."

"That's right," Gonzales said. "But the exit was fast. He must have made a running jump out of the window and landed on the cement drive. It was the entry that left the prints. Collins, shoot your flash under the window again."

Collins was the man in uniform who stood guarding the important discovery beneath the window. He responded to Gonzales' order by pointing a bright finger of light down on the narrow strip of earth that separated house from the driveway. It was a plot barely eighteen inches wide, but somebody had worked it over for planting, and because of that a pair of footprints was distinctly visible on the soft earth.

"We're in luck," Gonzales explained. "The landlord worked that ground yesterday morning. Set out some petunia plants—ruffled petunias. Too bad. A couple of them will never bloom."

A couple of them were slightly demolished from trampling, but between the withered green the two indentations were embedded, like an anonymous signature. Briscoe shoved the screen forward and peered farther out of the window.

"It must be nearly six feet to the ground," he remarked.

"Sixty-eight inches," Gonzales said. "The footprints don't seem very deep."

"They aren't—no heels. If you were down where Collins is, you'd see what I saw a few minutes before you walked in. Those prints are from rubber-soled shoes, 'sneakers' we used to call them when I was a kid. At closer view you can pick up the imprint of some of the tread, but not much. Those particular soles were pretty well worn. But you're thinking, Briscoe, as usual. That earth is soft. We'll have to measure the moisture content to get an idea of how much weight stood above those prints to make them the depth they are, but at first guess I'd say we're looking for a tall, slender lad."

"A juvenile?" Briscoe asked.

"Why not? Like I told my wife when she came home from her shopping trip last week, no wonder so many kids are going wrong. They come home from school and find their mothers dressed up in a sack with a belt at the bottom. That's enough to drive anyone out on the streets."

Keith Briscoe pulled his head in out of the window and ran a searching hand over the cut screen. It was a clean job. A sharp blade of a pocket knife could do the job. Gonzales could be right about the juvenile angle.

"You sound like a detective," he said.

"Gee, thanks," Gonzales grinned. "Maybe I'll grow up to be a hot reporter someday. Who can tell?"

There was no sarcasm in the exchange. Gonzales and Briscoe had been friends long enough to be able to insult one another with respect and affection. Gonzales had a good mind and an eye for detail. He also had imagination, which was to building a police case what mortar is to a bricklayer.

"We found a purse—black felt—on the driveway near the curb," he added. "People in the building identified it as belonging to the deceased. There's no money in it except some small change in the coin purse, but there's this that we found on the top of the bureau—"

Gonzales had a slip of blue paper in his hand. He handed it to Briscoe. It was the deduction slip from a company paycheck. After deductions, Violet Hammerman had received a check for $61.56.

"Payday was Friday," Gonzales continued. "The landlord told me that. He knows because he's had to wait for his rent a few times. Violet Hammerman didn't have time to get to the bank Friday—she worked late—but she cashed her check at the Sav-Mor Market on Saturday." Gonzales had another slip of paper in his hand now, a long, narrow strip from a cash register. "When she bought groceries to the sum of $14.82," he added.

There was such a thing as sounding too much like a detective. Briscoe returned the blue slip with a dubious expression. It was barely two-thirty. Gonzales was a fast worker, but the markets didn't open until nine. But Gonzales caught the expression before he could fit it with words.

"I'm guessing, of course," he said quickly, "but I'm guessing for a reason. $14.82 from $61.56 leaves $46.74. Assuming she spent a few dollars elsewhere and dropped a bill in the collection plate, we see that Violet Hammerman's killer escaped with the grand sum of $40 or, at the most, $45."

"A cheap death," Briscoe said.

"A very cheap death, and a very cheap and amateurish killer." Gonzales paused to glance at the slip of blue paper again, but it was no longer entirely blue. A red smear had been added to the corner. "What did you do, cut your hand on that screen?" he asked.

Briscoe didn't know what he was talking about, but he looked at his hand and it was bleeding.

"Better look in the bathroom for some mercurochrome," Gonzales said. "You could get a nasty infection from a rusty screen."

"It's nothing," Briscoe said. "I'll wash it off under the faucet when I get home."

"You'll wash it off under the faucet right now," Gonzales ordered. "There's the bathroom on the other side of the bureau."

Gonzales could be as fussy as a spinster. It was easier to humor him than to argue. The photographer was finished with the corpse now, and Briscoe pulled the sheet up over her face as he walked past the bed. A cheap death and a cheap way to wait for the ambulance. Violet Hammerman had lived a humble and inconspicuous life, but she might rate a conspicuous obituary if he could keep Gonzales talking. Of course, Violet Hammerman might not have approved of such an obituary, but she now belonged to the public.

"A cheap and amateurish killer," Briscoe said, with his hand under the faucet, "but he wore gloves, rubber-soled shoes and carried a gun."

Leaning against the bathroom doorway, Gonzales rose to the bait. "Which he fired too soon," he said. "That's my point, Briscoe. There's a pattern in every crime—something that gives us an edge on the criminal's weakness, and we know he has a weakness or he wouldn't be a criminal. It takes a mind, some kind of a mind, to plan a burglary; but it takes nerve to pull it off successfully. This killer is very short on nerve. One cry from the bed and he blazed away at close range. A professional wouldn't risk the gas chamber for a lousy forty bucks. Don't use that little red towel. Red dye's no good for an open cut."

Gonzales, with an eye for detail even when his mind was elsewhere. Briscoe put the guest towel back on the rack. A silly-looking thing—

red with a French poodle embroidered in black. It seemed out of place in Violet Hammerman's modest bathroom. It was more the sort of thing Elaine would buy. Elaine. He thought of her and slammed the faucet shut so hard the plumbing pipes shuddered.

"A killer short on nerve, but desperate enough to break into a house," Briscoe recapitulated, his mind busy forcing Elaine back where she belonged. "A forty-dollar murder." And then he had what he was groping for, and by that time he could face Gonzales without fear of anger showing in his face. "Sounds like a hophead," he suggested.

Gonzales nodded sadly.

"That's what I've been thinking," he said. "That's what worries me. How much of a joyride can he buy for so little fare? I only hope Violet Hammerman isn't starting a trend." Among his other characteristics, Sergeant Gonzales was a pessimist, and Keith Briscoe couldn't give him any cheer.

He had troubles of his own.

Judge Kermit Lacy's court hadn't changed in four years. The flag stood in the same place; the woodwork still needed varnishing; the chairs were just as hard. If the windows had been washed, the evidence was no longer visible. Courtrooms could be exciting arenas where combating attorneys fought out issues of life and death, but there was nothing exciting about a courtroom where tired old loves went to die, or to be exhumed for delayed postmortem.

The dead should stay dead. The thought tugged at Keith Briscoe's mind when he saw Faye sitting at her attorney's table. Faye had changed in four years. She looked younger, yet more mature, more poised. She wore a soft gray suit and a hat that was smart without being ridiculous. There had never been anything ridiculous about Faye—that was the only trouble with her; she always carried with her the faint aura of Old Boston. She looked up and saw him then. And when their eyes met, there was a kind of stop on time for just an instant, an almost imperceptible shadow crossed her eyes, and then she smiled. Keith walked to the table. He didn't quite know what to do. Was it customary to shake hands with an ex-wife—the sort of thing tennis players do after vaulting the net? He kept his hands at his side.

"You're looking good, Faye," he said, "—great, in fact."

Clumsy words, as if he were just learning the language.

"Thank you," Faye responded. "You look well, too, Keith. You've lost weight."

Keith started to say "No more home cooking" and thought better of it. And he didn't look well. It wasn't just because he'd been up most of the night delving into the violent departure of one Violet Hammerman from this vale of fears; it was because he had that depth-fatigue look of a man who's gradually working up to an extended hangover.

"I keep busy," he said.

"And how is Elaine?"

That question had to come. Keith searched in vain for a twinge of emotion in Faye's voice. There was none. Elaine was a knife that had cut between them a long time ago, and old wounds heal.

"Elaine's fine," he said, and then he couldn't be evasive any longer. "Faye—" The bailiff had entered the courtroom. In a few moments the judge would walk in and there would be no more time to talk. "—I wish you'd reconsider this action. We have a good arrangement now. If you take the boys east, I'll never get to see them."

"But that's not true," Faye objected. "They can visit with you on vacations."

"Vacations! A few weeks out of a year—that's not like every weekend!"

"Every weekend, Keith?" Faye's voice was soft, but her eyes were steady. Faye's eyes were always steady. "You've had four years of weekends to visit the boys. How many times have you taken advantage of them?"

"Every weekend I possibly could! You know how my job is!"

Faye knew. The half-smile that came to her lips had a sadness in it. Now that he really looked at her, Keith could see the sadness. She was lonely. She must be lonely, bringing up two boys with nothing but an alimony check for companionship. Now she was bringing suit for permission to take the boys east—ostensibly to enroll them in prep school; but Keith Briscoe suddenly knew the real reason. There were old friends back east to wipe out the memories—perhaps even an old flame.

Keith felt a quick jab of pain he didn't understand. "I'm going to fight you, Faye," he said. "I'm sorry, but I'm going to fight you every inch of the way."

It was nearly eight o'clock that night before Keith got home to his apartment. Nobody came to greet him at the door except Gus, Elaine's dachshund. Gus growled at him, which was standard procedure, and made a couple of wild snaps at his ankles as he passed through the dark living room and made his way to the patch of brightness showing down the hall. At the doorway of Elaine's bedroom, he paused and listened to the music coming from the record player at her bedside. It was something Latin with a very low spinal beat. He listened to it until she came out of the bathroom wearing something French with an equally low spinal beat. Keith was no couturier, but he could see at a glance that Elaine's dress wasn't percale and hadn't been designed for a quiet evening at home. He could also see that it was expensive. He would know how expensive at the first of the month.

She looked up and saw him in the doorway. "Oh," she said. "I didn't hear you come in."

Keith didn't answer immediately. He just stood there looking at her—all of her, outside and inside. The outside was still attractive. He could feel the tug of her body clear across the room.

"Do you ever?" he asked.

Elaine turned around and picked up an ear clip from her dressing table. She raised her arms to fasten it to her ear.

"Going out?" he asked again.

"It's Thelma's birthday," she said.

"I thought it was Thelma's birthday last week."

That made her turn around.

"All right," she said, "what's eating you? Have you been playing with martinis again?"

"I'm old enough," Keith said. He came across the room. She not only looked good, she smelled good. "I just thought you might want to stay home for one evening."

"Why? So I can sit in the dark alone and watch Wyatt Earp? This lousy apartment—"

"This lousy apartment," Keith interrupted, "costs me $175 every month. Considering certain other expenditures I have to meet, it's no wonder I devote a little extra time to doing what is known among the peasants as being gainfully employed. If I didn't, you couldn't look so provocative for Thelma's birthday."

Elaine picked up the other ear clip and fastened it in place. It was as though he hadn't spoken, hadn't reprimanded her. And then her face in the mirror took on a kind of animal cunning. She turned back toward him with knowing eyes.

"How did you make out in court?" she asked.

"We got a continuance," Keith said.

"A continuance? Why? So you can suffer a little longer?"

"I want my boys—"

"You want Faye! Why can't you be honest enough to admit it? You've always wanted Faye. You only married me because you couldn't have your cake and eat it, too. That's your big weakness, Keith. You want to have your cake and eat it, too!"

"I want a divorce," Keith said.

He hadn't meant to say it—not yet, not this way. But once it was said, there was nothing to do but let the words stand there like a wall between them, or like a wall with a door in it that was opening. And then Elaine slammed the door.

"You," she said quietly, "can go to hell."

That was the night Keith Briscoe moved out of the apartment. He'd been spending most of his nights in a furnished room anyway, a room, a bath, a hot plate for the coffee and a desk for his typewriter. And a table for the shortwave radio alongside the bed. The typewriter had bothered Elaine at night, and that was when Keith did most of his work. He could pick up extra money turning police cases into fabrications for the mystery magazines. Extra money was important with two boys growing their way toward college.

But on the night he moved into the room to stay, Keith didn't work. He just sat and stared at the calendar on the desk and tried to get things straight in his mind. He had a one week's continuance. One week until he'd walk back into Judge Lacy's courtroom and see Faye sitting there calm and proud and lonely. Elaine was a stupid woman, but even the biggest fools made sense when the time was right. It was Faye that he wanted—Faye, the boys, everything that he'd thrown away. Elaine was a bad dream. Elaine was an emotional storm he'd been lost in, and now the storm was over and he was trying to find his way home through the debris. But a week wasn't very long. Perhaps his lawyer could find a loophole and get another stay. It was actually only six days until Monday....

On Sunday night, at a half hour past midnight, the shortwave radio rousted him out again.

Dorothy McGannon had a cheerful face even in death. She must have smiled a lot in life. Once her moment of terror was over, the muscles of her face had relaxed into their normal position, and she might have been sleeping through a happy dream if it hadn't been for the dark stain seeping through the blanket.

She was alone in the room, except for Sergeant Gonzales and company. She had lived alone, an unmarried woman in her late twenties. The apartment was small—living room, kitchen, and bedroom. It was on the second floor, rear, one of eight apartments in the unit. The service landing stopped about eighteen inches from the window where the screen was cut three ways and now poked awkwardly out into the night. It had taken agility to balance on the railing and slit that screen; it had taken even more to swing out onto the railing and escape after the fatal shot had been fired.

"Our boy's getting daring," Gonzales reflected. "Still nervous with the trigger, but daring."

"Do you think it's the same killer who got Violet Hammerman last week?" Keith asked.

Up until this point, nobody had mentioned Violet Hammerman. She was just last week's headline, forgotten by everyone but next of kin. But the cut screen and swift death were familiar. Gonzales, the pattern-maker, was already at work.

"That was a .45 slug ballistics got out of the Hammerman woman," he answered. "When we see what killed this one, I'll give you a definite answer. Unfortunately, there's no soft earth out on that porch landing—no footprints; but the method of entry is the same. That's a peculiar way to cut a screen, you know. It takes longer that way."

"But makes for a safer exit," Keith said.

"That's true—and this caller always leaves in a hurry." Gonzales turned back toward the bed, scowling. "I wonder if he kills them just for the fun of it," he mused. "Nobody heard a scream tonight. The shot, but no scream. Still, with five out of eight television sets still going, it's a wonder they heard anything."

"Did he get what he came for?" Keith asked.

Still scowling, Gonzales turned and looked at him. Then he nodded his head in a beckoning gesture.

"Follow me," he said.

They crossed the small bedroom and went into the living room. They turned to the right and entered the kitchen alcove, which had one wall common to the bedroom and faced the living room door. The far wall of the kitchen was cupboard space, and one door stood open. On the sink top, lying on its side as if it had been opened hurriedly, was a sugar can which contained no sugar—or anything else.

"What does that look like?" Gonzales asked.

"It looks like Dorothy McGannon kept her money in a sugar can," Keith said.

"Exactly. She worked as a legal secretary. She was paid Friday and gave $10 to the manager of this place Friday night in payment for $10 she'd borrowed earlier in the week. He saw a roll of bills in her purse at the time—$50 or $60, he thinks. We found the purse in a bureau drawer in the bedroom—there was $5 and some change in it."

"The killer missed it."

"The killer didn't even look for it. That drawer stuck—it made enough noise to wake the dead, well, almost. It's obvious he didn't bother with the bureau, and that's interesting because it's what he did bother with last week. Instead, he came straight to the kitchen, opened the cupboard door, and now it's bare."

What Sergeant Gonzales was saying explained the frown that had grown on his forehead. It meant another piece of the pattern of guilt was being fitted to an unknown killer.

"He might have been a friend of the woman," Keith said, "—someone who had been in the apartment and knew where she kept the money. A boyfriend, possibly. She was single."

"So was the Hammerman woman," Gonzales reflected. "But no boyfriend. We questioned the landlord about that, definitely no boyfriend. But you're right, she was single. They were both single and both killed on Sunday night. It's beginning to add up, isn't it? Two murders, each victim a woman who lived alone, each one killed on a weekend after a Friday payday. Do you want to lay a small bet that's a .45 slug in the corpse?"

"No bet," Keith said. "What about groceries?"

"Groceries? What groceries?"

"McGannon's. Does she have any? Hammerman did, as I recall. Over $14.00 worth."

Gonzales looked interested. He glanced behind him at the living room door clearly visible from the kitchen.

"You're thinking again, Briscoe," he said. "A delivery boy—but wait, Hammerman's groceries were paid for at the market. Still, it might have been a delivery boy. Tall, skinny. The lab says not over 150 pounds. It's worth looking into. I don't like the idea of a murder every weekend."

Dorothy McGannon did Keith a big favor getting herself killed when she did. It was a good enough story to keep him away from court until another continuance had been called, and that meant another week to try to reach Faye. He caught her coming down the courthouse steps. She was annoyed that he hadn't shown up—obviously, she thought it was deliberate, and Keith wasn't certain but what she was right.

"If we can go somewhere and have a drink, I'll explain," he suggested.

"I'm sorry, Keith. I've wasted enough time as it is."

"But I couldn't help not showing. I was on a big story—look."

He unfolded the late edition and handed it to her. She hesitated.

"One drink to show there's no hard feelings," Keith said.

She consented, finally. It wasn't a warm consent, but Keith took it as a major victory. He drove her to a small bar near the news building where she used to meet him in the old days, when their marriage, and the world, was young. Faye had always been a little on the sentimental side. He led the way to their old booth at the back of the room and ordered a Scotch on the rocks and a Pink Lady. That was supposed to indicate that he hadn't forgotten.

"Make it a vodka martini," Faye said.

"You've changed drinks," Keith observed.

"I've changed a lot of things, Keith."

That was true. Now that they were alone, he could see it. This wasn't going to be easy. Faye took a cigarette from her purse. He fumbled in his pocket for a lighter, and then studied the situation in her eyes, lustrous over the flame.

"I've changed, too," he told her. "I'm working nights now, Faye. Real industrious. I've been doing a little writing on the side—may even get at that novel I used to talk about."

"That's good," Faye said. "I'm glad to hear it." And then she paused. "How does Elaine like it?"

Keith snapped the lighter shut and played it back and forth in his hands.

"Elaine and I aren't living together anymore," he said. "I moved out last week."

He watched for a reaction, but Faye was good at concealing emotions. She was like the proverbial iceberg—nine-tenths submerged. If he'd realized that four years sooner, he wouldn't have been sitting there like a troubled schoolboy waiting for the report on a test paper.

"I'm sorry, Keith," she said.

"I'm not. It's been coming for a long time. It was a mistake from the beginning—the whole mess. I don't know how I could have been so blind."

One drink together. He didn't say much more; he didn't dare push her. Faye was the kind who would walk away from him the minute he did. But at least he had said the important things, and she could think about them for another week.

Not until he was back in that small, furnished room did it occur to Keith that he was playing the fool. He was trying to get Faye back when he didn't even know how to get rid of Elaine. He sat down to work. He pushed the problem back in his mind and concentrated on Sergeant Gonzales' problem. The case was beginning to fascinate him. What kind of a killer was it who would operate in this way? A half-crazy hophead, yes; but with enough animal cunning to make some kind of plan of operation. Now he understood what Gonzales meant by that pattern talk. If it were possible to think as the killer thought … Obviously, he'd been in Dorothy McGannon's apartment prior to the murder. Very few people kept household money in sugar cans anymore. Elaine kept money anywhere scattered about the bedroom in half a dozen purses. The "cat-killer," as Keith had dubbed him in his latest story, would have a holiday if he slashed her window screen.

But how would he know? He thought of Elaine again—she wouldn't stay in the back of his mind. He thought of her alone in the apartment. What did she do all day? She never went to the market; she telephoned for groceries. But she didn't pay for them, except to give the delivery boy a tip. The bill, along with many, many others, came in at the first of the month. There were other deliveries: the cleaner, the liquor store … And what else? And then he remembered that in the early days of their marriage, before Elaine learned to go outside for her amusements, she'd been a pushover for all the gadgets peddled by the door-to-door trade. It was a thought, and an impelling one.

A gadget. It would have to be something easy to sell; getting the door slammed in his face wouldn't help the killer at all. He had to have a few minutes, at least, to size up the possibilities: learn if the woman lived alone, see where she went for the money when he made the sale. Perhaps he had a gimmick—the "I just need 100 more points" routine. There were other approaches, legitimate ones that could have been borrowed: items made by the blind, items made by the crippled or mentally retarded. Something a woman would buy whether she needed it or not.

The next day, Keith went to Gonzales with his idea. Together they paid another visit to the McGannon woman's apartment. They examined the drawers in that kitchen cupboard—all standard items from bottle opener to egg beater, but nothing that looked new. Gonzales moved to the broom closet.

"Sometimes peddlers handle cosmetic items," Keith reflected. "I'll have a look in the bathroom."

He went through the tiny bedroom and into an even tinier bath. There was no tub, just a stall shower and a Pullman lavatory. He pulled open one of the lavatory drawers and then called to Gonzales. When Gonzales came into the room, Keith stood with a small guest towel in his hand. It was green this time, a sort of chartreuse green with a black French poodle embroidered at the bottom.

"Familiar?" he asked.

And Gonzales remembered, because a red towel was bad for an open cut.

They made an inquiry at every apartment in the building where anyone was at home. Afterwards, they went to the apartment on Curson and interviewed all of the available tenants there. Out of it all, a picture emerged. In both cases, on the Saturday prior to the murder, at least one tenant at each address remembered seeing a peddler with a basket on his arm entering the premises. One tenant at the Hammerman address, an elderly woman living with her retired husband, actually stopped the peddler on the walk and conversed with him.

"He was selling little towels and things," she reported. "Real pretty and cheap, too. I bought two for a quarter apiece. Would have bought more, but a pension don't go far these days." But did she remember how the peddler looked? Indeed, she did. A tall, gawky young man— hardly more than a boy. "Not much of a salesman," she added. "He didn't even seem to care about selling his things. I had to stop him or he would have gone right past my door."

He had gone right past all of the doors, apparently, except two— Violet Hammerman's and Dorothy McGannon's. A check on the mail boxes at each unit indicated an explanation. All of the other apartments in each building were occupied by two or more tenants. The cat killer concentrated on women living alone.

"That's great," Gonzales concluded. "In this particular area we have the largest concentration of unmarried people of any section of the city. Now all we have to do is locate every woman living alone and warn her not to buy a guest towel from a door-to-door peddler."

"Aren't peddlers licensed?" Keith said.

"Licensed peddlers are licensed," Gonzales said. "But what's more important, merchandise of this sort is manufactured. There's a code number on the tag inside. Keep your hat on this operation for a few days, Briscoe, and you may have an exclusive. In the meantime, this whole area will be searched for a tall, thin peddler carrying a basket."

"Or not carrying a basket," Keith suggested. "I don't think your man entered these buildings blind. I think he had his victims selected days before the Saturday checkup. I think he watched them, studied the location of the apartments—planned everything in advance. He's probably out lining up next Sunday night's target right now. He's making headlines, Gonzales. Everybody has an ego."

Gonzales made no argument.

"You've really been doing some head work on this," he said.

"Yes," Keith answered, "I have." There was more head work to do.

Keith went shopping. He left Gonzales and found his way to one of the large department stores. He located the linen department and wandered about the aisles, avoiding salesladies until he found what he was looking for: guest towels in all the assorted colors, guest towels with jaunty French poodles embroidered at the bottom.

"Something for you, sir?"

A voice at his shoulder brought his mind back to the moment.

"No, no thanks," he said. "I was just looking."

He walked away quickly. He was doing too much head work; he needed some air.

That evening he went to see Elaine. He still had his key and could let himself in. Nobody met him at the door, not even Gus.

"He's at the vet's," Elaine explained. "He caught a cold. They're keeping him under observation for a week."

She was in the bedroom doing her nails. She sat on the bed, sprawled back against the pillows. She barely looked at him when she spoke.

"I thought you weren't coming back," she said.

"I'm not," he told her. "I only came tonight so we could talk things over."

"Talk? What is there to talk about?"

"A divorce."

The hand operating the nail polish brush hesitated a moment.

"We did talk about that—last week," Elaine said.

He waited for several seconds and there was no sign of interest in his presence. He might have been a piece of furniture she was ready to give to the salvage truck. He walked past the bed and over to the window. Elaine's carpet was thick; he couldn't have heard his footsteps with a stethoscope. He went to the window and pulled aside the soft drapes. It was a casement window and both panels were cranked out to let in the night air. The apartment was on the second floor. Directly below, the moonlight washed over the flat roof of the long carport and caught on the smooth curve of the service ladder spilling over the side. The window itself was a scant five feet above the roof.

"You should keep this window locked," he said. "It's dangerous this way."

The change of subject brought her eyes up from her nails. "What do you mean?"

"Haven't you been reading the papers?"

"Oh, that!"

"It's nothing to scoff at. Two women are very dead." She stared at him then, because this wasn't just conversation and she was beginning to know it.

"Stop wishing so hard," she said. "You're almost drooling."

"Don't be stupid, Elaine."

"I'm not stupid—and I'm not going to let you scare me into letting you off the hook. What do you think I am, Keith? A substitute wife you can use for a while until you decide to go back to the home fires and slippers routine? Well, I'm not! I told you before, you can't have your cake and eat it. You walked out on me—I didn't send you away. Just try to get a divorce on that and see what it costs you!"

It was two days later that Sergeant Gonzales called Keith to his office. There had been a new development in the case, one of those unexpected breaks that could mean everything or nothing, depending on how it went. A call had come in from a resident of a court in West Hollywood. A woman had reported seeing a prowler outside her bedroom windows. Bedroom windows were a critical area with Gonzales by this time, and when it developed that the woman lived alone, worked five days a week and spent weekends at home, what might have been a routine complaint became important enough for a personal interview. True to his words, he was cutting Keith in on the story if there was one, and there was. Nettie Swanson was a robust, middle-aged woman of definite opinions on acceptable and inacceptable human conduct.

"I don't like snoopers," she reported. "If anybody's curious about how I live, let him come to the door and ask. Snoopers I can't abide. That's why I called the police when I saw this fellow hanging around out back."

"Can you describe the man, Miss Swanson," Gonzales asked.

"I sure can. He was tall—like a beanpole. Would have been taller if he hadn't slouched so much. Young, too. Not that I really saw his face, but I thought he must be young by the way he slouched. Can you give me any reason why young folks today walk around like they been hit in the stomach? And their faces! All calf-eyed like a bunch of strays trying to find their way back to the barn!"

"Miss Swanson," Gonzales cut in, "how are your nerves?"

Some people talked big and folded easily. Nettie Swanson was as collapsible as a cast iron accordion. She listened to Sergeant Gonzales explain the situation and a fire began to kindle in her eyes. The prowler might come back, he told her. He might appear at her door sometime Saturday carrying a basket of items to sell. Would she allow a police officer to wait in her apartment and nab him?

"That's not necessary," she said. "I got a rifle back in my closet that I used to shoot rattlesnakes with when I was a girl in Oklahoma. I can handle that prowler."

"But he's not just a prowler," Gonzales protested. "If he's the man we think he is, he's already killed two women that we know of."

She took the information soberly. She wasn't blind, and she could read. And then her eyes brightened again as the truth sank home.

"The 'cat-killer'! Now, isn't that something! Well, in that case I guess I'd better leave things to you, Sergeant. But I've got my rifle if you need another gun."

Gonzales couldn't have found a more cooperative citizen.

Saturday, Keith sat with Gonzales in a small, unmarked sedan across the street from the apartment house where Nettie Swanson lived. It was an old two-story affair flanked on one side by a new multiple unit and on the other by a shaggy hedge that separated the edge of the lot from a narrow alleyway. The hedge was at least five feet high and only the mouth of the alleyway was visible from the sedan.

But the entrance to the building was visible and had been visible for over an hour. Inside the building, one of Gonzales' men had been waiting since nine o'clock. It was nearly eleven.

Keith was perspiring. He opened the door next to him to let a little more air into the sedan. Gonzales watched him with curious eyes.

"You're even more nervous than I am," he remarked, "and I'm always an old woman about these things. You're working too hard on this, Briscoe."

"I always work hard," Keith said. "I like it that way."

"And nights, too?"

"Nights, too."

"That's bad business. We're not as young as we used to be. There comes a time when we have to taper off a little." Gonzales pushed his hat back on his bead and stretched his legs out in front of him giving the seat a tug backward. "At least that's what they tell me," he added, "but with five kids they don't tell me how. You've got kids, haven't you?"

Keith didn't answer. He looked for a cigarette in his pocket, but the package was empty. Down on the corner, just beyond the alleyway, he could see a drugstore. Drugstores carried cigarettes and no conversation about things he didn't care to discuss.

"I'm going for some smokes," he said. "Tell our friend not to peddle his towels until I get back."

The drugstore was on the same side of the street as the apartment house they were watching. Out of curiosity, he crossed over and walked past the front door. It was open to let in the air, but the hall was empty. He walked past the alley and on to the drugstore. He bought the cigarettes and walked back, still walking slowly because he was in no hurry to get back into that hot sedan. Gonzales was right: he was nervous. His bands trembled as he slit the tax stamp on the cigarette box. At the mouth of the alley he paused to light a cigarette, and then promptly forgot about it and let it fall to the ground.

A few minutes earlier, the alley had been deserted. Now a battered gray coupe was parked against the hedges about twenty feet back from the street. He looked up. The sidewalk in front of him was empty, but across the street Gonzales was climbing out of the sedan. Gonzales walked hurriedly toward the front door of the building, a man with his mind on his business. He didn't see Keith at all. The picture fell into place. Keith went directly to the coupe. It was an old Chevy, license number KUJ770. He stepped around to the door and looked for the card holder on the steering post. It had slipped out of focus, but the door was unlocked. When he opened the door, he saw something that had dropped to the floor of the car and was half hidden under the seat. It was dirty from being kicked about, but it was blue and it had a black French poodle on it. He dropped the towel to the floor and went to work on the card holder. The registration tab slid into view: George Kawalik, 1376¼ N. 3rd Street. Keith had the whole story in his hand. Gonzales hadn't seen the coupe; he couldn't have seen it from the far side of the hedge. He stepped back, intending to go after Gonzales, and it was then that he heard the shot. He waited. There may have been a shout from within the building. He was never sure because what happened, when it did happen, it happened very fast. He had started around the edge of the hedge when suddenly the hedge burst open to erupt a head—blond, close-cropped, a face—wild, contorted with fear—and then a body, long but bent almost double as it stumbled and fell forward toward the coupe. The door was wrenched open, and the face appeared above the steering wheel before Keith could orient himself for action. He was already at the curb twenty feet away from the car. He turned back just as the coupe leaped forward and was forced to scramble in fast retreat to avoid being run down. The retreat came to a sudden stop as he collided with about a hundred and eighty pounds of mobile power which turned out to be Gonzales.

"Was that him in the coupe? Did you see him?"

The coupe was a gray blur racing toward the corner.

"Did you see the car? Did you get the number?" Gonzales had a right to shout. A killer had slipped through his fingers. A two-time murderer was getting away. "That fool woman and her rattlesnake gun!"

Keith recovered his breath.

"Did she fire the shot?" he asked.

"No—but she had the gun in her hand when she opened the door. Clancy, inside, didn't catch her in time. The peddler saw it and ran for the back door. It was Clancy who fired. Did you get the license number?"

Gonzales's face was a big, sweaty mask in front of Keith's eyes. A big, homely, sweating face. A cop, a friend, a man in trouble. And Keith had the whole story on a tiny slip of paper in his hand.

He didn't hesitate.

"No," he said. "I didn't get it. I didn't have time."

Who could tell when decisions were made? An opportunity came, an answer was given—but that wasn't the time. Time was a fabric; the instant called now was only a thread. But it was done. The moment Keith spoke, he knew that something his mind had been planning all this time was already done. The fabric was already woven. He had only to follow the threads.

There was a murderer named George Kawalik who killed by pattern. He found an apartment where a woman lived alone. He watched the apartment, located the bedroom window, waited until Saturday when it was most likely he would find her home and made his scouting expedition under the pretext of peddling pretty towels. Sunday night was payoff night. He came, he stole, he killed.

There was another man named Keith Briscoe who had made a mistake. He didn't like to think about how or why he'd made it, but he had to think of a way out. He wasn't a young man anymore. A little gray had begun to appear at his temples, and he was beginning to feel his limitations. It didn't seem fair that he had to pay for the rest of his life for a flirtation that had gone too far. It seemed less fair that his sons had no father, and that Faye was becoming a lonely woman who took her drinks stronger and who was running away to find the love he wanted to give her.

After leaving Gonzales, Keith had time to think about all these things. He sat alone in the furnished room and laid them out logically, mathematically in his mind. He put it into a simple formula: Keith plus Faye equaled home and happiness; Keith minus Elaine equaled Faye. The second part was no certainty, but it was at least a gamble and Keith not minus Elaine was no chance at all.

He knew the odds against murder. George Kawalik would be caught. He was no longer a footprint on the earth or a faceless shadow tall enough to reach up and slit a window screen, lean and agile enough to hoist himself into a room. He now had a face as well as a body; he had a method of operation; more important, he had a car. Gonzales had seen the gray coupe fleetingly, but he'd seen it with eyes trained to absorb details. And Gonzales had an organization to work with. Even as he sat thinking about it, Keith knew what forces were being put into operation. The coupe would be found. It might take days or even weeks, but it would be found. In the meantime, George Kawalik would kill again. That was inevitable. The compulsion that drove him to the act, whether it was a mental quirk or an addict's desperate need for money, would drive him again.

And Sunday was the night for murder.

On Saturday evening, as soon as it was dark, Keith went on an expedition. The address in Kawalik's registration slip wasn't easy to find in the dark; it wouldn't have been easy by daylight. It was a run-down, cluttered neighborhood ripe for a mass invasion of house movers. Old frame residences with the backyards cluttered by as many haphazard units as the building code would permit. Far to the rear of the lot he found Kawalik's number. The unit was dark and the shades drawn. He wanted to try the door, but it was too risky. This was no time to activate Kawalik's nervous trigger finger. He walked quietly around to the rear of the unit. All of the shades were drawn, but one window was open. He stood close to it for a few moments, and it seemed he could hear someone breathing inside. He moved on. The back door had an old-fashioned lock that any skeleton key would open. He fingered the key ring in his pocket and then decided to wait. He left the unit and walked back to the garages, a barrackslike row of open-front cubicles facing a narrow alley. The gray coupe was there.

Kawalik was holed in, the natural reaction to his narrow escape. That was good. Keith wasn't ready for him yet; he merely wanted to know where to find him at the proper time. He found his way back through the maze of units to the street, always with the uneasy knowledge that a crazed killer might be watching from behind those shaded windows. He'd almost reached the sidewalk when a voice out of the darkness brought him to a sudden halt.

"Looking for somebody, mister?"

A man's voice. Keith turned about slowly and then breathed easier. An old man stood in the lighted doorway of the front apartment. He had the suspicious eyes and possessive stance of a landlord protecting his property.

"I guess I had the wrong address," Keith said.

"What address you looking for?"

"A place to rent. A friend of mine told me he saw an empty unit here."

"Nothing to rent here," the old man answered.

"A unit with the shades rolled down," he said.

"That place's rented. The man rents it works nights."

Keith went home then. The old man still looked suspicious; Keith was satisfied.

There was only one thing to do before returning to Kawalik. In the morning, Keith called Elaine. It was nearly noon, but she sounded sleepy. Elaine's nights were unusually long. He'd worked out his story carefully. He was working late that night, he told her, but he had to see her. It was important. How about midnight? Elaine protested. Thelma was giving a party.

"Not another birthday?" he challenged.

She still protested. What did he want that couldn't wait? Freedom, he told her.

"And you know what I told you," she said.

"That it would cost me. Well, I may have a way of raising the fare. You don't dislike cash, do you?"

She fell for it. She would be home by midnight.

He watched the apartment from the street. At midnight all of the lights were blazing. At one o'clock the front lights went out, and he moved around to the rear. At one-thirty, the bedroom light went out. Elaine thought he'd stood her up and had gone to bed. She couldn't have made a bigger mistake.

Twenty minutes later, Keith entered Kawalik's apartment by way of the back door. The place was dark. For a few seconds, he was afraid Kawalik had more nerve than he'd been given credit for and was out calling on some other victim chosen in advance, but the fear left him when he reached the bedroom. A faint glow of moonlight penetrated the window blind outlining a long body under the sheet on the bed. Keith had his own gun in his hand. He switched on the flashlight. It was Kawalik, but he didn't stir. Keith moved closer to the bed. Kawalik's eyes were closed and his breathing heavy. One arm was thrown outside the sheet. Keith's first hunch had been correct. The arm was tattooed with needle marks and the last jolt must have been a big one. Kawalik wouldn't awaken for hours.

It was a better break than he'd bargained for. He played the flash around the room, not wanting to risk the lights because of the eagle-eyed landlord up front. Item by item, he found what be needed: Kawalik's .45 in a bureau drawer, a pair of canvas shoes with smooth rubber soles in the closet, a pair of gloves, a basketful of colored guest towels. Keith thumbed through the basket until he found a pink one. Shocking pink. It seemed appropriate for Elaine.

In the bathroom, he located the pocket knife among other interesting items: a hypodermic needle, a spoon with a fireblackened bowl, the remnants of an old shirt torn in strips. One of the strips was stained with blood. Kawalik must have gone deeper than he intended locating the vein. Another blood-spotted strip dangled over the edge of the lavatory. He started to play the light downward and then switched it off instead. He didn't breathe again until he was convinced it was a cat he'd heard outside the building. He left the place then, without a light, locking the back door behind him.

Half an hour later, Keith climbed through Elaine's bedroom window. He was breathless and scared. A dozen times he'd expected her to hear him sawing away at the screen and ruin everything; but the other tenants of their building had always been thoughtful about such things as late, late television movies at full volume, or all-night parties of vibrant vocal range. This night was no exception and so Elaine would be sleeping, as usual, with ear plugs and eye mask. He really didn't need Kawalik's rubber-soled shoes on the deep-piled rug, but he did need Kawalik's signature—the pink towel to deposit in the linen closet in the bathroom. In the dressing room he found two purses in plain sight. He took the money from them, jamming the smaller, an evening bag, in his pocket for subsequent deposit in the driveway below. That done, he went to the bed, leaned over Elaine and raised the eye mask. She awakened with a start, but she didn't scream. Elaine had nerve—nerve enough to stare at the shadowy figure standing over her bed until recognition came.

"Oh, it's you—"

And then she saw the gun in his hand. That was when Keith fired.

It was easy. Murder was easy. By the time he was safely in his car again, Keith was in the throes of an almost delirious elation. His nerves had been tauter than he knew; now they were unwinding with the power of a strong spring bursting its webbing. He knew how Kawalik felt when the shot in his bloodstream took effect: wild and free and about ten thousand feet up. Elaine was dead, and there wasn't a thing anyone could ever do to him. The noisy neighbors hadn't heard the shot, the evening bag had been dropped at the foot of the service ladder on the garage, the pink towel was in the linen closet and ballistics would match the bullet in Elaine's body to the two other bullets they were holding from two other identical crimes. And the beauty of it all was that Kawalik, when they caught him, wouldn't be able to remember but what he really had killed her. There was nothing left to do, but get the gun, gloves, shoes and the money back into Kawalik's apartment. After that, he belonged to the inevitable. The inevitable was Sergeant Gonzales. Keith didn't see the police car in front of Kawalik's place until it was too late to drive on. He had slowed down to park, and Gonzales recognized him.

"I see you got my message," Gonzales called.

Keith shut off the motor. He had no idea how Gonzales had located Kawalik so quickly, but he could play dumb. Dumb meant silence.

"I told them at headquarters to call you just as I was leaving. It seemed a shame for you to miss out on the finish."

"The cat-killer?" Keith asked, his mind racing.

"We got him. I tell you, Briscoe, I've had an angel on my shoulder on this case. Another lucky break. The landlord here got suspicious. Said a fellow had been prowling around the place last night and he heard somebody again tonight, so he called the police. The boys didn't find a prowler, but out in the garage they found something more interesting—"

Keith's mind raced ahead of Gonzales's words. He wasn't ten thousand feet up anymore, but he was still free. They'd have to look for the gun. He could help them do that; in the dark he could be a big help.

"—an old coupe," Gonzales added, "like the one they've been alerted for all day. They took a look. The front seat was full of blood."

In the dark he could help them find the gun and the gloves and the rubber-soled shoes—And then Keith's mind stopped racing and listened to Gonzales' words.

"Blood?" he echoed.

Blood, as on a strip of torn cloth in the bathroom. Blood, as what was soaking into Elaine's bedclothes and beginning to stain Keith's hands.

Gonzales nodded.

"I guess Clancy's a better shot than we knew. The catkiller won't climb tonight, Briscoe, or any other night. He's in there now so doped up he doesn't even know we've found him. It's a good way to kill the pain when somebody's blown a chunk out of your leg."

It wasn't really blood on Keith's hands; it was a gun. When he couldn't stand the weight of it any longer, he handed it to Gonzales. Gonzales would figure it out. A thread, a fabric, a pattern. Elaine had been right: he had a weakness, and a man with a weakness shouldn't play with guns.

Murder and Lonely Hearts

Herbert Gibson was the last man who would have been suspected of wanting to kill his wife. He was the prototype of the good citizen: he belonged to the local Chamber of Commerce, two service organizations, the Athletic Club—which he hadn't visited in ten years and thirty pounds—and attended church every Easter, Christmas, and Mother's Day. The latter was a concession to Irene (Mrs. Gibson) who, in their twenty-six years of marriage, had mothered three cocker spaniels and a French poodle.

On the surface, the Gibson marriage was a happy one. None of their neighbors on Acacia Lane, that suburban paradise for the middle-income group, could say anything against them. They were a quiet, conservative couple in their mid-forties, who kept their house painted, their two Chevrolets polished, and their lawns clipped and green, which was a matter of great significance on Acacia Lane. Residents of long tenure might have noted, had their memories been equally green, that Herbert Gibson had worn a somewhat bitter expression when he began walking the earliest cocker spaniel; but with succeeding years and successive spaniels this expression had gradually altered to resignation, benign resignation and finally, by the time Irene switched to the poodle, a kind of absent-minded serenity which, in the latter months, approached nirvana.

There was, however, nothing absent-minded about the manner in which Herbert conducted his business. He was a C.P.A.—twenty-five years in the same location: Room 408 Handley Building. It was an old building. The offices were small, dingy, but inexpensive, and Herbert saw no object in providing luxurious surroundings merely for the purpose of telling clients how much they owed the government. Irene, who wasn't interested in business, was vaguely aware that he went off somewhere or other every day to do something or other, for which he received a fairly adequate income.

Herbert wasn't ambitious. If he occasionally felt a vague stirring or uneasiness within, he stopped off at the drugstore for a bicarbonate and forgot about it. But that was before Rodney Dumbarton, Business Management, moved into the adjoining office. Whatever business

Dumbarton managed was none of Herbert's—they met only on occasions when the postman erred as to his choice of mail slots—until the day his neighbor departed mere minutes ahead of the police. It developed that Mr. Dumbarton had managed to collect substantial sums of money from clients for services never rendered, a practice considered anti-social in law enforcement circles.

The fact that he'd been in contact with an absconded criminal was one of the most exciting things that had ever happened to Herbert. He tried to share the experience with Irene at dinner, but anything pertaining to his business bored Irene. All he had to say was—

"An interesting thing happened at the office today."

—and her face, never really attentive, took on an expression of complete remoteness. She stirred her asparagus with a fork and stared over the top of Herbert's slightly balding head.

"I'm getting awfully tired of that Currier and Ives over the mantel," she remarked.

Herbert tried again.

"Mr. Dumbarton, next door to me, left just ahead of the police. He was mixed up in the darndest—"

"I think it's the snow I dislike," Irene added. "It's so cold looking."

"—scheme," Herbert said. "He'd distributed a lot of phony advertising for something called a 'Friendship Cruise.' Here, I brought one of his brochures home with me."

Irene paid no more heed to the brochure than she had to Herbert. "The room needs more color."

"His idea was to get unmarried men and women corresponding with one another through his office and then sell them passage on one of his cruises. It was a sort of floating lonely hearts club."

Herbert paused, smiling at his own feeble attempt at humor. Finally, Irene did look at him.

"Herbert," she said, "eat your lamb chop. Celeste is waiting for the bone. She's been very patient."

Herbert sighed and put the brochure down on the table. The conversation had gone the way of all their conversations; Irene hadn't heard a word he'd said.

With no one to talk to, Herbert soon forgot about Rodney Dumbarton and his extravagant scheme until one morning a week later when he was going through the morning mail and came across the following letter:

Friendship Cruises, Inc.

Dear Sir:

I am writing in response to your interesting brochure only because you sound as if you are a highly respectable organization and would have a highly respectable clientele ...

At this point Herbert realized the postman had erred again, and that he had compounded the postman's error with his letter opener; but two typewritten stationery sheets remained, and curiosity got the better of virtue. He continued:

... This is very important to me as I am a respectable lady, over thirty, who has never traveled abroad, and the idea of getting acquainted with someone on shipboard before sailing seems wonderful.

You suggest a brief autobiography and information on my likes and dislikes. There really isn't much to tell about me. I make my living from tax accounting; but I would prefer companionship with someone in some other kind of work, preferably a writer or an artist, but most of all someone who is an interesting conversationalist. I would love to have someone to talk to.

It is difficult to say what I like to do, because I've never had time to do it and find out. I can only tell you what I've always dreamed of doing if I ever went abroad. Most of all, I want to go to Paris. I want to visit the Louvre and see the famous paintings, and visit Notre Dame Cathedral and see the Rose Window, and sit at one of those little tables outside a sidewalk cafe and have whatever people have at sidewalk cafes. I even want to take the elevator to the top of the Eifel Tower!

I suppose I sound just like the typical tourist, but I will be waiting to hear from any of your clients whom you think might be interested in knowing me.

Respectfully,
Sylvia Sagan Box 1477, City

P.S. I am a blonde with hazel eyes and have what my friends tell me is a good figure.

What had started as curiosity blossomed into astonishment by the time Herbert finished reading the letter. Was there actually such a woman as Sylvia Sagan? I would love to have someone to talk to. The words had a poignant quality that aroused Herbert's sympathy. It's difficult to say what I'd like to do, because I've never had time to do it and find out. At this point the writer placed a mirror to Herbert's soul. He raised his eyes. The door to his office stood open. The gold lettering, chipped with the passing years, told him his identity: Herbert Gibson, Certified Public Accountant. Somewhere in the city was another office: Sylvia Sagan, Tax Accountant. It might even be very much like his own—one desk, two chairs, a water cooler in the corner, and a calendar on the wall with a picture of puppies at play.

Herbert's eyes followed the direction of his thoughts and suddenly came to an arresting halt. The calendar didn't have a picture of puppies at play, Irene's perennial selection; it had a picture of a sea coast—and a wild one at that! And then he remembered why he'd done the choosing this year. There were two lines underneath the picture that had struck his fancy:

"I must go down to the sea again,
To the lonely sea and the sky—"

They were from a poem he'd memorized in High School English. He'd been darned good at English, come to think of it. He'd written several A compositions and tried his hand at a few short stories before he married Irene. I would prefer companionship with someone in some other kind of work, preferably a writer ... Herbert reined in his imagination and replaced the letter in its envelope. He would return it to the sender, of course, with a note of explanation the first time he had a few minutes to spare.

And that is exactly what he would have done, if Irene's brother Lennie hadn't been parked in his favorite chair in front of the television when he got home that night.

Lennie was a problem. He had won a Purple Heart in World War II and was still bleeding. He was getting a bit old to be a member of the Lost Generation; and anyhow, Lennie wasn't lost. He just didn't know what had become of everybody else. He did, however, know the way to Herbert's house whenever he was in need, and his unheralded appearance precipitated another fruitless conversation.

"I suppose Lennie's lost his job again," Herbert said to Irene irritably.

"You didn't even notice the new picture I bought for over the mantel," Irene said to Herbert.

"Or is his wound bothering him again—that nicked finger he got on the target range in Georgia?"

"I think the coloring is much nicer, don't you?"

"Hang it all, Irene, you know how he monopolizes the television, and this is my night for Foreign Escapade!"

"It's a genuine reproduction of a genuine Matisse, Herbert. Just think, a genuine Matisse!"

Herbert took Celeste for a walk.

It was a foggy night, and he almost enjoyed walking Celeste on a foggy night. She was less conspicuous and so was Acacia Lane. The houses of the neighbors—the Meekers, the Swansons, Dr. Pettigrew— were just so many dim forms behind the mist; and with a little imagination the street could become the Limehouse District, or a coastal town in Normandy, or any other place where mystery stalked the shadows.

"Who is Silvia, who is she
That all her swains commend her ...?"

He hadn't thought of those lines since he was courting Irene and they sang them together at her mother's upright. It seemed impossible now that they had ever done anything together. To Irene he was just a man who walked the dog, while Lennie watched television. What kind of a man would he be, if he'd ever had time to do what he wanted to do? A letter began to write itself in his mind.

Dear Miss Sagan,
Your letter has been forwarded to me by Friendship Cruises. I must say that it is a very interesting letter with certain passages that lead me to believe we have much in common. Oddly enough, we're in almost the same business—

No, the last sentence wouldn't do. Sylvia wanted to correspond with someone in a different field, preferably a writer or an artist. Herbert made a mental erasure.

Oddly enough, in view of your request, I am a writer of short stories. Not a very successful one, I'm afraid; but then, like yourself, I've never had anyone I could really talk to or have share my dreams. That's important, don't you think? To know someone who cares about what you are doing—who believes in you and wants to be a part of your life?

Your ideas on travel are charming, Miss Sagan; but not nearly as charming, I'm sure, as you must be. I hope you will honor me by acknowledging this letter and telling me more about yourself.

Respectfully Yours—

Herbert Gibson didn't sound proper at the end of the letter any more than the letter sounded like Herbert Gibson. It was more in the style of Rodney Dumbarton's romantic brochure. His name hadn't appeared anywhere on the piece—still, he wanted something crisper.

Respectfully Yours, Rodney Barton

That was better. Celeste stopped and Herbert stopped. A shapely blonde emerged out of the fog and walked past them. Herbert stared, remembering a postscript and adding it to his own mental missile.

P.S. I am a little past 40. I have light brown hair, blue eyes, and work out regularly at the Athletic Club.

It was only a letter in his mind, but it was astonishing how much satisfaction it gave him. It wouldn't be fair to actually write it. Or would it? It wasn't as if there really were a cruise. What harm could one letter do? He might give the poor woman a bright day in her drab little office with the water cooler and the calendar on the wall. He wouldn't have to risk exposure by using his own address; he could take a Post Office box ...

The fog gave Herbert daring, but it was Lennie who gave him decision. He returned to the house just in time for Foreign Escapade. Lennie was watching wrestling.

"My gosh, Herbie, what do you want with that kid stuff? Watch this now! Abdullah's got a sleeper hold on the Cowboy. Ride 'em Cowboy!"

Herbert unsnapped Celeste's leash and went upstairs. Irene was in her bedroom reading a novel. She didn't so much a look up when he came to the door.

"I just want to borrow your typewriter to write a letter," he said. She didn't answer, naturally.

The correspondence between Rodney Barton and Sylvia Sagan began innocently enough. It was all very well to write one letter and then terminate the correspondence, but why just one letter? As long as nothing could come of it anyway, what harm could be done? Herbert needed some entertainment now that Lennie had settled down with the television.

And certain things demanded an answer.

> ... I can tell by your letter, Mr. Barton, that you are a very interesting person. You must meet fascinating people in your work, and I'm flattered that you would even think of writing to me. You've no idea how dull my life is! How I, too, long for someone to share my dreams!
>
> Have you decided definitely on the cruise? I still want to visit Paris, but there's also Rome ...
>
> P.S. I'm enclosing a recent snapshot. It's not very good, but it will give you some idea of what I'm like.

The snapshot wasn't very good—Sylvia was too far from the camera to give any distinct features to her face. But it had been taken on a beach, and although the bathing suit might have been a little out of fashion—Herbert wasn't an expert on such matters—the contents were arranged in a quite satisfactory way. This troubled him. He'd written to her only out of the kindness of his heart to give the poor woman something to dream on a bit longer. Why was her life so dull? And then he read the letter again. "... you are a very interesting person ..." Perhaps that was true. Perhaps all he needed was for someone to hold up the mirror and let him see himself for what he could be. That might be the case with Sylvia, too. There could be no harm in one more letter.

> Dear Miss Sagan,
> Do you really imagine that my life is exciting, or that I have met anyone more interesting than you? Your letters are like a breath of fresh air on a stifling day. What a marvelous thing to have found a woman who is interesting and interested in others.
>
> It would be criminal to go abroad and not visit the Eternal City. I would love to be able to escort you through the galleries, the cathedrals and the old ruins.

Incidentally, have you ever been married? I ask only because your snapshot makes it seem incredible that you were not.

Cordially,
Rodney

P.S. May I call you Sylvia?

The postscript was accidental; it seemed to write itself. This wasn't turning out at all the way Herbert intended. He had the vague sensation of being sucked into a whirlpool, but he mailed the letter anyway.

Dear Rodney,
You're right, we must be honest with one another. Yes, I have been married—unhappily. I hope you won't be angry with me, for not having told you of this sooner; but I did want to make your acquaintance, and was afraid you would think me forward. After all, the past is the past, don't you agree? When two people have so much in common they should enjoy one another and no questions asked.
Have you thought of Spain?

Dearest Sylvia,
I think of nothing but Spain—and you! But now I, too, must make a confession. It was only by accident that I opened your first letter. You see, I work in an office adjoining Friendship Cruises and received it by mistake when the company went out of business several weeks ago. I meant only to return your letter with an explanation of why it had been opened, but you sounded like someone I wanted to know. I realize that I shouldn't have continued this long without telling you the truth, but I hope we are close enough friends now that you can forgive.
There are no Friendship Cruises, Sylvia dear, but there are still friendships that sometimes become life voyages. We can escape the humdrum world. Fortunately, I have a little property
...

It was madness. Even as he posted the letter, Herbert knew that. Irene would never consent to a divorce, and even if she did they would have to divide the property. The house was clear and would realize a nice profit, but half of that profit, less court fees ... and he might not even get half if Irene learned about Sylvia! No, it was stark madness. It was what happened to a man after having his wife's brother planted in front of the television for six weeks. But he couldn't put all the blame on Lennie. There was still that stormy seascape on the calendar—the omen. And now everything hinged on Sylvia's answer. Perhaps she wouldn't answer. The thought came with both pain and relief, for even then Herbert knew what he really had in mind.

Sylvia did answer.

> Rod, my dearest,
> How can I be so lucky? Or was it only luck? Do you believe in Fate? Now I can tell you how timid I was about writing to Friendship Cruises. Their brochure made everything sound so wonderful, and I was simply dying of loneliness; but I was afraid of the type of person who might answer their offer. Now I don't have to be afraid because you weren't even a client. I suppose it's cruel of me, but I'm really happy the company went out of business.
> You write that you have a little property you could dispose of. So have I. It may take a few weeks to liquidate my holdings, but I've waited a lifetime. A few weeks longer won't kill me ...

The language of Sylvia's letter was almost brutal. What had started as an innocent prank, had reached an irrevocable conclusion: Irene had to go.

But how? Herbert had never contemplated murder—in spite of Lennie's visits. How many means were there? Irene looked at him suspiciously when she found him tampering with the kitchen window. And he decided a faked robbery and shooting wouldn't work anyway. Irene was annoyed when he managed to bump into her a few times at the head of the stairs. That sort of thing was much too risky, really. The fall might not kill her. He'd be in a worse position than ever then, with an invalid on his hands. The axe in the garage was out of the question. Herbert always felt nauseous at the sight of blood.

The solution, unexpectedly, came from Irene herself.

"The rose bushes are getting a blight," she remarked over the breakfast table.

Herbert was deep in his problem.

"You're putting on a little weight, Irene," he said. "Why don't you do something for exercise—horseback riding, for instance?"

"Horseback?" It was the first time she'd heard him in years. "You know I'm terrified of horses. I was thrown when I was a girl."

"I know, but I don't think you should go through life being afraid of anything. I'll go with you."

Irene stared at him strangely. She'd been staring at him strangely ever since the window episode.

"I am afraid of nothing," she said firmly, "except the blight on the roses. Are you listening to me, Herbert? I want you to stop off and buy some arsenic—"

Herbert was listening.

"—and while you're about it, pick up a bottle of wine for dinner. It's Lennie's birthday."

"Wine?" Herbert echoed. Irene's voice softened.

"I know it's an extravagance, Herbert, but I want the dinner to be something special. I didn't tell you before, but Lennie's leaving soon. This may be the last time we're all together on his birthday."

Irene had become a prophetess.

Arsenic and wine—the classic means of murder. There was still a matter of mechanics to work out. But when the fates were with you, what could go wrong? Herbert sat in his office and listened to the surf pounding on the rocky shore in the calendar picture—the omen. Now he understood what had been happening to him when he chose that calendar—happening long before he'd heard of Friendship Cruises or gone walking Celeste in the fog. Sylvia had only roused the dormant senses; he really was Rodney Barton—always had been. He had only been slumbering all through the years and now he was awakening.

And Rodney Barton could do anything. Arsenic and wine ... he needed a small container. He left his office and walked down a flight to the dentist in 304. He complained of a toothache he didn't have, and then returned to his own office with a small bottle of oil of cloves which he promptly dumped down the drain. The small bottle was what he needed.

At noon, Herbert went out for lunch and stopped at the gardening shop where he'd traded for years. They made up a special arsenic solution of their own that came bottled, boxed, wrapped in paper and sealed with a strip of gummed advertising tape. The tape was never very tight. As soon as he left the shop, Herbert peeled off the strip being careful not to tear it, and returned to his office. There he managed to unwrap the bottle without damaging the paper or the box and—careful not to get his fingerprints on the bottle—transferred a small portion of the contents into the empty oil of cloves bottle. That done, he rewrapped the bottle, retaped the seal—with the aid of the office mucilage—and surveyed his work with smug satisfaction. He knew Irene. She opened every package the moment it was placed in her hands; only her fingerprints would be on the arsenic.

He envisioned himself, shocked and grief-stricken, telling the police how Irene had asked him to buy the arsenic and the wine, and he, in all innocence, had done so without realizing the dark significance of her parting words:

"This may be the last time we're all together ..."

Suicide was much more tragic than an accident. The neighbors would see nothing strange in a quick sale of the property so he could get away from bitter memories—away to Spain, warm and exciting with dark-eyed beauties dancing in the sunlight, and Sylvia, of course. Sylvia who really understood him—and if it turned out that she didn't, there were always the dark-eyed beauties. Herbert leaned back in his chair, and, for the first time in his life, put his feet up on his desk. He was going to enjoy being Rodney Barton.

On birthdays, holidays, and festive occasions, Irene used candles on the table. Herbert counted on that and wasn't disappointed. For contemplated sleight of hand, the less light the better. He didn't open the wine bottle. Lennie was more proficient at that art, and the search for a corkscrew took him safely off to the kitchen. Irene—to whom Herbert had given the arsenic, and who ripped the covering from the bottle in order to make certain he hadn't made a stupid mistake and bought the wrong preparation, was busy with her dinner. There was plenty of time during one of her absences from the room to transfer a few drops of poison from the small bottle in his pocket to the wine glass in front of her plate. It was a colorless liquid—not noticeable in the candlelight.

It was done. Herbert replaced the bottle in his pocket and stepped back from the table. Strange how he could hear that surf on the rocks again—louder than it had been before. It was actually done. It wasn't something dreamed up on a foggy night's walk; it wasn't something lurking in the back of his mind as he typed out mad letters to Sylvia. And they were mad letters. He realized that now with a sudden, sharp clarity that came like a lifting of the fog. Who was Sylvia? Who was she to make Herbert Gibson a murderer? No, not Herbert. It was

Rodney who had done it—Rodney Barton.

"Herbert—Herbert, do sit down. We're waiting for you."

Herbert looked up, startled. He hadn't even heard Irene and Lennie come into the room, and there they were seated at the table ready to begin dinner. Lennie was pouring the wine.

"Wait, Lennie—" Irene said. "I think there's something in this glass."

He saw her hand reach out—but to his glass, not to hers.

"Dust," she said. "I was sure that I washed out those glasses."

Irene left the table, glass in hand, and in a moment there was the sound of the faucet running in the kitchen. And it was then Herbert became aware of a terrible loss: Rodney Barton was gone! He couldn't go through with it; he simply didn't have the nerve. But Lennie was still pouring wine. Irene's glass was full—blood red and full. He had to get that glass somehow; but she returned too soon. Lennie filled Herbert's glass. It was time for the toast. Herbert's hand was trembling as he reached forward. If there was nothing short of snatching the poisoned drink from Irene's hand, he'd have to do just that. And then he thought of a way.

"Celeste!" he said sharply. "Where's Celeste? We have to get the whole family in on this."

When Celeste bounded up to the table, there was a momentary distraction, one just long enough for Herbert to switch glasses with Irene. They could proceed with the festivities then—Herbert so shaken from his brush with homicide, he nearly forgot himself and drank along with the others. Just in time, he realized what he was doing and made a splendid job of spilling the contents of his glass all over the damask cloth.

"Herbert, what have you done?"

The voice of a shrew, but music to his ears. Irene's glass was empty and she could still berate him.

"You've spilled your wine, you clumsy fool! You've spilled it all!"

Sheer music. Herbert made his way to the kitchen, for a towel, and Irene's chosen phrases followed him all the way. He didn't care. She could scold for the rest of their days just as long as he could hear her voice. And then it stopped. He listened, but the voice didn't come again—only the thud.

When Dr. Pettigrew and the policeman came down the stairs, Herbert was sitting in his chair with his face buried in his hands. He pulled the hands away slowly and looked up at them with haggard eyes. Lennie was with them, too, standing a few steps behind. He held something in his hands.

"I don't know what happened," Herbert said vaguely. "I just don't know—"

"It was arsenic poisoning," the policeman said. "One sniff of the glass was enough to convince me, and the doctor agrees. Your wife died of arsenic poisoning."

"But she couldn't have! I spilled—"

Dr. Pettigrew stepped forward and placed a restraining hand on his shoulder.

"Take it easy, Mr. Gibson. I know how you feel. This is incredible to me, too. Why, I've known you and Irene for years. I was just telling the sergeant, here, that I couldn't imagine what could get into a woman to do what she did."

"What she did?"

Pettigrew's face was grave.

"You've got to brace yourself, Herbert. Irene put the arsenic in the wine. We know that because Lennie tells us she'd been after him for days to buy it, but he never got around to it. I suppose she thought she could count on her own brother to cover for her. And tonight at the table, she found an excuse to take your glass out to the kitchen, didn't she? And when you spilled your wine, she was terribly upset, wasn't she? Don't you see, Herbert? Somehow or another Irene made a mistake with the glasses, but the poisoned drink was meant for you."

"For me?" Herbert echoed. "But why—?"

Three faces looked at him with varying degrees of pity, and then Lennie handed him a package of letters.

"We found these in Irene's room," he said. "Read them and you'll know why."

But Herbert didn't have to read the letters. The address was sufficient: Sylvia Sagan, Box 4770, City.

"Mr. Gibson! Mr. Gibson, are you all right?"

Herbert looked up with the eyes of a small boy trying to comprehend. Celeste, the French poodle, the Matisse over the mantel, the brochure he'd left on the dining table. Slowly, he understood.

"She wanted someone to talk to," he said.

Death Scene

The woman who had driven in with the black Duesenberg fascinated Leo Manfred. She stood well, as if she might be a model or a dancer. Her ankles were arched and her calves firm. Leo wriggled out from under the car he was working on in order to examine her more closely.

She was dressed all in white—white hat with a wide, schoolgirl brim; white dress, fitted enough to make her body beckon him further; white shoes with high, spiked heels.

But it was more than the way she dressed and the way she stood. There was something strange about her, almost mysterious, and mystery didn't go well in the grease-and-grime society of Wagner's Garage. Leo got to his feet.

Carl Wagner, who was half again Leo's thirty years, and far more interested in the motor he'd uncovered than in any woman, blocked the view of her face. But her voice, when she spoke, was soft and resonant.

"Mr. Wagner," she said, "can you tell me when my automobile will be ready?"

Automobile—not car. Leo's active mind took note.

By this time Wagner was peering under the hood with the enthusiasm of a picnicker who had just opened a boxed banquet.

"It's a big motor, Miss Revere," he answered, "and every cylinder has to be synchronized. Your father's always been very particular about that."

"My father—" She hesitated. There was the ghost of a smile. It couldn't be seen, but it was felt—the way some perfumes, Leo reflected, are felt. "—my father is very particular, Mr. Wagner. But it's such a warm day, and I don't feel like shopping."

Carl Wagner wasted neither words nor time. The fingers of one hand went poking into the pocket of his coveralls and dug up a set of keys at the same instant that he glanced up and saw Leo.

"My helper will take you home," he said. "You can tell your father that we'll deliver the car just as soon as it's ready."

If Leo Manfred had believed in fate, he would have thought this was it; but Leo believed in Leo Manfred and a thing called opportunity.

Women were Leo's specialty. He possessed a small black book containing the telephone numbers—of more than 57 varieties; but no one listed in his book was anything like the passenger who occupied the back seat of the boss's new Pontiac as it nosed up into the hills above the boulevard.

Leo tried to catch her face in the rearview mirror. She never looked at him. She stared out of the window or fussed with her purse. Her face was always half lost beneath the shadow of the hat. She seemed shy, and shyness was a refreshing challenge.

At her direction, the Pontiac wound higher and higher, beyond one new real estate development after another, until, at the crest of long private driveway, it came to a stop at the entrance of a huge house. Architecturally, the house was a combination of Mediterranean and late Moorish, with several touches of early Hollywood. Not being architecturally inclined, Leo didn't recognize this; but he did recognize that it must have cost a pretty penny when it was built, and that the gardener toiling over a pasture-sized lawn couldn't have been supplied by the Department of Parks and Beaches.

And yet, there was a shabbiness about the place—a kind of weariness, a kind of nostalgia, that struck home as Leo escorted his passenger to the door.

"I know this house!" he exclaimed. "I've seen pictures of it. It has a name—" And then he stared at the woman in white, who had been given a name by Carl Wagner: "Revere," he remembered aloud. "Gordon Revere."

"Gavin Revere," she corrected.

"Gavin Revere," Leo repeated.

"That's it! This is the house that the big film director Gavin Revere built for his bride, Monica Parrish. It's called—"

The woman in white had taken a key out of her purse.

"Mon-Vere," she said.

Leo watched her insert the key into the lock of the massive door and then, suddenly, the answer to the mystery broke over him.

"If you're Miss Revere" he said, "then you must be the daughter of Monica Parrish. No wonder I couldn't take my eyes off you."

"Couldn't you?"

She turned toward him, briefly, before entering the house. Out of her purse she took a dollar bill and offered it; but Leo had glimpsed more than a stretch of long, drab hall behind her. Much more.

"I couldn't take money," he protested, "not from you. Your mother was an idol of mine. I used to beg dimes from my uncle—I was an orphan—to go to the movies whenever a Monica Parrish was playing." Leo allowed a note of reverence to creep into his voice.

"When you were a very small boy, I suppose," Miss Revere said.

"Eleven or twelve," Leo answered. "I never missed a film your mother and father made—"

The door closed before Leo could say more; and the last thing he saw was that almost smile under the shadow of the hat.

Back at the garage, Carl Wagner had questions to answer.

"Why didn't you tell me who she was?" Leo demanded. "You knew."

Wagner knew motors. The singing cylinders of the Duesenberg were to him what a paycheck and a beautiful woman, in the order named, were to Leo Manfred. He pulled his head out from under the raised hood and reminisced dreamily.

"I remember the first time Gavin Revere drove this car in for an oil change," he mused. "It was three weeks old, and not one more scratch on it now than there was then."

"What ever happened to him?" Leo persisted.

"Polo," Wagner said. "There was a time when everybody who was anybody had to play polo. Revere wasn't made for it. Cracked his spine and ended up in a wheelchair. He was in and out of hospitals for a couple of years before he tried a comeback. By that time everything had changed. He made a couple of flops and retired."

"And Monica Parrish?"

"Like Siamese twins," Wagner said. "Their careers were tied together. Revere went down, Parrish went down. I think she finally got a divorce and married a Count Somebody—or maybe she was the one who went into that Hindu religion. What does it matter? Stars rise and stars fall, Leo, but a good motor ..."

Twelve cylinders of delight for Carl Wagner; but for Leo Manfred a sweet thought growing in the fertile soil of his rich, black mind.

"I'll take the car back when it's ready," he said.

And then Wagner gave him one long stare and a piece of advice that wasn't going to be heeded.

"Leo," he said, "stick to those numbers in your little black book."

For a man like Leo Manfred, time was short. He had a long way to travel to get where he wanted to go, and no qualms about the means of transportation. When he drove the Duesenberg up into the hills, he observed more carefully the new developments along the way. The hills were being whittled down, leveled off, terraced and turned into neat pocket-estates as fast as the tractors could make new roads and the trucks could haul away surplus dirt. Each estate sold for $25,000 to $35,000, exclusive of buildings, and, he would have needed an adding machine to calculate how much the vast grounds of Mon-Vere would bring on the open market.

As for the house itself—he considered that as he nosed the machine up the steep driveway. It might have some value as a museum or a landmark—Mon-Vere Estates, with the famous old house in the center. But who cared about relics anymore? Raze the house and there would be room for more estates. It didn't occur to Leo that he might be premature in his thinking.

He had showered and changed into his new imported sports shirt; he was wearing his narrowest trousers, and had carefully groomed his mop of near-black hair. He was, as the rearview mirror reassured him, a handsome devil, and the daughter of Gavin Revere, in spite of a somewhat ethereal quality, was a woman—and unless all his instincts, which were usually sound, had failed him, a lonely woman. Celebrities reared their children carefully, as if they might be contaminated by the common herd, which made them all the more susceptible to anyone with nerve and vitality.

When Leo rang the bell of the old house, it was the woman in white who answered the door, smiling graciously and holding out her hand for the keys. Leo had other plans. Wagner insisted that the car be in perfect order, he told her. She would have to take a test drive around the grounds. His job was at stake—he might get fired if he didn't obey the boss's orders. With that, she consented, and while they drove Leo was able to communicate more of his awe and respect and to make a closer evaluation of the property, which was even larger than he had hoped. Not until they returned and were preparing to enter the garage did she manage to flood the motor and stall the car.

"It must be the carburetor," he said "I'll have a look."

Adjusting the carburetor gave him additional time and an opportunity to get his hands dirty. They were in that condition when a man's voice called out from the patio near the garage.

"Monica? What's wrong? Who is that man?"

Gavin Revere was a commanding figure, even in a wheelchair. A handsome man with a mane of pure white hair, clear eyes, and strong features. The woman in white responded to his call like an obedient child.

When the occasion demanded, Leo could wear humility with the grace of his imported sports shirt. He approached Revere in an attitude of deep respect; Mr. Revere's car had to be in perfect condition. Would he care to have his chair rolled closer so that he could hear the motor? Would he like to take a test drive? Had he really put more than 90,000 miles on that machine himself?

Revere's eyes brightened, and hostility and suspicion drained away. For a time, then, he went reminiscing through the past, talking fluently while Leo studied the reserved Monica Revere at an ever-decreasing distance. When talk wore thin, there was only the excuse of his soiled hands. The servants were on vacation, he was told, and the water in their quarters had been shut off. The gardener, then, had been a day man.

Leo was shown to a guest bath inside the house—ornate, dated, and noisy. A few minutes inside the building was all he needed to reassure himself that his initial reaction to the front hall had been correct: the place was a gigantic white elephant built before income taxes and the high cost of living. An aging house, an aging car—props for an old man's memories.

Down the hall from the bathroom he found even more interesting props. One huge room was a kind of gallery. The walls were hung with stills from old RevereParrish films—love scenes, action scenes, close-ups of Monica Parrish. Beauty was still there—not quite lost behind too much make-up; but the whole display reeked of an outdated past culminating in a shrinelike exhibition of an agonized death scene—exaggerated to the point of the ridiculous—beneath which, standing on a marble pedestal, stood a gleaming Oscar.

Absorbed, Leo became only gradually aware of a presence behind him. He turned. The afternoon light was beginning to fade and against it, half shadow and half substance, stood Monica Revere. "I thought I might find you here," she said. She looked toward the death scene with something like reverence in her eyes. "This was his greatest one," she said. "He comes here often to remember."

"He" was pronounced as if in reference to a deity.

"He created her," Leo said.

"Yes," she answered softly.

"And now both of them are destroying you."

It was the only way to approach her. In a matter of moments she would have shown him graciously to the door. It was better to be thrown out trying, he thought. She was suddenly at the edge of anger.

"Burying you," Leo added quickly. "Your youth, your beauty—"

"No, please," she protested.

Leo took her by the shoulders. "Yes, please," he said firmly. "Why do you think I came back? Wagner could have sent someone else. But today I saw a woman come into that garage such as I'd never seen before. A lovely, lonely woman—"

She tried to pull away, but Leo's arms were strong. He pulled her closer and found her mouth. She struggled free and glanced back over her shoulder toward the hall.

"What are you afraid of?" he asked. "Hasn't he ever allowed you to be kissed?"

She seemed bewildered.

"You don't understand," she said.

"Don't I? How long do you think it takes for me to see the truth? A twenty-five-year-old car, a thirtyyear-old house, servants on 'vacation.' No, don't deny it. I've got to tell you the truth about yourself. You're living in a mausoleum. Look at this room! Look at that stupid shrine!"

"Stupid!" she gasped.

"Stupid," Leo repeated. "A silly piece of metal and an old photograph of an overdone act by a defunct ham. Monica, listen. Don't you hear my heart beating?" He pulled her close again. "That's the sound of life, Monica—all the life that's waiting for you outside these walls. Monica—"

There was a moment when she could have either screamed or melted in his arms. The moment hovered—and then she melted. It was some time before she spoke again. "What is your name?" she murmured.

"Later," Leo said. "Details come later."

The swiftness of his conquest didn't surprise Leo. Monica Revere had been sheltered enough to make her ripe for a man who could recognize and grasp opportunity.

The courtship proved easier than he dared hope. At first they met, somewhat furtively, at small, out-of-the-way places where Monica liked to sit in a half dark booth or at candlelit tables. She shunned popular clubs and bright lights, and this modesty Leo found both refreshing and economical.

Then, at his suggestion, further trouble developed with the Duesenberg, necessitating trips to MonVere where he toiled over the motor while Gavin Revere, from his wheelchair, watched, directed, and reminisced. In due time Leo learned that Revere was firmly entrenched at Mon-Vere. "I will leave," he said, "in a hearse and not before"—which, when Leo pondered on it, seemed a splendid suggestion.

A man in a wheelchair. The situation posed interesting possibilities, particularly when the grounds on which he used the chair were situated so high above the city—so remote, so rugged, and so neglected. The gardener had been only for the frontage. Further inspection of the property revealed a sad state of disrepair in the rear, including the patio where Revere was so fond of sunning himself and which overlooked a sheer drop of at least 200 feet to a superhighway someone had thoughtfully constructed below. Testing the area with an old croquet ball found in the garage, Leo discovered a definite slope toward the drop and only a very low and shaky stucco wall as an obstacle.

Turning from a minute study of this shaky wall, Leo found Monica, mere yards away, watching him from under the shadow of a wide-brimmed straw hat. He rose to the occasion instantly.

"I hoped you would follow me," he said. "I had to see you alone. This can't go on, Monica. I can't go on seeing you, hearing you, touching you—but never possessing you. I want to marry you, Monica—I want to marry you now."

Leo had a special way of illustrating "now" that always left a woman somewhat dazed. Monica Revere was no exception. She clung to him submissively and promised to speak with Gavin Revere as soon as she could.

Two days later, Leo was summoned to a command performance in the gallery of Mon-Vere. The hallowed stills surrounded him; the gleaming Oscar and the grotesque death scene formed a background for Gavin Revere's wheelchair. Monica stood discreetly in the shadows. She had pleaded the case well. Marriage was agreeable to Gavin Revere—with one condition.

"You see around us the mementoes of a faded glory," Revere said. "I know it seems foolish to you, but, aside from the sentimental value, these relics indicate that Monica has lived well. I had hoped to see to it that she always would; but since my accident I am no longer considered a good insurance risk. I must be certain that Monica is protected when I leave this world, and a sick man can't do that. If you are healthy enough to pass the physical examination and obtain a life insurance policy for $50,000, taken out with Monica Revere named as beneficiary, I will give my consent to the marriage. Not otherwise.

"You may apply at any company you desire," he added, "provided, of course, that it is a reputable one. Monica, dear, isn't our old friend, Jeremy Hodges, a representative for Pacific Coast Mutual? See if his card is in my desk."

The card was in the desk.

"I'll call him and make the appointment, if you wish," Revere concluded, "but if you do go to Hodges, please, for the sake of an old man's pride, say nothing of why you are doing this. I don't want it gossiped around that Gavin Revere is reduced to making deals."

His voice broke. He was farther gone than Leo had expected—which would make everything so much easier! Leo accepted the card and waited while the appointment was made on the phone. It was a small thing for Leo to do—to humor an old man not long for this world.

While he waited, Leo mentally calculated the value of the huge ceiling beams and hardwood paneling, which would have to come out before the wreckers disposed of Gavin Revere's faded glory.

Being as perfect a physical specimen as nature would allow, Leo had no difficulty getting insurance. Revere was satisfied. The marriage date was set, and nothing remained except discussion of plans for a simple ceremony and honeymoon.

One bright afternoon on the patio, Leo and Monica, her face shaded by another large-brimmed hat, and Gavin Revere in his wheelchair, discussed the details. As Revere talked, recalling his own honeymoon in Honolulu, Monica steered him about. The air was warm, but a strong breeze came in from the open end of the area where the paving sloped gently toward the precipice.

At one point, Monica took her hands from the chair to catch at her hat, and the chair rolled almost a foot closer to the edge before she recaptured it. Leo controlled his emotion. It could have happened then, without any action on his part. The thought pierced his mind that she might have seen more than she pretended to see the day she found him at the low wall. Could it be that she too wanted Gavin Revere out of the way?

Monica had now reached the end of the patio and swung the chair about.

"Volcanic peaks," Revere intoned, "rising like jagged fingers pointing Godward from the fertile, tropical Paradise ..."

Monica, wearied, sank to rest on the shelf of the low wall. Leo wanted to cry out.

"A veritable Eden for young lovers," Gavin mused. "I remember it well ..."

Unnoticed by Monica, who was busy arranging the folds of her skirt, the old wall had cracked under her weight and was beginning to bow outward toward the sheer drop. Leo moved forward quickly. This was all wrong—Monica was his deed to Mon-Vere. All those magnificent estates were poised on the edge of oblivion. The crack widened. "Look out—"

The last words of Leo Manfred ended in a kind of eerie wail, for, in lunging forward, he managed somehow—probably because Gavin Revere, as if on cue, chose that instant to grasp the wheels of the chair and push himself about—to collide with the chair and thereby lose his balance at the very edge of the crumbling wall.

At the same instant, Monica rose to her feet to catch at her wind snatched hat, and Leo had a blurred view of her turning toward him as he hurtled past in his headlong lunge into eternity.

At such moments, time stands as still as the horrible photos in Gavin Revere's gallery of faded glory; and in one awful moment Leo saw what he had been too self-centered to see previously—Monica Revere's face without a hat and without shadows. She smiled in a serene, satisfied sort of way, and in some detached manner of self-observation he was quite certain that his own agonized features were an exact duplication of the face in the death scene.

Leo Manfred was never able to make an accurate measurement; but it was well over 100 feet to the busy superhighway below.

In policies of high amounts, the Pacific Coast Mutual always con ducted a thorough investigation. Jeremy Hodges, being an old friend, was extremely helpful. The young man, he reported, had been insistent that Monica Revere be named his sole beneficiary; he had refused to say why. "It's a personal matter," he had stated. "What difference does it make?" It had made no difference to Hodges, when such a high commission was at stake.

"It's very touching," Gavin Revere said. "We had known the young man such a short time. He came to deliver my automobile from the garage. He seemed quite taken with Monica."

Monica stood beside the statuette, next to the enlarged still of the death scene. She smiled softly.

"He told me that he was a great fan of Monica Parrish when he was a little boy," she said.

Jeremy handed the insurance check to Gavin and then gallantly kissed Monica's hand.

"We are all fans ... and little boys ... in the presence of Monica Parrish," he said. "How do you do it, my dear? What is your secret? The years have taken their toll of Gavin, as they have of me, but they never seem to touch you at all."

It was a sweet lie. The years had touched her—about the eyes, which she liked to keep shaded, and the mouth, which sometimes went hard—as it did when Jeremy left and Gavin examined the check.

"A great tragedy," he mused. "But as you explained to me at rehearsal, my dear, it really was his own idea. And we can use the money. I've been thinking of trying to find a good script."

Monica Parrish hardly listened. Gavin could have his dreams; she had her revenge. Her head rose proudly.

"All the critics agreed," she said. "I was magnificent in the death scene."

The Master's Touch

Ambrose Du Page had billed himself as the World's Greatest Hypnotist for ten years. Then the flurry of interest in his craft, roused by the much-publicized Bridey Murphy incident, waned and Ambrose went into an immediate professional decline which culminated in the establishment of the Du Page School of Hypnotism on the second floor of an aging medical building on Melrose Avenue.

It was from his office in his unintentionally non-profit establishment that he observed the razing of a furniture storage building on the adjoining lot which, in turn, made visible the Blue Front discount store on the next lot. Screened only by narrow wrought iron grillwork, the rear window exposed an extra-large safe inside the manager's office. With little to occupy time except a growing stack of unpaid bills, the safe in the window became magnetic. Long before Du Page, master of the unconscious, knew what his own gray cells were plotting, he had ascertained that the Blue Front did an astonishingly high volume of business on weekends and, due to banking hours, the cash receipts were locked in the safe from closing time Sunday until the banks opened Monday morning. With the aid of a pair of high-powered binoculars (purchased at Blue Front) he was further able to estimate the average weekend gross at somewhere near twenty thousand dollars, not including the unreadable checks.

It was an inspiring view.

Du Page's passion for the safe grew stronger. A mind trained to dazzle and delight audiences could conceive a thousand delights purchasable with the contents: new equipment, a new assistant with the proper body structure and a projecting personality of equal proportions, a new agent and contracts, a grand tour—Spain. The big money, the smart money was in Spain. Du Page's slender fingers stroked the gray beginning to show at his temples. Distinguished; and he had kept his figure—not a pound gained in twenty years. As for talent, that was never lost. It was locked inside, waiting only for the sound of the overture and the parting of the curtains to bring it out.

On the fourth Sunday after the razing, Du Page lifted the binoculars to his eyes and watched a man carefully count a stack of twenty-dollar bills. It was the sixth such stack and Du Page had noted the sum of each on the memo pad before him. Engrossed in his work, he wasn't aware of the entry into his office until roused by a loud hiccough. He whirled about, the binoculars still in his hands.

"I'm sorry to (hic) disturb you," gasped a slightly built man with a blue face, "but I saw your (hic) light and I've (hic, hic) tried everything!" The last word ended in a pathetic wail as the man slumped against the desk. Frantic fingers clawed at the mahogany and reddened eyes begged for assistance. Du Page understood. The man was suffering from a severe case of hiccoughs and sought aid through hypnosis.

"Not everyone can be hypnotized," Du Page explained. "You must be willing—"

"I am!" the man cried.

Reluctantly, Du Page turned his back on the safe in the Blue Front window. He began with the revolving disc, and the results were almost instantaneous. In his desperation, the patient had no resistance.

"Now you can relax," Du Page said. "You are breathing normally. You have no hiccoughs. When my fingers snap you will awaken and be perfectly free."

Du Page snapped his fingers and the man's eyes opened. Normal color returned to his face and he smiled wanly.

"Thanks, Doc," he said. "You saved my life. You're a genius!"

It was a slight exaggeration but Du Page was appreciative. Now that the hiccoughs were healed and the man's face no longer blue, he looked familiar.

"My name is Wing," he explained. "Carmichael Wing."

"D.D.S.," Du Page added. "You're the dentist who took over the office directly under—" He paused and glanced back at the lighted window where the manager was still counting money. "—mine," he added thoughtfully. "And it's strange that you would have your office open Sunday evening, particularly when I never hear drills."

"I can't practice," Wing said. "I have no license."

"But you rented—"

"Bought," Wing corrected. "I bought the dental office downstairs. I was practicing in Arizona but for family reasons, namely my ex-wife, I moved to California. Now I can't get a license."

Automatically, Carmichael Wing's eyes sought the lighted windows of the Blue Front. Then he noted the binoculars on Du Page's desk, the column of figures on the memo pad, and two minds met in perfect rapport.

"I still have my army binoculars," Wing added. "I like them better than the ones the Blue Front sells. Do you know that last week they peddled twenty-two thousand and fifty-six dollars' worth of that discount junk, not including coin?"

Twenty-two thousand and fifty-six dollars.

Ambrose Du Page picked up the binoculars and turned back to the window. Now the money was counted. He watched the manager place it in a series of bank sacks and go to the safe.

"And have you noticed," Wing said, as if there had been no pause in the conversation, "that the skylight on the roof is directly over the manager's office. It's fire glass—double thickness with steel mesh and heavy gauge steel framing."

"Mr. Wing," Du Page began.

"Call me doctor, please," Wing said.

"Dr. Wing, do you realize that what you're suggesting is grand larceny?"

"Not," Wing reflected, "unless we can figure a way to open that safe."

Some partnerships were made in heaven. Once he had recognized the thievery in Carmichael Wing's heart, Du Page found it easier to live with his own. Neither Du Page nor Wing knew how to open the safe. The store undoubtedly had an alarm system and was protected by a commercial night patrol. The job clearly called for the services of a professional. But safecrackers didn't have guilds, nor were they listed in the yellow book.

Then Du Page recalled that he had once done a series of benefits for the state penal system and dredged up from his subconscious the name of Willie Evans, burglar, who served as a subject during the demonstration of the master's hypnotic powers. He contacted the institution where Willie served his time and learned that he was paroled eight months ago and subsequently employed by Hover's Machine Tools in Culver City. By this time the magnetism in the Blue Front safe was overpowering. Ambrose Du Page donned his least threadbare suit, rented a small sedan and drove to Hover's.

Except for acquiring a suntan, Willie hadn't changed. He was a stocky, blunt-featured young man with a small vocabulary and a stubborn mind. Du Page picked him up at the employee's gate at quitting time, and drove to Artie's Beer Bar in the next block. Over a pair of cold lagers they discussed the business at hand.

"Who sent you?" Willie asked suspiciously, scrutinizing him.

"Nobody sent me, Willie," Du Page insisted. "You remember me, the Great Du Page. We worked together at a San Quentin Christmas Party."

"I remember," Willie admitted, "but somebody must have sent you. The safe jobs are all syndicate now. You gotta have a contract."

"Not for this safe job. This is something only two people know about, myself and my partner. We want to cut you in."

"Why?"

"Because we need you. Is that honest enough?"

"I'm retired," Willie said.

"We split three ways, Willie. Twenty thousand minimum, and no risk."

"I'm retired and reformed," Willie said. "I gave my word to Genevieve, my fiancée, that I'd never go near a safe again. I served one stretch. That's enough."

"Genevieve," Du Page reflected. "She sounds shrewish."

"Genevieve is a lady!" Willie explained. "I'll prove it to you. Hey, Artie!"

The bartender looked up expectantly.

"Artie, another round," Willie said, "and have Genevieve serve 'em. I want her to meet a celebrity."

So Willie's Genevieve was a waitress at Artie's Beer Bar. Du Page was due for a surprise when she came to the table. She was very lovely. Her smile was warm. Her eyes were blue. Her hair was a soft yellow-gold. Had Du Page been in a position then to hire an assistant for his Spanish tour, he would have looked no farther than Genevieve.

Willie made the introductions and then said, "Genevieve only works in this place evenings. Her real job is teaching in a private school. Teaching retarded children."

"That's a highly specialized field," Du Page said. "You're to be congratulated."

Willie beamed. "After we're married, Genevieve is going to try teaching me. I'm the most retarded student she'll ever have."

"Willie!" Genevieve scolded. "Don't say such things! You have a very bright mind."

"Sure," Willie agreed. "Why not? It's never been used."

Genevieve's nose wrinkled deliciously when she frowned at Willie. She gave every evidence of being a woman in love. Mother instinct, Du Page surmised. There were women like that—always attracted to some pitiful underdog they could rehabilitate. He wondered if Willie would be up to it. When Genevieve walked back to the bar, her hips swaying in innocent abandon, Du Page turned to Willie with feigned understanding.

"Well, I guess that's that, Willie," he sighed. "Now that I've seen Genevieve, I can understand your retirement."

"She's really something, isn't she?" Willie agreed.

She was behind the bar now, smiling and exchanging light banter with half a dozen admiring male customers. Willie seemed very sure of himself, to leave her so exposed.

"When are you to be married?" Du Page asked.

"As soon as I save a grand," Willie said. "Genevieve has already saved a grand, but she wants us to start out equal in every way. I've only been out of stir eight months and I've already saved three hundred and twenty bucks."

"Splendid," Du Page mused. "At that rate, Willie, it will be only nineteen and one-half months until you and fair Genevieve are wed. My congratulations to you both."

Du Page pushed aside his beer and came to his feet. He had planted seed in fertile soil. He could feel Willie's suddenly anxious eyes pulling him back.

"Nineteen and one-half months?" Willie echoed.

"Or," Du Page added, "one year and seven and one-half months." He glanced at the gay gathering at the bar and smiled knowingly. "I hope," he said pointedly, "your Genevieve is a patient filly."

It was just forty-eight hours later that Willie Evers came to Du Page's office. He hadn't even taken time to go home after work. He still wore shop clothes and carried a lunch pail.

"Nineteen and one-half months is a long time to wait," he admitted. "I've been thinking—that's almost as long as I was in stir."

"It's like serving a second sentence, Willie," Du Page agreed.

"It sure is. And you know something? I don't think I can sweat out a stretch like this one. I mean, seeing Genevieve every day—"

"—and with all those other men around her."

"That's what I mean. Du Page, where is that safe you were talking about?"

Du Page got out the binoculars and handed them to Willie. He pointed out the right window and gave Willie his head. It was still daylight, but the lights burned inside the manager's office in the Blue Front building and this time there was no one to block the view of the safe. After several minutes, Willie lowered the glasses.

"It's child's play," he said. "I cut my teeth on a safe like that. How do I get in?"

"Through the skylight on the roof," Du Page said. "After we get the skylight open, I'll lower you by rope into the office. Wing will watch for the night patrol. We've kept a schedule for the past week and know when it's due."

"All right," Willie said. "I'll do it—but you've got to promise me that Genevieve will never know. I gave her my word."

"No one will know," Du Page said. "They'll blame juvenile delinquents. Be careful you don't make it look too professional."

Willie flexed his fingers. "My hands are stiff," he said. "If I could just practice a little ..."

It so happened that Du Page had a small safe in his back room. There was little in it but dust, but he led Willie back and let him practice. Willie spun the dial on the combination a few times and confidence began to animate his body.

"I haven't lost it!" he cried. "It's like old times. You watch. In thirty seconds I'll have this box open."

He took hold of the dial again and then froze. Thirty seconds passed without a muscle moving. "What's wrong?" Du Page said. "What is it?"

"I don't know," Willie said. "I can't move my doggone fingers."

"You can't move—Are they cramped?"

"No. I just can't make them work."

Willie looked up pathetically. Until Du Page saw his eyes, he suspected a trick. Willie might want a bigger cut. Willie might be stalling. But he wasn't. He was paralyzed. He got up and smoked a cigarette and tried again. Again he hit that same block. He was crouched before the safe, staring blankly at the lock, when Carmichael Wing came in and was briefed on the situation.

"He doesn't want to open the safe," Wing said.

"You're crazy!" Willie cried. "Of course I want to open the safe. That's why I came here, even if I did promise Genevieve I'd never pull another job."

"That's it," Wing insisted. "He doesn't really want to open the safe. In his subconscious mind he's afraid that opening the safe will cause him to lose his girl."

Willie Evers didn't know if he had a subconscious mind. He only knew that he couldn't marry Genevieve until he had a thousand dollars, and that he couldn't wait more than a year and a half to get it. He tried the safe once more but his fingers were as stiff as nails.

"Willie, sit down and relax," Du Page said. "Take my chair—it's softer. Now, lean back. Close your eyes and relax. You're among friends here and there's no danger. You're Willie Evers, the World's Greatest Safe Cracker, and you've never failed. You never would have served time if some fink hadn't squealed."

Willie hovered at the brink of a comatose state. "That's the truth," he mumbled. "How did you know?"

"Because I know you, Willie. You're the best in your field, and you have nerves of steel. But you lack confidence. Now listen to me, Willie. I want to tell you about that safe. Inside it is Genevieve's dowry—one thousand dollars that belongs to you. But you have to prove you're worthy of Genevieve by opening the safe to get it. When I snap my fingers you will get out of the chair and open the safe."

Du Page snapped his fingers.

Willie awakened, went directly to the safe and opened it.

"You really are a genius!" Carmichael Wing exclaimed. "You're a regular Svengali!"

"I'm lucky," Du Page answered. "Willie's reformation is one of convenience rather than conviction. If he'd been morally opposed to opening the safe, we'd be right back where we started. Now, Willie, close the safe and let's rehearse once more."

Hypnotic suggestion was all Willie needed. He ran through the safe opening routine two more times before Du Page brought him out of the trance, and on the Saturday night before the scheduled burglary the three partners returned for a dress rehearsal. Du Page had found a quantity of stage money in his prop trunk and placed it inside the safe. He also purchased a leather attaché case. Willie's tool kit, to be used in the event the Blue Front safe didn't respond to his magic fingers, would supply leverage for the skylight. Carmichael Wing appropriated thirty feet of somebody's extra-strength clothesline for Willie's descent from the roof to the safe.

"Willie," Du Page said, seating the subject in his chair, "this is our last dry run. Tomorrow night everything has to be perfect the first time because there will be only one performance. We all have our parts, and we all have motivation. You need money so you can marry Genevieve. Dr. Wing needs money so he can get his license. I need money so—" Du Page restrained a shudder "—I can get out from under these falling walls. Now lean back and relax. When I snap my fingers you take this attaché case and go to the safe. You will open the safe, transfer the money to the case, close the safe and return to me.

You will do everything I instruct you to do until I snap my fingers a second time, and when I do you will remember nothing of what you have done."

Du Page snapped his fingers.

Willie rose from the chair, opened the safe, transferred the stage money to the attaché case, closed the safe and returned to Du Page.

"He did it!" Wing exclaimed.

"Like clockwork," Du Page answered.

"What you said about him not remembering—is that true?"

"Of course it is! It's post-hypnotic suggestion."

"But if he doesn't remember robbing the safe tomorrow night, he won't—"

"Willie," Du Page said sharply, "we won't need the stage money anymore, and I don't want it here if the police come around on Monday asking questions. There's an incinerator for trash at the back of the empty lot. Take the stage money downstairs and burn it."

Willie was still under hypnosis. He obeyed without protest. As soon as he had gone Du Page answered Dr. Wing's almost-phrased question.

"Willie won't remember his cut," he said. "That's the master's touch, Dr. Wing. Post-hypnotic suggestion. If Willie can't remember, he can't inform. But I'm not a heartless man. I intend to mail him one thousand dollars so he can marry his Genevieve. He won't know where it came from, but he'll know what to do with it."

Willie returned with the empty attaché case, and Du Page brought him out of the trance. Willie looked about, puzzled. He was still in a semi-dazed state and seemed unable to recall what he had done. Du Page explained again about the Blue Front safe and then drove Willie home. But first they drove to the alleyway and stopped behind the incinerator.

"I want you to remember this, Willie," Du Page said. "Tomorrow night I'll park the car here. The manager finishes counting the money by eight, and the patrol doesn't make its first check until nine. That leaves us one hour to do the job. Dr. Wing will stay downstairs in front of the building as our lookout. We'll open the skylight and I will lower you by rope. When you have the money, I'll haul you up. Then we part company. You take the attaché case and leave it here in the car. We all meet at my place at ten."

Willie absorbed all the instructions and seemed to understand, but there was trouble on his doorstep when Du Page drove him home.

Trouble was Genevieve, militant as an Amazon in her anxiety for Willie.

"Willie, we had a date tonight!" she scolded. "You promised—"

"Willie is doing some alteration work in my office," Du Page explained quickly. "It has to be done after hours. We finish tomorrow night, Willie. Don't forget. Eight o'clock sharp."

He left Willie to soothe the lovely Genevieve, an enviable chore, and devoted the rest of the evening to planning new tricks to delight the Iberians. At eight o'clock on the following evening Willie and Dr. Wing appeared in Du Page's office. Across the vacant lot the manager of the Blue Front was locking up the take from a heavy weekend trade. Du Page immediately put Willie into deep hypnosis and repeated each step of the operation ahead.

"Do exactly what I told you to do last night," he said. "Everything exactly as I told you. Then go home and go to bed. You will sleep soundly, and in the morning you will remember nothing of this night. Nothing at all. Now," Du Page snapped his fingers. "Let's go."

Everything worked as planned. The window of the manager's office had been hidden behind the walls of the old storage building so long everyone had grown careless. The skylight frame was loose and popped up at the first application of leverage. Willie was lowered into the office carrying his tool kit, but sent it back up immediately. The safe opened easily. He filled the attaché case and tugged on the rope. Du Page hauled him up to the roof and Willie retrieved his tool kit.

"Now do exactly what I told you to do last night," Du Page reminded. "The car is parked in the alley."

Willie went off into the darkness and Du Page replaced the skylight. He coiled the clothesline and made an unhurried descent from the roof. Reaching the sidewalk, he signaled Wing and then walked back to the sedan in the alley. Willie had remembered. The attaché case was on the front seat. Du Page got into the car and slipped the key into the ignition. It was eight-fifty by the dashboard clock—just ten minutes before the patrol was due. He rolled down the window and listened. Dr. Wing climbed into the front seat and placed the attaché case on his lap. Du Page switched on the ignition as Wing snapped the catches of the case.

And then Dr. Wing howled. "Du Page—it's empty! The case is empty!"

Carmichael Wing was right. There wasn't even dust in the case.

"What happened? Willie was under hypnosis! You told him to do exactly what he was told to do last night. Exactly." Then Wing paused and sniffed the air. "Du Page," he said hollowly, "do you smell smoke?"

They raced to the incinerator, where bright orange flames were feasting on a pile of greenbacks. Du Page watched in horror as one clearly identifiable fifty-dollar bill caught fire and was quickly reduced to ash. He made a wild grab for a stack of twenties and pulled back a handful of scorched fingers.

"Everything exactly as he did it last night!" Wing screamed. "Exactly! ... But last night you told Willie to burn the money in the incinerator!"

Du Page was weeping softly when the bright spotlight of the night patrol made a white runway of the alley and sent them scampering back to the sedan. There was nothing to do but drive away while the incinerator completed cremating twenty thousand dollars....

Twenty thousand, six hundred and seventy. Willie concluded counting the take from the Blue Front safe and replaced it in his tool case, all but the one thousand dollars he would deposit in the bank before he bought Genevieve's ring. The rest of the money would go into a safety deposit box. It was always a good idea for a bridegroom to have a little money tucked away somewhere.

Willie locked the tool kit in the dresser and faced his own image in the mirror.

"Relax, Willie," he said, in imitation of Du Page. "Just relax and put yourself in my power." Willie laughed sharply. "Okay, so I needed hypnosis the first time. I was out of practice. But I got smart, Du Page. You said there was one thousand in the safe for me. Why not my full one third? But you never noticed that little slip. Willie is just a dumb ex-con too stupid to suspect a frame." He lapsed into the Du Page voice again. "Do everything I tell you to do, Willie. Open the safe. Take out the money. Go down to the incinerator and burn it while I tell the dentist how we're going to cheat you out of your share—and don't listen at the door. Don't think for yourself and stash that stage money in the tool box so the Great Du Page will think you goofed and burned the real money."

Willie was tired. He stretched out on the bed and smiled happily at Genevieve's photograph on the dresser.

"And if Du Page ever comes around asking questions—what then, Willie?" Willie closed his eyes. "You will sleep soundly and in the morning ... you will remember nothing ... nothing at all."

Henry Lowden Alias Henry Taylor

As the train neared Kirkland, the land leveled out and took on the look of river country. It was a long time since Henry Lowden had been so far downstate. The coming brought memories of Sunday School picnics with ripe watermelons and bottled pop kept cool in gunny sacks plunged into the water; of girls' laughter and the plop of a baseball in a catcher's mitt, and of all the other rich remembrances that hadn't been so far behind Arnold Mathias when he died with a bullet in his back.

When he thought of that, Henry Lowden could feel the weight of the snub-nosed .38 hugging his ribs. It wasn't as if he had never killed a man before. A convict who attempts to break out of prison asks for death; and a man whose job is seeing to it that convicts don't break out of prison has to do that job as mechanically as the engineer who was now slowing the train for the Kirkland stop. What troubled Henry Lowden about having fired the shot that killed Mathias was the thing he knew about him. Arnold Mathias hadn't belonged in prison. He was an innocent man.

Ripe watermelons, girls' laughter, the plop of a baseball in a mitt … Memories faded as the train came to a stop. Henry Lowden looked at his wristwatch: 2:10 p.m. Only twenty minutes late, and still time to do what must be done. He stood up and took down a small black suitcase from the rack above the seat. He held it firmly as he descended from the train; for it, like the gun whose weight he felt under his coat, was important. The state didn't know it yet, but the case of Arnold Mathias wasn't closed.

Lowden was the sole passenger to alight from the train. It was July, hot, clear sky and sultry air, with the dust long undisturbed on the wide leaves of the burdock weeds skirting the station platform, and the sun raising sudden streams of perspiration on his grave, forty-year-old face. He left the sun quickly and stepped inside the station house. The waiting room seemed as devoid of life as the platform had been, until his ears caught a sound from the baggage room. He walked to the doorway. An elderly man in shirt sleeves and baggy trousers was shoving a large crate across the floor. He paused at the sight of the newcomer.

"Are you the station master?" Lowden asked.

The old man gave the crate a final shove with his foot.

"Fragile," he muttered. "How can anything so danged big be fragile?" Then, remembering the question, "I reckon you could call me that. Stationmaster, ticket seller, baggage clerk. Anything to be done around here, I'm the one to do it."

"Can you tell me where to get a taxi?"

The old man scratched his graying head. "I do believe I've seen one or two uptown," he answered. "Nobody comes to Kirkland as a rule except those that have family to fetch them. You're the first stranger I've seen come in on the train since old State Senator Dawes died and all his kin come to see what he left in his will." He eased through the doorway and shuffled across the room to a small office with a grilled window. "Got a telephone book in here somewhere," he added. "Whereabouts did you want to go in the taxi?"

"The Grand Hotel on Maple Avenue," Lowden said.

The old man stopped searching the clutter on a rolltop desk and peered quizzically through the grill. "How long since you was in Kirkland, mister?" he asked.

"This is the first time. A friend who used to live here told me about the Grand."

"Then your friend must not have lived here for at least two years. The Grand Hotel on Maple Avenue burned to the ground two years ago last March."

"Is there another hotel?"

"There sure is. There's the Grand—"

"But you just said—"

"The new Grand. They rebuilt on Center Street, two blocks north of the post office. You can't miss it. Six blocks straight ahead as you leave the station. But I can go on looking for that telephone book—"

"Never mind," Lowden said, "I'll walk." He started to turn away; then paused. "Are you sure there's been no one you didn't recognize come off the train in the past two days?"

"No, sir! Not since old Senator Dawes died, and he didn't leave hardly enough to bury himself. Served them right!" The old man chuckled over the joke on Senator Dawes's greedy relatives, and then sobered as his eyes were drawn to the touch of green being slipped under the grill of the ticket window. He took it up in his hands, tenderly.

"It's yours if you can remember to do one thing for me," Lowden said. "If any stranger—anyone you can't identify—does come in on the train before I leave Kirkland, you're to call the Grand Hotel and ask for Henry Taylor. That's my name—Henry Taylor. If I'm out, leave the message with the room clerk. Understand?"

There was a great deal of understanding in a twenty-dollar bill.

"Henry Taylor," the old man repeated.

"Maybe you should write it down."

"No, sir! I never forget a name. A name or a face. Don't you worry about that, Mr. Taylor."

"And you needn't mention this to anyone."

"Not anyone, Mr. Taylor. Not a soul!"

Any stranger to Kirkland would have recognized Center Street on sight, because of its location. The narrow artery Henry Lowden had taken—neatly divided into blocks of unassuming frame bungalows shaded by oaks—emerged onto a wide circle of green containing more oaks and a bronze union soldier charging south. Threading out from the circle, twin rows of stern red brick and gray stone business houses faced one another like scowling adversaries across an asphalt aisle. The new Grand Hotel differed from its unimaginative brethren only in the concession to modernity of a stainless-steel edged canopy and a pair of plate glass doors. Henry Lowden went inside. The small foyer was dotted with simulated leather chairs holding occupants who, reassuringly, evinced only mild curiosity as he made his way to the desk and requested a room.

There were questions. "Name?"

"Henry Taylor."

"Home address?"

Lowden hesitated. "Chicago."

"Business?"

Lowden smiled wryly. "Historian," he said.

"Historian," the clerk repeated soberly. "I don't believe we've had a historian staying here before."

"That's odd," Lowden said. "It seems that big flood control dam down at the basin would lure every sort of tourist."

"I beg pardon?"

"Three years ago this town was humming. The payroll, locally, ran over a million dollars."

The room clerk was a boyish lad who had only shaved a few times.

"I guess I don't remember," he said.

"Many things are forgotten in three years," Lowden remarked. He glanced at the wall clock above the clerk's head. It was almost two-thirty. "Here," he added, depositing the small black suitcase on the desk, "send this up to my room. I have to get to a bank before it closes."

"Don't you want to see the room?" the clerk queried.

"Does it have a bed?"

"Why, yes. Of course."

"Then I don't need to see it. Tell the boy to take good care of the bag."

Tossing a fifty-cent piece on the counter, Lowden turned and walked back to the street. Outside, he stepped into the first doorway beyond the hotel and waited until he was certain no one had followed him out of the hotel, and then proceeded toward the circle of green which was always called the square. There was only one bank in Kirkland—the Farmer's and Merchant's on the southeast corner of the square. It was a two-story, gray stone building with a high arched doorway and a cornerstone dated 1898. Gold lettering on one window advertised the impressive assets within, a figure Henry Lowden studied while straightening a few wrinkles out of his coat and giving a reassuring pat to the area of the shoulder holster. He then went inside.

In 1898, banks were designed with high ceilings, marble floors, and piano-mahogany furnishings. Six people were within range of vision: three tellers, one secretary, female, behind a waist-high counter to the left, a farmer at one of the teller's windows and a small boy on tiptoe playing with a pen at one of the customers' desks. No bank guard was in sight; but at the end of the room, behind a brass-barred entry, stood the huge circle of the vault.

Henry Lowden turned to his left.

"I'd like to see someone about opening a new account," he said.

A nameplate on the secretary's desk informed him that it was Miss Foster who looked up with tortoiseshell rimmed eyes.

"Mr. Kern handles new accounts. Won't you wait?" Mr. Sam Kern— Vice President was the nameplate on a deserted desk. Behind it was a mahogany door lettered: Wm. O. Spengler—President.

"Mr. Spengler will do nicely," Henry Lowden said.

"Mr. Spengler is in conference with Mr. Kern—"

Before further enlightenment on this impasse could come, the mahogany door swung open, violently, and the loud, rasping voice of an old man shattered conversation.

"If I didn't keep check on you, William, you'd have my bank in

receivership! No, I won't have you handling my chair! You take me out,
Sam. Should have left you in charge of the bank instead of my idiot
son-in-law!"

The occupant of the wheelchair was the last remaining fragment of
a man, white hair, piercing eyes, a face withered with age until the
skin stretched like parchment over the sharp bones.

"Out to the street, Sam," he ordered. "Ralph is waiting with the car.
Don't you jostle me now. I've got a bad heart and can't stand being
jostled. Open that gate, young lady—"

The stream of orders being issued from the wheelchair ceased
abruptly as Henry Lowden reached out and opened the small gate in
the counter. The piercing eyes looked upward.

"You're not an employee," the fragment snapped.

"That's right," Henry Lowden said, "I'm not."

"Couldn't be an employee. Too wide awake. You're a customer."

"I hope to be," Henry Lowden said.

"A new account? William—" The old man twisted about in the
wheelchair. "Come out here and take care of this man! Fifty-five years
I was president of this bank, and I never failed to shake hands with
every new customer. That's one thing folks could say for Josiah
Wingate. Sam, roll me over to that desk where the boy is. Boy, you're
getting off to a fine start. Here's a silver dollar for you. Ask your Daddy
to put it in the Kirkland Farmer's and Merchant's Bank and watch
it grow. All right, Sam. Don't dawdle! Roll me out to the car!"

Sam Kern, the chair, and its vociferous occupant rolled out of sight,
leaving behind a bewildered boy with a silver coin, promptly deposited
in a trouser pocket. Henry Lowden turned back to Miss Foster, but
now the doorway behind her was filled by someone who could only be
William, William Spengler. Tall, graying, an expression of smoldering
fury darkening his face, he became aware of Lowden and smothered
the fury.

"Miss Foster, is this gentleman here to see me?"

"Why—yes, Mr. Spengler. Unless Mr. Kern—"

"Mr. Kern is busy. Don't keep the gentleman waiting."

The office of W. O. Spengler—President—was as dated as the rest
of the building; mahogany paneling, a massive desk, tall leather
chairs. Spengler had gone to the window and stood peering down at
the street below, his hands making fists at his side. Over his shoulder,
Henry Taylor caught a glimpse of the invalid's chair being folded into
the back seat of a limousine. When Spengler turned about and caught

him watching, Henry Lowden smiled.

"They get difficult as they grow older," he observed.

"Yes, they do," Spengler said. "I have to humor him. Not only is he my father-in-law, but he founded this bank. He can't seem to adjust to retirement. Won't you sit down, Mr.—"

"Taylor," he said, as he sat down in one of the leather chairs. "Henry Taylor. I have a letter of credit." He reached under his coat, felt the cold steel in his holster, and then found the inner pocket— "from my bank in Chicago," he added. "I wish to transfer some funds to this bank while I'm here doing research."

"Research?" Spengler returned to his desk and accepted the letter. "In what field, Mr. Taylor? Perhaps I can be of assistance."

"I'm sure you can," Lowden said. "It's for a book I'm doing on the subject of unsolved crimes."

William Spengler had a peculiar face. One emotion could overlap another like a double exposure. What was left of the fury folded into an alerted curiosity which finally became articulate.

"And you have come to Kirkland to do research for such a project?"

"I'm surprised that I'm the first," Lowden said. "You read the newspapers, don't you?"

"I have little time—"

"But you must know that Arnold Mathias is dead. He was shot down by a guard while attempting to break out of State Prison two days ago. His cellmate escaped, but Mathias was killed."

"Yes," Spengler reflected. "I did hear a newscast—"

"And this is the Kirkland Farmer's and Merchant's Bank where Arnold Mathias was employed in December of 1956."

William Spengler was no longer interested in the letter of credit. His eyes were almost as sharp as those of his father-in-law, and they were fixed on the face of the man who called himself Henry Taylor.

"You didn't have to come to Kirkland to learn that," he said.

"No, I didn't. But there are some things I did have to come here to learn. Let's recapitulate. Mathias was a trusted employee—"

"Hired by my father-in-law the year before he retired." Spengler added, "And against my advice."

"Because Mathias had a record?"

"A juvenile record. Let's not make it sound worse than it was, Mr. Taylor. My father-in-law has a philanthropic streak where young people are concerned. You saw him just now with the boy out front. Mathias had come from a broken home—the usual sad story. Mr.

Wingate wanted to give him a chance. I wanted to protect the bank."

"But you kept him on after you succeeded Mr. Wingate."

"There was no reason not to keep him on. He was a willing worker, seemingly honest. Then, in '56, the Dyer Construction Company transferred $500,000 in cash from their St. Louis bank to meet the local payroll on the dam project. We kept it in the vault. Only Mr. Kern and myself had keys, and only Mr. Kern and myself handled the payroll. But Arnold took to working late. I never suspected the reason until after the theft. You know the story, Mr. Taylor. Arnold took $200,000 from that vault."

"He never admitted taking it."

"But he was convicted in a court of law. I hired Ira Casey to defend him—the best defense attorney in the state. He was convicted, nevertheless."

"On a plea of not guilty," Lowden said. "Do you know what Mathias was doing at State Prison, Mr. Spengler? He'd gotten hold of a set of court records of that trial, and he'd gone over every word of testimony again and again until he found something he was looking for. He marked it off and then drew some maps. Maps of this bank."

Spengler's face was interesting to watch. It was as if an unseen hand had wiped away all expression. But his voice had a cutting edge.

"How do you know all this?" he demanded.

Henry Lowden smiled. "Now, I couldn't tell you that, Mr. Spengler. A writer can't reveal his sources of information. They might dry up."

"Then why should I believe you?"

"Because I'm in possession of those court records—and the maps. I was hoping you might find time to go over them with me—that is, if you really are interested in my book."

Spengler was silent for several seconds. One hand reached down and pulled at the long desk drawer in front of him. He seemed about to take something out of it; then changed his mind.

"Do you think there's a market for such a book, Mr. Henry?" he asked.

"Taylor," Henry Lowden corrected. "Mr. Taylor. Yes, I'm sure there is. Consider the fact that the theft occurred on the afternoon you were called home because your wife was dying—that gives the story emotional appeal. And then there was Mr. Kern's early departure because his only son was playing his first varsity basketball game forty miles away, and he had to drive over icy roads to watch him play. That gives the story family appeal. But what makes it most interesting, and what has bewildered the authorities for two and a half years, is the fact that—even if Mathias did commit the crime for which he was convicted—no trace has ever been found of the $200,000. What's the trouble, Mr. Spengler? Is something wrong with my letter of credit?"

William Spengler had closed the desk drawer and picked up the letter of credit. He came to his feet.

"I'll see if Mr. Kern is back," he said. Then, as he started toward the door, he looked back and added: "Mr. Taylor, perhaps you will have dinner with me in my home tonight."

"That's very kind of you," Henry Lowden said. "Very kind indeed."

"And perhaps you will bring those court records and maps so we can study them together."

"Now, that's more than kind. I was sure you would be cooperative, Mr. Spengler."

When Spengler left the room, Henry Lowden went quickly from his chair to the opposite side of the desk. He opened the long drawer to find what had held Spengler's interest. It was a newspaper two days old, folded to a feature story—

ARNOLD MATHIAS SLAIN

Arnold Mathias, 24, convicted of stealing $200,000 from the Kirkwood Farmer's and Merchant's Bank in 1956, was shot and killed early this morning while attempting to escape from State Prison. H. T. Lowden, the guard who shot Mathias, stated that Mathias had always insisted he was framed.

"I don't know why he broke for it," Lowden told reporters. "I believed in his innocence, too."

A cellmate, Thomas Henry, 40, made good his escape in a laundry truck ...

The man who called himself Henry Taylor read no further. He closed the drawer quietly.

It was very old brandy. It lay golden amber in the bottom of the snifter, moving in lazy circles as Henry Lowden gently shook the glass. The dinner had been as heavy and unimaginative as the square-faced housekeeper who prepared and served it, but within William Spengler's study the atmosphere changed. The architecture was still

Midwestern Victorian, and the furnishings slightly rural English, but above an ugly mantelpiece hung a surprisingly good French painting. In William Spengler's house—to be more exact, Josiah Wingate's house—the painting was as conspicuous as a carrousel in a mausoleum.

Spengler didn't touch his brandy. His eyes were fixed on the small black suitcase at Henry Taylor's feet.

"It's a pity Mathias attempted to escape," he remarked. "He might have been up for parole soon."

"Parole boards are notoriously slow in this state," Henry Lowden mused, "and Mathias had no friends to prod from the outside."

"That's not true! I hired Ira Casey—"

"Who was a college classmate of yours and friend of almost thirty years standing."

"What's wrong with that?"

"Nothing. I would say it was very convenient. I would have considered myself lucky to have such a friend if $200,000 had disappeared from my bank."

"I hired Casey to defend Mathias!" Spengler protested.

"And the Kirkland Farmer's and Merchant's Bank," Lowden added quietly. "This is excellent brandy, Mr. Spengler. I don't suppose you buy this in Kirkland."

"I'm not chained to Kirkland! I get out occasionally."

"Out," Lowden repeated. "That's an apt word. It's what Mathias wanted—and a chance to clear his name."

"Or to recover the $200,000 from wherever he had it hidden," Spengler said.

Henry Lowden drained the contents of the brandy snifter and lifted his eyes to meet Spengler's. There was a speculative smile in them.

"But where could he have hidden it, Mr. Spengler? That's what makes this case so interesting. Two hundred thousand dollars is a difficult sum to dispose of—or to acquire unobtrusively—in a town as small as Kirkland. Let's assume that Mathias did take the money, but wasn't convicted. What could he have done? He couldn't use it locally without creating suspicion. He was a bank teller on a fixed income, just as Sam Kern is a bank official on a fixed income."

"And just as I am a bank president on a fixed income," Spengler interposed.

"That's my point. The man who took that money from the vault would have had to do one of three things. He could have left town—

which, obviously, he didn't. None of the three men who were in the vault the day the money was taken went anywhere—except, one of them, to prison."

"The three men," Spengler repeated.

"Mathias, Kern and yourself, Mr. Spengler. It's all here in the court records." Lowden took up the suitcase and carried it to Spengler's desk. He opened it and took out a sheaf of papers. "It was the last Friday before Christmas," he continued. "The bank closed at three. The tellers, Mathias, Peterson—"

"Pierson," Spengler corrected. "Lee Pierson. He's still with the bank, and so is Goddard. I was a witness at the trial, Mr. Taylor. I know what is in the records. When the bank closed, the tellers began to count their cash. Pierson and Goddard were finished and out of the bank by three-thirty. Mathias had trouble getting his cash to balance. I went over it with him twice before we caught the error. Sam Kern was in the vault checking the Dyer payroll against the remaining funds. The payroll went out on Friday, and the balancing usually kept us at the bank until four or later."

"But at three-forty," Lowden said, "you received a telephone call from your housekeeper, Mrs. Holmes. Now here's a section of testimony Mathias had bracketed. Mrs. Holmes was on the stand being examined by the District Attorney. His object was to pinpoint the situation which resulted in Mathias being left alone in the bank.

Q. Mrs. Holmes, will you please tell the court what you did following Mrs. Spengler's heart attack on the date in question?

A. I got the medicine Dr. Clinton had left and gave her a spoonful.

Q. Was Mrs. Spengler subject to such attacks?

A. Yes, sir. Mrs. Spengler had been a semi-invalid for more than twenty years. We knew it was only a matter of time. I gave her the medicine and got her into bed, and then I called Dr. Clinton and told him this one seemed worse than the others. He asked me to call Mr. Spengler right away, and that's what I did.

"Mr. Taylor," Spengler interrupted. "I told you that I'm familiar with the testimony at the trial. What are you trying to prove?"

"I'm not trying to prove anything," Lowden answered quietly. "I'm only trying to discover what Arnold Mathias wanted to prove. A few pages later in the transcript is another bracketed section. It's the testimony of Samuel Kern being questioned by the District Attorney. Kern states that he, Mathias, and yourself were alone in the bank when Mrs. Holmes called. He was in the vault. Hearing the telephone, he stepped outside because he thought it might be his wife calling to remind him of the basketball game.

> Q. When you stepped outside, Mr. Kern, did you lock the vault?
> A. No, I didn't. I wasn't finished checking the payroll. The call was from Spengler's housekeeper informing him that his wife had just suffered another heart attack. He left for home immediately. That is, he started to leave. He put on his hat and coat and went out to the parking lot at the side of the bank; but he came right back. He couldn't get his car started. I offered to push him, but he said it would be better if Arnold pushed him. I had a new car with an automatic shift. Arnold had an old one with a standard shift. When the pavement is icy, it's hard to get a start from an automatic drive.
> Q. And so Mr. Spengler left the second time with Arnold Mathias.
> A. No, sir. Not then. Arnold never parked in the lot behind the bank. I think he was sensitive because Mr. Spengler had kidded him about his old car giving the bank a bad name. He always parked on the side street around the corner. While he went to get his car and drive it back, Mr. Spengler came into the vault to help me; but he was too upset. Finally, he asked me to call Dr. Clinton for him. I did, but the doctor had already left for Mrs. Spengler's house. By the time I finished the call, Arnold was back. Before Mr. Spengler went out with him he said to me, "I know how much it means to you to see your son play his first game tonight, Sam. You clear out and let Arnold lock up."

Henry Lowden finished reading. When he looked up Spengler was watching him closely. "That section of testimony is not only bracketed," Taylor added, "but a few words of it are underlined. '... Mr. Spengler came back into the vault to help me,' and again, '... he asked me to call Dr. Clinton for him.' That makes an interesting coupling, don't you think?"

Spengler simply ignored the question.

"What about your second point, Mr. Taylor? You said that Mathias could have done three things with the money."

Lowden smiled. "A subject does get tedious when it's pursued too hotly, doesn't it? The second thing Mathias could have done was to hide the money, as you suggested. But where? His room was thoroughly searched by the police at the time of his arrest, and his car was all but torn apart. Moreover, although the theft occurred on Friday when Mathias locked the vault, and wasn't discovered until the following Monday, Mathias made no attempt to leave town—as would have been expected of a man with a very warm $200,000 on his hands. He went to a movie Friday night, alone. He caught cold and, according to his landlady's testimony, stayed in his room Saturday and Sunday. On his way to the movie, he had the tank of his car filled at the Center Street station. Less than a gallon of fuel had been consumed when the police examined his car. By their tests, that car made less than fourteen miles to the gallon, which means that Arnold Mathias drove less than fourteen miles after the money was taken from the vault. Where—and when—did he hide it, Mr. Spengler?"

"You're quoting almost verbatim from Ira Casey's summation to the jury," Spengler said sharply. "All you've omitted was the sentimental reference to his tragic childhood."

"Sentimental? Does that denote disapproval?"

"I hired Casey!"

"Unfortunately for Mathias. Casey was your personal friend, with a friend's loyalty and a friend's blindness. William Spengler, respectable citizen, had lost his wife on the day a large piece of the Dyer payroll was stolen. Convention wrapped him in immunity. Another lawyer, to whom William Spengler was just one of three men who had access to the vault, would have pounced on what Mathias discovered after three years in prison. Mrs. Holmes, under oath, testified that she had called Dr. Clinton and then, at his request, called you at the bank. Samuel Kern, under oath, testified that you asked Mathias to start your car in spite of his offer—"

"Because Sam had a car with an automatic drive!"

"Because Mathias had parked his car around the corner, and you knew it! He had to walk—let's say 200 feet, get his car started, drive around the lot and then come back inside the bank for you, Mr. Spengler. It was cold and so, naturally, you waited inside for him. You went to the vault to help Kern; then you asked him to call Dr. Clinton.

Didn't Mrs. Holmes tell you that she had called the doctor? It must have been a tremendous oversight if she didn't. But Kern, another sympathetic friend, was willing to do anything to help. He left the vault and made the telephone call. Now here's a map Mathias drew of the bank—exterior and interior. He marked the location of the telephone Kern used, and the location of where his car was parked when he went to get it. With Mathias outside and Kern on the telephone, there must have been a period of several minutes when you were alone in the vault."

William Spengler hadn't touched his brandy. Now he lifted the glass and drank slowly, never taking his eyes from Henry Lowden's face. When he put the glass down, empty, he said, "And what was your third possibility, Mr. Taylor?" Lowden placed the sheet of paper back in his suitcase.

"I wasn't certain until I came to Kirkland this afternoon," he said, "but the stationmaster gave me a clue. I understand that the late Senator Dawes had a great many mourners at his funeral."

"Senator Dawes—?"

"And even deeper mourners when it developed that he had left no fortune. But what if one of those wouldbe beneficiaries had stolen $200,000 and wanted to pass it off as an inheritance? The idea has possibilities, don't you think?"

Tightly, Spengler replied, "If you're thinking of the coincidence of my wife's death at the time of the theft, you can forget it. She left me nothing. Everything, even this house, is in her father's name."

"But he won't live forever, will he? A tight-fisted old tyrant like Wingate must have accumulated quite a fortune."

"That's not true! My father-in-law has been ill for many years, and my wife was an invalid for most of our married life. Illness is expensive even in Kirkland."

"And frustrating," Lowden reflected, "particularly for a man with a taste for fine brandy and French painting."

"The third possibility," Spengler insisted.

"The obvious, Mr. Spengler. The Dyer deposit must have been a temptation from the beginning, knowing that you had a ready-made suspect working in the bank. A record is tough to live down, even a juvenile record. The public is seldom in a forgiving mood when someone has made off with its unearned cash. And then your wife had a heart attack on Friday afternoon. Her timing was perfect."

"My wife was dying—"

"That couldn't have surprised you. She'd been near death for twenty years. But it did give you an excuse to leave the bank early on the same day Sam Kern was eager to get off to a basketball game. All you had to do was get Kern and Mathias out of the way for a few minutes—just long enough to transfer $200,000 from the Dyer account to your own box. The money was never found, Mr. Spengler, because it never left the vault."

Henry Lowden might have been reading from the court records. He finished his quiet accusation and waited. Spengler's response was electric.

"Is that what Arnold Mathias told you when you were cellmates at State Prison, Mr. Henry?"

"You made that mistake once before. The name is Taylor. Henry Taylor."

"There is no Henry Taylor! I suppose you thought it was too late for me to check on that letter of credit this afternoon. It wasn't. I telephoned the Chicago bank while you were waiting in my office. That letter was a fake."

"You were frightened, Mr. Spengler."

"I'm a good businessman!"

"Who keeps a two-day old newspaper in his desk. You didn't hear of Mathias' death on a newscast. You read about it over and over—"

"What are you trying to do, Henry? Sell me those records and that ridiculous map? Do you think I care what a dead convict suspected?"

The man who called himself Henry Taylor didn't lose control.

"We're not discussing what a dead convict suspected," he said. "Innocent or guilty, when a man tries to break out of prison he's courting sudden death. But there's something you don't know about Thomas Henry, who did escape. He wasn't serving time for anything as minor as grand theft. He was in for murder. He's got nothing to lose."

"All I have to do is pick up this telephone—"

"Absolutely nothing, Mr. Spengler. And he's rough. He could make the Sphinx talk if the Sphinx could lead him to $200,000. Go ahead and pick up the telephone. The number of the police station is 110. I looked it up in the directory in my hotel room."

William Spengler was reaching toward the telephone. He paused, bewildered, and in the instant of hesitation Henry Lowden's right hand flicked inside his coat pocket and came out grasping the snub-nosed .38.

"No—don't," Spengler said weakly.

"Have you ever been worked over by a desperate man, Mr. Spengler? A really desperate man?"

"But I don't have the money here!" Spengler gasped.

"Where is it?"

"At the bank. I can't get it until tomorrow."

"Is it all there?"

"Most of it. Henry, be reasonable. Everyone thinks Mathias took the money, and he's dead. We can make a deal."

"Thank you, Mr. Spengler. We already have."

The man who called himself Henry Taylor shifted the gun to his left hand and took up the telephone with his right. Carefully, he dialed 110. There was time to explain while the operator rang.

"I'm not Thomas Henry, Mr. Spengler; but I knew I could get a confession out of you and clear Mathias if I reached you before Henry. Lucky for you, I succeeded. My name is Lowden. Henry Taylor Lowden. I'm the guard at State Prison who had to shoot Mathias."

On the other end of the wire, a voice was answering. Lowden's mouth set in a grim smile. The case of Arnold Mathias was almost closed.

The Very Hard Sell

The call came over the loudspeaker above the used car lot at 3:00 p.m. "Mr. Cornell, you're wanted on the telephone. Mr. Cornell, telephone—please."

It was a godsend, Cornell felt. Mr. Garcy was in a bad mood and so somebody had to take a beating. Here of late that somebody always seemed to be him. It wasn't fair and Garcy knew it. There were slack periods in the auto market when nothing moved. Sales were down in the new car showroom, too. What was he supposed to do—hypnotize the customers? The woman hadn't wanted the blue Olds; she didn't like blue. Even Jack Richards, who was almost twenty years younger than Glenn Cornell and who always wore a perky little bow tie that charmed the feminine trade, couldn't sell a blue car to a woman who didn't like blue no matter how good a buy it was.

"Mr. Cornell, you're wanted on the telephone ..."

Cornell took advantage of the chance to break away from Garcy and made it to the office before the girl on the switchboard could finish her second call. The voice on the telephone was masculine—young, definite.

"Is this Garcy Motors on Sutter Street? Mr. Cornell? You had a black Cadillac on the used car lot a few days ago—a '57 sedan. I think it had a card on it—$3750. Yes, that's the one I mean. Is it still there? It is? Good. I'm coming by to look it over as soon as I get off work. If it runs as good as it looks, you've got a sale."

"It does," Cornell insisted. "It handles like a new car and carries a new car guarantee. What time will you be in? 5:30? Fine, I'll have her warmed up and ready. Say, what's your name so I'll know you? Berra? Okay, Mr. Berra, I'll see you at 5:30."

When Mr. Berra hung up, Glenn dropped the telephone in the cradle. He raised his head and found himself eye level with the salesmen's rating chart Mr. Garcy always kept in plain sight. There had been six names on the chart, but the last two had lines drawn through them. Mr. Garcy never erased a name when he let a man go. He left it there, cancelled out by a chalk line, as a grim reminder of what could happen to anyone whose sales dropped too low. The name just above the last chalk line was Glenn Cornell. He turned around and saw Mr. Garcy standing in the doorway.

"A customer of mine," Cornell said with forced brightness. "He's been looking at the black Caddy. I'm taking him out on a demonstration ride at 5:30."

It wasn't much of a lie. Cornell had never laid eyes on Mr. Berra; but Garcy didn't know that, and it was worth stretching the story a bit to see the way his expression altered from surprise to near disappointment and then to one of the leers he used for a smile.

"Good man!" Garcy said. "He's really interested. Sell him, Cornell. Don't let him get away. He's on the hook. All you have to do is reel him in."

It was more than a pep talk; it was an order. Cornell vowed then and there that he'd sell the black Caddy to Mr. Berra if it was the last thing he did.

Exactly one week later, at a few minutes before 11:00 p.m., a patrol car answering a neighborhood complaint found a black Cadillac parked in an alley behind a lumber yard, about two miles across town from Garcy Motors. A man was slumped over the steering wheel, his chin pressing down on the horn rim and the horn, according to the complainant, had been sounding for nearly an hour. The first officer out of the patrol car opened the right front door of the Cadillac.

"Hey, mister," he called above the din of the horn, "this is no way to sleep off a drunk. You're keeping people awake." And then he paused and leaned forward, sniffing at the interior of the sedan. "Bring your flash over here!" he shouted to his companion. "I think this car's full of fumes!"

The second officer appeared at his shoulder and inhaled deeply. "Not gas," he said. "Smells more like burnt alfalfa."

But when the light from the flash caught the man slumped over the steering wheel, both officers fell silent. He wasn't drunk; he was dead. Glenn Cornell would never sell anything to anyone after what the .45 slug had done to the right side of his head.

Hazel Cornell was a nice-looking woman in spite of the grief in her eyes. Twenty years ago, Police Detective Sommers decided, she must have been the prettiest bride of the season. Now she was a widow. She didn't cry—praise heaven for that! There were dark shadows under her eyes and a tightness about her mouth; otherwise, she might have been a typical housewife who had donned her best cotton dress and a small hat with blue flowers on the brim that was usually worn only to church, and come down to report a mischievous neighborhood child, or some other minor disturbance.

But Police Detective Sommers handled homicide cases.

"I know what I told the police officers last night," she said, "and I know how it all looks. But I knew my husband, too. It isn't true what was printed in the papers this morning. Glenn didn't kill himself. He was a religious man. He wouldn't take his life."

Her voice was low but firm, the inner tension held in careful check. Sommers glanced down at the Cornell file open on his desk. All of her statements of the previous night were there.

"But Mrs. Cornell," he remonstrated, "you admitted that your husband had been depressed and in ill health."

"Not really ill health," she said. "His cough had been bothering him some. Glenn had bronchitis when he was a child. Every so often, his cough came back. It was nothing new. He wouldn't have killed himself for that."

"But you also said that he was worried about the prospective customer for the car he was trying to sell. He'd been working on the deal all week without getting a definite answer. He came home for dinner last night and refused to eat."

"He had a headache," she explained.

"He went to his room for about ten minutes and then came out again, saying that he was going to meet Mr. Berra and—" Sommers glanced down at the report again "—put an end to the indecision."

"'I've got him on the hook,' he told me. 'All I have to do is reel him in.'"

"Ten minutes," Sommers repeated, ignoring the interpolation. "Now, Mrs. Cornell, didn't you identify the gun found on the seat beside your husband's body as his own gun, which, you stated, was kept in his bureau drawer?"

"Yes, but Glenn—"

"And the ballistic test has proved that your husband was killed by a bullet fired from that gun."

"But Glenn didn't fire the gun!"

She wasn't excited, she was adamant. She hadn't come alone. Sprawled in the chair beside her, a teen-age youth stirred restlessly at her words.

"Mom, I wish you wouldn't get so worked up," he said.

"I'm not worked up, Andy," she replied quietly. "I'm merely telling this officer the truth. Your father didn't commit suicide."

It wasn't going to be easy to talk her out of such conviction. She was a firm woman. She must have been a devoted wife, and must be a good mother, an uncomplicated personality who was still in a state of semi-shock from learning that such an evil as violent death could happen in her orderly life.

Sommers tried again. "Mrs. Cornell," he said, "do you realize what your statement means? If your husband didn't commit suicide, he must have been murdered. Do you know anyone who might have wanted to murder your husband?"

"Oh, no. Glenn had no enemies."

"And yet you insist that he was murdered."

"It might have been a holdup. He was driving that expensive car. Someone might have thought he had money."

She was grasping at straws, illusory straws.

"But you identified Mr. Cornell's personal effects at the morgue," he reminded. "His wallet, containing $17, his key case, his cough drops—"

"That cough of his," she said. "He was never without them."

"—his wrist watch and his wedding ring. Nothing was taken. Men have been murdered for much less than $17, Mrs. Cornell, but your husband wasn't one of them."

"Then it must have been a madman," she said. "One of those crazed fiends we read about."

If she wasn't going to change her mind, Sommers could at least take the out offered him.

"It might have been," he admitted.

"Or Mr. Berra. Have you found Mr. Berra?"

Her eyes were accusing him across the desk. But Sommers had never seen a clearer case of self-inflicted death. There had been no indication of a struggle in the car. He'd gone there himself as soon as the patrol car radioed in. No struggle, obviously. And there were no fingerprints on the gun except Glenn Cornell's. He opened his mouth to answer, but Andy beat him to it.

"Mom," he pleaded, "the police know what they're doing. Leave it be."

"No, they don't know. Not when they tell the reporters that your father committed suicide. They should at least talk to Mr. Berra."

She stood up, a small, determined woman without tears.

"Glenn Cornell did not kill himself," she said.

She turned and left the office, and Andy scrambled to his feet to follow. He hesitated in front of the desk.

"Don't mind my mother," he said. "She's all upset, you see. She just can't believe it."

He was a good-looking kid, ruddy-faced, short pale blond hair, broad shoulders encased in a school sweater with a huge S over his chest.

"But you can believe it, is that it?" Sommers asked.

"Sure, I understand. A man's confidence can go. His pride. I mean, maybe this customer he was trying to sell cracked wise, or maybe old Garcy was riding him too hard. Some bosses are like that. As soon as they smell chicken, they're like a wolf sniffing blood."

"Chicken?" Sommers echoed. "Are you trying to tell me that you think your father was chicken?"

Andy Cornell flushed red up to his close-cropped hair.

"Look, I didn't mean— Well, anyhow, I know he could be pushed around."

"How old are you, Andy?"

"Sixteen."

"And nobody pushes you around, do they?" Sommers asked.

"I'll say they don't."

Sommers' eyes held the boy's for a few seconds and then dismissed him. Andy went out, but long after he'd gone Sommers stared after him. At least the boy had inadvertently explained what was behind his mother's refusal to face the obvious. "Chicken," he repeated to himself. It wasn't much of an obituary. He could at least talk to Mr. Berra.

A row of red and white pennants dangled listlessly above the used car lot of Darcy Motors on Sutter Street, limp reminders of a sale that wasn't being patronized. Inside the showroom office, Mr. Garcy showed a similar lack of enthusiasm for his inquisitive caller. He'd already had to cope with a couple of reporters. Suicide. That was a bad subject to fool around with. Morbid. Could give a place a bad name.

"To be honest with you, Officer," he said, "and I am honest with everyone, I wasn't too surprised when the police called me down last night to identify Cornell's body and my Cadillac. Not surprised that he'd killed himself, I mean. The man was on the downgrade—not up to par at all. A few years ago he topped the list on that sales chart month after month, slack season and heavy; but lately he'd lost his drive. Brought his problems to work with him. That's bad. When a man can't leave his problems at home, he's bound to hit the skids."

"Problems? What problems?"

"Any problems. We all have them, don't we? Family problems, health problems, money problems; but we learn to keep them out of our work. Not Cornell. Excuses, always excuses. His boy stayed out too late at night so he couldn't get any sleep. His boy was getting in with a bad crowd at high school. He didn't want his boy going wrong. I tell you, Officer, if Glenn Cornell had had five or six kids he'd have been alive today. He'd have had to give up worrying long ago."

Sommers thought of Andy Cornell—tall, blond, handsome.

"His son hasn't been in trouble, has he?"

"Andy? Of course not. Good kid, Andy. Wish I had a son just like him. My luck—four girls. But Cornell worried just the same. Maybe it was physical. He had headaches a lot—took pills all the time, and always had trouble with his throat. Never smoked. But he'd been with me for nearly eleven years, and I hate to let a man go."

Garcy's eyes inadvertently strayed to the chart on the wall. Sommers' followed. "Moroni, Taber—" he read aloud. "What does the chalk line indicate, Mr. Garcy?"

Garcy scowled. "I can't carry dead weight. I've got a business to run."

Sommers nodded.

"Cornell," he added, reading the next name above the discharged salesmen. Silence filled in for the things nobody said. "So you think he was sufficiently depressed to have committed suicide."

"Depressed, unstable—use whatever term you want to use, Officer. The fact is still the same. He did kill himself, didn't he?"

Of course he'd killed himself. Nothing had ever been more obvious, and yet Sommers, irritated by one derisive word, had to keep asking questions. "What about Mr. Berra?" he queried. "Did you talk to him?"

Garcy's expression changed from bridled impatience to momentary bewilderment.

"Who?" he asked.

"Berra. Cornell's customer for the Cadillac. Mrs. Cornell has told us that her husband had taken the death car from the lot in order to close a deal with a Mr. Berra."

Garcy met Sommers' gaze with unblinking eyes.

"I don't think there was a Mr. Berra," he said. "I'm serious, Officer. I know, I told your men the same story Mrs. Cornell told them last night; but I've had time to think it over, and I'm convinced the whole thing was a fabrication. I'll tell you why I think it. It began last Friday—a week ago yesterday. Cornell had muffed what should have been a sure sale—that was just before noon. I had a luncheon date at my club and had to leave, but I told him I wanted to have a talk with him when I returned. He was in trouble, and he knew it. It was almost three o'clock before I got back. I'd no more than gone out to the lot to speak with Cornell—he was in charge of the used car sales—than a call came over the loudspeaker for Mr. Cornell to go to the telephone. I followed him back to the office and got there in time to hear him making an appointment with a Mr. Berra to demonstrate the black Caddy at 5:30."

"Didn't Berra show?" Sommers asked.

"He did not. At about 5:15 there was another call. I usually go home at 5, but I was staying around to see how Cornell would handle this sale. The second call was from Berra again. He couldn't make it down to the lot in time, but if Cornell would drive over to a service station at the corner of Third and Fremont he could pick him up and demonstrate the car from there. It sounded all right, so I let him go."

"When did he come back?"

"I don't know," Garcy said. "I went on home. In the morning, the Caddy was back on the lot, but Cornell told me he had a sure sale just as soon as Mr. Berra raised the cash. I got after him about pushing for a low down payment, but he said Berra didn't want to finance— that he only did business on a cash basis and would have the money in a few days. I didn't think much about it at the time, but now, thinking back, I realize that Cornell was acting strange even then."

"Strange?" Sommers echoed. "In what way?"

"I don't know exactly. He didn't seem to want to talk about Berra, except to assure me that he was sold on the car and would raise the money. Usually the salesmen chew the fat a little about their clients, brag on how they handle them, or even have a few anecdotes; but Cornell was like a clam. I even tried to pump him. I asked him if Berra worked at the service station where he'd picked him up. He said no, he didn't think so, and that was all I got out of him. Three days later— no, four, Tuesday, it was. Last Tuesday I asked him if he'd heard from Berra and told him to get on the ball and not let the customer get cold. That afternoon he took the Caddy and said he was going to drive over to Berra's house. He came back about half an hour later saying that nobody was home and he'd try again."

"And did he?"

"I don't know. I only know that on Thursday—day before yesterday—Mr. Berra called back. This time he said that he'd raised the money. His mother, who lived in Pasadena, was putting up the full amount on the condition Cornell would drive him over to her house and let her inspect the car first. I thought then that it sounded fishy, but a $3750 cash sale isn't something you toss in the waste basket, and I trusted Cornell. I told him to go ahead, but to—"

Garcy hesitated and a little color came up in his face.

"But what?" Sommers prodded.

"I was only kidding, of course."

"But what, Mr. Garcy?"

"But not to come back until he'd closed the deal."

The silence in the shop was broken only by the distant sound of voices in the back lot garage.

"And did he come back?" Sommers asked.

"No. He called in yesterday morning and said he'd run into a little difficulty, but would get it straightened out before the day was over. He still had the Caddy with him." Garcy's face was no longer red; it was chalk white. "Damn it, it was only a figure of speech! I didn't mean for the man to blow out his brains!"

Sommers let Mr. Garcy indulge in his anguish without interruption. The well-adjusted machinery of his own mind was tabulating and arranging certain facts. All of them led him to one question.

"Mr. Garcy," he said, "you've just told me that this man, Berra, telephoned Cornell here at the office three different times, and yet you started out by saying that you didn't think the man existed. How do you account for that?"

"Timing," Garcy responded, grateful for a change of thought. "I got to thinking about it this morning. Cornell got that first call just after I'd started dressing him down for fluffing the other sale—at a time when he knew I'd be talking to him because I'd told him as much before I went to lunch. And then there's the way he dragged out this deal for a whole week, all the time insisting the car was as good as sold. I think he'd already flipped, Officer. I think he'd so lost his confidence that he rigged up Mr. Berra out of his imagination and fixed it with some friend to make the calls just to make it look good. I never saw the man. Nobody on the premises saw him, and Cornell never told us anything about him. The switchboard girl heard his voice—a young man, she says. Maybe it was his son. But I still think Mr. Berra doesn't exist."

Garcy could be right, but something stuck in Sommers' mind. No, not his mind; his senses. The senses absorbed and retained in an instant what the mind needed time to analyze. Some small thing. He scowled over the nagging thought of it.

"You say that Cornell took the car to Berra's house," he said. "Did he tell you where the house was?"

"No, he didn't. He said it wasn't far, and he was back in half an hour."

"Could he have jotted down the address somewhere—in his sales book, for instance?"

Garcy shrugged.

"You can look through his desk if you want to. Believe me, if I could locate this Berra I'd have a few questions for him myself. Do you know how many miles Cornell put on that Caddy last week? Nearly two hundred. I checked the mileage down at the police garage last night. I have to keep an eye on that kind of thing. Some of the young salesmen like to take a late model out on their dates at night and eat up the fuel. Little things like that can wipe out a businessman's profits. It only takes one leak to sink a ship, if it's neglected long enough."

Sommers ignored the lecture and went to work on Cornell's desk. There was ample evidence of other customers—names, addresses and telephone numbers, but nothing concerning Mr. Berra.

"You see," Garcy told him. "He made up this customer out of whole cloth. It's tragic when a man's so weak he has to resort to lies to keep up a front."

Chicken. Garcy's vocabulary was thirty years removed from Andy Cornell's, but they were saying the same thing. For Sommers, it was just another goad to keep looking.

"Third and Fremont," he mused aloud.

"What's that?" Garcy asked.

"The location of the gas station where Cornell was to meet Berra."

"Oh, sure. That's what he said. Look, Officer—" Garcy's words stopped Sommers at the door. "If you want to go on looking for Mr. Berra, that's your business. Selling cars is mine. I'd like to get that Caddy back on the lot in time for the Sunday display."

"I'll have it cleaned up and brought over to you, Mr. Garcy," Sommers answered. "In the meantime, there's something you can do to jack up your sales force and keep them on their toes."

"Yes? What's that?"

"Draw a line through Cornell's name," he said. "On that chart."

According to the lettering on the canopy, the manager of the service station at the corner of Third and Fremont was a man named Max Fuller. It was a busy intersection and several minutes elapsed before Detective Sommers could command Fuller's attention. Even then it was hardly undivided. They stepped inside the office, but Fuller kept a wary eye on his assistant.

"New kid on the pumps," he explained. "Have to watch 'em the first few days. Police, isn't it? What's on your mind? Selling tickets to something?"

Sommers wasn't selling tickets to anything. He explained what was on his mind, and, as he did so, Fuller forgot about his pumps.

"Berra?" he echoed, at the sound of the name. "Say, what's this guy done, anyway?"

It was an interesting response.

"What do you mean?" Sommers asked.

"Well, there was a fellow in here yesterday asking for the same man. Wanted to know if anyone of that name worked here, or if I knew where he could find him. I told him I'd never heard of the name, so he described him to me. A young fellow, he said. Twenty, maybe, but no more. Swarthy skin, dark hair and eyes, expensive-looking clothes. The description didn't ring any bells, so he goes on to tell me a story about having picked up this Berra here at my station nearly a week ago. Craziest thing I ever heard."

"Crazy," Sommers echoed. "In what way?"

"In every way. The way he picked up Berra. He drove over to the side of the building, see, so as not to block off my pumps. He cut the motor, figuring he'd have to come inside the office to find the person he was supposed to meet; but before he could get out of the car, the door of the men's room opened and Berra came out of it—running, he said, with his head ducked down. Berra pulled open the car door, asked if he was Mr. Cornell—"

"Cornell?" Sommers repeated.

"That's the name of the fellow who came in here yesterday asking about Berra. Cornell said he was, and so Berra got into the car. 'Okay,' he says, 'let's go.' Cornell is a car salesman, you see. The fellow who came running out of the restroom had called him about buying a black Cadillac—"

Max Fuller's voice broke abruptly. He'd been cleaning his hands on a wipe cloth as he talked. When he dropped it on the desk, his eyes caught the front page of the morning paper that had been staring up at him all this time. One story had a black headline: Auto Salesman

Suicide Victim. He followed the story for a few lines and then looked up, puzzled.

"Why, that's the guy," he said. "The same one who was in here yesterday."

"The same one," Sommers agreed. "Tell me, did you see the man Cornell described—the day he was supposed to have come running out of the men's room?"

"No, sir, I didn't. Late in the afternoon—this was at 5:30, he said— things are really jumping around here. People coming home from work, you know. I don't have a chance to watch anything but the pump meters. To tell you the truth, I don't even remember Cornell driving in, but he sure could have without me noticing. You can see for yourself. There's plenty of area out there for a man to park a car clear of the pumps."

Sommers moved back to the doorway. Fuller was right. It must have been thirty feet from the station office to the edge of the lot—an inner edge where a two-story commercial building rose up like a tall, windowless wall. A man could park his car clear of the pump area and not be noticed by anyone during the rush hours. By the same token, a man coming out of the restroom, which was in the rear end of the station building, would have been shielded from view.

"And you keep the restrooms locked, I suppose," Sommers said.

"Have to," Fuller answered. "Company orders. Sure wish I didn't. Those darned rooms give me more trouble than the rest of the business put together. I could write a book!"

"Mind if I look at it?"

"Go ahead. I've got to get back to my customers. If I can be of any help, let me know. I doubt it though. I couldn't help Cornell. He left here saying he was going to the other station."

Sommers had started to leave. He paused outside the doorway. "The other station?" he echoed.

"The other service station," Fuller explained. "The one down at Eighth and California. He told me that was where he left Berra after demonstrating the car. He sure seemed anxious to find that guy Berra. Crazy story, isn't it? Stories, when they're crazy like that, they stick in your mind."

It was a crazy story. Sommers wondered how Garcy would have reacted to the tale he'd just heard. Would he still believe Berra didn't exist, or would he point out what was still an annoying fact: that nobody except the dead man had seen Berra? He went around the building and proceeded to inspect the men's room. It was exceptionally clean. The company could give the management a seal of approval for cleanliness. There wasn't a thing out of order or out of place. Not a thing. The waste basket was in full view, the towel dispenser was filled, there wasn't so much as a leaky faucet or a dripping plumbing pipe. And there was no apparent evidence of Berra's having been in the room a week ago. Sommers made a careful inspection of the lavatory. It was an inexpensive casting with a hollow rim. He ran an exploratory finger along the under edge until it touched something unfamiliar. He squatted on his heels and examined the area by the flame of his cigarette lighter. There was a lump of something that looked a little like hardened chewing gum, but that scraped off on his fingernail into slivers of lead. Solder. Liquid solder. There were fragments of several lumps of it dotting the underside of the fixture. He didn't scrape off any more of it. He snapped off the lighter and stood up.

What did it mean? Chewing gum he would have understood, but not liquid solder. He left the restroom and went back to his car. For a few moments he sat parked in view of the spot where Cornell must have parked a week before his death. The door of the restroom was in full view. If it had been ajar when Cornell arrived, it would have been an easy matter for anyone waiting inside to see and recognize a specific model that had been requested to call for him. A very special form of taxi service—but to where? Max Fuller had told him. Another service station at the corner of Eighth and California.

The station at Eighth and California was an independent—not so modern or so clean as the one Sommers had just visited, but twice as busy. The reason for that was the garage about twenty-five yards behind the pump area. It was there that Sommers located a stout, balding man in overalls whose name was Donnegan, and who owned the business. Like Max Fuller, Donnegan had a story to tell. Cornell had been in the previous day inquiring after the same party—a man named Berra.

"I don't know anybody by that name, let alone employ him," Donnegan explained. "All I've got on the payroll are relatives. I don't say they work, mind you, but they're on the payroll. Might as well be. I feed them anyway."

"What did Cornell say about Berra?" Sommers asked.

"Just what I told you," Donnegan said. "Asked if I knew him. Told me how he looked—young, dark, well dressed. Said he'd dropped him off here a week ago after taking him for a demonstration ride in the '57 Cad Cornell was driving. Berra wanted to buy it, he said. Made him promise not to sell it to anyone else. Said he was going to meet his father here and put the bite on him."

"Here?" Sommers echoed.

"Yeah. That's a good one, isn't it? The car salesman fell for it, too. You'd think those guys would get used to deadbeats playing them for suckers. Still, for a commission I guess a man will go a long way."

"Two hundred miles," Sommers said.

"How's that?"

Sommers didn't bother to explain, but it was hardly more than half a mile from Fuller's garage to Donnegan's. Allowing for a demonstration ride, there were still a lot of miles to account for to reach that two hundred total Garcy had complained about.

"Did Cornell tell you anything else?" he asked. "Did he mention where he was going when he left here?"

"No, he didn't say anything about that," Donnegan answered, "but he did tell me one peculiar thing. He said this fellow Berra, when he got out of the Cad to meet his father here, ducked his head and ran for the men's room. 'Maybe he was carsick,' I cracked, but Cornell didn't laugh. He seemed worried or puzzled. Maybe that's a better word—puzzled."

It was a good word because Sommers was puzzled, too. Something was beginning to take shape, some vague pattern—but of what? The man Garcy had insisted didn't exist was becoming more real. A young man—a young voice on the telephone. A perturbed salesman retracing his route a week after he'd first taken it, and a day after Berra's second call. He wouldn't have gone to those lengths to search for someone he'd put up to concocting a prospective sale in order to get him off the hook with Garcy. Sommers had one more thing to do before leaving Donnegan's station, and after he'd inspected the men's room he was even more puzzled. On the underside of the lavatory he found several lumps of hardened liquid solder. There was a pattern, all right, but he needed more pieces before it could be meaningful.

Assuming that Mr. Berra did exist—why had he used Cornell for a chauffeur, and where else had they gone? Cornell had told his employer that he'd driven out to Berra's home, but that Berra wasn't in. Unless this was an outright lie, Berra must have given an address. It hadn't been in Cornell's desk, but there was a possibility that he'd jotted it down on a scrap of paper in his wallet. Sommers returned to headquarters and examined the dead man's effects. Nothing. A trail that had started out so promisingly had come to a dead end. There was only one other place to look.

Downstairs in the garage, Mr. Garcy's well-traveled Cadillac was ready to be returned to its owner. Cornell had been very neat with his dying. The upholstery wasn't bloodstained and the bullet had lodged in his skull, thereby saving the door's glass. Properly advertised, the car would make a quick sale to some morbid individual. Sommers wasn't morbid; he was determined.

The instant he opened the door of the Cadillac, he was again aware of that sense of something known, but not recognized. He'd done this very thing not more than twelve hours ago—opened the door of the death car, to which he'd been summoned, and peered into the front seat. Was it something seen? No. Only Cornell and the gun that had fallen to the floorboards at his feet had been seen. But something smelled—yes, that was it: a pungent, smoky odor as if something had been burned. He opened the glove compartment. Nothing to explain the odor there—no oily rags or singed material of any kind; only one detailed price ticket from Garcy Motors and one city map.

One city map. Sommers was excited the instant he drew it out into the light. It was a new map, but it had been marked with a red pencil. Crosses, small red crosses at various locations. The more he studied the locations, the more interesting they became. One cross was at the corner of Third and Fremont; one at Eighth and California. There were three others at widely separated locations: two on corners and one in the middle of the block. Add the distances together and double for round trips and a good piece was gone out of the missing two hundred miles. Now, he had three more chances to locate the elusive Mr. Berra.

Sommers pocketed the map and closed the glove compartment. The car was ready to roll now—cleaned, vacuumed, the ashtrays pushed in. Ashtrays. Now there was something to be seen. Last night the ashtray on the instrument panel had been open. Sommers yanked it out and examined the contents, overlooked in the cleaning of the car, perhaps, because someone had pushed the ashtrays in. Glenn Cornell didn't smoke because of his delicate throat, and Garcy Motors would surely be more careful of a display model than to leave an ashtray full of stubs still faintly smelling of the weedy scent Sommers remembered from the previous night. And these were not standard cigarette stubs either; this was marijuana.

The pieces of the pattern were gathering fast. Sommers turned the contents of the ashtray over to the lab for analysis and got set for a tour of the city. There were three locations on the map to be identified. The first turned out to be a small independent grocery located across the street from a high school—the Charles Steinmetz High School. Sommers noted the name of the school with interest. He didn't linger at the grocery. Strolling in for pack of cigarettes was enough to show him there was no one working inside answering the description of Mr. Berra. He didn't expect there would be. The second location on the map was even more interesting—an herb and health food shop operated by an oriental who, if not inscrutable, was at least self-possessed. Sommers didn't know what he was going to do with the wheat germ flour he bought, but he did know the pattern was beginning to form a most interesting picture.

The third red cross on the map was in the middle of the block on a residential street, where aging bungalows were being replaced by modern multiple-unit apartments. Without a house number, it would have been difficult to learn just what the third cross indicated except for the pattern in Sommers' mind. A man who didn't want to be found wouldn't give a correct address; he would give, if possible, an address where nobody lived. Vacant lots were the rule in such cases, but in this instance there was something even better. A house about to be moved stood like an empty shell with uncurtained windows and a collection of advertising throwaways cluttering the lawn and the front porch. Nobody was home. This is what Cornell had reported back to Mr. Garcy after calling on Berra. Nobody, certainly, was at home here. Sommers parked the car and began to examine the property for some sign of ownership.

At a casual glance, the building might have been only temporarily vacant; closer inspection showed the wreckers had already been at the porch foundations. Several brick pillars were in ruins and the brick fireplace just around the corner of the house was half-demolished. It was there that Sommers discovered the man with a wheelbarrow. The man looked up, surprised, a brick in each hand. These he promptly added to the growing pile on the wheelbarrow. When Sommers showed his badge, the man grinned.

"It's okay, Officer," he said. "I've got Mr. Peterson's permission to take these bricks. It's his house. We were neighbors for years. 'Go ahead, take 'em when they move the building,' he said. 'Finish your patio.' I don't know why I bother, to tell you the truth. One of these days, one of the buyers is going to offer me a price I can't resist and they'll be hauling my house away."

"Where's Mr. Peterson?"

"Gone to Carmel. Retired. Suppose that's where I'll be going someday."

"How long has it been since Mr. Peterson moved away?"

"From here, you mean? Oh, he hasn't lived in this old house for seven or eight years. Rented it out. The last tenants left about three weeks ago. Glad to see 'em go, too. Most people in this world are fine—just fine. All nationalities, all races. But once in a while you run across some bad neighbors. This Berrini family—"

"Berrini?" Sommers echoed.

"That's right. Not a family, really. Couldn't blame the mother so much. She was a widow who had to work. Three young girls in elementary school to support, and two sons who should have been a help and never thought of anything but hot-rods and flashy clothes. The older one—Bruno—even served time at one of those juvenile delinquent work farms a few years ago. I don't know about Joe. He's still in high school."

"How about Bruno?" Sommers prodded. "How old is he now? What sort of looking fellow is he?"

The man with the wheelbarrow stared at him thoughtfully.

"Is Bruno in trouble again?" he asked. "He must be in trouble again. A man was here yesterday asking those very same questions. I don't think he was a police officer though. He was driving a big car, a big black Cadillac."

Cornell again. A trail that had started with a trip to Third and Fremont was almost completed. Only one more location was needed to fill in the gap that stretched between an abandoned dwelling and an alley behind a lumber company.

"Bruno's a nice enough looking young fellow," the man was saying. "About twenty, I'd say, and a real flashy dresser. I don't know where he gets his money."

"I think I do," Sommers said grimly. "Do you know the Berrinis' new address?"

"Couldn't tell you that, Officer, but I suppose the Post Office people could. Wherever they moved, they have to get mail."

"That they do," Sommers said. "I've got something for Bruno Berrini myself—special delivery."

It was a very neat plan. Back at headquarters, Sommers conferred with Lieutenant Graves of Narcotics, and the little red crosses on the map found in the glove compartment took on significance.

"The way it looks to me," Sommers said, "the car salesman, Cornell, marked this map himself. Berrini—or Berra, as he called himself—would have been more careful. Cornell was used—that much must have been obvious to him yesterday morning when he called Garcy and said that he'd run into difficulty with the sale, but would have it straightened out before the day was over."

Graves nodded agreement.

"The used car routine is a new switch," he admitted. "We haven't run into it before. Berrini couldn't use his own car; if we spotted those delivery stations and watched them, it could be traced to him. The way he ducked his head and ran in and out of the restrooms indicates how afraid he was of being seen. This scheme beats the stolen car method where there's always a resulting investigation that might lead to an arrest. Who would think of reporting a reluctant car buyer to the police?"

"Exactly," Sommers said. "Cornell didn't even dare report him to his employer. Imagine his feelings when he realized he'd been tricked into chauffeuring a marijuana peddler on his rounds. He must have spent that last day of his life retracing the places to which the elusive Mr. Berra had caused him to drive: the station at the corner of Third and Fremont, the station at Eighth and California—that was the first day's route. Then he repeated the second trip: to the grocery store across from the high school and to the health food shop, checking the map as he went. By this time he knew what those locations meant. Berrini made one mistake. Maybe he was just too cocky, but on that second drive he smoked some of his own product. Cornell didn't smoke at all, and the fumes must have bothered his throat; in any event, something happened to draw his attention to the stubs I found in that ashtray."

Graves had listened intently; now he asked, "Why—?"

"Because Cornell was shot with his own gun, a gun usually kept in his room. He went home, according to what his wife said, just long enough to have gone into his room and taken the gun. By that time, he must have located Berrini. He told his wife that he was going out to meet Berra and 'put an end to the indecision.'"

"'I've got him on the hook,' he told me. 'All I have to do is reel him in.'"

Mrs. Cornell's words intruded in Sommers' mind. They fit into the pattern too.

"A man doesn't go home to get his gun," he added, "if he's only going out to sell a car. The going was rough for Cornell, but not that rough."

"That's one thing I don't understand," Graves remarked. "Granting that you're right and that Cornell did realize that he'd been used to deliver marijuana to the supply points on this map, why did he go after Berra himself? Why didn't he go to the police?"

There were alternative reasons. There was the possibility of attempted blackmail—that was the obvious one. Cornell had needed that sale badly enough to cling to it all week. He had enough on Berra to make him buy the car.

There was also the possibility of anticipating a reward if he nailed a marijuana peddler; Cornell could have used a reward. But to know why a man does anything, it is necessary to know something about the man himself; and everything Sommers had learned about Glenn Cornell suggested that he was a good citizen and a conscientious father. He was risking his life when he went after Berrini. He must have known that a hopped-up person was capable of anything. The only reason a man like Cornell would do such a thing was the kind of reason that stood tall and broad-shouldered in a high school jersey with a big S on the chest. S for Steinmetz.

Graves listened to that possibility spelled out, and then asked, "Do you think Cornell's son is mixed up in this?"

"It isn't what I think that matters," Sommers said. "It's what Cornell feared. I'm going to do a little checking at Steinmetz. Right now, I'd be willing to give odds that Andy Cornell and Joe Berrini are pals and that Glenn Cornell knew about it and worried about it. I'm not looking into a crystal ball when I say that, either. The man who called Garcy Motors asked for Cornell by name. If Bruno Berrini's kid brother pals around with Andy Cornell, chances are he knew Andy's father was a salesman at Garcy's. He might even have known that he was easygoing—'he could be pushed around' was the way Andy put it. I think that's your answer, Lieutenant. I think Cornell took his gun and went after Berrini on his own because he was afraid police action might hurt his son. Guilt can rub off on the innocent, too, especially when the innocent is an adolescent with more bravado than brains."

At least it was a reason, and there had to be a reason—even as there had to be a reason for the lumps of solder on the undersides of the two rest-room lavatories.

"You may be right," Graves said. "It shouldn't be too difficult to find out what happened last night. We know the deposit points for the marijuana—all we have to do is watch. Berrini's used them before, the multiplicity of the soldering lumps indicate that some kind of packet or container has been hidden under the lavatories more than once, and he'll use them again. Cornell's dead—a published suicide. What does he have to fear?"

Sommers was thoughtful. Lieutenant Graves' job seemed simple; his wasn't so easy.

"He may use the car salesman method of transportation again," he suggested. "You've got to admit, it's a good one. If it hadn't been for Cornell's curiosity and that marked map, we'd never have traced the black Caddy to him."

"And Berrini knows nothing of the map," Graves added.

"Of course not. He'd have destroyed it if he'd known. Lieutenant, I've got a request to make of your department. I want you to contact the used car dealers in this area and alert them to Berra's pitch. Chances are he'll be going through this same routine within the week."

"Within the week?" Graves echoed.

"It's the football season," Sommers said. "What's a logical place to peddle marijuana—particularly marijuana that's been delivered to the pushers before Saturday?"

Graves grinned.

"You've been nosing around in my detail," he said. "You know we've been getting reports from the football games."

"It's a report from a used car dealer that I'm interested in," Sommers said. "You want Berrini for passing narcotics—that's an easy job. I want him for something that's going to take a little doing. I'm going out now and take some instructions in how to sell an automobile."

"You?" Graves asked.

"Who else, Lieutenant? I'm the man who wants Berrini for murder."

Bruno Berrini was watched. Before the day was over, his new residence had been located in a stucco duplex within a few blocks of the house about to be moved. The school office was closed over the weekend, but on Monday it was learned that Joe Berrini, the younger brother, was a junior at Steinmetz High and a classmate of Andy Cornell. The two boys were seen together in the schoolyard on the day after Glenn Cornell's funeral, which was on Tuesday. It was the same day when Lieutenant Graves reported on the results of notifying the local used car dealers of Berrini's routine. He'd wasted no time in trying his trick again. He used his own product, and that gave him more daring than sense. This time it was a salesman named Hamilton from Economy Motors who had the same story to tell that Sommers had already pieced out of interviews with Max Fuller and the man named Donnegan. A man who called himself Mr. Baron had telephoned in on the previous Friday and inquired about a '58 Buick displayed on the lot. Told it was still there, he expressed great interest and asked that a salesman pick him up for a demonstration ride at a service station on the corner of Third and Fremont. From there on the story was the same. Baron's peculiar conduct had puzzled the salesman, but customers could be peculiar.

"Friday," Sommers mused. "That's the same day he used Cornell the first time. I was right. He works on a schedule. He should call back about the Buick on Thursday. He had to divide these trips up. No salesman would fall for making four stops on a trip. He'd be suspicious."

"So Berrini divides his distribution points into two parts and services them a week apart," Graves concluded.

They were right. On Thursday, Hamilton called in to report that Mr. Baron had decided to buy the Buick, but had to get the money—the full amount—from his mother, who insisted on seeing what he was buying before writing the check. Sommers and Graves went out to the lot together. By that time, Mr. Baron had called back to say he couldn't make it in, but would meet Mr. Hamilton in front of his home. The address given was the empty house.

Sommers got into the Buick.

"I'll be behind you," Graves told him. "Berrini will have the stuff on him, but I don't want to take him until he's made his deliveries. I want the receivers as well as the distributor."

"I want more than that," Sommers said. "I want a murderer."

He picked up Berrini in front of the house that still looked as if somebody had just washed the curtains and forgotten to pick up the throwaways from the porch. Berrini was a man of habit. He'd worked out a means of transportation to his delivery spots, but he wasn't prepared for a stranger behind the steering wheel. He balked at the curb.

"Where's Mr. Hamilton'?" he demanded.

A young, dark, good-looking kid in a very sharp tweed jacket and slacks. He might have been all slicked up to go paying court to his girl, but Sommers knew a killer could look like an angel.

"Sick," he answered, trying to sound convincing. "He asked me to take his place."

Berrini hesitated. Was the word "cop" written all over Sommers' face, putting the lie to his story? If it was, he should be reaching for the holster under his coat. He didn't. He let the weight of the gun lean against his ribs, while Berrini's suspicious eyes passed judgment. The eyes were a little glassy. He was about ready to make that almost inevitable switch from reefers to something more potent. His judgment wasn't good. Almost a week had passed since Cornell's death, and there had been no public notice of anything but obvious suicide. Berrini felt safe. He crawled into the front seat and gave an address. He said very little during the half hour that passed before Sommers pulled up before a ranch-style home in one of the better districts. This was supposed to be where Berrini's mother lived. He waited for the story and it came.

"I don't see her car in the driveway," he said. "She must have gone to a little store a few blocks down the street. She buys a lot of this health food stuff. Let's drive down and see."

"Maybe you should ring the bell," Sommers suggested. "She might have left the car in the garage."

"She never leaves the car in the garage—never! She's at this store—I'll bet ten dollars. Just a few blocks—"

It was a thin story, but to a commission-hungry salesman eager for a cash sale it would have been convincing. Sommers listened to the directions and then proceeded to the herb shop. He pulled up to the curb and parked about half a block ahead of the unmarked car in which Lieutenant Graves was waiting. Berrini went inside alone. Through the front window, Sommers observed him in earnest conversation with the proprietor, after which they went into the back room for a few moments. When Berrini came back into view, Sommers knew the first delivery had been completed; but the lieutenant wouldn't make his move until they had proceeded on the delivery route. That was the agreement between them. Berrini's supply points were the lieutenant's concern, but Berrini belonged to Sommers.

Berrini returned to the Buick with another story.

"She was in here a little while ago," he reported, "but they were out of what she wanted. The clerk sent her to another store. If you don't mind driving a little farther, we'll catch her there. This car's what I've been looking for."

So a man with a lagging sales record and a family to support would go along with the pitch. He'd come this far; he had to keep riding that sale. Sommers was beginning to get the feel of the part he was playing. Be pleasant, be nice, keep smiling. Pretend you don't know the next stop is a small independent market across the street from the Steinmetz High School. He glanced in the rearview mirror as the Buick edged away from the curb. Lieutenant Graves was sliding across the seat to get out of the unmarked sedan. Within minutes, he'd have relieved the herb shop proprietor of his latest consignment. So far, everything was working out according to plan.

It was almost dark when they reached the store. The schoolyard was deserted and the streets empty. Berrini went inside and Sommers, as he had done before, watched from the Buick. Five minutes passed, ten minutes, fifteen. Nobody else went into the store or came out of the store. Little independents didn't do a volume business, particularly not at an hour when housewives were already preparing the dinners their families were waiting to devour. Twenty minutes. Sommers crawled out of the Buick and scanned the street behind him. Something must have delayed Graves back at the herb store; there was no sign of his sedan. By this time Sommers knew what Glenn Cornell had learned at the end of his long drive. Berrini, Berra, Baron—whatever he called himself—wasn't coming back. This was the end of the line. Thanks for the ride, sucker, but I don't need you anymore. Sommers gave the lieutenant five more minutes and then went into the store alone.

The balding proprietor was adamant. The gentleman must be mistaken. A dark young man in a tweed jacket? Here, in this store? Nobody had come into the store in almost an hour. Business was slow; it was closing time.

"I don't think so," Sommers said. "I think it's opening time."

He pulled his badge from his pocket and thrust it under the man's startled eyes.

"Open!" he ordered. "Where's Bruno Berrini?"

The man's face reddened. "Who?" he stammered.

"Bruno Berrini. He's in trouble—big trouble. You don't want to cover for a killer, do you?"

It was one thing to peddle marijuana to high school students, one thing to twist young lives so that they might never be whole again; but it was something entirely different to face a detective from

Homicide and risk your own sweet freedom. One wild glance toward the rear of the store and Sommers had his answer.

"What's back there?" he demanded.

"Only the stockroom," the man protested. "Nothing else!"

There was only one reason for the man to scream the words. Sommers wouldn't listen to him, but Berrini would. There was no time to waste. The stockroom was dark, but beyond it a ribbon of light showed beneath a closed door. As Sommers moved toward it, the light disappeared. Now there was only a door—vague in the shadows—and behind it a man who knew why Glenn Cornell had died with his chin on the horn rim of a Cadillac he hadn't sold.

"Berrini!"

Sommers fired the word at the silence and dropped back against the wall beside the door.

He waited a few seconds and then—

"I'll give you to the count of three to come out, Berrini. If you don't want twice the trouble you've got now, you'll come quietly. We know you killed Glenn Cornell. We found a nice, clear print you forgot to wipe off his gun. One—two—"

It was a lie. There hadn't been a print on Cornell's gun that hadn't matched Cornell's own; but Sommers got no farther with his threat. The first interruption was an undistinguishable oath, and then the walls seemed to split open with the sound of gunfire. But Berrini wasn't shooting at the door. Berrini wasn't shooting at all. Sommers discovered that when he jerked open the door and let the fading finger of light from the front of the store stretch to the place where Berrini crouched with his arms folded over his face as if they could stop the .45 leveled at the back of his head from splitting open his skull.

"Drop the gun!" Sommers ordered. "Drop it on the floor!"

For about five seconds Berrini's life expectancy hovered at zero and then the barrel of the .45 drooped, lowered, and finally fell to the floor.

"Okay, kick it this way," Sommers said,

The gun slid across the floor. Not until it was safely under his foot, did Sommers draw an easy breath. It was no small thing to have talked down the hatred blazing in the eyes of a tall, blond kid with a big S on his sweater.

Back at headquarters, Bruno Berrini made his confession. He hadn't meant to kill Cornell. Cornell had sought him out and insisted on one more demonstration ride. Not until they were under way did he reveal his knowledge of his brother Joe's use of him and demand information about his brother's association with Andy. They quarreled then, and Cornell pulled his gun. It was self-defense, Berrini insisted. It was an accident. A guy has a right to defend himself, doesn't he? So the gun went off while he was struggling for it and killed a guy. It was self-defense. That was the story he would take into court, and whether or not he succeeded in selling it to a jury wasn't in Sommers' department. What was in his department, in his office, in fact, was a kid with a story to tell.

Andy Cornell was shaken and subdued.

"It was a crack Joe Berrini made the day after my father's funeral that made me suspicious," he admitted. "He was trying to be nice, I guess. 'Your old man had to have a lot of guts to put a .45 to his head,' he said. I got to thinking about it later. I even looked through all the old newspapers to make sure, but nobody had mentioned that my dad's gun was a .45. I didn't know it myself until the police returned the gun to my mother and I got hold of it. Dad would never let me near it. Too many kids got killed playing with empty guns, he always said. But it was a .45 all right, and how did Joe know that unless he knew a lot more? Then I got to thinking about this Mr. Berra and how much the name sounded like Berrini.

"I knew my dad didn't like me hanging around with Joe because of his brother's record. I didn't see what that had to do with Joe, but it had worried him and so I got to thinking that maybe he'd had a fight with Bruno, or something. I knew Bruno was mixed up in what was going on at the grocery store across from the school. Kids know more about that kind of thing than cops, I guess. I just kept watching and waiting for my chance to talk to Bruno, which happened to be today."

"A talk with Bruno," Sommers repeated, "at the point of a gun." He was scowling when he said it. The kid might have been killed, taking that gun away from Bruno. "Haven't you Cornells ever heard of going to the police?" he demanded.

Andy ducked his head. It was time for a lecture on the folly of a citizen taking the law into his own hands; but Andy Cornell suddenly wilted, as if the excitement of his search for Bruno was all that had held back the grief of his father's death and now that barrier was gone. He would be remembering the warnings his father had given him about the Berrinis and picking up that burden, too. The kid had too much hard living ahead of him to be handicapped by additional crosses of guilt.

"Well, there's one thing I'll have to hand to you," Sommers admitted, having decided to forego the lecture. "You're not it any more than your father was."

Andy looked up, puzzled.

"What's that?" he asked.

"Chicken," Sommers said.

Don't Sit Under the Apple Tree

It was exactly ten minutes before three when Loren returned to her apartment. The foyer was empty—a glistening, white and black tile emptiness of Grecian simplicity which left no convenient nooks or alcoves where a late party-goer could linger with her escort in a prolonged embrace, or where the manager—in the unlikely event that he was concerned—could spy out the nocturnal habits of his tenants. Loren moved swiftly across the foyer, punctuating its silence with the sharp tattoo of her heels on the tile and the soft rustling of her black taffeta evening coat. Black for darkness; black for stealth. She stepped into the automatic elevator and pressed the button for the seventeenth floor. The door closed and the elevator began its silent climb. Only then did she breathe a bit easier, reassuring herself that she was almost safe.

There was an apex of terror, a crisis at which everything and every place became a pulsing threat. Loren wore her terror well. A watcher—had there been an invisible watcher in the elevator— would not have been aware of it. He would have seen only a magnetically attractive woman—mature, poised, a faint dusting of premature gray feathering her almost black hair. The trace of tension in her face and eyes would have been attributed to fatigue. The slight impatience which prompted her repeated glances at the floor indicator above the doors would have passed for a natural desire to get home and put an end to an overlong, wearisome day.

In a sense, the watcher would have been right.

The elevator doors opened at the seventeenth floor, and Loren stepped out into a carpeted corridor of emptiness. Pausing only to verify the emptiness, she hurried to the door of her apartment. The key was in her gloved hand before she reached it. She let herself in, closed the door behind her, and leaned against it until she could hear the latch click. For a moment her body sagged and clung to the door as if nailed there, and then she pulled herself upright.

Above the lamp on the hall table—the light turned softly, as she had left it—a sunburst clock splashed against the wall in glittering elegance. The time was eight minutes before three. There was work to be done. Loren switched off the lamp. The long room ahead became an arrangement of grays and off-blacks set against the slightly paler bank of fully draped windows at the end of it; but halfway between the hall and the windows, a narrow rectangle of light cut a pattern across the grays. The light came from the bedroom. Loren moved toward it, catching, as she did so, the sound of a carefully modulated feminine voice dictating letters.

To Axel Torberg and Sons,
Kungsgaten 47,
Stockholm, Sweden.

Gentlemen:
In regard to your inquiry of February 11, last: I am sorry to inform you that full payment for your last shipment cannot be made until the damaged merchandise (see our correspondence of Jan. 5) has been replaced.

Having done satisfactory business with your firm for the past twenty years, we feel confident that you will maintain this good will by taking immediate action.

Very Truly Yours,
Loren Banion, Vice President
John O. Banion, Inc.

Loren entered the bedroom. The voice came again, now in a warmer and more informal tone.

Katy, get this off airmail the first thing in the morning. Poor old Axel's getting forgetful in his dotage and has to be prodded. Okay, Doll—?

Next letter:

To Signor Luigi Manfredi,
Via Proconsolo, Florence …

The room was heavily carpeted. Loren made no sound as she crossed quickly to the French windows, barely glancing at the dictograph which stood on the bedside worktable. It was still partly open. The night wind worried the edge of the soft drapes which gave concealment as Loren, pulling them aside only a finger width, peered out at the scene below. The seventeenth floor was one floor higher than the recreation deck. The pool lights were out; but there was a moon, and young Cherry Morgan's shapely legs were clearly visible stretched out from the sheltering canvas sides of one of the swinging lounges. There were legs other than Cherry's—trousered legs; identity unknown. With her parents abroad, Cherry was playing the field.

... if you will wire this office on the date of shipment, we will have our representative at the docks to make inspection on arrival....

The voice of Loren Banion continued to dictate behind her. Loren listened and slowly relaxed. She had, she now realized, been gripping at the draperies until her fingers were aching. She released the cloth and walked back to the bed—no longer swiftly, but with a great weariness as if she had come a very long distance, running all the way. She sank down slowly and sat on the edge of the bed. The dictograph was now a droning nuisance, but a necessary one. Cherry Morgan could hear it, and that was important.

"... Honestly, Mrs. Banion, I don't know how you can work as late as you do! Sometimes I hear you up there dictating all night long."

"Not all night, Cherry. I never work past three. Doctor's orders."

"Doctor's orders? What a drag! I'm glad I don't have your doctor. If I'm going to work until three in the morning it's got to be at something more interesting than business correspondence!"

And the fact that Cherry Morgan frequently worked past three was the reason the dictograph continued to play.

... Very Truly Yours,
   Oh, you know the rest, Katy. On second thought, give the sign-off more flourish. Signor Manfredi probably sings Don Jose in his shower.

A small crystal clock stood beside the dictating machine. Loren glanced at it; it was six minutes before three. She had done well. A year of catching planes, meeting trains and keeping spot appointments, had paid off in timing. It was all over, and she was safe. The tension could ebb away now, and the heaviness lift; and yet: it was all she could do to raise up the small black evening bag she had been clutching in her left hand, open it, and withdraw the gun. She held the gun cupped in the palm of her right hand. She looked about the room for some place to hide it; then, unable to look at it any longer, jammed it back into the bag and tossed it on the table beside the clock. The time—five minutes before three. It was close enough. She got up and switched off the machine. Then she removed her gloves, shoes, coat, and went into the bathroom. She left the door open—the shower could be heard for some distance at this hour—and returned exactly five minutes later wearing a filmy gown and negligee. She got into bed and switched off the light; but now her eyes were caught by a glittering object that would not let them go. It was such a frivolous telephone—French styling sprayed with gold. It was magnetic and compelling. It seemed almost a living thing; and a living thing could be denounced.

"Not tonight," Loren said. "You won't ring tonight."

It had all started with a telephone call—long distance, Cairo to New York City.

"Mr. Banion calling Miss Loren Danell … thank you. Here's your party, Mr. Banion."

And then John's voice, annihilating miles.

"Loren—? Hold on tight. I've got one question: will you marry me?"

It could have happened only that way. John wasted neither time nor words. She had clung to the telephone, suddenly feeling quite schoolgirlish and dizzy.

"But, John, what about Celeste?"

"What about her? She's flipped over a Spanish bullfighter, and he's expensive. We've finally struck a deal. She's in Paris now getting a divorce."

"I can't believe it!"

"Neither can I, but it's true. I thought I'd never get rid of that—of my dear wife, Celeste." And then John's voice had become very serious. "You know what it's been like for me these past years, Loren. Celeste trapped me—I admit that. She wanted status and money, and she got both. I got—well, now I'm getting free and I suppose I should just be grateful for the education. Loren, I don't say these things well—but I love you."

At that moment, the telephone had been a lifeline pulling Loren out of the quicksand of loneliness. She clung to it until John's voice blasted her silence.

"Well! I want an answer! Will you marry me?"

Laughing and crying, she had answered, "Yes, yes, yes, yes—"

"Hold it!" John ordered. While you're talking, I can be flying. See you tomorrow."

Tomorrow …

Rain at Kennedy—hard, slanting, and completely unnoticed as John bounded off the plane like a schoolboy. There was much to be done before the cable from Paris announced the divorce had been granted, and one of the many things concerned a change in office procedure. Loren discovered it one morning when she found her old office cleaned out, and, investigating, a new name on the door of the office next to John's.

LOREN BANION
VICE-PRESIDENT

"Only a little premature," he explained. "You might as well get used to the name."

"It's not the name—it's the title!" Loren exclaimed.

"Why not the title? You've been doing the job for years; I've only belatedly given you the status. Belatedly," he repeated, "this, too." It was then that he gave her the ring, almost shyly. "Oh, Loren why does it take so long to learn to distinguish the real from the phony? You are real, aren't you, Loren? You're not one of those scheming females."

"Oh, but I am," Loren insisted. "I've been deliberately getting under your nose for years."

John had laughed. Under his nose meant only one thing at the moment. He kissed her, quickly.

"That I like. That I'll buy any day. That's not what I meant. I meant that you're not one of the phonies—the honky-tonk phonies. All out front and nothing to live with. I want to grow old with you, Loren. You're the only—" He hesitated, groping for a word. "—the only pure woman I've ever known."

It was terrible how grave John's face had become; Loren drew away.

"Please—no pedestals," she protested. "It's so cold up there!"

"It's not cold here!"

He had taken her in his arms, then, and he was right. It was warm; it was a place to rest at last. But then his arms tightened, and his fingers dug into her arms until she wanted to cry out. It was the first shadow of fear to come.

"You're real," he said. "You have to be real. I couldn't stand being fooled again!"

"I couldn't stand being fooled again!"

Loren stared at the telephone on the table. It was silent; but John's words were ringing in her mind. She glanced at the clock. Sleep was impossible, but nothing could be unusual tonight, and within ten minutes after Loren Banion concluded her dictation, she always turned off the lamp. The darkness came—complete at first, and then a finger of moonlight from the open window probed across the carpet. Below, the silver sound of a girl's laughter was quickly muffled in sudden remembrance of the hour.

The hour. The hour was only ten minutes spent. The long hour before four ...

The honeymoon had been in Miami and off-Miami waters. John was a fisherman—unsuccessful but incorrigible. Monday, Tuesday, Wednesday without a catch. It was no wonder Sam McGregor, an Atlanta account they had discovered vacationing at their hotel, had insisted on an hour of solace at the Flotsam and Jetsam on the beach. It was a shanty-type bar—one of the higher bracket shanties— where the drinks were long and the shadows cool. Loren was too happy to see details in the Grotto-like shadows; but someone had seen clearly. Very clearly. It was an informal place for customers in shorts and bathing suits, and the only entertainment rippled from the busy fingers of a pianist in T-shirt and dungarees who wheeled his diminutive instrument from booth to booth. He wasn't meant to be heard or noticed, and only rarely tipped; and Loren wasn't really aware of him at all until, above John's and Sam's ribbing laughter, a tinkling sound became a melody. She looked up. The small piano was no more than three feet away, and behind it sat a man she had never expected to see again.

"Don't sit under the apple tree with anyone else but me ..."

He played not too well; but he did enjoy his work. His smile seemed to indicate that he enjoyed it very much. His smile ...

"Loren—are you all right?"

John's voice brought Loren back from the faraway place Loren's mind had gone reeling.

"You look shook up, honey. Don't tell me that you got seasick today."

Honestly, Sam, this woman can take more punishment ..."

When John's voice stopped, he couldn't have known too much then. That was impossible. But he seemed to sense that the piano player had something to do with Loren being disturbed. He pulled a bill out of his pocket and placed it on top of the piano.

"How about hoisting anchor, sailor?" he said. "I'm afraid we're not very musical in this booth."

The piano player's smile broadened and one hand closed over the bill. "Anything you say, Mr. Banion. I only thought it would be nice to salute the newlyweds."

"You know me?" John asked.

"Why, everybody knows you, Mr. Banion. Didn't you see your picture in the paper the day you flew down? Nice catch, Mr. Banion." And then, with another smile for Loren. "Nice catch, Mrs. Banion. A very nice catch."

The piano rolled on, picking up something with a calypso beat. The incident had taken only a moment, but having sensed that something was amiss, Sam had said brightly—

"Enterprising chap. They don't miss a trick down here. How about another round?"

Loren stood up. "You two—yes," she said. "No more for me. I'm going back to the hotel."

"Loren—why? What's wrong?"

John must not ask that question; he must not look that concerned. She laughed her gayest and confessed—

"I'm afraid you'll have to stop bragging about me, John. I did get seasick this afternoon, and now I'm almost hung on one drink. No— not hung enough for you to break this up. You stay on with Sam. I'm going to get some air."

Air, wind, and a long walk along the beach—nothing erased Ted Lockard. He should be dead. Men died in a war. They stopped answering letters, and they never came back. One assumed they had died. But not Ted. Ted was alive, and his smooth voice, so thrilling to a girl, had an oily quality maturity could identify. There were men who lived off their charms, even as did some women.

"A nice catch, Mrs. Banion. A very nice catch."

Loren wasn't intoxicated, but she was sick. A girl had written wild, foolish letters, and Ted Lockard probably kept all of his love letters the way some men kept hunting trophies—or securities. He would try to reach her some way—she knew that. And she was vulnerable; not because of a youthful human failure, but because of John's conception of her. She had to be perfect in order to compensate his pride, for having been so deceived by Celeste.

Luck was with her. That night, a wire from Mexico City sending John south. Loren returned to New York. But it was only a reprieve.

Celeste returned from Europe just before Christmas, sans bullfighter and sans cash. There were telephone calls and wires, all ignored, and then, one day Celeste came to the office. John saw her. Loren wasn't aware of the meeting until it was over. John had asked her to go down to the docks and see Signor Manfredi's shipment through customs. The Signor's shipping department had only a vague idea of the transoceanic hazards for breakable materials. It was a task usually delegated to an employee of lesser status; but Loren thought nothing of it until she returned in time to pass Celeste in the outer office.

Celeste was icily majestic.

"Congratulations, Mrs. Banion," she said. "John looks in the pink. You always were a good manager."

Not too much—just enough. Celeste could make a prayer sound insulting.

Inside, Loren found John not at all in the pink. He was remote and grave.

"What was Celeste doing here?" she demanded.

"She came to wish us a Merry Christmas," John said bitterly.

Loren glanced down. John's checkbook was still on his desk.

"John—you gave her money!" He didn't answer.

"Why? Hasn't she cost you enough? You don't owe her a thing!"

"Loyalty," John said.

His voice was strange.

"What?" Loren demanded.

"It's a word," John explained. "Just a word."

Then, suddenly, he turned toward her and grasped her shoulders with both hands, holding so tightly that she remembered what had happened the day he gave her the ring. For just an instant, she was actually afraid; and then he smiled sadly and let her go.

"Forget Celeste," he said. "It's a holiday season. I felt charitable."

Loren didn't. She left John abruptly and hurried back to the front office. Celeste was nowhere in sight. Katy sat at her desk, typing letters. She looked up as Loren spoke—

"Mrs. Ban—" she began, and then corrected herself. "The former Mrs. Banion—where did she go?"

"Out," Katy said.

Katy, sweet, wholesome, naive. What did she expect to learn from Katy? She strode across the reception room and entered the hall, arriving just in time to glimpse Celeste as she was being assisted into the elevator by an attentive man. They turned and faced her, and just before the doors closed Loren got a frontal view of Celeste's new adornment. Ted looked very handsome, and he smiled.

Merry Christmas, Loren. Merry Christmas and a Happy New Year. Santa had come early. It was the beginning of a long wait, of not knowing what Ted might have told Celeste, or what Celeste might have told John, or when Ted would make his move. John said nothing. Her own tension was the only change between them. After a time, she began to think she was suffering from nothing but the ancient feminine penchant for borrowing guilt.

Then, in the middle of January, John took the night plane to Cleveland.

"You could leave in the morning and still make that meeting in time," Loren protested.

John was adamant.

"I like to fly at night. It's smoother and I sleep all the way."

"Then I'll work on the correspondence."

"You work too hard, Loren. Why don't you let Katy do that?"

"John—please. I know these people. I've been handling your correspondence with them since dear Katy was taking her first typing lessons and getting used to having teeth without braces. Don't you know that I'm jealous of my work?"

"I should know," John said. "I'm jealous, too—of you. But I don't have to worry, do I?" His fingers stroked her cheek lightly. "No, I don't have to worry—not about Loren."

Loren, who lived on a pedestal where the life expectancy was so short.

She had worked that night until almost three, showered, and gone to bed. Sleep came immediately after work. She had to fight her way out of it when the telephone rang. Groping for the instrument, she noticed the illuminated face of the clock. It was exactly four. Nobody ever called anyone at four o'clock in the morning unless something terrible had happened.

"John—?"

She waited, suddenly fully awake and afraid. There was no answer. And then it began, so brightly, so spritely—one full chorus of a piano rendition of an old wartime melody:

"Don't Sit Under The Apple Tree With Anyone Else But Me ..."

That was all.

The clock had always been silent. There was no reason for it to tick so loudly now. Loren stirred restlessly against the pillows and turned her head toward the source of her torment. Sleep was impossible. She pulled herself up higher against the pillows. Aside from the clock, there was no other sound. Silence from the deck below. Cherry had closed up shop for the night. The moonlight brought objects on the table out of darkness. Loren's fingers found a cigarette, lighted it, and then she sat back smoking and remembering ...

She never told John about the four o'clock call. It was Ted's signature, obviously; but what did he have in mind? For days and nights after that call she waited for his next move. Nothing happened. John returned from Cleveland to find her thinner and tense.

"Working too hard," he scolded. "Loren, I won't allow this to go on! Katy's going to take on at least a small part of your work."

She wanted to tell him about the call; but she couldn't tell a part without revealing the whole.

"Then reveal the whole, Loren. John is a sane, adult human being. He'll laugh about it and send Ted packing."

"Do you remember the McGregors?" John asked suddenly. "Miami—our honeymoon?"

Loren remembered. Her mind had just been in the same vicinity.

"I met Sam in Cleveland. He's broken—literally broken. His wife has gone to Reno, and Sam's shot. I've seen that man fight his way through tight spots that would have staggered Superman; but this has got him. You women don't know what you can do to a man."

"Reno?" Loren echoed. "Why?"

John's face hardened. "The usual reason. Sam's a busy man. Little time to play Casanova. They don't have bullfighters in Atlanta; but they do have Casanovas. You would think a woman could tell the difference between love and flattery wouldn't you? But no, it seems they all have the same weakness." And then the bitterness ebbed out of John's voice. "Except one," he added.

She told him nothing.

She continued to wait; but there was no word from Ted. Early in

February, John flew to Denver on the night plane. Loren worked on correspondence until three and then retired; but she couldn't sleep. A vague uneasiness gnawed at her mind until four o'clock when the telephone rang and the uneasiness ceased to be vague.

The call was just as it had been before. No words at all—just that same gay piano serenade ...

For the next few months, John's trips were frequent. It was the busy time of the year. On the first night of his next departure, she didn't try to sleep. At four o'clock, the telephone rang.

"... don't sit under the apple tree with anyone else but me."

She tried having the call traced. It was useless. The caller was too clever. Clever, but purposeless. Aside from starting her nerves on a process of disintegration, the calls were inane. Ted was too practical minded to torture without a purpose. It was the kind of sadistic trick she might expect of a jealous rival.

"Celeste!"

At one minute past four, on a morning when John was planing to Omaha, Loren placed the telephone back in the cradle convinced that she'd hit upon the source of her troubles. Ted was more clever than she'd imagined. He'd gone to John Banion's ex-wife, rather than his present wife. He'd told her his story, and now Celeste was trying to break up John's marriage by torturing his wife into a breakdown. At one minute past four a.m., immediately following the fourth of the maddening calls, the scheme seemed obvious to Loren. Wear her down, weaken her, unnerve her, and then—She wasn't quite sure what Celeste meant to do then; but there was no reason to wait and see. Two could play this game!

Loren's mind became quite clear. She began to analyze. The calls came only on the first night of John's trips. Reason: had John been at home he might have intercepted the calls. Furthermore, there was never any way of knowing how long he would be gone. The only way of avoiding him was to make the call immediately after his departure. This meant that Celeste had access to John's plans.

On the following day, Loren spoke to Katy.

"Do you remember the day the former Mrs. Banion had an interview with Mr. Banion?" she asked.

Katy considered her answer only a moment. "Yes, I do, Mrs. Banion."

"Did she come in alone?"

This time, Katy considered a bit longer.

"I don't think I remember—yes, I do. A man came with her. He waited in the reception room."

Ted, obviously.

"Have you seen him since?"

"No, Mrs. Banion."

But there were other girls in the office-young, impressionable. Ideal bait for Ted's charms.

"Katy, I want you to do something for me. Talk to the girls, casually, of course, and try to learn if any of them has a new, dreamy boyfriend."

Katy laughed.

"According to what I pick up in the lounge, most of them have a new, dreamy boyfriend every week."

"That's not what I mean! I mean one certain boyfriend."

She was making a mess of it. A casual inquiry was becoming an inquisition; but there was still one thing she must know.

"And Katy, on the day when the former Mrs. Banion had the interview with Mr. Banion, did you, by any chance, overhear anything that was said?"

"Overhear, Mrs. Banion?"

There was such a thing as being too naive, and Loren's patience had worn thin.

"Accidentally or otherwise," she snapped. "Oh, don't look so wounded. I had your job once, and I was ambitious and human. I listened; I spied. I know what goes on in an office. This is important to me, Katy. I'll make it worth your while if you can tell me anything—anything at all."

It was a foolish, weak, female thing to do, and Loren regretted her words as soon as they were spoken.

Had Katy been shocked, it wouldn't have been so bad; but it was all Loren could do to suppress the desire to slap the hint of a smile she saw on Katy's face.

You're cracking up, Loren. You're losing control.

She held on tight, and Katy's smile faded.

"I'm sorry, Mrs. Banion; I didn't hear anything. But if I do hear anything, I'll let you know."

Loren went back to her office shaken at her own self-betrayal. Celeste was succeeding. Whatever her diabolical plan, she was succeeding. Never had she spoken to an employee as she had spoken to Katy. Never …

When John returned from Omaha, he found Loren confined to her bed.

"It's nothing," she insisted. "I think I had a touch of flu."

"You've had more than a touch of overwork," John said. "I warned you, Loren. Now I'm going to send you off on a vacation."

So Celeste can have a clear field. That's her game. It must be her game.

"No!" Loren protested. "Not now! Not at a time like this!"

John's face became very grave. He sat down on the edge of the bed, still wearing his topcoat—his briefcase and newspaper in his hand. These he placed on the bed beside her.

"You've heard, then," he said. "Loren, there's no reason to be upset. It isn't as if she meant anything to me—or had meant anything to me for years. In fact—" There were times when John's mouth hardened and became almost cruel. "—I'd be a liar if I pretended to be sorry."

The newspaper had fallen open on the bed. While she was still trying to understand John, Loren's glance dropped and was held by the photograph of a familiar face. Celeste. She drew the paper closer until she could read the story. Celeste had been in an auto accident upstate. Celeste was dead.

Celeste was dead. It was horrible to feel so happy; and impossible not to. The pressure was gone. Her diabolical scheme would never materialize. Within a few days, Loren was herself again.

Three weeks later, John flew to San Francisco. Loren worked late, as usual, retired, and slept soundly—until four o'clock in the morning when the telephone rang.

The serenade continued.

A siren was sobbing somewhere in the street below. The sound brought Loren through time back to the immediate. She snuffed out her cigarette in a now cluttered tray and her eyes found the clock again. Three forty-five. The sound of the siren faded; but now she sat upright, her heart pounding. Why was she afraid? She had been methodical and efficient and decisive. That was the important thing—decisive.

"The thing to remember about business, Miss Donell, is that an executive must learn to make decisions and stand by them. You may be right, you may be wrong—but make the decision!"

That had been John Banion instructing his new secretary—eager, ambitious, and—why not face it—already in love with her boss. It had taken six years for him to recognize that love and turn to her when he finally discovered what everyone else had known about Celeste all along; and in the meantime, Loren had learned to be decisive.

Decisive. The first four o'clock call after Celeste's death removed all doubts. It was Ted; and it was her move. But where was Ted? It would have been easy enough to trace Celeste; but Ted was another matter. She didn't want to use a private investigator and leave a trail that could be traced. The solution to her problem came from an unexpected source: Katy.

"Mrs. Banion, do you recall asking about the man who was with the former Mrs. Banion when she came to the office just before Christmas?"

It was two weeks after Celeste's death. Loren didn't look up from her desk; she mustn't betray her excitement.

"What about him?" she asked casually.

"It's a peculiar coincidence; but I had to run an errand for Mr. Banion across town yesterday, and I saw the man. He was going into a small hotel—The Lancer. I think he must live there. He had a bundle under his arm that looked like laundry."

"You're very observant," Loren said dryly.

"You did ask—"

Loren looked up, smiling.

"Ancient history," she said, "but thanks, anyway. You're a diligent girl."

Loren wasn't so casual later when she drove to the Lancer Hotel, parked across the street and watched the entrance until she saw Ted come out. It was a shabby hotel in a shabby neighborhood; Celeste hadn't, obviously, contributed much to Ted's economic security. This wasn't a condition Ted could long endure. She watched him walk from the hotel to a bowling alley at the end of the block, and then went into a drugstore phone booth to verify his registration at the hotel. That done, she went to work.

The first thing to be done was to obtain a recording of a piano solo of Ted's theme. This, for a small fee, was easily accomplished. For a somewhat larger fee, she then obtained a small wire recorder of a type that could be carried in a handbag or a coat pocket. At home, she transferred the record onto the tape, adding a personal touch at the conclusion:

"We can reach an understanding if you will meet me behind the bowling alley at 2 a.m."

She destroyed the record and put the wire recorder away until

John's next business trip. On the first Thursday in March, he took the night plane to Chicago. As soon as she knew he was leaving, Loren did two things: she recorded two hours of correspondence on the dictating machine in her bedroom, and reserved two tickets at a playhouse.

Katy begged off from the theatre.

"I'd love to, Mrs. Banion, but it's the wrong night. You see, I have a friend—"

"Then hang on to him," Loren said. "A good man's hard to find. I'll ask someone else."

An out-of-town customer had nothing to do for the evening. Anyone was acceptable as long as she had a companion. She drove to the theatre in her own car. During the first intermission, she excused herself and went to a telephone booth in the lobby. She took the wire recorder from her bag, dialed Ted's hotel, and waited for his voice. As soon as he answered, she switched on the recorder and held it to the mouthpiece. When the recording was concluded, she hung up the telephone, replaced the recorder in her bag, and returned to her place in the theatre.

It was twelve-thirty, when Loren returned to her apartment the first time. She left her car parked in the street, as she frequently did after the garage attendant had gone off duty. It was safe. Every hour on the hour, Officer Hanlon made his rounds. She wanted the car to be seen. In the lobby, she met other theatre and party-going tenants returning home, and rode up in the elevator with them. She went directly to her room and put the wire recorder away in the drawer of the work table in her bedroom, transferring the gun to her handbag in its place. Then she set up the dictating machine, opened the bedroom windows enough to make certain the words would be heard on the deck below and waited until exactly one o'clock before turning on the machine. It was time to go.

She went down in the service elevator and left the building through the alley—unseen. She didn't take the car. She walked a distance and caught a cab, took the cab to within six blocks of Ted's hotel and walked the rest of the way. At two o'clock, she was waiting in the shadows behind the bowling alley. Ted was only a few minutes late. He advanced close enough for her to see the surprised recognition in his eyes before she fired. A strike in the bowling alley covered the shots. Ted fell and didn't move again. When she was certain that he was dead, Loren walked away—not hurriedly, but at a normal pace.

The streets were almost empty at this hour, but within a few blocks she found a cab, rode to within six blocks of her apartment, and walked the rest of the way. The service entrance was locked, but the front lobby was empty.

It was exactly ten minutes before three when Loren returned to her apartment ...

... The sound of the siren faded away, but not the pounding of Loren's heart. It was as if she had been in a kind of sleepwalker's trance, and now she became horribly aware of the fact that she was a murderess. The horror didn't lie in the fact that Ted was dead—she cared no more for that than John had cared about Celeste's death. It was something else. Fear—but what could go wrong? She'd been at the theatre, with an escort, when the hotel switchboard had handled Ted's call. She'd left her windows open so Cherry Morgan could hear her voice. She'd left her car on the street, and come up in the elevator with friends. She'd destroyed the record—the wire recorder. Loren was out of bed in an instant. She ripped open the table drawer, opened the recorder, and pulled free the wire. She wiped it clean on the skirts of her negligee. No evidence. There was no way to connect her with the body the police would find behind a bowling alley in a shabby neighborhood across town; but there must be no evidence. The wire was clean. What else? Katy had told her where to find Ted; but she didn't even know his name. John—? No matter what Celeste might have told John, he would never connect her with Ted's murder.

But the gun. She should have gotten rid of the gun. She snatched it out of the handbag and began to look about for a hiding place. The echo of the police siren was still in her ears, and reason wouldn't still it. The gun was the one damning piece of evidence. She stood with it in her hands, turning about, directionlessly—and the doorbell rang.

When Loren went to the door, it was with a gun in her hands and doom in her mind. Just in time, she remembered to stuff the weapon under a cushion of the divan, and then go on to open the door. Officer Hanlon stood in the lighted hall looking all of nine feet tall.

"Mrs. Banion," he said, "I'm sure sorry to disturb you at this hour, but there was no one on duty downstairs."

She couldn't speak a word. Not one.

"I didn't know where to leave this."

He held up a set of keys, dangling them before her eyes. It was some seconds before she recognized them.

"You left them in your car, Mrs. Banion. I noticed the window was down when I went past at one o'clock, but I didn't think I could do anything about it without some way to turn on the ignition. It started to sprinkle a few minutes ago, so I stopped to see what I could do. I found these. You're getting careless, Mrs. Banion."

Loren saw her hand reach out and take the keys; it might have been detached from her body.

"Thank you," she said. "Is that all?"

"That's all, Mrs. Banion. Sorry to get you out of bed, but I didn't know what else to do."

Loren closed the door; then leaned against it—listening until she could hear Hanlon go down in the elevator. Only the keys? She wanted to laugh, and she wanted to cry. Most of all, she wanted John. She wanted to cling to him, to bury her head on his shoulder and be safe. The weeks of terror were over, and all Hanlon had wanted was to give her the keys! John was gone, but his room was next to hers. She ran to it, turned on the light, and went to the chair behind his desk. Soft, rich leather with the feel of John in it—the contour of his back, the worn places where he'd gripped the arm rests. And then Loren's eyes fell on the desk. For a moment, she was afraid John had gone off without his ticket. The airline envelope was there. She looked inside. The ticket was gone. I'm becoming a neurotic woman who worries about everything, she thought. And then she noticed what was written on the envelope in the time of departure line: 8:00 a.m. 1/6/.

The sixth was Friday. 8:00 a.m. was in the morning. This morning—not Thursday night.

It had to be a mistake. The airline office was open all night. She dialed quickly.

"John Banion? ... What flight did you say? No, there was no John Banion on the nine o'clock flight to Chicago ... The eight o'clock this morning? ... Yes. We have a reservation for John Banion ... Who is this calling? ... Oh, Mrs. Banion. Your husband flies with us frequently. He always takes the daytime flights. Always."

Loren put the telephone back on John's desk, and stood listening to the words of a story. It had begun with John's fingers digging into her arms.

"I couldn't stand being fooled again!" he'd said.

And—then, on the day Celeste had come to see him—

"Loyalty," John said. "It's a word. Just a word."

"Oh, no, John," Loren whispered.

"I like to fly at night," John said. "It's smoother and I—"

"John, no—"

But it had to be John. He'd seen her face that day in Miami when Ted played an old melody. He'd gotten some story from Celeste— enough of a story to induce him to buy her silence, and immediately afterwards the calls had begun. And where was John when he didn't take the night flights he was supposed to take? With a cold certainty, Loren knew. Men lived by patterns. He had turned to his secretary once, and now—hadn't Katy been the one who had told her where to find Ted? Katy, who couldn't go to the theatre because she was expecting a friend? Katy, that not so naive child who did listen at the boss' door …

And Ted Lockard was dead. Loren remembered that when the telephone in her bedroom started ringing. She turned and walked slowly and obediently into her room. She picked up the telephone and listened to the music with an expressionless face. It was four o'clock. It was time for John's serenade.

The Affair Upstairs

Mrs. Emily Procter had the nicest roses on Roxbury Avenue, and that was because she never allowed the gardener near them. Samuel, her husband, could—under careful direction—spade the earth at fertilizing time; but the hired Japanese was required to confine his activities to the small patch of front lawn and the hedges.

Mrs. Emily Proctor always tended the roses herself. There were many of them. The climbers started at the entrance to the driveway and extended the entire length of the white brick wall that stretched to the rear of the lot. The bushes were at the corners of the building, front and rear, and the rose trees were in the patio that filled in the L created by the architectural design of Roxbury Haven, a ten-unit stucco, singles and doubles by lease only. Emily and Samuel Proctor resided in apartment 5A, the lower rear at the end of the patio where the small sign "Manager" was affixed to the, door.

All of the lower apartments opened into the patio and all of the upper apartments had small balconies with neat wrought iron railings in front of sliding glass doors. From the rose trees in the patio, and from the corner bushes at the entrance and at the approach to the garage area, and from the climbers on the wall, Mrs. Emily Proctor, attired in smock, gardening gloves and straw coolie hat, had visual command of every doorway, every garage stall, and every person who entered or left Roxbury Haven. There was nothing about any tenant that she didn't know.

Mrs. Emily Proctor was happy.

On the day Haynes versus Haynes made its initial appearance on Judge Carmichael's docket, Emily timed her activities carefully. She had been spraying the Mary Margaret McBride at the entrance to the driveway for nearly thirty minutes, when Todd Haynes returned. She saw the black convertible come slowly down the street—very slowly for Tod Haynes, who was usually fast about everything. Fast, she mused darkly, in every way. The car was barely moving as it turned into the driveway, and his face, which she saw clearly before he saw her; was that of a man driving in his sleep—or one who had just been hit by a falling wall. And then a disturbing thing occurred. Tod

Haynes saw Emily. He looked at her, glared at her; and then the convertible leaped forward, swerving slightly so as to force her back against the rose bush, and roared past on its way to the garage.

"Oh," Emily gasped. "That man!"

She didn't expect the Mary Margaret McBride to answer. The voice came as a surprise.

"Now, what's got into him? Is he drunk?"

"I wouldn't be surprised," Emily answered. "He drinks like a fish."

And then she remembered herself. Turning, she saw Mr. Kiley, the postman, who had just crossed the lawn and was arriving, mail in hand. Automatically, Emily reached up to brush back her hair and straighten the coolie hat.

"Oh, good morning, Mr. Kiley," she said. Her voice softened. "Now, I shouldn't have said that about Mr. Haynes. He's been having so much trouble."

"Sickness?" Kiley asked.

"Worse trouble than that, I'm afraid. Poor Mr. Haynes was sued for divorce by Mrs. Haynes only this morning."

Mr. Kiley shook his head sadly.

"Moral deterioration," he said. "There's a new series running in the evening paper that tells all about it. Homes breaking up. Children running wild. Moral deterioration. Gonna wreck the whole country."

And Emily Procter smiled knowingly.

"You don't have to tell me!" she declared. "If you managed an apartment building, you wouldn't need to read the newspapers."

From where he stood, Mr. Kiley could see the row of balconies extending along the upper floor of the unit. Now, out of 4B, emerged Patti Parr—young, silver blonde, her body still clad in a flimsy white negligee. She stretched luxuriously and stared up at the sky. Mr. Kiley watched appreciatively.

"I'll bet I wouldn't!" he said.

Emily glanced up at 4B, frowned and then reached for the mail in Mr. Kiley's hand. "Anything for me?" she asked brightly. "Oh, just another old bill! At least I can put the rest of it in the boxes for you."

"Lord knows, you're on your feet enough, Mr. Kiley! And I haven't another thing to do." By this time, Emily was nudging Mr. Kiley toward the sidewalk. "And I do hope you won't repeat anything I said about poor Mr. Haynes," she added. "If there's anything I can't stand, it's gossip."

Mr. Kiley moved on down the street, and Emily paused a moment to look after him. It was a lovely morning. The preschool children were playing in the yards, and she wondered, idly, what these young mothers were thinking of to let their children leave such expensive toys scattered over the neighborhood and why Mrs. Williams didn't do something about her daughter. The child ate constantly and looked like a baby blimp.

When Emily turned back to the patio, she noted that Patti Parr had gone inside again: That was a relief. Her appearance had such bad timing. Tod Haynes would be returning from the garage at any moment. She went to the row of mail boxes and busied herself, listening without turning when the heavy footsteps came from the rear of the driveway. They came closer, and then stopped.

"Do you censor it for us, too?" Tod Haynes asked.

Emily, with most of the mail still in her hands, was trying pitifully to stuff old Miss Brady's New Romances into a mail slot designed for letters. When it dropped from her hands, Tod bent down quickly, retrieved it, and returned it to her. Her lips tried to form the words, "Thank you," but her voice didn't respond at all. Tod stared at her darkly and then stalked off toward the inside stairwell, leaving Emily Proctor with a peculiar feeling she would later recognize as the beginning of terror.

The marriage of Tod and Ann Haynes had disturbed Emily from the beginning. She was certain it would never last. Tod Haynes wasn't the husband type ...

"Do you mean he doesn't look beat enough?" Sam asked. "Give him time."

It wasn't at all what Emily meant. Tod Haynes had a roving eye—any woman could see that—and Ann Haynes was nobody's fool. She was attractive in a self-assured way that Emily secretly envied. A businesswoman who assumed responsibilities and would expect a mate to do the same. Oh, Emily didn't guess or deduce all this. When apartments are as close as the apartments at Roxbury Haven; and when one of the legitimate duties of the co-manager is to inspect the units when they are vacated for new occupancy and when—as it developed—such a situation occurred shortly after the Haynes moved into 5B, Emily couldn't avoid hearing one significant conversation which took place on the balcony one summer evening at dusk.

The magnolia tree Sam was always going to get trimmed grew up beside that balcony. Because of it, Emily, who was near the sliding doors inside 4B, heard when Tod and Ann stepped outside.

"Ouch!" Tod said. "So help me, someday I'll get an axe—"

Then Ann laughed softly, and there was one of those interesting silences when Emily's imagination made her feel slightly uncomfortable.

After a little while, Tod said, "No regrets, Mrs. Haynes?"

"No regrets," Ann answered. "What about you?"

"Oh, I'm getting used to the harness," Tod said. "I told you when I applied for the job—'experienced: no references.'"

"Tod—"

"—but a willingness to learn. Ann, this has to work."

"It will," Ann said.

"I mean, it has to. Life has to start making sense somewhere along the line."

By this time, Emily knew she was eavesdropping; but she always made herself believe that it was a part of her duty as manager to learn what kind of tenants she had. Credentials meant nothing. She could never see past anyone's teeth. And so she listened carefully as Tod Haynes continued.

"I blew it once," Tod said. "But I'm not going to blow it again. My luck changed the day l walked into Curtis's office and found you at the reception desk. Do you remember what you said to me?"

Ann's voice became professional.

"Mr. Curtis will see you in a few minutes, Mr. Haynes."

"No," Tod said. "I mean that wonderful thing you told me just before I went in to see Curtis. You must have known my knees were shaking. 'Mr. Haynes,' you said, 'I want you to know I have a book in my library that's dogeared and loved. It's called A Summer Ago.'"

Ann laughed softly.

"You would remember that!"

"A book that sold exactly 622 copies," Tod added. "The one good thing I did before I became a one-shot genius. Ann—" Now his voice became quietly tense. "—hang on tight. I'm going to deliver for Curtis. I'm going up there again."

The silence came again. Now Emily could smell the magnolias; she began to feel guilty. She started to draw away from the door, filing away in her mind all she knew about the new tenants in 5B; and then Ann spoke once more.

"Tod, you didn't marry me for that, did you?"

"What?"

"Because I won't be used. I love you too much to be just the woman you need until you're on top again."

"Don't be silly."

Inside the doorway of 4B, Emily heard and nodded knowingly. Her instincts were always right. Tod Haynes wasn't the husband type.

The proof of Emily's forebodings came in due time. Each morning Ann Haynes went off to the office while her husband stayed at home, a situation Emily found deplorable.

"If he's got his wife trained to work for him, don't knock it," Sam said. But Sam didn't understand. It was dangerous to leave a man like Tod Haynes alone. He was too attractive, as was duly noted by every female in Roxbury Haven. There was Mrs. Abrams, in her late sixties, whose sole interest in Tod Haynes was because he reminded her of grandson Robert, stationed in Germany.

"With NATO," she told Tod, "very close to General Norstadt."

And Tod was so charming, Mrs. Abrams dropped a stitch on the sweater she was knitting for Robert, and Mr. Abrams raised his eyes from the Wall Street Journal for all of thirty seconds—more than anyone had seen of him in months.

There was Miss Fanny Brady, who had been a fixture in bit parts since the days of the crank and megaphone and would never retire. Fanny had a weakness for flame-colored capris and pink bra tops, and her hair coloring varied from orange to silver. She had no more than heard Tod's typewriter at work, than she attempted to interest him in doing the story of her life.

"It won't be dull," she promised. "I have memories."

"Only memories?" Tod teased. "I should think your future would be even more interesting."

Thereafter, Miss Fanny Brady glowed every time Tod walked across the patio, or appeared on his balcony for a cigarette and coffee break.

Emily missed none of these things. Long before apartment 4B was rented, she had learned to resent Tod Haynes. She never allowed herself the luxury—or the pain—of understanding why. She never considered, as she shared a dull breakfast with Sam, that it might really be Ann Haynes whom she resented. But one thing Emily knew, by means of that ancient art known as feminine intuition, and that was that trouble came to Roxbury Haven on the day Patti Parr rented 4B.

Usually, Emily showed the apartments. Sam confined his activities to the maintenance work in morning hours before going off to his part-time job. But on the morning Patti Parr's heels clicked smartly across the patio, and her determined finger rang the bell marked "Manager," Sam adjusted his suspenders, donned the handsome Italian sweater (similar to one of Tod Haynes') Emily had given him, over protests that he wouldn't be found dead in it, and escorted Miss Parr upstairs. They were gone an inordinately long time. When Emily went up, ostensibly to see if the drapery rods were in working order, she found a merry threesome in the hall. Tod Haynes' door was open. He stood just outside chatting with Patti Parr as if they were old friends.

"I think the apartment is darling," she cried, as Emily approached, "but I wanted to see how it looked furnished. Mr. Haynes was on his balcony and heard me."

"Anything to be neighborly," Tod said. "What about it, Mrs. Proctor? Do I get a commission for renting the apartment?" And then he laughed. "Just joking. I get a new neighbor—that's commission enough."

When Patti Parr moved in, Tod Haynes was very helpful with the drapes. Emily doubted that Patti was the literary type, but he was also very helpful with the crates of books. On one occasion, when a special delivery package came for Patti, Emily took it up to 4B and found Tod in a strange situation. He was sprawled on the divan, a drink in one hand and a sheaf of typewritten paper in the other. He looked up when he saw her at the door. Her disapproval must have showed. He frowned—then smiled crookedly.

"Patti," he said, "shall I read that chapter to Mrs. Proctor, the one that bugged me? I told you I wanted a woman's reaction."

Patti shook her head quickly. Emily wasn't supposed to see, but she did. It was some kind of signal between them. Emily didn't understand; but she wasn't surprised when—a few days later—she heard Tod and Ann quarreling bitterly in the garage.

"Tod, I warned you," Ann said. "I won't be used!"

And Tod's voice answered, "You're making a fuss over nothing. I just had a few drinks—"

"You know what drinking did to you once—"

Discretion forbade Emily hearing any more, but she was prepared for the big break when it came. It began with Tod selling his book. He came home driving a black convertible: second hand, but big. It roared magnificently down the driveway and into the garage. Moments later, Tod came striding across the patio. It was November. The rains would start any time now. Overhead, the sky was leaden.

Emily began to gather up her gardening tools.

"Here, let me help you," Tod said, taking up the bag of fertilizer. "Tell me, Mrs. Proctor, do you put little umbrellas over your plants when it rains, or do you leave them standing out in the cruel world?"

Emily was a bit startled, and then she realized that Tod had been drinking again. At her door, he added, "Now, don't worry about me. I'm going right upstairs like a good boy and call my wife and then I'm going to take her to dinner and dancing, and we may even take a rocket to the moon."

He bounded up the stairs, leaving Emily a little breathless.

But Tod Haynes didn't go out with his wife that night. He didn't go out at all for some time.

It was almost dusk when Patti Parr came downstairs and got her small foreign car out of the garage. Midway out of the driveway, the motor stalled. Emily heard Patti trying to start it again until, finally, Tod came down and tried to help. It was no use. By that time, the rain had started. Amid much laughing, Tod pushed the small car back into the garage and returned in his own. Emily saw Patti get in Tod's car and the two of them drive away.

At the usual time, Ann Haynes came home from work. Being a sensible woman, who read weather forecasts before going to work, she was wearing her hooded raincoat. Emily watched her go upstairs. After that, Emily continued to watch the Haynes' window. She saw Ann come to the balcony several times. It rained harder. As the hours passed, Emily was tortured with indecision. Should she tell poor Mrs. Haynes her husband had gone out in his car after drinking? On a rainy night, there was even more chance he might crack up. With Sam off at work, there was no one to advise her. While Emily sat beside the telephone deliberating, it rang. She picked it up.

"Mrs. Proctor," Ann Haynes asked, somewhat timidly, "I wonder if you saw my husband go out any time this afternoon?"

"Why, yes," Emily answered. "You mustn't worry, dear. He went out in his car."

"His car?" Ann Haynes echoed.

"The car he drove home. He seemed quite happy over it. And then, a little later, that sweet Miss Page next door to you started to go out in her car, but it stalled. Your husband came down and took her—"

"Thank you!" Ann Haynes said, abruptly.

The sound of her receiver clicked in Emily's ear. She was uneasily aware, as she replaced the telephone on the cradle, that she might have said too much. But she was also aware of a vague sense of vicarious pleasure.

On the following morning, Mrs. Haynes didn't go to work. In the middle of the morning, clear after the rain, so that all the patio regulars were in their places, Patti Parr returned in a cab. Two hours later, Tod Haynes black convertible roared up the drive. Ten minutes later, the battle began. No one on the patio was spared any of the details, until Tod remembered the glass doors to the balcony and slammed them shut.

Emily was replacing a bulb in the lower hall when Ann Haynes came out of 5B, suitcase in hand, and started down the stairs. Tod was at her heels.

"This is insane!" he roared. "I went out to celebrate the book being accepted; I meant to pick you up at the office, but I met an old pal—"

"Not such an old pal, according to what I heard!" Ann called over her shoulder.

"What you heard? What did you hear? It's a lie!"

"I have a witness. You'll find out in court!"

Tod came bounding down the stairs.

"I won't let you go, Ann," he insisted. "I won't let you leave me!"

But Ann left, figuratively slamming the door in Tod's face. He cursed under his breath, turned and saw Emily on the ladder. He looked at her strangely for several seconds, and then stalked back upstairs.

The look Tod had given Emily the day Ann left him was a smile compared to the sullen glare she absorbed and held with her, along with the tenant's morning mail. No one had ever given her such a fright; no one, certainly, had ever tried to run her down in the driveway. She wanted to discuss it with someone; but Sam was still asleep, and when the patio regulars appeared, Mr. Abrams buried himself behind his newspaper, and Mrs. Abrams found delight in a new letter from Robert. Fanny Brady had a new magazine, and the normalcy that came to Roxbury Haven deceived Emily into believing the two incidents were of no importance. She returned to work on the roses, only to become uneasily aware that somebody was staring at the nape of her neck. She turned, slowly. Tod Haynes was out on the balcony of 5B. He didn't have a cup of coffee; he wasn't smoking a cigarette. He was staring at her in that same malevolent manner. And even when she faced him, boldly, he continued to stare. Had she been inclined to believe such things, Emily would have thought he had the Evil Eye.

After a while, Tod went inside. Emily was relieved until that strange feeling came again, the uneasy feeling of being watched. She glanced up at the balcony. No one was there.

"Emily—"

She whirled about. Tod Haynes was standing not two feet away. It was all Emily could do to refrain from screaming.

"Oh, did I frighten you, dear?" he said warmly. "I'm sorry."

Emily was temporarily paralyzed. In spite of his familiarity with other women, Tod had never addressed her by her first name. As if that wasn't enough, he took her arm and drew her toward him.

"I just came down," he said, "to see if you would ask Sam to help me get my trunk from the garage."

"Your trunk?" Emily echoed, weakly. "Are you going away?"

Then Tod Haynes smiled in a strange and frightening way.

"We never know, do we, Emily?" he said.

Sam picked up the lunch pail and started for the door. Emily thought he was going to leave without saying anything at all. At the doorway, he looked back.

"Haynes actually tried to run you down?" he asked.

"This morning in the driveway. And I'm not making it up. The postman saw it, too. And, Sam, if you had seen the way he looked at me at the mail boxes—"

"Have you been reading other people's postcards again?"

"I wasn't reading anything! And then a little while ago—out on the patio." Emily lowered her voice. "He was so familiar."

"With you?" Sam asked.

Emily didn't like the sound of his voice. He wasn't impressed. Maybe she did look at the mail sometimes, but it was only to see where the postmarks were from. Some people had interesting friends in interesting places, not just a husband who didn't care if she was threatened and insulted.

"The way he looks at me," she said. "Sam, I think the divorce has affected his mind."

"He seemed all right when I took his trunk up," Sam said. "I don't know why a divorce should bother a man."

"Sam Proctor!"

But Sam was completely unsympathetic. As he turned and left her, he said, "And I've got a piece of advice for you, Emily. Don't stand around in driveways."

Sam went to work and wouldn't be back until after midnight. Emily was left with her doubts, which she tried to reason away. Mrs. Haynes had left in a rush, carrying only a bag. It wasn't unreasonable to think she'd left things behind to be packed. She listened to the sound of the trunk being dragged across the floor upstairs, and it seemed that noises were much sharper now.

A little later, another strange thing happened. Emily heard Tod Haynes come down the stairs. He went out on the patio and began to talk to old Mr. Abrams, who had been setting in the sun alone. Nobody ever talked to Mr. Abrams. Emily's curiosity compelled her to go outside.

"... thirty-seven years," the old man was saying, excitedly. "Thirty-seven years in the hardware business. Tools, plumbing fixtures. Yes, sir. Anything you want to know about in the hardware line, I can tell you."

"Where can I buy a good saw?" Tod asked.

"All kinds of saws," Mr. Abrams said. "What kind of saw do you want?"

Tod hesitated. He turned slowly and saw Emily standing a few yards away. He looked at her steadily, until she began to have the same sensation she had experienced when he looked down at her from the balcony.

"What do you want the saw for?" Mr. Abrams prodded.

"When something is too large," Tod said, still staring at Emily, "it has to be cut down."

Then he walked away without saying anything more to anyone. When he came back, he carried a new saw and a coil of rope. Emily didn't see him again until after dark. In the meantime, she listened. She listened for the sound of the saw and heard nothing. She listened for the sound of the trunk and heard nothing. What she did hear was the sound of pacing. Heavy, thoughtful pacing. When she was very quiet, all the sounds in the building were magnified. She heard Patti Parr come downstairs and go off on a date. The Smiths came home. Harry Stokes came home and went out again. Still, overhead, the pacing. Once it stopped and she heard the shower run for just a few seconds. Later, there was the sound of a glass breaking in the kitchen. A few minutes later, she heard heavy footsteps come down the stairs and stop at her door. Emily didn't know she was so tense until the bell rang.

She opened the door and faced Tod Haynes.

"Emily," he said. And then he smiled strangely. "I knew you would be waiting by the door."

He had been drinking. His hair was mussed and his tie awry. When he took a step forward, she leaned on the door.

"Don't be afraid of me, Emily," he said. "I'm not going to come in." He carried a bundle which he shifted from one arm to another. "Laundry," he explained. "Keep forgetting to take it out now that I'm a bachelor again ... Emily, I know how you notice things, so I thought I'd save you some trouble. There's a woman coming to my apartment tonight. No, don't say anything yet," he protested, as her mouth opened. "I'm telling you because she may come while I'm out, and I don't want you worrying your mind about it. You worry about all of us so much."

When Emily found her voice, it was unexpectedly shrill.

"Mr. Haynes," she said, "you've been drinking."

"I know," Tod answered. "It's terrible, isn't it? I have all kinds of bad habits—like giving a pretty girl a ride when her car won't start."

"And not coming back until the next day!"

Tod beamed. "There, I knew you hadn't missed that! Who else could have known, I asked myself. Who else but dear Emily?"

There was nothing happy in his smile. Behind it, in his eyes, was that same look that had frightened her all day.

"Mr. Haynes," she said firmly, "you can't blame me for your misconduct."

"Indeed I can't," he confessed. "Indeed I can't. But when the woman I'm expecting comes—if she comes before I get back—just close your eyes and let her go upstairs unmolested—please. She'll have a key. She's only coming to pick up her trunk."

"Do you mean it's your wife?" Emily asked.

Tod shook his head sadly.

"Emily, dear," he said. "I have no wife ..."

His words trailed behind him as he walked away. Not until he was gone did Emily begin to wonder how Ann Haynes was going to carry that large trunk downstairs.

It was almost two hours later that Emily heard the sound of footsteps on the patio. She scurried to the window and peeked out to see Mrs. Haynes, wearing her familiar hooded raincoat, enter the building. The footsteps went up the stairs. Moments later, the door opened and Mrs. Haynes walked inside. She proceeded slowly through the apartment. Emily waited for the sound of the trunk that didn't come. After a few moments, the footsteps went out on the balcony. Quietly, Emily slid open her door. Now she caught the smell of a cigarette. Then the sound came—a quick gasp of surprise.

"I thought you were smarter than that," Tod said quietly. "Did you think I was going to let you get away with it?"

There was no time for an answer. While Emily stood frozen below, thinking Tod must have returned without her knowing it, there was a dull thud, a scraping sound and the quick closing of the glass doors. Simultaneously, a tiny red spark spiraled down from above and dropped at her feet. She picked it up. It was a cigarette, still smoldering and marked with lip rouge.

Emily hurried inside and locked the door behind her. She hardly dared to breathe. Her mind raced back over the day: the anger in Tod's face when he came home from court; the incident in the driveway; his strange changes of mood; the trunk, the rope and the saw— At that point her mind balked. Then she heard the sounds again: a scuffling, something that might have been a chair being moved, a crash—finally, a heavy thud that made the ceiling shudder.

She waited. It was all over. No. Now the pacing began again. When it stopped, she heard the trunk being dragged across the floor; after that, more pacing. Then the shower began to run—hard. It ran for a long time. What was the shower for? To wash away—what? Alone in her world of sounds, Emily panicked. She ran to the telephone. The police? She hesitated. That might be brash. Sam. Yes, she'd call Sam at work and try to make him understand. And then she stopped, telephone in hand. The shower was still running, but now there was a closer sound. The door directly above slammed shut, and heavy footsteps came down the stairs. They stopped in front of her door, and there was a silence of several seconds before they slowly walked away. Emily dropped the telephone into the cradle and hurried to the window. Tod Haynes was crossing the patio. His shoulders sagged and his head was down, and under one arm he carried something wrapped in a newspaper. It could have been a saw.

Emily was terrified, but she had to know. She waited until he disappeared down the driveway; then she got the pass key. She slipped upstairs unnoticed and unlocked the door of 5B. Inside, all was darkness except for the light showing in the bathroom. She waited until her eyes adjusted to the shadows. Standing near the door was a trunk. Around it, tied tightly, was the rope. Hanging from the rope was a shipping tag addressed—as she could see by the light from the bathroom—to Mrs. Haynes. She moved forward, giving the trunk a wide margin. The bathroom was a magnet. Proceeding toward it, her foot touched something glittering on the floor. She picked it up. It was a liquor glass, still smelling of whisky.

Emily stepped inside the bathroom. The shower was going at full pressure; steam billowed over the top of the enclosure until it was difficult to see across the small room. She had to learn what was behind those frosted doors; but, for the moment, she was paralyzed. Nowhere in her journey to the shower had she seen anything of Mrs. Haynes.

But Emily wasn't alone in the apartment. She knew that the instant the bathroom door slammed shut behind her. She screamed and whirled about. The doorknob was still turning. She grabbed it with both hands and pulled with all her strength against whoever might be outside—trying to pull it open—until her fingers found the lock …

Emily's scream was penetrating, and it went on for a long time. Long enough for all the residents of Roxbury Haven to crowd outside apartment 5B, where they stood helpless before a locked door until Tod Haynes came bounding up the stairs two steps at a time. As he hurriedly unlocked the door, the two policemen Fanny Brady had thoughtfully summoned from a passing patrol car, shouldered through the group. They went directly to the bathroom, the source of the now weakening screams, and pounded on the door with an authority that brought response. Bedraggled, dripping and babbling hysterically, Emily emerged from the steaming interior.

"Why, Mrs. Proctor," Tod exclaimed, "whatever have you been doing in my shower?"

She stared at him—horrified.

"Murderer!" she gasped.

All around Emily was a tight ring of faces—her incredulous and astonished tenants. Nobody seemed to understand.

"Murderer!" she repeated. "He cut her up in the shower with a saw. He's got her remains stuffed in a trunk!"

Tod Haynes said nothing at all. One of the policemen went into the bathroom and turned off the shower, revealing a stall completely free of bloodstains or bone fragments. The saw was found on the kitchen sink.

"I got it to trim that magnolia branch hanging over the balcony," Tod explained. "It's been knocking me in the head for a year."

Now everything seemed to be happening in a dream. One of the officers peeked outside and came back rubbing his forehead where it had contacted the magnolia tree. That left only the trunk—which was opened to reveal nothing but Mrs. Haynes' clothing, including the hooded raincoat. While truth seeped slowly through the confusion in Emily's mind, Tod casually lit a cigarette, glanced at the mouthpiece and then wiped the last trace of lipstick from a corner of his mouth.

"It was you!" Emily cried. "You're the one who came back! You're Mrs. Haynes!"

Everybody stared at Emily, strangely.

"I think we've got a live one," said the officer who took Emily's arm. "Come along, lady. I know a nice doctor who'll enjoy talking to you."

Emily was helpless. She felt herself being drawn along through the group of her astonished tenants, and she knew Tod Haynes had contrived the whole affair in order to discredit her. Nobody, she was sure, would ever believe anything she said again.

But at the doorway, they were stopped by a man in a raincoat who was almost as confused as Emily.

"I've been ringing the bell downstairs," he said, "but nobody answers. I've got a subpoena for —" He paused to read from the paper in his hand. "—Mrs. Emily Proctor—witness: Haynes versus Haynes."

Emily looked quickly at Tod—in time to catch what no one else saw or could have understood: a smile of deep satisfaction.

Won't Somebody Help Me?

It was like any other hospital except for the bars over the windows. The bars over the windows, the lock on the door, and the heavy wire cage where they put patients who became violent. But beyond violence is a quiet place where all cries fade to muted whimpers in the mind—until nothing remains but staring silence and no hope at all ...

The first time the strange thing happened to Lonnie, his wife, Venita, was more puzzled than afraid. It wasn't easy to be afraid of Lonnie, quiet and gentle as he was. Those were the things that had attracted her to him that night at the dance on Ocean Park pier. She had been a conspicuous extra—the visiting cousin from Tulare taken along because there was nothing else to do with her; and he had been the only male on the stag line who seemed to notice her. Venita was an almost pretty girl, but shy; Lonnie was tall and sort of good-looking in an awkward way, and when he asked her to dance she felt an excitement she'd never known in all her seventeen years. They had three dances in virtual silence, then went out to inspect his new Chevy. Lonnie was quiet there, too, but persuasive.

On the following Saturday they drove the Chevy to Las Vegas and were married. All Venita knew about her husband was that his father was a preacher in a small town in Texas, that he'd run away from home when he was fifteen, had been working in an aircraft plant for the past five years, and had saved enough money for the down payment on a six-room stucco house. All he knew about Venita was that she was an orphan from Tulare who didn't want to go back. It wasn't much to begin with, but in four and a half years Venita hadn't been sorry—or afraid.

Sometimes she did worry. Lonnie worked too hard. It was as if he had someone standing over him, whip in hand, driving him every waking moment. Dr. Barbour noticed it the time Lonnie got the flu and had to stay home for a week. It was when Stevie, the first baby, was only a few months old and the unpaid bills were still cluttering up the buffet. Lonnie wanted to keep on working. He was getting sick leave, but no overtime.

"Your husband is a driving man, Mrs. Payne," the doctor told her. "He wants to stay on his feet until he drops. Where does he think he's going in such a hurry?"

That might have been the first trouble sign; but Venita didn't realize it, and Dr. Barbour was a nice old man who spent more time with his rose bushes than with the patients and wasn't looking for complications. And Lonnie never drove anyone but himself. He was wonderful to her and kind to the children. After the twins were born, Venita had been weak and nervous. Lonnie was still getting overtime then, but he'd come home after a long day at the factory and do the babies' laundry while she put dinner on the table, and then, on nice evenings, ask Mrs. Mandell next door to stay with the children while he took her for a drive in the hills. There was one favorite spot where they could park under the trees, open a few cans of beer, and watch the moon come up. Lonnie would talk then—talk about his big plans, of all he was going to do for her and the children. That was Lonnie—a sweet guy with no temper at all. That's why she was puzzled the first time the strangeness came over him.

It was one evening at dinner. Bobby was in his high chair, crying. Stevie and the twins had been good-natured, healthy babies; but Bobby was fussy and inclined to catch everything that came along. Maybe babies could catch things that hadn't come yet, that were just on the way. Venita thought of that later; but on this particular evening she knew exactly what was wrong.

"It's the shots," she told Lonnie. "I took Bobby down to the clinic for shots today. I took all the children. It's free you know."

Lonnie didn't so much as look up. He was eating his franks and beans without seeming to hear, see, or even taste anything.

"It's a good thing something's free," he muttered.

"I asked why Bobby doesn't gain weight as fast as the other children did," Venita added, "and they said it was too early to tell—that I should come back when he gets over the shots."

"Maybe he isn't supposed to gain weight," Lonnie said.

That was the first strange thing. The words were surprising; they didn't seem to make sense.

"Not supposed to—?" she echoed.

"The Lord giveth and the Lord taketh away."

"Lonnie! What an awful thing to say!"

Lonnie put down his fork. He looked at her for several seconds—just as if he'd never seen her before and then he looked at each of the children in the same way.

"Lonnie—"

She thought he was sick, but she couldn't reach him. He pushed back his chair and left the table. Before she could come to her feet, the front door had slammed behind him.

It was late when Lonnie returned—almost midnight. He came in quietly, the way he'd done during the years when there was so much overtime, and undressed in the bathroom so as not to awaken anyone. The room remained dark when he came in and got into bed beside her.

"Lonnie—"

He was flat on his back staring at the ceiling. She pulled closer to him, brushing her face against his bare shoulder. It was a signal they had. They were human beings and sometimes they quarreled—to be exact, sometimes Venita quarreled. Lonnie wouldn't really quarrel. He'd go off alone, as he'd done this night, and not return until he was all over being offended. Then, when they were alone, she'd draw near to him and soon everything would be all right. But it was different this night. When she reached out and placed her arm across his chest, she could feel his body go rigid. He didn't actually pull away from her, but he didn't respond. After a while Venita drew back her arm and leaned away from his shoulder. The last time she looked at him before falling asleep, he was still staring at the ceiling.

On payday Venita learned that Lonnie had received his notice.

If it hadn't happened so suddenly, it might have been easier on Lonnie; but the cancellation of a government contract was somehow as final as death.

"It's the same for everybody," Lonnie explained. "The Chief Engineer got severance just like the rest of us."

"Maybe the company will get a new contract," Venita said. "Or maybe those men from Seattle—"

Lonnie cut her short.

"That was last winter when they started the layoffs. Seattle is in worse shape than Los Angeles now. Nobody's hiring. That's all the guys have been talking about for months. Nobody's hiring anymore."

"Then there'll be some other kind of job."

"I'm a tail assembler," Lonnie said. "That's all I've ever been—a tail assembler."

He was frightened. When Venita realized that, she tried to encourage him. There was the employment insurance—twenty-six weeks it would run. That was six months—something would turn up in half a year. Wasn't that what the Employment Office was for—to find jobs for men and men for jobs? The state didn't want to pay out that money any more than Lonnie wanted to accept it; they'd place him in no time at all. Meanwhile, it would be fun to have him around the house. They'd never had much chance to get acquainted, with him working such long hours for so many years. Besides, there were things to do: screens to paint, a garden to spade—

In the fourth week of the layoff, Mrs. Mandell spoke to Venita over the back fence.

"I never seen a man with such energy," she said. "Look at your husband, Mrs. Payne. All afternoon digging in the hot sun!"

Venita left the fence and walked back to him. Some men worked in a garden to relax; Lonnie might have been digging for gold. He stopped to wipe the sweat from his face as she reached him, and the sun in his eyes gave him a glassy stare.

"My old man used to say I was the laziest boy he knew," he re marked. "I'd chop more cotton in half a day than he could chop in two, but he still said I was lazy."

"Lonnie," Venita said softly, "don't—"

"I'm not lazy, Venita."

"I know that, Lonnie."

"They just don't have a job for me."

"They will have soon. The papers keep saying they will."

"But next week's Stevie's birthday, and we promised him a three wheeler."

"And he'll get one later. Maybe for Christmas."

"Christmas—"

Lonnie leaned on the spade, staring off at something only he could see. Just when Venita had decided he wasn't going to speak again, he said:

"I never did believe it."

"Believe what, Lonnie?"

"That stuff about Joseph and Mary and the angel of the Lord. My old man said I was a black sinner and would suffer for sure. A real black sinner."

And then Lonnie went back to punishing the earth with his spade.

On the sixteenth week of the layoff, Lonnie drew a job reference. It didn't materialize. He had started working when jobs were easy and all anybody needed was an able body and enough common sense to follow orders. Now times had changed.

"They wanted a college man," Lonnie told her. "Can you imagine—a college man! High School at the very least. I could have done the work. I've worked since I was fourteen."

"Maybe you could go to night school," Venita suggested.

"At my age? I'd feel silly."

"But people lots older than you go to night school. You have the time—"

She didn't say anymore. There was a darkness that came over Lonnie's face at times and a sudden turning away. It wasn't fun to have him home anymore.

Lonnie's birthday fell on the twenty-fifth week. Finances were getting awfully tight by that time; but Venita asked Mrs. Mandell to stay with the children, then splurged on a couple of steaks and half a dozen cans of beer so they could drive up to the mountains and be alone again. It had been a long time, but the old camping spot and its magic hadn't changed. The tension between them ebbed away, and as the beer ran low and the moon lifted high, Lonnie came back to her. It was good. It was so good that all the evil days fell away and there was nothing to fear ...

Three weeks after the unemployment insurance ran out, Venita went to Dr. Barbour. Lonnie drove her to the office in his old Chevy. One of the pistons had been knocking badly for months, but there wasn't anything they could do about it. It was tough because it meant less would come of the For Sale sign that Lonnie had lettered on the rear window.

He was sitting in the waiting room when she came out. He looked up at her and for the first time Venita was afraid. His eyes had a cornered look—like those of an animal that's been kicked and beaten and awaits the next blow. Dr. Barbour was so cheerful with his congratulations that she had the dread suspicion Lonnie would have liked to kill him on the spot. Driving home, she tried to be optimistic. She still had relatives in Tulare. Maybe they could borrow—

"I used to make a hundred dollars a week," Lonnie said. "More with overtime. Remember the week I got so much extra time there was a hundred and sixty bucks?"

Lonnie's knuckles were white on the steering wheel.

"I remember," she said. "And you'll make that again—more even."

"No, not anymore."

"Lonnie, don't say such things! We're so young—"

"Not anymore," he repeated. "It's the judgment. The sins of the fathers visited on the children."

By this time Venita had learned there was nothing to do when Lonnie got into such a mood but let him talk it out. Later it would be as if nothing had happened. That evening, after dinner, he went out and came back with a quart of ice cream for the children, and they had a little celebration and the usual instructions about helping Mama by being good. Lonnie was in high spirits then.

"I've been thinking," he told Venita, after all the children were in bed, "and I've got this thing figured out. It's been in my mind, see? I hated taking that insurance money. It hurt my pride being lined up and asked all those questions every week. Well, that's all over now. I'm my own free man again and now I've really got something to work for. I'll get a job this week. You'll see. I'll get a swell job this week—a hundred, a hundred and a quarter at least!"

He almost sobbed the last words, and that was the real beginning of her fear. From that night on Venita never relaxed.

The first time Venita spoke to Dr. Barbour about Lonnie, the old man almost laughed in her face. Something wrong with Lonnie? Why, he'd known the young man since the first time they came to see him, when she was expecting Stevie. A fine young man—loyal, dependable, hard-working.

"But that's just it," Venita protested. "He isn't working. He hasn't worked for such a long time that he's lost confidence in himself. He acts so strange and says such strange things—things I don't understand. Then, when I ask him what he means, he doesn't remember having said anything at all."

Dr. Barbour stopped laughing, but his eyes still smiled. "Do you know," he said, "that Mrs. Barbour is always accusing me of that very thing? Now, Mrs. Payne, you've been in a family way often enough to know how your nerves can play tricks on you at such a time. Lonnie has a lot on his mind, that's all. If he's worrying about my fee, tell him to stop. His credit's good with me. I have faith in that young man, and I think you had better have faith in him too."

Faith. The word sounded fine and strong in Dr. Barbour's office; but Lonnie was sick. No matter what anyone said, Venita knew that. There are sicknesses people recognize and understand: measles or chicken pox or something organic; but Lonnie's sickness was more dangerous. He was like a man drowning on dry land, with no way to reach him because he didn't know anything was wrong.

After a while he stopped looking for work, and something inside him began to die. He never left the house, except to work in the yard or play with the children. He seemed to be ashamed for the neighbors to see him at home. In the evening he took to watching an evangelist on television until it was a relief when a tube blew out and there was no money to replace it. Once in a while he talked big again, reminding her of all the money he used to make and of all the money he would make when that good job came along. It was no use trying to talk him into settling for anything less. Lonnie would just close up and not talk at all. It was a time of terrible tension and strain, never knowing when or how the breaking point would come.

And then Bobby took sick. He'd never been really well, and when the cough developed, nothing Dr. Barbour or the clinic could do seemed to help at all. It was a torturous thing—hard on the baby and nerve-wracking for everyone else. They moved the crib into their own bedroom so he wouldn't disturb the other children, and that only brought it closer to them.

On the third night Venita awakened with a start. She always slept at the edge of awareness now. She turned her head and saw that Lonnie wasn't in the bed bedside her. Bobby! The thought came with a sharp wrench of panic that brought her up to a sitting position in the bed. The night light wasn't on; but she could see Lonnie's tall shadow standing over the crib looking down. Bobby was quiet.

"Lonnie—"

She whispered the word, sliding out of bed to stand beside him.

"Lonnie, what's wrong?"

She thought at first that he hadn't heard her. He didn't move and his face was an expressionless mask in the pale window light. Then he said, "Do you remember Job?"

"Who?" Venita asked.

"A man in the Bible—a rich man. Then the Devil came and took everything away from him—his riches, his wife, his children. One by one, they were all taken away."

"Lonnie!"

She almost screamed his name. It was terrifying to hear him say such things over Bobby's crib. The sound startled him. She saw the dazed shock come into his eyes as he stared first at the crib, then back at the bed, trying to realize why he was on his feet. Then Bobby, awakened by the sound, began to whimper. Instantly, Lonnie had the child in his arms.

"Poor little fellow—Daddy's little fellow. Hush, now. You're safe, sonny. You're safe with Daddy. Venita, where's that medicine the doctor left? No, don't you go looking for it in your nightgown. You get back into bed. I'll take care of it—"

Lonnie trailed off down the hall to the bathroom, still consoling the baby on his shoulder, and Venita stood alone with the dread flowing through her like cold poison. Lonnie was two men! She'd seen it— there in the darkened room she'd seen two men in one. He was sweet and gentle and kind; but way down in the depth of him was an awful darkness that the worry and strain were bringing to the surface. And what if the dark Lonnie came all the way? What if the Lonnie she loved—the Lonnie who loved her and his children—was lost completely?

She couldn't go back to bed—not now. The things he'd been saying at Bobby's crib wouldn't let her. She found her robe and slippers, hurrying in order to get away before he returned from the bathroom. He'd ask questions for which there were no answers.

The telephone had been taken out months ago; but Mrs. Mandell knew Bobby wasn't well and had said they could use hers any time, day or night. Because it was night, Venita came to the door with her now heavy body encased in a loose flannel robe and her graying hair wound up in curlers. Of course Mrs. Payne could use the telephone! Was it Bobby? Was the poor dear worse? Venita didn't try to explain. She was half crying by the time her ringing aroused Dr. Barbour and her mind fumbled for words.

"Dr. Barbour, could you come please. No, it's not Bobby. I mean, yes, he's still got the cough, but that's not why I called you. It's the other— what we talked about before."

He was an old man and he didn't awaken easily. She tried again, but she couldn't say too much with Mrs. Mandell hovering anxiously at her shoulder.

"Don't you remember, Doctor? I told you I was afraid, terribly afraid—"

"Now, Mrs. Payne, have you been having a bad dream? Why don't you take some of those sleeping pills I left with you and have a good night's sleep?"

"But I'm afraid. I have to talk to you—"

"Tomorrow, Mrs. Payne. I'll stop by first thing in the morning. We'll all sit down together over a pot of hot coffee and talk this thing out. Everything will be all right. You'll see."

There was nothing more she could do. Could she tell him Lonnie had frightened her, talking about a man named Job? He would laugh at her again. She was only an overwrought expectant mother having the usual foolish fears. She placed the telephone back on its cradle. It was too heavy to hold any longer.

"Such a shame," Mrs. Mandell said, "such an awful shame! A nice young couple with so much trouble coming all at once. You can be grateful you got such a considerate husband."

"Yes," Venita said numbly.

"I always say, a woman with a considerate husband—she's rich no matter what happens. You look tired, my dear. A cup of tea, maybe?"

Mrs. Mandell waited for an answer, her head cocked to one side like a motherly hen clucking over her flock. Warm, sympathetic—and so far away there was no use even trying to reach her.

"No," Venita said. "No, thank you. I have to get back now. Thank you for the use of the telephone."

She was more than tired; she was defeated. She went back to a house that was completely quiet again, and that made the whole thing seem just a bad dream. Perhaps Dr. Barbour was right after all. Just a bad dream. Lonnie had left the light burning in the bathroom, and a part of her weary mind remembered the need to keep the bills down. She turned it out on her way back to bed. In the bedroom the nightlight was burning and by its dim light she could see Lonnie putting Bobby back into the crib. She watched him from the doorway, his long, lanky body bent nearly double over the low bed. The baby was quiet now, but Lonnie didn't move. Puzzled, Venita walked closer to the crib until she could look down into it— and then she screamed.

"No—Lonnie! No!"

For just an instant she was paralyzed with horror—but instants were precious. Lonnie was pressing the pillow down against Bobby's face. It took all her strength to drag him away. He was like a robot that had been set to do a certain task and couldn't hear or respond to anything but force. All her strength—and where it came from she didn't know. Only one thing did she know then—the pillow. She had to get that pillow away from Lonnie ...

It was just like any other hospital if she didn't look at the windows, and she didn't. She looked at Lonnie. He stood beside the bed gazing down at her with love, pity, and something vague and faraway in his eyes. She was too sleepy to analyze it. The sedation they'd given her was taking hold, and she couldn't remember very much anymore.

When he stooped down and kissed her lightly on the forehead, it seemed as if she must have had the baby already and this was the customary first visit.

But that wasn't right. There was still something nagging at her mind, something left over from the turmoil and violence that had preceded silence. A scene. Three people in the scene. No, just two people at first—just Lonnie standing beside her at Bobby's crib with a wild, bewildered expression in his eyes.

"Venita, what are you doing with that pillow? What are you doing?"

She did have the pillow by then. She had it after ripping it out of his hands.

"What are you doing, Venita? What have you done?"

He didn't remember. The struggle for the pillow had brought him to his senses, and now he believed only what he saw. The pillow was in her hands, not his. He turned back to the crib. Bobby was alive and whimpering. Bobby was safe.

"Thank God for that!" Mrs. Mandell exclaimed. "Thank God, Mr. Payne! Thank God you stopped her in time!"

Now the third person was in the scene, summoned by Venita's scream; but she had everything wrong, too. It wasn't that way, Mrs. Mandell. It wasn't the way it looks!

"The poor dear. We should have realized that she was going to pieces. Call the doctor, Mr. Payne. Call him now—right away. The poor, poor dear—"

But it wasn't that way—it wasn't that way at all!

The scene faded into warm, creeping nothingness until there was nothing but Lonnie's face above her. Sweet Lonnie. Gentle Lonnie. Loyal in spite of all the things she'd said and sobbed about him. Useless things because nobody believed her. Hadn't Mrs. Mandell seen her with the pillow still in her hands, and didn't Dr. Barbour remember how upset she had been on the telephone? He knew what had to be done.

Lonnie's face began to float away.

"Now you have a good rest, honey," he said. "That's all the doctors say you need—a real good rest. And don't you worry about anything at home. You know I'll take good care of the children. You know that, don't you?"

He smiled and even through the smile that strange thing was in his eyes. He turned and walked down the aisle toward the door that would lock him out and lock her in, and with every step she wanted to cry out and run after him; but the drug was as strong as a straitjacket, and there was nothing left of protest but the whimper in her mind.

"Don't let him go—please don't let him go to the children! He's the sick one—can't you see? Won't somebody see? Won't somebody help me?"

Cop's Day Off

Sam Ward had worked hard for the Detective Lieutenant's badge in his pocket, and he never stopped working. That was the mystery around headquarters—what made Sammy run so hard?

He didn't seem particularly ambitious. He wasn't prodding Captain Norton for his job, or aspiring to a place on the D.A.'s staff; and he'd never been a glory boy looking for headlines. He was just a cop who worked hard. He never stopped, he never relaxed, he seldom smiled.

"Sam," Captain Norton said, "what are you doing down here today? Isn't this supposed to be your day off?"

Sam, who was thirty-six, but appeared older because of the pinched lines about his eyes and mouth, looked up from his desk with an almost guilty cringe.

"I'm just running through some of the unsolved files," he said.

"Well, stop running through them," the Captain snapped. "You look terrible. You've got bags under your eyes, and your skin's the color of old library paste. I want you out of here. Ray, take Sam with you."

Ray Moreno had the same kind of badge in his pocket, but he'd come by it with less strain. His face could still smile—wide, with the white teeth flashing.

"I'm meeting my wife at the airport, Captain. She's coming in from Mexico City."

"Okay. So take Sam down to meet your wife. Or drop him off at the ballpark. Do something. I'm getting tired of seeing him in here every day. You'd think a married man might at least have a lawn to mow."

When the Captain was in that kind of mood there was only one thing to do about it. Sam got up from his desk and followed Moreno outside. It was a nice day—clear, no haze, with a fair wind blowing in off the ocean that would grow stronger as they drove south.

"Don't let the Captain burn you," Moreno said. "He rides me, too. But this time, he's right. The taxpayers aren't going to remember you one day longer if you kill yourself on the job."

Sam stared out of the window and said nothing. It was the best way he knew to change the subject of an unwanted conversation and it worked. Moreno went on.

"I know what I'm going to find at that airport—a basket full of bottles. Every time my wife flies down to visit her family, she comes back with another one of those hand-woven baskets full of bottles from the glass-blowing factory. Blue bottles, brown bottles, purple bottles—the house is so full of them now that I've been threatening to add another wing. Does your wife collect anything, Sam?"

There was the old standard reply, "Nothing but my pay check,"—but Sam didn't give it. "No, she doesn't," he said.

"You're a lucky man," Moreno said. "When a woman gets started collecting something there's just no—hey, what's going on up there? Looks like somebody's hurt."

Moreno disliked the Freeway. He'd turned off on a side street—one of the numerous shortcuts he knew so well—and now, sliding up over a small rise, they were suddenly in the midst of a mob scene in the middle of the street. Moreno touched the siren button to clear passage and wheeled the sedan to the curb. By this time they could see a tiny form lying in the street. Moreno had his door open before he cut the motor. Even so, Sam beat him to the spot.

The victim was a child—a seven or eight-year-old girl. She had been struck down by an auto—that was obvious even before the volunteered information erupted from the spectators. She was unconscious. No visible wounds but possible internal injuries. Kneeling beside the child, a panic-stricken woman clenched her own hands together to keep them from reaching out to the victim.

"Don't move her," someone called out from the crowd. "She may have a broken neck."

"Oh, Kathy—"

Moreno knelt beside the woman.

"That's right, lady," he said. "You mustn't move her. Has anyone called for an ambulance?"

"I did," a man said.

The voice was deep and commanding. Sam, who now stood beside Moreno, was forced to turn his eyes away from the child. It was an old man who had spoken the words—tall, white-haired, majestic in appearance. He wore a loose-fitting sweater coat, baggy trousers, and heavy felt slippers on his feet; but there was an authority about him that commanded instant attention.

"I called for the ambulance and the police as soon as I saw it happen," he said. "You came a lot faster than I expected."

"We didn't come in answer to the call," Moreno explained. "We were just passing by."

"That explains it," the man said. "I'm getting too old to stand the shock of seeing the public served by its employees."

Moreno stood up. "The public's employees are spread pretty thin in a growing city," he said. He whipped out a notebook and a pencil. "What's your name, sir?" he asked.

The old man lost a shade of majesty.

"Just because I made a remark about public employees—"

"Forget it," Moreno said. "Everybody makes remarks about public employees. We'd feel neglected if they didn't. I want your name because you said that you saw what happened here."

"Oh. Yes, sir. Yes, sir, I did. My name's Max Schiller. I live right across the street—that's my house with the rocker on the front porch. Ask anyone around here—they'll tell you who I am."

With a murmur of assent behind him, Moreno made note of Schiller's name and. address.

"And you, lady?"

When the woman who had knelt beside the child tried to rise, Sam stepped forward and helped her to her feet. She was light—a small woman and young. Not over twenty-five, Sam guessed. She trembled slightly against his arm.

"Sally Grossman," she said. "I live here." She nodded at the house behind Moreno's shoulder. "But Kathy isn't my child. She's Kathy Lambert. She lives down in the corner house. Her parents are divorced. Her mother works. Kathy ran out into the street after Susie—that's her cat, her Siamese cat."

Suddenly fear leaped into her eyes.

"Bobby—?" she called. "Where's Bobby?"

"I'm here, Mom."

A boy wriggled through the crowd to reach his mother. He was possibly ten—thin and awkward in his tee shirt and denims. The woman's hands grasped his shoulders protectively and he grimaced in disgust.

"I came out to call Bobby," Mrs. Grossman continued, "and I saw Kathy up the street playing with her cat. She's such a sweet girl and alone so much. The cat is a companion to her. Then, all of a sudden, Susie jumped out of Kathy's arms and darted across the street. I think Kathy must have seen the car corning and was afraid for Susie. She ran after her. I screamed and Kathy went down in front of the car. I think I screamed." The woman looked about for confirmation.

"Somebody screamed—I think it was me."

"What kind of car was it?" Moreno asked.

"Car?" Mrs. Grossman seemed helpless.

"A '59 Impala convertible," Bobby Grossman announced loudly. "Pale blue—"

"Bobby, be quiet," his mother ordered. "That's all he talks about, Officer. He wants his father to buy a blue Impala convertible. As for the car that struck poor Kathy—oh, I don't know. It happened so fast and all I could think of was the child."

"The driver didn't stop?"

"Oh, no! That's what makes it all so horrible. The car just kept right on going."

Moreno turned to Max Schiller, who stood all this time like a prophet waiting to be called for testimony. Before the question could be asked he said, "It was a sedan. A big, gray sedan. A Buick. Not a new one—six, seven years old, maybe. I sat there on my porch across the street and watched him come up over the rise. He never slacked speed—never thought about a child playing in the street."

"He?" Moreno echoed. "Are you sure it was a man?"

"Look," Schiller said. "Do you see that delivery truck backing out of the driveway three doors down? What's the lettering on the side of it?"

Moreno was puzzled. Sam followed the direction of his gaze. A truck was pulling out of a driveway, but it was old and unwashed. The lettering was indistinct.

"Ralph's TV Repair Service," the old man read aloud. "Call MA 6-078—Oops, there he goes and I missed the last number. And that's without glasses. Seventy-two years old and no glasses. Ask anyone around here."

"That's true," Mrs. Grossman volunteered. "Mr. Schiller reads the finest print—the Bible, even, without glasses. If he says it was a Buick—"

"It was an Impala," Bobby protested.

"A gray Buick," Schiller repeated, "driven by a man. A young man. They think of nothing but themselves, these young men. They don't care how many children they kill—"

The sound of the ambulance siren cut off Schiller's commentary. The crowd fanned out and flattened against the curb. Grim men had grim work to do. Moments later, a police car arrived. By this time Moreno had the story organized. They could get out an immediate alert for a gray Buick sedan, six or seven years old, driven by a young man. It would show signs of an accident—the impact had been hard and there were fragments of glass on the street. Moreno was ready to continue to the airport.

"Go ahead," Sam said, "I'm too late for the ball game now. I'll go back in the other car ..."

"The Captain won't be happy to see you," Moreno cautioned.

"He can look the other way," Sam answered.

Moreno drove away and Sam waited on the curb until the ambulance had gone. The questioning over, old Max Schiller ambled across the street and sat down in his rocking chair. He looked like a white-crowned eagle on self-imposed sentry duty over the street. Mrs. Grossman, Bobby in tow, started back to her own house.

"Does he always sit like that?" Sam asked.

"Mr. Schiller?" The woman paused and looked back over her shoulder. "Yes, most of the time," she said.

"Ever since Johnny ran off with that old woman," Bobby piped.

"Bobby! You get into the house this instant! Scoot, now!" A slap on the rear sent Bobby on his way, but not soon enough.

"Johnny," Sam repeated. "Who is Johnny?"

"Old Mr. Schiller's grandson."

"And he ran away?"

- "Yes, about four months ago. He'd been keeping company with an older woman. It upset the old man, naturally. Johnny's parents were killed when he was a child. Johnny was all Mr. Schiller had."

"So that's why he sits on the front porch," Sam mused. "Johnny—"

It was all in the Missing Persons file—among the unclosed cases. John Schiller—20. White. Dark brown hair. Gray eyes. Height—5'-9". Weight—140 pounds. Distinguishing marks: anchor and coiled serpent tattooed on right forearm. Believed to have eloped with Sandy Downes, sometimes known as Andrea Dawn, entertainer. Schiller has served one hitch in the Navy. Radio technician. Has worked as drummer in nightclubs, gas station attendant, radio repairman. Believed to have gone to Las Vegas.

The report was accompanied by a photograph of a dark-haired, good-looking young man in the uniform of an apprentice seaman. In spite of his youth, John Schiller had very solemn, searching eyes. A woman would consider them romantic.

That was all. There was no indication of any investigation or subsequent reports. The case was dated nearly six months past—Mrs.

Grossman had been a little off in her memory. Sam Ward studied the file for a few minutes and then went to Captain Norton.

"I thought I told you to go to a ball game," Norton admonished.

"I was with Moreno when he came across the hit-and-run," Sam explained. "The Lambert girl."

Norton's face darkened. "I just heard from the hospital. She's in a critical condition. If she dies, it means a manslaughter charge."

"Against a young man driving a gray Buick sedan," Sam said.

It was the way he said it that caused Norton to look at him in a listening way. Sam Ward wasn't a great talker. When he did talk, it meant that something was on his mind.

"What do you want?" Norton asked.

Sam handed him the file.

"I want to look for John Schiller," he said.

"Any particular reason?"

Sam hesitated. "Call it a hunch," he said.

"All right," Norton sighed. "If that's what you'd rather do than go to a ball game, go ahead. It's your day off."

The trouble with missing person cases, was that there were too many of them. If John Schiller had been a minor teenage girl, for example—more of a search would have been made. But he wasn't a minor, and he'd committed no crime except to break an old man's heart.

In this case, a call to the Las Vegas police for a check of the marriage mills would have covered the situation.

But when a grown man and woman went off together, it didn't necessarily mean Las Vegas. One thing was certain: in nearly six months' time, two people had to eat. John Schiller hadn't come from a fashionable neighborhood—there was no reason to believe he'd gone off with a bankroll. And who was this Sandy Downes—or Andrea Dawn? An entertainer, the report said. But no one Sam had ever heard of. Entertainers weren't exactly a scarcity in Los Angeles; but if an entertainer worked, she had to be registered somewhere.

Sam spent the next half hour on the telephone and came up with the information that Sandy Downes, a singer, had last been booked at the Blue Pussycat, a night club in Santa Monica. Sam put on his hat and started traveling.

The Blue Pussycat was as uninviting in mid-afternoon as any similar establishment. It was a place designed for the lower echelon trade. The bar was open but deserted, except for a bartender and one customer who appeared to be a permanent fixture. Sam flashed his badge and was directed to the owner, who was in his office with his tax accountant.

"My master," the owner explained. "In the old days, Lieutenant, a man with no education except from the school of hard knocks could take a few dollars, plus a lot of guts, and make out in this world; but those days are gone forever. Sit down and have a cigar, Lieutenant. And, Roger, be sure and make a note—one cigar in the deductions for good will."

Roger was a neatly dressed young man with an Ivy League haircut and heavy, black-rimmed glasses. He seemed completely humorless. By contrast, the owner, whose name was Mike Adamic, was in shirt sleeves, had no hair except a gray shadow circling above his ears, and laughed as easily as a man who's about to lose his last dollar. When Sam stated his mission, Adamic's forced joviality faded.

"Sandy?" he said. "Sure, I remember her. I've booked Sandy in and out ever since she was a kid. She had plenty of spark in those days. This last engagement was pitiful. I wanted to cancel after the first week, but what can you do? If I didn't have such a big heart, Roger wouldn't have me handcuffed. I let her stay the full six weeks—just for old times' sake."

"When was that?" Sam asked.

Adamic turned to Roger. "Tell the lieutenant when," he said.

"Last name?" Roger queried. Adamic grinned up at Sam.

"You see? Just like Univac. The last name, Roger, is Downes. Sandy Downes."

Roger picked up a ledger from the stack on the desk and thumbed through it until his index finger came to rest under a certain notation.

"Downes, Sandy," he read aloud. "April 7, '59 through May 12, '59. Salary—$200 per week. Total paid out: $1200, less federal income tax and unemployment insurance."

"Beautiful," Adamic said.

"April to May," Sam mused. "That makes it almost six months since she terminated. Tell me, Mr. Adamic, was Miss Downes keeping company with anyone at the time she worked here?"

Adamic raised his eyebrows. "Lieutenant, I'm not a chaperone—" he began. But by this time Sam had pulled the photograph of John Schiller out of his coat pocket, and at the sight of it Adamic's expression changed.

"Sure, I remember. The kid," he said. "Johnny something-or-other.

What's wrong, Lieutenant, is he in trouble?"

"I wouldn't be surprised," Sam said.

He stayed just long enough to get Sandy Downes' address when she was employed at the Blue Pussycat, plus a publicity still which showed what happened to a once lovely blonde who had stood under the spotlights and listened to the loud music a little too long. Her smile already had a trace of hardness, and the retoucher couldn't take the disillusionment out of her eyes. She was at the stage where she needed the love of youth, and John Schiller was an orphan looking for his mother.

The address was that of a fashionable apartment hotel fronting on the ocean, and the story was short and sad. Sandy Downes had lived there until three months ago, only to leave suddenly, owing to the embarrassing inability to pay her rent. She had left no forwarding address, and a considerable amount of mail had accumulated consisting chiefly of inquiries from skip-tracers.

"Her brother was with her most of the time she was here," the manager concluded. "He left no forwarding address, either."

"Her brother?" Sam brought out the photo of John Schiller and handed it to the manager.

"Yes, that's the young man. Nice looking—but you can't tell by faces, can you?"

"You can't tell by faces," Sam agreed.

As Sam prepared to leave the building, the afternoon papers were delivered to the foyer. He paused to read the front page. The Kathy Lambert story was in it. Her condition was still critical—she had yet to regain consciousness. The police were searching for a gray Buick sedan as described by an eyewitness. Sam scanned the story quickly and put the paper aside. He was still searching for two people who had to eat.

Mike Adamic's human Univac had noted two deductions from Sandy Downes' salary. The federal government didn't give out information; but the California Department of Employment was more cooperative. Sam consulted a telephone directory for the location of the local branch and continued his search.

Beyond the multiple lines of weary humanity edging toward the cashiers' windows were offices; and inside one of the offices was another human Univac—Sam was struck by how little they differed from one another in appearance—who, in due time, divulged that the department had no Sandy Downes listed among its clientele. But it did have an Andrea Dawn.

"Currently collecting?" Sam asked.

"Currently," he was told. "But not for long. She has only three weeks compensation still due her."

"And when does she receive the next payment?"

"Are you familiar with Miss Down's or Downes' appearance, Lieutenant?"

"I have her photograph," Sam said.

"Then, if you're not too late or she's not too early, you should be able to spot her in the lineup at window four. I'll check with the cashier—"

Sam didn't wait for more. Outside the office, the lines of weary humanity now became individuals with faces and bodies. Sometimes luck was with you; sometimes it wasn't. It hadn't been with Kathy Lambert; but it was with Sam when he took a spectator's position in view of window four.

It was getting late in the afternoon; the line was short. He hadn't long to wait before a tall, blonde woman marched through the front doors and headed toward the window. Even without the publicity photo he would have recognized Sandy Downes. Faded she might be, but she still made the others in the room look dowdy by comparison. Her Capri pants were skintight; her blouse was blazing red; and her blonde head tossed back like a startled colt when he stepped forward and called her by name.

"Miss Downes—"

She didn't speak. She gave him one penetrating stare and reached an immediate decision. The decision was to leave—suddenly.

She wheeled past him and hurried toward the side exit. The few seconds in timing that her move cost Sam were enough. By the time he reached the street she was climbing into a car waiting at the curb. He caught a glimpse of the blazing red blouse before the vehicle swung out into the traffic.

A man was driving, and for a moment Sam saw his face clearly. It was John Schiller, and the car he drove was an old gray Buick sedan.

Moreno was back from the airport.

"What do you know?" he was saying. "No bottles this trip! This trip my wife brought back a bongo drum. A four-foot-high bongo drum. When my teenage boy comes home and sees that—wow! I don't think I dare go home."

"Moreno—"

Captain Norton's voice broke up Moreno's tale. He had a message. Sam Ward was waiting at the Employment Office in Santa Monica. He had some interesting information; but he needed a warrant and clearance with the Santa Monica police to make an arrest.

Moreno listened to the story and forgot his bongo troubles. It was a different kind of trouble that sent him speeding out Wilshire.

Sam was waiting with an address he'd obtained from the office— inside.

"What do you use, a crystal ball or a seventh sense?" Moreno demanded. "The old man's grandson! Did he tip you in some way? Is there something I missed?"

"Later," Sam answered, "I'll write my memoirs. Right now—" He shoved the address under Moreno's nose and got in the car.

It wasn't far and it wasn't fashionable. It was one of the older two-story apartment buildings on a street of multiple units that faced one another like evenly matched sparring partners divided by two lanes of spasmodic traffic. Inside, an entry hall and a row of mailboxes.

Sam's finger ran along the names carefully and finally stopped.

"Mr. and Mrs. John Schuyler," he read. "What do you think?"

"I think you've hit it," Moreno said,

"Apartment 7B," Sam said.

They went up together. Daylight was fading, and the upper hall, still unlighted, was deeply shadowed.

They groped their way to the far end of it before finding the right door. Sam listened. Behind the door, the faint sound of jazz came to meet him—a bass viol, a probing trumpet, and the dominating throb of drums. John Schiller was a drummer. Sam listened a moment longer and Moreno pulled his gun.

"I don't trust a hit-and-run," he said. "It takes an unbalanced mind to do a thing like that. This character may be a psycho."

"This character," Sam said quietly, "is a fool." Then he rapped loudly on the door. "Schiller! John Schiller—open the door!"

The jazz stopped instantly. "Schiller—"

There was another sound, a scrambling sound—as if furniture had got in someone's way.

"Okay, Moreno," Sam said.

Moreno was an expert on locks. A professional housebreaker couldn't have done the job more quickly, although he would have done it more quietly. One well-placed shot at close range, and it was only a matter of picking away the splinters.

When Sam kicked open the door, Moreno had the room covered. They were none too soon. A tall, dark-haired youth with a frightened face had scrambled as far as the kitchen door before Moreno's command, backed up by the gun, swung him about and pinned him against the wall.

John Schiller looked more like sixteen than twenty. He stared at the gun in Moreno's hand.

"Don't shoot," he said. "I haven't done anything!"

"Where's the woman?" Moreno demanded.

"I—I don't know what you mean."

"You know what we mean," Sam said. "Where is she, Schiller?"

"My name is Schuyler. John Schuyler. There's been some mistake—"

"Where is she?"

He stopped fighting. "She's gone out," he said.

"Where?"

"To the store—for groceries."

"When?"

"Not long ago. Ten, fifteen minutes."

"Did she take the car?"

"Yes, sure."

"Better get downstairs, Moreno" Sam said. "She may spot the police car when she comes back. And don't worry about Johnny. He isn't going anywhere."

Sam opened his coat to reach for a handkerchief in his back pocket. He wore his service revolver in a shoulder holster. It looked ominous enough to keep John Schiller pinned to the wall even after Moreno had gone.

"Sit down," Sam ordered.

Obediently, Schiller moved to the nearest chair and perched nervously on the edge of the seat.

"Are you happy, Johnny?" Sam asked.

The question wasn't expected. Schiller stared at him.

"What?" he said.

"You've had nearly six months of her. Are you still happy?"

"I don't dig you," the boy began.

"You dig me, all right. You're not married, are you?"

"Not yet. Her divorce isn't final."

"Then clear out."

Schiller half rose from the chair. "Now wait a minute—"

"No, you wait and you listen," Sam said. "Don't try to be noble about this because you're not. You're a silly kid who fell for the flattering attentions of an older woman. But it's not love, Johnny. Not yours and not hers—"

"I do love Sandy!" Schiller protested.

"You loathe her," Sam said. "If it hasn't hit you yet, it will. One of these mornings you'll wake up and go into the bathroom and throw up what's left of your big love affair, and then you'll clear out, Johnny. That's exactly what you'll do, unless you're fool enough to wait around for that divorce."

He was hitting home, hard—he knew that Schiller didn't want to hear the truth.

"But she's down on her luck just now. I can't walk out when she's down on her luck!"

"Why not? Have you got a broken leg? Stop trying to be a hero, Johnny. You're out of uniform now. Sandy Downes is a grown woman. Her luck is what she made it with her big blue eyes wide open. Yours aren't quite open yet—or are they beginning to see the light? The rest of your life, Johnny. That's all you have at stake—the rest of your life."

The lecture ended when Moreno walked in with Sandy Downes. He'd intercepted her in the driveway, and she wasn't happy.

"What is all this?" she demanded.

"What is all this about an accident? Johnny, does it make any sense to you?"

Moreno wasn't happy either.

"Sam," he said, "the gray Buick is down in the driveway, but there's not the slightest indication of it ever hitting Kathy Lambert."

"I know," Sam said. "It didn't."

And while Moreno looked incredulous, Sam explained it to him.

"We're taking Schiller and the woman in on Max Schiller's old complaint—missing persons. Kathy Lambert was struck down by some one driving an Impala convertible—light blue."

Kathy Lambert regained consciousness a little after six p.m. She was young and healthy; she could absorb a lot of punishment and still survive.

An hour later a man who couldn't get along with his conscience saved the police a lot of work by turning himself in. He had been upset about his failing marriage and careless in his driving. The proof of his confession was written on the right front fender of his light blue Impala convertible.

"No crystal ball and no seventh sense," Sam explained to Moreno and Captain Norton. "Just common sense. Who knows more about the different makes and models of cars than any expert in the world?"

"My ten-year-old son," Moreno admitted.

"Exactly. A kid can recognize the make and model of any automobile a block away, and an accident like that doesn't mean to a child what it meant to Mrs. Grossman, for instance. She's a mother. She probably never saw the car. Her only thought was for the child. Max Schiller, on the other hand, is an old man with an obsession. He'd been sitting on his front porch for the past six months with only one thing on his mind—the return of his grandson. How would his grandson return?"

"In a gray Buick sedan?" Captain Norton suggested.

"That was my hunch. The old man must have seen John Schiller and Sandy Downes together in that car. We know he'd seen them together somewhere because of the mention of her in the missing persons report. But there was no more reason to think that he could recognize the make and model of the collision car in the midst of that emotional crisis than Mrs. Grossman could—less reason, perhaps. I doubt if Max Schiller ever owned a car. And yet he gave a positive identification not only of the car but of the driver. I couldn't buy that, Captain. I couldn't believe that old Max Schiller had seen what he claimed to have seen—at least, not with his eyes."

"Not with his eyes?" Norton echoed.

"With his mind," Sam explained. "In his mind, Captain, his grandson was a killer of children when he ran off with that woman—his own children."

"Not only a crystal ball," Moreno remarked, "an analyst as well."

Sam shook his head. "No crystal ball and no analyst—just files. I ran across the Schiller case in the unsolved files just before the Captain ordered me out of the office. Something about it stuck in my mind. When we came across that accident, and one of the witnesses had the same name, I just had to follow my hunch." And then Sam Ward, who never stopped working and never relaxed, gave them one of his rare, sad smiles. "After all, as the Captain said, it was my day off."

It was late when Sam left for home, but he didn't stop to eat on the way. Dixie would have supper warm and ready no matter how late he came in, and she would be eagerly waiting to hear what important case Captain Norton had needed him for this time. He always had to have a good story for Dixie. Tonight he was lucky. Kathy Lambert had made the front pages.

Some of the story he left out—some of the details about John Schiller and the woman he'd gone off with.

"And you found the poor old man's grandson and sent him home!" Dixie exclaimed. "Sammy, aren't you proud of yourself?"

Sam Ward cringed inside every time his wife called him "Sammy." Seventeen years ago, when they had eloped to Las Vegas, it had been a term of endearment; but seventeen years ago Sam had been only nineteen and Dixie only thirty-three. She wasn't exciting or glamorous anymore. She was only a ridiculous woman with the over-pampered face of a rapidly aging child.

"What will they do to the man who confessed?" she demanded.

She didn't really care. It was only a game they played—a pretense that there was something of interest left between them.

"The rest of his life," Sam said sadly.

"The rest of his life? Do you mean he'll get life for an accident that wasn't even fatal?"

For a moment Sam had difficulty remembering who Dixie was talking about. He'd had only one thing on his mind from the time he found the missing person report in the unsolved file.

"No, of course not," he said. "I was thinking of another case—another case, entirely."

The Deadly Mrs. Haversham

The lettering on the door was clear and black: LT. O'KONSKY-HOMICIDE. The woman outside the door hesitated, one neatly gloved hand resting on the doorknob, while her eyes studied the words as carefully as if she were silently spelling out each letter. She was a small woman—slender, smartly dressed in black, and with a certain poise that suggested she might have been a debutante—and a lovely one—some thirty years earlier. Her face was soft, her eyes were sad, and a ghost of a smile touched her lips as she turned the knob with a determined gesture.

Detective Lieutenant O'Konsky sat at his desk reading a newspaper with a lurid headline: HAMMER SLAYER SOUGHT. The door opened quietly, but O'Konsky was suddenly aware of the incongruous aroma of expensive cologne. He looked up and stared at the woman, a mixture of surprise and apprehension struggling with the long-practiced objectivity in his eyes. The newspaper dropped to the desk as he came slowly to his feet. There were occasions when O'Konsky subconsciously remembered that a gentleman was required to rise in the presence of a lady, in spite of the scarcity of ladies encountered on his job.

There was over six feet of O'Konsky standing, but he might have been invisible. The woman came to the desk and looked down at the headline on the abandoned newspaper.

"A terrible thing," she said in a barely audible voice. "A wicked thing!"

O'Konsky inhaled the cologne. "Yes ma'am," he said.

"Murder is such a wicked thing—and this one with a hammer." She shuddered inwardly. "So untidy."

O'Konsky hadn't taken his eyes from the woman, and his eyes weren't happy. She raised her head and gave him a faint smile.

"Do you remember me, Lieutenant?"

O'Konsky nodded.

"The fireplace poker murder last June," she said brightly.

O'Konsky cleared his throat.

"And the rat poison in July," he added.

"July? Was it really July?" The woman frowned over the thought—

then nodded. "Yes, you're right. It was July—but it wasn't rat poison. It was insecticide. Nasty fluid. I've warned our gardener time and time again—" Her voice faded as she looked around the room. A side chair stood on the far side of the lieutenant's desk. "Do you mind if I sit down?"

O'Konsky remembered the rest of his manners. He bounded around the corner of the desk and came back with the chair. He even held it in place for her while she sat down.

"Excuse me," he said. "I was just surprised, Mrs. Haversham—"

"To see me again? Thank you, Lieutenant. Yes, that's much better. I'm a little tired. The stairs—"

"And the heat," O'Konsky suggested.

"Yes, it is warm for September, isn't it? I remarked to my brother only yesterday—"

O'Konsky was back in his own chair by this time. One hand furtively pressed the buzzer on his desk. The woman's eyes caught the action and clouded momentarily, but her voice remained unchanged.

"Do you remember my brother, Lieutenant?"

O'Konsky's eyebrows huddled over the question.

"Brother—" he mused. "Thin chap—pale moustache—not much hair."

The woman nodded.

"Charles began losing his hair when he was a very young man. It upset him terribly. He never mentioned it to me, of course. Charles isn't the communicative type—but I could tell. I've often wondered if he might not have married and been quite different if only he hadn't lost his hair. Men are so sensitive about such things."

The woman paused—suddenly embarrassed. "Oh, I'm sorry. No offense, Lieutenant."

O'Konsky's hand came back from the receding hairline he'd unconsciously caressed.

"Don't worry about me," he said. "I gave up this battle long ago."

"But you're a married man—and a police officer. I don't suppose police officers are troubled by a sense of inferiority. But poor Charles— and his sister married to such a handsome and successful man!"

A door at the back of the room opened and a man came over to O'Konsky's desk. O'Konsky turned in his chair to greet him.

"Sergeant Peters, you remember Mrs. Haversham, don't you? Mrs. Harlan Haversham—widow of the late Harlan Haversham."

There was a note of pleading in O'Konsky's voice. Peters stared hard at the woman on the chair, and then his gaze dropped momentarily to the headline on the newspaper spread across O'Konsky's desk.

"Oh, that Mrs. Haversham!" he said.

O'Konsky sighed as if he'd just made the last payment on the mortgage, and then he scribbled something on a slip of paper and handed it to the man.

"This is why I buzzed you," he said. "Mrs. Haversham and I are having a little chat just now, so I thought maybe you could take care of this for me."

Peters scanned the paper and then shoved it into his coat pocket.

"Right away," he said. But at the doorway he paused to cast one long look back at Mrs. Haversham. He didn't appear any happier than O'Konsky.

Mrs. Haversham endured the interruption in patient but observing silence. When it was over, she continued the conversation as if nothing had taken place.

"Did you know my husband, Lieutenant?"

"I never had the pleasure," O'Konsky answered.

"That's a pity. You would have admired him—everyone did. He was so intelligent and kind, but his heart ..."

Her voice broke off huskily. In the brief silence that followed she seemed almost at the verge of tears, and then, as if remembering that grief was a private matter not to be aired in a police detective's office, her back stiffened and her chin came up higher.

"But then," she continued, "I believe I asked you if you knew my husband the first time we met. Let's see now, that was the time when—"

"A man fell down an elevator shaft," O'Konsky broke in. "Accidental death."

A fleeting smile crossed Mrs. Haversham's lips.

"According to the police," she said.

"Now, Mrs. Haversham—"

"Oh—" One gloved hand drifted up in protest. "I won't argue the point, Lieutenant—not now. After all, the case is closed."

"And the poker case is closed," O'Konsky said, "—and the rat poison."

"Insecticide," Mrs. Haversham corrected. Her glance fell to the headline again. "But not the hammer murder," she added. "There were no fingerprints, of course."

"No fingerprints," O'Konsky sighed.

Mrs. Haversham spread her hands out on her lap—palms up and

then palms down. She wore extremely smart gloves. Black.

"So few women wear gloves anymore," she said quietly, "but I always have—even before Mr. Haversham's tragic death. It's a matter of the way in which one has been reared, I suppose."

O'Konsky took a handkerchief out of his breast pocket and patted his neck. He was beginning to squirm in his chair.

"There were no fingerprints on the poker, either," Mrs. Haversham reflected.

"The case was open and shut—" O'Konsky began.

"—or on the bottle of insecticide."

"Mrs. Haversham—" O'Konsky's voice was troubled. The handkerchief was now a wadded ball in his hand. "—I know that you must have read all about this new murder in the newspapers."

She smiled vaguely.

"Oh, I have, Lieutenant, but they haven't reported all of it right. Newspapers never do."

"Then—" O'Konsky's face was haggard. "—I don't need to ask why you've come to see me."

"I always try to cooperate with the police," she said quietly.

"That you do, Mrs. Haversham. That you most certainly do!"

At that very moment the door opened and Sergeant Peters returned with another man—older, taller, dressed in an expensively tailored suit. The newcomer smiled at Mrs. Haversham, and she returned the smile in recognition.

"Dr. Armstrong! How well you're looking!"

"Thank you," the doctor said.

"And your wife? She's well, too?"

"Never better."

"That's nice. I've been meaning to drop a card, but I've been so busy."

"I'll bet you have, Mrs. Haversham. Do you want to tell us about it now?"

The woman hesitated. She looked at the doctor; she looked at O'Konsky. For the first time, her eyes were anxious.

"Where's the other one—with the notebook?" she asked.

"I don't think that will be necessary this time," the doctor said.

"Oh, yes. Things must be done in an efficient manner. That's one of the things my late husband taught me. I didn't learn too well, I'm afraid. But then, I have Charles. He's so very efficient about everything."

Mrs. Haversham paused. One hand went to her forehead in a

meaningless gesture; then she noticed the sergeant and smiled again.

"Oh, you do have a notebook," she said. "That's better, now we can proceed." She wriggled straight in her chair while O'Konsky wriggled down in his. Then she began to dictate in a calm, clear voice:

"I, Lydia Haversham, being of sound mind and under no duress whatsoever, do hereby confess to the hammer murder ..."

The lettering on the door was bright gold: DR. J. M. ARMSTRONG—PSYCHIATRIST. Behind the door, a thin, middle-aged man with a pale moustache and little hair on his head sat nervously on the edge of a chair. His light blue eyes, worried but attentive, were focused on the doctor's face. Only occasionally did he cast a quick, apprehensive glance in the direction of his sister—deep in a leather armchair alongside the doctor's desk. The conversation was about Lydia Haversham, although it seemed hardly to concern her.

"It all goes back to the shock of your brother-in-law's tragic death, Mr. Lacy," the doctor explained. "The implication of violence—"

Charles Lacy reacted in immediate protest.

"But there was no violence. Harlan Haversham suffered a heart attack. My sister knows that. He'd had these attacks several times prior to his death. We all knew—"

Dr. Armstrong's voice remained calm. "I said the implication of violence, Mr. Lacy. Unfortunately, this last attack occurred on a staircase. Mr. Haversham collapsed and fell over the balustrade, plunging a possible eight floors—"

The doctor raised the clip end of his gold-plated pen in a gesture of silence as Charles Lacy opened his mouth to protest again.

"No, we do not run away from things anymore. We do not pretend this horror hasn't occurred. Your sister and I have been having some very frank talks these past few days, and she's a much stronger person now."

Charles Lacy looked toward his sister for reassurance. She sat very small in the huge chair, an expression of tired resignation on her face.

"Harlan plunged eight floors," she repeated dully. "He was crushed and bleeding. It was because the elevators weren't running and he had to take the stairs."

"The elevators," Dr. Armstrong repeated. "Do you see the significance? A few months after her husband's tragic death, your sister came to the police and confessed to having pushed a man down an elevator shaft. There was no murder at all—it was merely an accident—but she'd read the account in her newspaper and a subconscious feeling of guilt compelled her to that ridiculous confession."

"For better or for worse, in sickness and in health—" Lydia murmured.

The doctor nodded sympathetically.

"A wife always feels an exaggerated responsibility for her husband— especially a wife who loves deeply. The confession was ridiculous, and your sister knew that, but it fulfilled—temporarily—her need for punishment stemming from this mistaken sense of guilt."

"It was Saturday," Lydia recalled. "The repair men were working on the elevators because it was Saturday. Harlan shouldn't have been in his office when they started working, but I had asked him to go—"

She spoke slowly and deliberately—like a child talking to herself. Dr. Armstrong caught Charles Lacy's eye and nodded. A signal of understanding passed between them.

"A month later a second confession," the doctor continued. "This time to a crime of a violent nature. A brutal slaying with a poker—"

"Eight floors," Lydia repeated. "Crushed and bleeding."

"—and then, a month later, another confession. Unfortunately, Lt. O'Konsky didn't call me in for consultation until this third disturbance. He thought then—and I concurred as you will recall— that the confessions were merely a manifestation of loneliness—an attempt to draw attention to herself."

Charles Lacy fidgeted on the edge of his chair. Lydia was watching him. She'd been watching him all this time. He'd just become aware of that.

"I've tried to follow your suggestions," he said defensively. "I've tried to get Lydia to go out more—and to have friends in. I've made sacrifices, too. I'm a busy man, doctor. Since my brother-in-law's death, the business keeps me working all hours."

"Charles always worked all hours," Lydia remarked, "—even before Harlan's death. He was Harlan's secretary—his right-hand man. Harlan used to tell me that he wouldn't know how to find anything in the office if it weren't for Charles."

Nobody noticed her. Dr. Armstrong didn't so much as turn his head.

"I'm not blaming you, Mr. Lacy," he insisted. "If anyone's to blame it's myself for not going into this matter more thoroughly at the time of the last confession. I took too much for granted. I've worked with the police on such cases before, but never—" He hesitated. "—never with one of your sister's sensibilities. I should have probed deeper." And then he smiled and leaned back in his chair.

"But I believe we've gotten to the very root of the trouble this time," he added. "We understand it all now, don't we, Mrs. Haversham?"

Lydia Haversham smiled vaguely. "Yes, I'm sure we do," she said.

"And you realize that you couldn't possibly have committed that hammer murder any more than you could have committed any of the other crimes to which you have confessed. You didn't even know the victim."

"It's all preposterous!" Charles exploded. "My sister was at home the entire evening the crime occurred. I telephoned her from the office at ten o'clock sharp. I always telephone when I work late."

Lydia nodded.

"Charles always telephones," she said. "He never forgets. It was only that he forgot to get his passport out of the safe—"

Charles swung about and faced his sister, but his words were for the doctor.

"She should forget about that!" he said. "Now that you've probed the past—or however you put it, Doctor, she should forget—shouldn't she?"

"She should—and will," the doctor answered, "—now that she really understands why she felt compelled to confess to crimes her nature would never have allowed her to commit. You see, Mrs. Haversham—" and now the doctor faced Lydia for the first time "—you aren't guilty of anything. Your husband suffered a fatal heart attack on the stairway—that was all. It was no one's fault. It could have happened to you—or to your brother—or to myself, for that matter. Many people have no warning whatsoever about such things. It so happens that your husband did have a medical record. You are completely absolved."

Lydia Haversham's eyes didn't leave the doctor's face while he spoke. She might have been memorizing every word.

"It could have happened to anyone," she repeated softly.

"Anyone," the doctor agreed. "It's unfortunate that the workmen came to service the elevators while your husband was still in his office. It's unfortunate they didn't know he was there. It's unfortunate that he had to make an unexpected trip to his office, but none of these things are conclusive. His heart might have stopped that day anyway. You're not responsible."

His voice was firm and persuasive. Lydia listened attentively, but she didn't seem quite convinced.

"I asked him to get the passport—" she began.

"For me," Charles cut in. "You see, Dr. Armstrong, I received a wire late Friday night—an important business matter in our South American branch. My brother-in-law couldn't get away, so I offered to make the trip myself. But it all happened so quickly, and there were so many things to do. Packing—tickets— In the rush, I forgot my passport in the safe, and only Harlan and myself knew the combination. If anyone is to blame for what happened, I'm the guilty party—but I don't crucify myself, Lydia. I can't afford to. I have to carry on the business, as I know Harlan would want me to do. He'd want you to carry on, too. You know that."

It was a long speech for Charles. He'd put a lot into it. He was a bit out of breath at the finish.

Lydia nodded, her eyes far away.

"South America," she said. "You never did go, did you, Charles?"

"How could I? When Harlan was found—"

"I've never been to South America. Why don't we go, Charles? Why don't we just forget everything and take a holiday?"

Charles seemed startled. He looked at the doctor. The doctor smiled.

"I think that's an excellent idea, Mrs. Haversham."

"But the business—" Charles began.

"Your brother-in-law left you his wife to care for as well as his business, Mr. Lacy. Speaking professionally, I'd heartily recommend a holiday. It should make a good beginning for a newer and fuller life."

The doctor came to his feet as he spoke. His words were like a benediction, to which he added one thought as he helped Lydia from her chair.

"And I don't want to ever find you in Lieutenant O'Konsky's office again, Mrs. Haversham."

Lydia smiled as she took her brother's arm.

"You won't, Dr. Armstrong," she promised. "You won't."

The lettering above the entrance stood twenty feet high: HAVERSHAM INDUSTRIES, INC. The ancient building was qualified to serve as a museum piece, an example of the rococo. Eight stories up, the door to the executive suite opened and a man and a woman came out into the hall. It was late. The hall lights cut a path through the darkness; the stairwell was a black hole with a small bright path at the bottom. Lydia Haversham advanced to the balustrade and looked down.

"How far it is," she said softly, "—and how empty. Are we really so alone, Charles? Is there no one else in the building?"

Charles Lacy, topcoat over his arm, scanned a pair of small green books held in his free hand.

"Our passports seem to be in order," he remarked. "We'd better get going if you still want to catch that midnight plane ... I'll say this for you, Lydia, when you decide to do a thing you don't waste any time."

"No more than necessary," Lydia murmured.

Charles stuffed the passports into a pocket of the topcoat, and then, for the first time, became aware of his sister's position at the balustrade.

"Lydia! Come away from there!" But Lydia didn't move.

"It is a terrible fall, isn't it?" she said.

"You're not to think of that anymore. It's all over. We're going away on a holiday and forget everything."

"Is it really that easy, Charles? Have you forgotten? Don't you ever hear his scream as he fell? Surely, he must have screamed ..."

Lydia turned slowly as she spoke. Her eyes weren't sad anymore. Her eyes were hard. She looked at Charles—a thin man with a pale moustache and a face that had gone chalkwhite.

"Lydia—"

"But that wouldn't bother you, would it? You hated him. You were jealous of everything he had—everything he was. But you knew how to use him. You made yourself valuable to him with your great efficiency. That's what made me suspicious, Charles. After it was all over—the shock, and the funeral—I found myself wondering why my efficient brother made so many mistakes on one day. Why you forgot your passport in the office safe so Harlan had to go for it—why you forgot to tell him the men were coming to service the elevators that morning—why you neglected to reserve the ticket you supposedly had to pick up at the airline office."

A thin man with a chalk-white face. Charles's mouth chewed at words that wouldn't come. Lydia's wouldn't stop. "Yes, I checked on that. I discovered there was no record of a reservation for Charles Lacy on any airline in the city that morning."

Now Charles spewed out his words.

"You're talking nonsense! Airlines make mistakes. No record of a reservation isn't proof that none was made."

Lydia smiled.

"I knew you'd say that—that's why I didn't tell the police. You're so much more clever than I. You would have explained everything—even the wire from South America—if there was a wire."

She stood with her back against the balustrade, her hands grasping the railing at either side. She started to move slowly along the balustrade. She reached the first step ... the second ...

"This is the way it was, wasn't it?" she said.

"Harlan here—starting down the stairs—and you behind him."

"You don't know what you're saying!" Charles cried. "You're imagining things again!"

"But I never imagine things, Charles. I've only been playing a game. Don't you remember the story of the shepherd boy who cried 'wolf' so many times when there was no wolf, that nobody believed him when the wolf did come? I've been crying 'murder' ..."

"But why, Lydia? Why?"

Lydia looked at her brother. He was only a step away—a step that seemed to make him tower above her. She leaned back against the railing and looked at him long and hard.

"You wouldn't ask such a question if you could see your face, Charles. I've been watching it through all those confessions—watching, waiting for you to break. But not you! Not a man so wrapped up in hate! I think I might have forgiven you if you'd shown even a sign of regret—but it's too late now. I've played my game well. I could confess to a dozen crimes and nobody would believe me. But someday, somewhere—on a stairway, on the deck of a ship, on the mountain trail of some scenic tour, perhaps—someday I'll pay you back for killing my husband."

Lydia's voice was calm and deliberate. Then the quiet came, the hollow, empty quiet of the blazing hall and the black gulf behind her. Her hands tightened on the rail.

"You tell me that," Charles said. "You idiot! Do you think I'm going to wait for you to kill me? Do you think I'm as big a fool as Harlan?"

She didn't think he'd wait, of course. Her weight shifted as he lunged toward her. Afterward, she wasn't sure if her foot had come out in a school-day trip, or if Charles had stumbled because his legs had become entangled in his topcoat. She never forgot how he plunged forward, how he started tumbling wildly down the stairs, until he struck the fragile supports of the balustrade and went through ...

When the scream died away, Lydia Haversham opened her eyes.

Charles's topcoat still dangled on the railing. She extended one gloved hand and pushed it over.

Her face was soft, her eyes were sad, and a ghost of a smile touched her lips.

"It could have happened to anybody," she whispered.

Your Witness

It was murder, although slaughter was a better term for it—or even assassination. Naomi Shawn settled on murder because it was a word that felt strangely at home in her mind. The crime, by any name, was happening to a bewildered citizen, one Henry Babcock, whose place of execution was the witness stand in Judge Dutton's court. Henry Babcock was in a somewhat similar circumstance to the late Agnes Thompson, housewife, who had been struck down by a Mercedes-Benz and subsequently buried. Henry was being buried, too; but he had the uncomfortable disadvantage of not being dead.

From her seat among the courtroom spectators, Naomi watched the scene with fascinated eyes. Arnold Shawn was a man of electrifying virility, persuasive charm, and intellectual dexterity. He was a dramatist, a strategist, a psychologist, and could, if need be, display the touch of the poet. He was more handsome at fifty than he'd been at twenty-five, more confident, more successful, more feared and much more hated. He was a lawyer who selected his clients with scrupulous care, basing his decision solely on ability to pay. But once a retainer was given, the accused could sit back with whatever ease an accused can muster and know that his fate was in the hands of as shrewd a legal talent as money could buy.

And the biggest heel.

Naomi Shawn's vocabulary wasn't as extensive as her husband's. He would have found a more distinctive way of describing his own character. In fact, he had done that very thing only a few hours earlier. "I'm not cruel, Naomi; I'm honest. I could lie to you. It would be easy, easier than you know, my dear. I could prove to you, beyond your innermost feminine doubt, that I am an innocent, loyal, devoted husband who is passionately in love with you, and everything you think you've learned to the contrary is pure illusion. But I won't lie. There is another woman."

Naomi tried not to listen to echoes. Arnold was speaking, and Arnold commanded attention when he spoke.

"Now, Mr. Babcock," he was saying, "you have testified that you saw my client's automobile run a red light, strike the deceased, Agnes

Thompson, drive on for a space of some fifty yards, stop, back up to a spot parallel with the body, and then drive on again without my client, Mr. Jerome, so much as alighting from the vehicle ..."

Mr. Jerome. He was nineteen. A slight nineteen, with an almost childlike face and guilty blue eyes that stared disconsolately at his uncalloused hands laced together on the table before him. His blond hair was combed back neatly, and he wore a conservative tie, white shirt and dark suit, as per Arnold's instructions. Kenneth Jerome looked more like an honor Bible student than a cold-blooded hit and run killer. And he was that; Naomi was the one spectator in the courtroom who knew. She had gone to Arnold's office one morning. He hadn't been home all night, a situation that was becoming alarmingly frequent. It was time to have a showdown. But young Jerome and his father had come to the office that day, and she was shunted off to another room. She heard the story. Kenneth Jerome couldn't deny hitting his victim; the police had already traced his car to the garage where it was being repaired.

"I didn't know I'd hit a woman," Kenneth Jerome explained. "I didn't see anyone. I thought I felt a thud, but it's open country out near the airport. Sometimes you hit a rabbit or even a cat late at night. And it was late. Somewhere near three-thirty, I think. Anyway, I thought that's what happened when I got home and saw my right front fender. I thought I'd hit a rabbit or a cat."

And Arnold's voice, had queried him from across the desk.

"Is that what you told the police?"

"Sure, it is. What else could I tell them?"

"Is there a traffic signal at that intersection?"

"There is—but there wasn't another car in sight"

"Was the signal with you, or against you?"

"It was with me. It was green."

"Is that what you told the police?"

"Sure, it is. I said the woman must have tried to cross against the light. I didn't see her at all."

And then Arnold had smiled. From the next room, Naomi couldn't see the smile; but she could hear it in his words.

"Very good, Mr. Jerome. Now, unless you want me to throw this case back in your teeth, tell me what really happened last night. I don't deal with clients who aren't honest with me ..."

Honest was one of Arnold's favorite words. It had an exceptional meaning to him.

"To be perfectly honest with you, Naomi, I never did love you. Not the way a man wants to love a woman. Your father had influence and I needed a start. It was that simple."

Echoes. She pushed them from her mind. She had come to watch Henry Babcock take his punishment for being a good citizen.

Arnold's voice came again. "You were standing on the sidewalk near the intersection at the time of the accident, is that right?"

Henry Babcock was merely nervous at this stage of the cross-examination. He was a rather slight man, balding, had a clean-shaven face and wore thick lensed glasses that magnified his eyes owlishly. He might have been Arnold's age, Naomi realized with a sense of in credulity. There was no other similarity. Henry Babcock looked shabby and servile. There was a natural elite, Arnold had always maintained, that was predestined to govern any society. At the moment, the validity of his theory seemed self-evident.

"Not exactly," Henry Babcock answered. "I was sitting on a bench at the bus stop, waiting for a bus."

"And how far was the bench from the intersection, Mr. Babcock?"

Henry Babcock hesitated. "I don't know as I could say, exactly. Not very far."

"Not very far." Arnold smiled. He was always dangerous when he smiled. "That doesn't help the jury much, does it, Mr. Babcock? Can't you be more specific? Was it as far"—he turned slowly, his eyes sweeping the courtroom and finally coming to rest—"as from where you're sitting to where the defendant is sitting?"

"Well, now, I don't know—"

"Yes or no, Mr. Babcock?"

The question was like a whip. Henry Babcock straightened his glasses and sat at attention.

"Well, yes," he said.

"The bench was the same distance from the intersection as you are from Mr. Jerome at this moment?"

"Yes, sir."

"Very good. Now please continue and tell the jury just what happened ..."

What had happened? Naomi's mind would wander, no matter how she tried to keep it in line. Was it really as simple as Arnold had said—merely a marriage of convenience? It was difficult to believe. She knew why she'd married Arnold. She had loved him; she still loved him, in spite of what he'd become. Was she somehow responsible for that?

She'd tried to be a good wife and mother; she tried to keep up with Arnold's dazzling success …

"Mr. Babcock" —Arnold's voice intruded on the memories again— "I want you to clarify one detail. You say that you didn't see Agnes Thompson prior to the accident. You were sitting on the bench waiting for a bus. Mrs. Thompson approached the intersection from the east—"

Someone had set up a blackboard in view of the judge and the jury. On it was drawn the intersection with crosses indicating the location of the bench and Henry Babcock, the spot where the accident occurred, and now, at Arnold's instruction, another cross for Mrs. Thompson approaching the intersection.

"We know that she came from the east," Arnold continued, "because we know that she had been visiting a sick grandchild and was returning to her own home, six blocks distant, only after the grandchild had shown signs of recovery and gone to sleep. Presumably, Mrs. Thompson was weary after the strain of her vigil; presumably, she walked with a heavy tread—she was a rather heavy woman. How do you account for not hearing Mrs. Thompson approach the intersection, Mr. Babcock?"

Henry Babcock appeared puzzled. He rubbed his jaw thoughtfully with one hand, and the light glinted off the lens of his eyeglasses. The staring eyes of the jury and the courtroom seemed to bother him. The question bothered him, too.

"I didn't say that I didn't hear her," he answered.

"Then you did hear her."

"I didn't say that, either. Maybe I heard her. I don't remember. I was tired, too. I'd just come from work."

"At the Century Club?"

"Yes sir. I clean up there after the place closes at two o'clock."

"Two a.m., that is."

"Yes, sir."

Two a.m. It was difficult to find an accident witness in broad daylight; but when, a few days after taking the case, Arnold had received an urgent telephone call from Jerome Sr. at a similar hour of a different morning, he knew there was work ahead. It was in the downstairs hall. Arnold had just come in. He still wore his black Homburg and black topcoat over his tuxedo. Naomi had descended most of the way down the stairs, having started when she heard him come in. He took the call in silence, concluding it with a curt assurance that he would handle everything. He'd dropped the telephone back into the cradle for a moment; then took it up again and dialed.

"Fran? Arnold here. Sorry to call you now, but something's come up. The Jerome case—a witness. Yes, the police are keeping him under wraps; but old man Jerome just got wind of it at a cocktail party and passed the word along. Now, here's what I want you to do. Get the wheels rolling. Get everything you can on Henry Babcock. That's right. Babcock. He's a janitor, or porter, or some such thing at the Century Club. He was waiting for a bus to go home after work when the accident happened. I want him tabbed from the year One. You know how."

Arnold had dropped the telephone back into the cradle and turned around. Naomi was at the bottom of the stairs by that time. He stared at her without seeming to see her at all.

"Is that who she is?" Naomi had asked. "Is it Fran, your secretary?"

Arnold's eyebrows had a way of knitting together when he was annoyed. At that moment she hadn't been sure whether he was more annoyed with her question or with Jerome's call; but it was probably the latter. She didn't even possess nuisance value anymore.

"Is that who who is?" he'd asked.

"The woman you've been with tonight."

She'd reached out and straightened his tie. Old-fashioned as it was, and Arnold did hate being old-fashioned about anything.

"You're talking nonsense, Naomi. Go to bed."

It was the way to dismiss a child. He'd stalked upstairs, his mind busy with the problem of Henry Babcock, good citizen, bent on the folly of doing his duty ...

And so they were in the courtroom, and Arnold was solving his problem.

"... so, at approximately half-past three, having finished your work at the Century Club, you were sitting on a bench at the bus stop waiting for transportation to take you home. Where do you live, Mr. Babcock?"

It was an innocent question. Henry Babcock answered without hesitation.

"In Inglewood," he said. "I've got a three-room apartment."

"And do you live alone?"

"Yes, sir. Since my wife died three years ago."

"Since your wife died," Arnold repeated. "My sympathies, Mr. Babcock. It must be lonely, coming home to an empty apartment."

The prosecutor stirred uneasily. He seemed to sense some ulterior motivation behind the question. Before he could object, Henry Babcock, who sensed nothing but the discomfort of the witness box, had answered.

"Yes, sir, it is," he said.

"But you do have friends."

"Friends?"

"At your place of employment. I believe the Century Club employs entertainers, including several very attractive young ladies. I understand that you do little favors for them, such as bringing coffee to the dressing rooms—"

The prosecutor leaped to his feet.

"Your Honor, I object to this line of questioning. We aren't here to ascertain the witness's sociability, or to delve into his personal life."

Arnold turned toward him, smiling.

"And why aren't we?" he asked. "The witness has testified in direct contradiction to the sworn statement of my client. Obviously, one of these two men is either mistaken or an outright liar. I see nothing objectionable, in attempting to establish the character of the witness. For that matter, I see nothing objectionable—although the learned prosecutor seems to differ with me on this point—in a lonely widower bringing coffee to a ladies' dressing room."

There was something diabolical about Arnold in action. Naomi was beginning to realize that. In a few words, he'd turned the prosecutor into an unwitting counsel for the defense. The man sat down, chastened and confused.

Arnold turned back to Henry Babcock.

"Agnes Thompson approached the intersection from the east," he resumed. "That means that she came from behind you, doesn't it?"

"Yes, sir," Babcock answered.

"Yes, because you sat on a bench parallel to a street running north and south. The bench"—Arnold referred to the blackboard again—"is on the southeast corner of the intersection. The signal, which you have testified was red when my client's automobile struck Mrs. Thompson, is approximately ten feet north of the bench, which would have been to your right as you sat facing the street. Correct?"

Henry Babcock adjusted his glasses and leaned forward to follow Arnold's indications on the blackboard map.

"Yes, that's correct," he agreed.

"And so, you were sitting on the bench, tired after the night's work."

"Yes, sir."

"And alone?"

"Yes, sir."

"Waiting for a bus to take you home to your apartment where you live alone."

Babcock's forehead had corrugated into a puzzled frown, but he answered.

"Yes, sir."

"You looked at the signal, and saw that it was red."

"Yes, sir."

"And before it changed to green, my client's automobile raced past the intersection, striking down Mrs. Thompson, whom you hadn't noticed prior to the accident—" Arnold paused, as if only at that instant discovering a flaw in the testimony. "Now, that does seem strange," he mused aloud. "You turned your head to the right and saw that the signal was red. Why didn't you also see Mrs. Thompson preparing to step down into the crosswalk?"

There was a slight murmur in the courtroom. Arnold's strategy was beginning to take hold.

"I don't know," Babcock answered. "I guess she wasn't there yet when I looked."

"Then you must have looked away from the light for a time."

Babcock hesitated, sensing a trap.

"The light was red!" he insisted.

"But you didn't see Mrs. Thompson."

"It was dark."

"Isn't there a street lamp at that intersection? Think, Mr. Babcock."

"There's a street lamp, but it only shines so far. After that, it's dark."

"And yet Mrs. Thompson would have had to come into that arc of light, wouldn't she?"

"Maybe she came too fast for me to see her. Maybe she was running."

"Running?" Arnold caught up the word and dangled it before the ears of the court. "Now, why would she have been running, Mr. Babcock? Haven't we already established that it was late, very late, and that she must have been weary from sitting up with a sick grandchild?"

Henry Babcock was an uncomplicated man who, very likely, had never sat in a witness box before in his life. He'd come to do his duty, and yet, by answering extemporaneously a few minor questions he hadn't thought through, he'd gotten himself into trouble. He glanced pleadingly at the prosecutor, who was helpless at the moment, and then got himself into worse trouble.

"Maybe she was afraid."

"But why should she have been afraid?" Arnold demanded.

"Because it was so late. It's not safe for a woman out alone at that hour. Things happen. You read about it in the paper all the time."

Arnold listened carefully to Henry Babcock, so carefully that he caught up the entire courtroom in his attitude and everyone listened, carefully.

"I read about it?" he echoed. "What do I read about?"

The accentuated pronoun forced Henry Babcock to a correction.

"I mean, people do," he explained. "Anybody."

"I think what you mean," Arnold interpolated, "is that you read about it all the time. Now, just what do you read?"

Henry Babcock was perspiring freely. He didn't bother to wipe his brow.

"Things that happen," he said. "Robberies, attacks—"

"And you always read about these things, is that right, Mr. Babcock? When you're all finished bringing coffee to the ladies' dressing room, and cleaning up the deserted club, you go home to your apartment, alone, and read about terrible things that happen to women who go out on the streets at night—"

Arnold's voice was an instrument played with professional skill. It was impossible not to be drawn along with it. But he got no farther before the prosecutor was on his feet shouting an objection. Arnold smiled at him with an expression of tolerant patience, and only Naomi understood what was happening. The innocent must always be made to appear guilty. This was Arnold's secret of success.

" ... I don't want a scene, Naomi. This woman need never have come between us if you hadn't insisted on a showdown. I'm not planning to divorce you, or to allow you to divorce me. I can't afford a scandal, and you have the children to consider even if my career means nothing to you ..."

The innocent must always be made to appear guilty.

"Your Honor," Arnold continued, with mock humility, "I'm deeply sorry if my remarks have caused prejudice in the minds of the jury. It wasn't my intention to infer that the witness has socially undesirable tendencies. Nevertheless, I'm still curious as to how he could have turned his head to observe the traffic signal and not have seen a woman about to step out into the crosswalk. If he was tired, he might have been dozing; but then, he wouldn't have seen the signal. If, however, he was alert enough to notice the signal, why didn't he see Mrs. Thompson?"

With these words, Arnold swung back to Henry Babcock.

"Or did you see her, Mr. Babcock?"

Henry Babcock drew back in the box.

"No," he said.

"Are you sure, Mr. Babcock? A few moments ago you were positive that you didn't see her; a few moments later you thought that you might have heard her. Now you can't seem to explain why you didn't see her. Isn't it possible that you did see her? That perhaps you spoke to her?"

"No—"

"That you approached her?"

"No! I never left the bench!"

"You never left the bench, and yet, with an automobile approaching, and surely Mrs. Thompson could have seen the headlights, the victim stepped off the curb and into its path. Why did she do that, Mr. Babcock, unless, as you have suggested, she was startled out of her wits? Was there anyone else in the vicinity at the time?"

Babcock was no longer bewildered; he was furious.

"No!" he shouted.

"Then no one could have startled Mrs. Thompson unless it was yourself."

"I didn't say she was startled."

"But you suggested it. You suggested that she might have been running. These are interesting suggestions, in view of the fact that you knew no one other than yourself was in the vicinity. Since you've volunteered this much light on the mystery of what happened at that intersection the night Mrs. Thompson died, perhaps, remembering that you're under oath, you would like to tell the whole truth."

Arnold waited for an answer, and the court waited with him.

"I told the truth!" Babcock insisted. "The whole truth!"

"Thank you, Mr. Babcock."

Arnold stepped back. He seemed ready to release the witness; only Naomi knew it was a feint. There had been another telephone call only this morning. She'd overheard enough to know Henry Babcock wasn't going to get off so easily.

"... Yes, Fran, he's going to be tough to crack—too clean. Nothing on him unless I can color up that job of his. What? Do you have proof? Good girl! Of course, it's enough. I'll make it enough."

And then he'd looked up to find Naomi staring at him accusingly. "What are you going to do to that poor man?" she had asked.

"I'm going to win my case," he had answered.

"Your client is guilty."

"Not until the jury brings in a verdict. Don't look so shocked, Naomi. You can't be that naïve! A courtroom is just like a battlefield. When a soldier's ordered to take an objective, he can't consider if innocent people will be hurt. There are no innocent people; there are only the quick and the dead. I'm one of the quick. Because of that, you live in a beautiful home, wear lovely clothes, drive an expensive sedan—"

"Who is the woman, Arnold?"

And that was when he had stopped evading her. "I'm not cruel, Naomi; I'm honest. I could lie to you. It would be easy, easier than you know ..."

Sitting among the spectators in the courtroom, Naomi learned how easy it was.

"Mr. Babcock—" Arnold swung back to face the witness, his sudden movement and the sound of his voice magnetizing attention. "How long have you been employed at the Century Club?"

The change of tactic puzzled Babcock.

"Ten months," he said.

"I don't suppose your salary is anything remarkable."

"I don't need much."

"Still, it's not comparable to—let us say, an instructor of mathematics and mechanical drawing at Freeman High School, which position you held for fourteen years prior to your employment at the Century Club. Tell me, Mr. Babcock, why does a man of your background work as a porter in a cheap night club? Why are you reduced to pushing a broom and running errands for showgirls? Or does this explain it better?"

No one was prepared for Arnold's next move, least of all Henry Babcock. When Arnold reached out and snatched the glasses from his eyes, Babcock rose from the chair, grasped at empty air, and barely steadied himself against the side of the bench short of falling.

"My glasses—" he gasped.

"Your eyes, Mr. Babcock!" Arnold corrected. "Isn't it true that you relinquished your profession because you were going blind?"

"No! I had cataracts—"

"Because your vision was eighty-five percent impaired when you underwent surgery eight months ago? Because you were totally color blind?"

Arnold had won his case. Naomi could sense the feeling of the court even before her ears picked up the murmur. By that time, Henry Babcock was trying to explain that an operation had restored vision to one eye and he was awaiting the required full year before a second operation that would restore the other; but few people heard.

"I'll be good as new!" he insisted. "I'll get my teaching job back—"

"But you weren't 'good as new' the night you claim to have seen my client go through a red light!"

"With my glasses, I can see color!"

"Out of which eye?"

"The left eye. The one that had the operation."

"But the signal is to your right."

"I turned my head."

"But you didn't see Mrs. Thompson."

"I couldn't. I can't see out of the sides—only straight ahead."

"Only straight ahead!" Arnold pounced on the phrase, as if he had been waiting for it all this time. "And how far straight ahead, Mr. Babcock? As far as from where you are sitting to the defendant—that's what you said, didn't you?"

Henry Babcock leaned forward, a grotesque figure of a man trying to peer through a fog.

"With my glasses—" he began.

"Your Honor," Arnold announced, "I move that the testimony of the witness be stricken from the record. It's obvious to everyone in this courtroom that he is not capable of giving reliable information on anything of a visual nature. The distance from the witness stand to the defendant, which Mr. Babcock has, under oath, declared to be the same as the distance from the bench on which he was seated at the time of the accident to the point at which the accident occurred, can't possibly measure in excess of thirty feet. I invite the prosecution to check me on this." There was no need to check. Naomi, remembering, realized when Arnold had set his trap. He was always dangerous when he smiled. "I have already checked the distance between the bench and the place of the accident," he added, "and it is, ladies and gentlemen of the jury, exactly sixty-two feet! Not only is the witness color blind, not only is he incapable of seeing out of the sides of his eyes; he is also completely unable to estimate simple distances.

Unless he's deliberately lying about everything, unless he did leave the bench and does know some reason why Mrs. Thompson stepped out in front of a fast-moving automobile, the most charitable conclusion we can reach is that this poor man's mind has been enfeebled by the double tragedy of losing his wife and almost losing his sight, and is incompetent to testify in a court of law!"

The prosecution roared a protest. Arnold turned toward him with a gesture of contemptuous dismissal.

"Your witness!" he said.

The jury was out fifteen minutes. After the acquittal, Arnold received congratulations with his customary indifference. The courtroom emptied. Naomi watched a defeated little man make his way toward the corridor: Henry Babcock, ex-good citizen. She caught his eyes, magnified by the lenses of the glasses, as he went by. It had been murder. He went out and she waited alone for Arnold.

"So that's how you take an objective," she said. "Did you have to destroy his character as well as his testimony? Do you think he'll ever get that teaching job back now?"

"If he's man enough," Arnold said. "That's his problem, not mine."

"Your problem is only how to get rid of a bothersome wife, isn't it?"

Arnold didn't seem to consider the question worth answering. They went out together. The sidewalk was deserted now except for a dejected man waiting at the bus stop, a man for whom Arnold didn't have so much as a glance. At the entrance to the parking lot, he looked up and frowned at the sky. It was starting to rain lightly.

"I'm glad you decided to visit court today, Naomi," he said. "I've got a five o'clock appointment and it's the very devil to catch a cab in bad weather."

"Five o'clock?" Naomi echoed. "That gives you time to pick up flowers. Shall I stop at a florist?"

"No, thank you, Naomi. Just get your car, please. I'll wait."

And Arnold waited. He stood at the edge of the parking lot driveway, so supremely confident that he didn't so much as step back when Naomi brought the sedan around. He didn't even have time to change his self-satisfied expression to surprise when she suddenly cut the wheels and slammed her foot on the accelerator.

After the police officer had extracted Arnold's body from under the wheels, Naomi tried to explain.

"It was a mistake!" she sobbed. "I meant to put my foot on the brake, not the accelerator! It was a terrible mistake!"

A small crowd had gathered, but there was only one eyewitness. The officer turned to him, and for a moment Naomi caught a glimpse of the man's eyes. The sympathy she'd given him in the courtroom was in them.

"If this woman is the victim's wife, surely she's telling the truth," he said. "Anyway, what I might have seen couldn't contradict her." Henry Babcock removed his glasses and blinked at the blur which was the policeman. "It's a legal fact," he said, "that I'm not a reliable witness."

THE END

Helen Nielsen Bibliography
(1918-2002)

SIMON DRAKE SERIES
Gold Coast Nocturne (1951; reprinted as Dead on the Level, 1954; UK as
    Murder by Proxy, 1952)
After Midnight (1966)
A Killer in the Street (1967)
The Darkest Hour (1969)
The Severed Key (1973)
The Brink of Murder (1976)

NOVELS
The Kind Man (1951)
Obit Delayed (1952)
Detour (1953; reprinted as Detour to Death, 1955)
The Woman on the Roof (1954)
Stranger in the Dark (1955)
Borrow the Night (1956; reprinted as Seven Days Before Dying, 1958)
The Crime is Murder (1956)
False Witness (1959)
The Fifth Caller (1959)
Sing Me a Murder (1960)
Woman Missing and Other Stories (1961)
Verdict Suspended (1964)
Shot on Location (1971)

SHORT STORIES (listed alphabetically)
The Affair Upstairs (*Alfred Hitchcock's Mystery Magazine*, July 1961)
Angry Weather (*Alfred Hitchcock's Mystery Magazine*, March 1959)
A Bad Night for Murder (*Mantrap*, July 1956)
The Breaking Point (*Ellery Queen's Mystery Magazine*, August 1965)
The Chicken Feed Mine (*Ellery Queen's Mystery Magazine*, December 1966)
Compensation (*Manhunt*, November 1957)
Confession (*Ed McBain's Mystery Book #1*, 1960)
Cop's Day Off (*Ellery Queen's Mystery Magazine*, August 1961)
The Crime is Murder (*Star Weekly*, January 12, 1957)
The Deadly Guest (*Alfred Hitchcock's Mystery Magazine*, October 1958)
The Deadly Mrs. Haversham (*Alfred Hitchcock's Mystery Magazine*,
    October 1957)
Death in the Mirror (*Mantrap*, October 1956)
Death Scene (*Ellery Queen's Mystery Magazine*, May 1963)

Decision (*Manhunt*, June 1957)

A Degree of Innocence (*Alfred Hitchcock's Mystery Magazine*, March 1958)

Don't Live in a Coffin (*Alfred Hitchcock's Mystery Magazine*, March 1960)

Don't Sit Under the Apple Tree (*Alfred Hitchcock's Mystery Magazine*, October 1959)

False Witness (*Star Weekly*, April 13 1957)

First Kill (*Manhunt*, April 1956)

Henry Lowden alias Henry Taylor (*Alfred Hitchcock's Mystery Magazine*, July 1960)

The Hopeless Case (*Ellery Queen's Mystery Magazine*, June 1962)

Hunch (*Manhunt*, March 1956)

Line of Fire (*Ellery Queen's Mystery Magazine*, September 1987)

The Long Walk to Death (*Mike Shayne Mystery Magazine*, June 1957)

The Master's Touch (*Alfred Hitchcock's Mystery Magazine*, April 1966)

Murder and Lonely Hearts (*Alfred Hitchcock's Mystery Magazine*, May 1958)

The Murder Everybody Saw (*The Saint Detective Magazine*, October 1954)

Never Trust a Woman (*Alfred Hitchcock's Mystery Magazine*, December 1957)

No Legal Evidence (*Ellery Queen's Mystery Magazine*, March 1969)

Obituary (*Alfred Hitchcock's Mystery Magazine*, April 1959)

The One (*Ellery Queen's Mystery Magazine*, November 1991)

Pattern of Guilt (*Alfred Hitchcock's Mystery Magazine*, July 1958)

The Perfectionist (*Alfred Hitchcock's Mystery Magazine*, November 1967)

The Perfect Servant (*Ellery Queen's Mystery Magazine*, November 1971)

A Piece of Ground (*Manhunt*, July 1957)

The Room at the End of the Hall (*Alfred Hitchcock's Mystery Magazine*, October 1973)

The Seventh Man (*Alfred Hitchcock's Mystery Magazine*, September 1967)

Thirteen Avenida Muerte (*Star Weekly*, July 25 1959)

This Man Is Dangerous (*Ellery Queen's Mystery Magazine*, June 1958)

The Three-Ball Combination (*The Saint Detective Magazine*, July 1956)

To the Edge of Murder (*Alfred Hitchcock's Mystery Magazine*, July 1959)

Verdict Suspended (*Star Weekly*, Aug 15, Aug 22 1964)

The Very Hard Sell (*Alfred Hitchcock's Mystery Magazine*, May 1959)

What Shall We Do About Angela? (*Alfred Hitchcock's Mystery Magazine*, December 1973)

Who Has Been Sitting in My Chair? (*Alfred Hitchcock's Mystery Magazine*, February 1960)

Witness for the Defense (*Ellery Queen's Mystery Magazine*, September 1963)

Woman Missing (*Alfred Hitchcock's Mystery Magazine*, May 1960; reprinted as "A Woman is Missing")

The Woman on the Roof (*Star Weekly*, August 28 1954)

Won't Somebody Help Me? (*Ellery Queen's Mystery Magazine*, January 1959)

You Can't Trust a Man (*Manhunt*, January 1955)

You're Dead! (*Manhunt*, April 1958)

Your Witness (*Alfred Hitchcock's Mystery Magazine*, December 1958)

Suspense Classics from the Godmother of Noir...

ELISABETH SANXAY HOLDING

Lady Killer / Miasma $19.95
Murder is suspected aboard a cruise ship to the Caribbean, and a young doctor falls into a miasma of doubt when he agrees to become medical assistant in a house of mystery.

The Death Wish / Net of Cobwebs $19.95
Mr. Delancey is pulled into a murderous affair when he comes to the aid of a friend, and a merchant seaman suffering from battle trauma becomes the first suspect when Aunt Evie is found murdered.

Strange Crime in Bermuda / Too Many Bottles $19.95
An intriguing tale of a sudden disappearance on a Caribbean island, and a mysterious death by pills, which could have been accidental—or murder.

The Old Battle Ax / Dark Power $19.95
Mrs. Herriott spins a web of deception when her sister is found dead on the sidewalk, and a woman's vision of a family reunion is quickly shattered by feelings of dread when she answers her uncle's invitation to visit.

The Unfinished Crime / The Girl Who Had to Die $19.95
Priggish Andrew Branscombe tries to control everyone until he becomes caught up in his own tangled skein of lies. Jocelyn is convinced she is going to be murdered on the cruise ship—and she is.

Speak of the Devil / The Obstinate Murderer $17.95
Murder stalks the halls at a Caribbean resort hotel, and an aging alcoholic is called in to solve a murder that hasn't happened yet.

Kill Joy / The Virgin Huntress $19.95
A young lady finds trouble in a house where death seems to stalk its every visitor; and a young man tries to stay one step ahead of the huntress who tries to uncover his questionable past. ʼ

Widow's Mite / Who's Afraid? $19.95
Tilly finds herself under suspicion of murder when her rich cousin is found poisoned; and a new door-to-door job goes horribly wrong for a young woman when her first customer is found stabbed to death.

The Unlit Lamp & Selected Stories $19.95
A classic 1920s social drama, paired with a collection of six stories from the same period. "Subtle, psychologically nuanced portraits of conflicted relationships."
—Sarah Weinman, *Troubled Daughters, Twisted Wives*.

The Shoals of Honour & Early Stories $19.95
A novel from 1926 plus six stories. "Biting satire on modern society and a modern romance with some real comedy sandwiched in makes a fairly likeable tale."—*Springfield Republican*

The Thing Beyond Reason/Echo of a Careless Voice/Blotted Out $19.95
Three rare novelettes from the 1920s & 30s. "Holding wastes little time thrusting the reader into the conflict and narrative action."—Alan Cranis, *Bookgasm*

Stark House Press
1315 H Street, Eureka, CA 95501
griffinskye3@sbcglobal.net /
www.StarkHousePress.com
Available from your local bookstore, or order direct or via our website.